BEAUTY AND THE BILLIONAIRE

LAUREN LANDISH

Edited by VALORIE CLIFTON
Edited by STACI ETHERIDGE
Photography by MICHELLE LANCASTER

ALSO BY LAUREN LANDISH

If you enjoyed this book, stay in contact! You can join my mailing list here. You'll never miss a new release and you'll even get 2 FREE ebooks!

PROLOGUE

MIA

*T*he darkness is complete, wrapping around me like an ebony velvet blanket, cool and textural on my naked skin. I can feel it on my goosebumps, the air adding to my trembling.

My body, exhausted from the last ordeal, still quivers as I try to find the strength to move. It's so difficult, the waters of sleep still tugging at me even as instinct tells me there's something in the darkness.

A soft shuffle of feet on the carpet, and I can sense him. He's here, watching me, invisible, but his aura reaches out, awakening my body like a warm featherlight touch on the pleasure centers of my brain.

Arousal ripples up my thighs, fresh heat shimmering with the memories of last time. I've never felt anything like him before, my body used and taken, battered and driven insane . . . and completely, thoroughly pleasured in a way that I didn't think possible.

It was so much that I don't even remember coming down, just an explosion of ecstasy that drove me into unconsciousness . . . but now my senses have returned and I know he's still there, measuring me, hunting me, *desiring* me.

How can he have strength left? How, when every muscle from my neck to my toes has already been taken past the limit?

How can he still want more?

My nostrils flare, and I can smell him. Rich, masculine . . . feral. A man's man who could tear me apart without a second's effort. His breath, soft but shuddering, sipping at the air, savoring the conquest to come.

Another whisper in the darkness, and the fear melts away, replaced by a heightened sense of things.

The moonlight, dim now in the post-midnight morning, when the night's as deep as it will ever be.

The sweat on my skin and the fresh moisture gathering at the juncture between my thighs.

He steps forward, still cloaked in shadow, a shape from the depths of night, ready for a new kind of embrace.

He reaches for my calf, and at his touch, I start to tremble. I should resist, I should say I can't take any more. He's already had his fill. What more can he want?

He inhales, his nose taking in my scent, and the knowledge comes to me, a revelation that I've chosen to ignore.

He wants me to be his. Not just his bedmate, not simply a conquest to have and to discard. He wants to possess me fully, to own me, body and soul.

But can I?

Can I give myself to such a man, a being whose very presence inspires fear and dread?

Can I risk the fury that I've seen directed at others turned back upon me?

His tongue flicks out, touching that spot he's discovered behind my right knee that I wasn't even aware of before him, my left leg falling aside on its own as my hunger betrays me.

My mind is troubled, my heart races . . . but my body knows what it wants.

He chuckles, a rumble that tickles my soft inner thighs as he pauses, his breath warm over my pussy. He scoops his hands under my buttocks, and I feel him adjust himself on the mattress, preparing for his feast.

"Delicious," he growls, and then his tongue touches me . . . and I'm gone.

CHAPTER 1

MIA

*T*he electronic drumbeats thud through the air so hard that I can actually feel my chest vibrate as I look at my screen, my head bobbing as I let the pattern come to me.

I've had a lot of people ask me how I can work the way I do, but this is when the magic happens. I've got three computer screens, each of them split into halves with data flowing in each one. I'm finishing up my evaluations, I've done the grind, and now I'm bringing it all together.

For that, though, I need tunes, and nothing gets my brain working on the right frequency as well as good techno does.

I can hear the door to my office vibrate in its frame, and I'm glad I've got my own little paradise down here in the basement of the Gold-stone Building.

Sure, my methods are weird, and I'm sort of isolated considering that I'm in a corner office with two file rooms on either side of me, but that's because I need this to make the magic happen.

Frankly, I wasn't too sure if I'd be able to keep this job, considering the number of complaints I got my first six months working here.

Part of it, of course, is my occasional outbursts—to myself, mind you, and more often than not in gutter Russian so no one can understand me.

That, with the random singing along with my tunes, meant I was labeled as 'distracting' and 'difficult to work next to.'

But the powers that be saw the value that I bring with my data analysis.

So, as an experimental last gasp, I was sent down here, where the walls are thick, the neighbors are paper, and nobody minds that my singing voice is terrible.

It works for them, but more importantly, it works for me.

And here I've remained for almost six years, working metadata analysis and market trends, making people with money even more money.

Not that the company's treated me poorly. I've gotten a bonus for seven quarters straight, and I've always managed my own investments.

For a girl who still has a few years until she hits thirty, I'm doing well on the ol' nest egg.

But I'm pigeonholed. Other than dropping off files from time to time, I almost never see anyone in my day to day work, which I guess is okay with me. I've never been someone who likes the social scene of an office.

On the other hand, I can wear my pink and blue streaks in my hair and not have to see people's judging glares. And I don't have to explain what my lyrics mean when I decide to sing along.

"Another one for the Motherland!" I exclaim as I see what I've been looking for. This isn't a hard assignment, merely an optimization analysis for some of Goldstone's transport subsidiaries. But I prefer to celebrate each victory, no matter how small or large, with glee.

I swipe all the data to my side monitors and bring up a document in the center and start typing. I've already included most of the boiler-plate that the executives and VPs want to see, the 'check the box' sort of things that my father would understand with his background.

After all, he is Russian. He knows about bureaucracy.

Finally, just as the Elf Clock above my door dings noon, I save my file and fire it off to my supervisor.

"In Russia . . . report finishes *you*."

Okay, so it's not my best one-liner, but it's another quirk of mine. While I'm as American as apple pie, I pay homage to my roots, especially at work, for some reason. It seems to help, so I'm sticking to it.

Heading to the elevator, I go upstairs before punching out for lunch and jumping into my little Chevy to drive to my 'spot', a diner called The Gravy Train. An honest to goodness old-fashioned diner, it's got some of the best food in town, including a fried chicken sandwich that's to kill for.

As I drive, I look around my hometown, still surprised at how big it seems these days. The main reason, of course, is tied to the dark tower on the north side of town, Blackwell Industries.

Thirty years ago, Mr. Blackwell located his headquarters here in the sleepy town of Roseboro and proclaimed it to be the bridge between Portland and Seattle. A lot of people scoffed, but he was right, and Roseboro's been the beneficiary of his foresight.

I've been lucky, watching a city literally grow with me. Roseboro is big enough now that some people even call this a Tri-Cities area, lumping us in with Portland and Seattle.

I get to The Gravy Train just in time to see the other reason that I come to this place so frequently for lunch wave from the window. Isabella "Izzy" Turner has been my best friend since first grade, and I love her like she's my own flesh and blood.

As I enter, I see her untie the apron on her uniform and slump down into one of the booths. Her normally rich brown hair looks limp and stringy today, and the bags under her eyes are so big she could be carrying her after work clothes in them.

"Hey, babe, you look exhausted," I say in greeting, giving her a hug from the side as I slide in next to her. "Please don't tell me you're still working double shifts?"

"Have to," Izzy says as she leans into me and hugs back. "Gotta keep the bills paid, and doing double shifts gives me a chance to maybe get a little ahead. I'll need it once classes start up again."

"You know you don't have to," I tell her for the millionth time. "You can take out student loans like the rest of us."

"I'd rather not if I don't have to. I owe enough to other people as it is."

She's got a point. She's had a tough life and has seen tragedy that left more and more debt on her tab, and student loans are tough enough without all the other stuff in her life.

And even though she always turns me down, I have to offer once again, just on the off-chance she'll say yes this time. "Still, if you need anything . . . I mean, I've said it before, but you can always come live with me. I've got room at my place."

Izzy snorts, finally cracking a smile. "You mean you want someone to stay up with you until two in the morning on weekends playing video games."

Before I can elbow her in the side, the bell above the door rings and in walks the third member of our little party patrol, Charlotte Dunn. A stunning girl who turns heads everywhere she goes with her long, naturally bright and beautiful red hair, she slides into the booth opposite Izzy and me, looking exhausted herself.

She settles in, sighing heavily, and Izzy looks over at her. "Tough morning for you too?"

"I think walking in the back and sticking my head in a vat of hot oil might just be preferable to working reception on the ground floor of Satan's Skyscraper," she jokes. "It's not like anything bad happened either."

"So what's the deal?" I ask, and Charlotte shakes her head. "What?"

"I guess it's just that everyone there walks like they've got a hundred-pound albatross on their back as they come in. No smiles, no greetings, even though I try. It's just depressing," she replies. "You got lucky, landing in the shining palace."

"Girl, please. I work all by my lonesome in the deep, dark dungeon of a basement," I point out.

Charlotte snorts. "But that's how you like it!"

She's not wrong, so I don't bother arguing, instead teasingly gloating, "And I get to wear whatever and work however the hell I please."

Our waitress, one of Izzy's co-workers, comes over with her order pad. "So, what can I get you ladies?"

"Something with no onions or spice," Izzy replies, groaning. "Maybe Henry can whip up a grilled cheese for me?"

"Deal. And for you ladies?"

We place our orders, and the three of us lean back, relaxing. Charlotte looks me over enviously again, shaking her head. "Seriously, Mia, can't get over the outfit today. You trying to show off the curves?"

"What curves?" I ask, looking down at today's band T-shirt. It's just a BTS logo, twin columns rising on a black shirt.

"Hey, you're rockin' it." Charlotte laughs. "It fits the girls just right."

I roll my eyes. Charlotte always seems to see something in me that I don't. Men don't seem to find me interesting. Or at least, the men *I* find interesting don't find *me* interesting.

Deflecting back to her, I ask, "How're things looking for you? That guy in Accounting ever come back downstairs to get your number?"

Charlotte snorts. "Nope. I saw him the other day, but it's okay. It's his loss."

She does a little hair flip and I can't help but smile. She hasn't always had the best luck with guys, but she never gives up and always keeps a positive attitude about the whole dating game. Her motto is 'No Mr. Wrongs, only Mr. Rights and Mr. Right-Nows.' Maybe not the classiest, but a girl's got needs, and sometimes it's nice to have an orgasm from a guy not named B.O.B.

We eat our lunches, chatting and gossiping and bullshitting as always. It's never a big to-do since we share lunch together at least once a week, if not more, but it's still nice to catch up. Izzy and I have been friends for so long, and Charlotte and I met in college. They're important to me.

"So, when do classes start up again, Izz?" Charlotte asks. "So you can, I don't know, get some sleep and not have fallen arches?"

Izzy snorts. "Too soon, I think. But if I can string together another two semesters—"

"Wait, two?" I ask in shock. "Honey, you're like the super-duper-ooper senior at this point. Seriously, some of the professors are probably younger than you by now."

"Hey, we're the same age!" Izzy protests, but shrugs. "You know, I had a freshman ask me if I was a TA the other day?"

"Ouch, that had to hurt," Charlotte says. "What did you say?"

"I pointed him in the direction of the student union and turned him down when he asked for my number. Seriously, I'm not sure if he even needed to shave yet. I don't have time to teach eighteen-year-old man-boys what and where a clit is!"

Charlotte and I laugh, and I punch her in the shoulder. "You'll get there in your own time, girl. But still, why the wait?"

"Mostly the internship," Izzy admits. "I can juggle classes and work, or internship and work, but I can't do classes, internship, and work. There's just not enough hours in the day."

I nod, understanding that Izzy has plans and dreams. But unlike most, she's willing to sacrifice and work hard to reach hers.

We shift topics, like we always do, until we've covered all the usual topics and my tummy feels pleasantly happy without risk of an afternoon food coma.

Wiping our mouths with our napkins, I glance at my phone, checking the time. "So, Char . . . rock, paper, scissors?"

"Nope, this one's mine!" Charlotte says, giggling as I lean into Izzy, preventing her from moving as Charlotte grabs the check and runs up to the counter.

"Hey! Hey, dammit!" Izzy protests. "I—"

"Should be quiet and let your friends pay for lunch for once," I whisper. "Or else I'll use my secret Russian pressure point skills on you!"

"Oh, fine, since you put it that way!"

Charlotte comes back, and she smiles at Izzy. "Chill, Izz. You bust your ass, and you've snuck us an extra pickle more than once. You're allowed to let me buy you lunch every now and then."

"We could all use some more *pickle*." Izzy chuckles. "Seriously, at this point, I'd settle for a one-nighter. No commitment, no issues, just a good old-fashioned hookup. As long he's well into his twenties, at least," she says with an eye roll.

"Mr. Right Now?" Charlotte asks, and Izzy nods. "Hmph. You find him, send him my way. I keep finding good guys . . . two months after they've met the girl of their dreams. Only single men I find are dogs."

"You've just gotta make sure you give them a fake number and a flea dip, and enjoy the weekend," I tease, though she knows I would never do anything of the sort.

"I'm lonely, but I've got rechargeable batteries."

We all laugh, and my phone rings. I pull it out, checking the screen. "Shit, girls, it's my boss. Says he's got a rush job for me to complete."

"How's he working out, anyway?" Charlotte asks as I finish my drink quickly. "And have you started working for The Golden Child yet?"

"Nope, I've never seen him except for the publicity stuff," I reply honestly. "He's the penthouse. I'm the basement. Twenty-four floors in between us. Anyway, I gotta jet, so I'll talk to you girls soon, okay?"

"Yup . . . I'm going to relax for this next ten minutes before I need to clock back in myself," Izzy says, stretching out. "Gimme a call later?"

I nod, blowing them a kiss, and head back to work.

CHAPTER 2

THOMAS

*L*ooking out over Roseboro, I feel like I'm looking over my empire.

Of course, I'm joking . . . but maybe not so much.

Twenty-five years ago, this town was just a suburb of a suburb of Portland. Though it was already up and coming, I'd like to think that over the past six years I've added my fair share to this place.

I'd finished my MBA at Stanford and set up shop in the growing town, watching the landscape change and cultivating the business interests that serve me best. Because I haven't just watched. I've worked my ass off to get Goldstone where it is today.

Still, I made sure to keep the competition in sight, literally.

My office faces the Blackwell Building, a one-mile gap separating the two tallest buildings in the city. It helps me keep things in perspective. I came to town because I saw potential, even if Blackwell had already created something big here.

But this place is too fertile for him to fully take advantage of. A rose that, if tended right, can provide more blossoms than any one man could utilize.

I watch the morning sun hit the black tower. I'll give Blackwell grudging respect. His design might be morbid, but it's also cutting-edge. All that black is absorbing the solar energy and using it for electricity and heating. The man was environmental before environmental was actually cool.

Too bad you'll never be that. You're just a wannabe, another young upstart who'll never stand the test of time.

I growl, pushing away the voice from inside me, even though I know it'll be back. It never really goes away, not for long. No matter how much I achieve, that voice of insecurity still resides in my center, ready to cast doubt and shadows on each success.

The soft ding from my computer reminds me that my ten minutes of morning meditation are over, and I turn back around, looking at my desk and office. It's nothing lavish. I designed this space for maximum efficiency and productivity.

So my Herman Miller chair is not in my office for lapped luxury, or for its black and chrome styling, but for the fact that it's rated the best chair for productivity. Same with my desk, my computer, everything.

Everything is tuned toward efficient use of my time and my efforts.

I launch into it, going through my morning assignments, answering the emails that my secretary, Kerry, cannot answer for me, and making a flurry of decisions on projects that Goldstone is working on.

Finally, just as the clock on my third screen beeps one o'clock, I send off my final message and stand up. Locking my computer, I transfer everything to my server upstairs in case I need it.

I see Kerry sitting at her desk as I leave my office. She's well-dressed as usual, her sunkissed skin and black hair gleaming mellowly under the office lighting, the perfect epitome of a professional executive assistant. While she works for me, she has this older sibling protective instinct. It's not often that I need it, but I appreciate her looking out for me.

"Need something, Mr. Goldstone?" she asks.

"Just headed upstairs," I tell her.

"Of course," she replies, her eyes cutting to her computer screen. "Just a reminder, sir, the governor will be hosting his charity event tonight at seven. I've already had your tuxedo dry-cleaned, and your car detailer called. Your car will be ready and downstairs by three this afternoon."

I give her a nod. Three's plenty of time. "I just sent you a list of other projects to work on, by the way."

"Of course, Mr. Goldstone. I was looking that over, and I got an email from Hank also, the team leader you assigned the Taiwan shipping contract to. He said that he's going to have to take a day off Friday, sir. His daughter's going to college this year, and he promised her that he'd drive her up so she can get settled into the dorm."

I stop, pursing my lips. "What is her name?"

Kerry taps her desk for a moment, searching her memory. "Erica, sir."

"Tell Hank that I understand and wish Erica the best, but if he isn't at work on Friday, don't bother coming in on Monday."

My tone has grown serious, and Kerry's eyes tighten, but she knows Hank is crossing a line. He should've given notice, especially when he's working a contract this important.

He's usually a good employee. But he knew his daughter was starting classes. No excuse for that.

No excuse for you, you mean. Failure just drips down from the boss's office down to Hank, that's all.

Leaving the twenty-fifth floor of the Goldstone building, I take the stairs up a level to stretch my legs. Not many people even know about this floor other than the executives. To everyone else, the Goldstone Building has twenty-five floors.

The twenty-sixth is mine. It's my penthouse, and while it isn't quite as large as the other floors, it's still six thousand square feet of space that's just for me.

I strip off my dress shirt, tie, and slacks, depositing everything in the laundry chute before pulling on my workout clothes.

Today's upper body day, and as I go into my home gym, I swing my arms to loosen up my shoulders. They're going to be punished today. Starting with bench presses, I assault my body, pushing myself to press the bar one more time, to get the fucking dumbbells up despite the pain, despite gravity kicking my ass.

Just like everything kicks your ass.

The finisher for today is brutal, even for me. The 300 . . . 100 burpees, 100 dips, and 100 pullups, in sets of ten, nonstop. By the time I'm finished, sweat pools on the rubberized gym flooring beneath me.

I have to force myself to my feet because I refuse to be broken by anything, even something as meaningless as a workout that's supposed to do exactly that.

Instead, I jump in for a quick shower and meditate for twenty minutes after. I need to focus because running Goldstone is a mental exercise.

Closing my eyes, I force myself to push all the responsibilities away, to let it all fade into the background.

I push away the flashbacks, the voice in my head, the memories that threaten from time to time, and imagine my perfect world . . . my empire. My perfect Roseboro, deep red petals soft as velvet and eternally blooming, ready to be passed from my generation to the next for tending and care.

I know I can do it.

I *must* do it.

Changing into my tuxedo, I head downstairs to the freshly cleaned limo waiting to take me to this event. The Roseboro Civic Library is one of the newest public buildings in town, a beautiful hundred-thousand-square-foot building in three wings over two floors. The central wing is named for Horatio Roseboro, who founded the city in memory of his daughter, who died on the Oregon Trail, while the other two wings are named for the main benefactors . . . Goldstone and Blackwell. My only request was that the Goldstone wing contain the children's section, and they were more than willing to do that.

Tonight, though, it's the scene for a fundraiser for the governor's favorite charity. Governor Gary Langlee tends to ignore Roseboro most of the time—we're not his voter base—but when it comes time to get money, he'll go just about anywhere he can if someone will cross his palm with a little bit of green.

I arrive at just the right time, ten minutes before seven, in order to get the best of the press. I tolerate the leeches more than like them, but I do understand that the fourth estate has a purpose and a job to do.

And there are legit journalists who I respect. It's just the paparazzi and empty talking heads that I despise.

So I smile for the cameras, giving a little wave and shaking hands with our local state representative before heading into the foyer, where the party has already started.

"Ah, Thomas!" the mayor says, greeting me in that hearty way that really endears him to the locals. "I'm so glad you could make it."

"You know me, never pass up a chance to press the flesh," I reply, making him laugh. He knows I'm lying but thinks that I'm only here because of the press and good PR that Goldstone will get for tonight.

The reality is far different. While Governor Langlee and I might not see eye to eye on most public policies, I actually agree with the goals of tonight's event.

"I'm sure you'll enjoy yourself," the mayor says after a moment when I don't follow up.

Clearing his throat, he looks around. "If you don't mind telling me, Thomas, there's a rumor around town that Goldstone is looking into building a sea transportation hub in Roseboro. I'm not saying I wouldn't appreciate it, but if you are, I happen to know a man who's got about seven hundred and fifty acres just outside of town. It's county land, but I'm sure we could work something out."

That's the mayor . . . a good ol' boy to the voters, a sneaky dealmaker to those with money. The man would sell his grandmother's grave if it'd make him a buck.

Oh, like you've been such a good son.

"If we do move on such a project, I'll be sure to keep City Hall informed," I tell him with a smile that turns just a little predatory at the end. "But of course, I would do my due diligence on the property. No use wasting my money when it could be spent on a proper seaport instead of along the Columbia?"

The mayor blanches just a little, which is what I want. A tiny reminder that while he may hold office, I hold the funds that make this city thrive or fail. Or at least a large share of the finances that do so.

Leaving him, I do my best to 'mingle'. I know the faces. I've seen it all before.

A pat on the back here for a friend.

A backhanded compliment for the enemy whom you can't quite man up and call out in public. The icy stare from across the room at those whose families have somehow found the time to engage in feuds despite not having the time to make a difference in the world.

It's all old hat, and while some might find it interesting, I just tolerate it to get my goal here tonight done.

Finally, at nine o'clock, I can't do it any longer. I retreat to the children's section, which is relatively quiet in comparison, and I look over the newest books on the display.

"You know, I'm not too sure if *Long Way Down* really belongs in the children's section," a throaty voice says behind me, and I turn to see Meghan Langlee, Governor Langlee's daughter.

She's wearing a Chanel cocktail dress that fits her like a glove, highlighting a very fit body and a camera grabbing face. A former beauty queen like her mother, Meghan's parlayed her looks into a budding career as a political pundit.

"Actually, I personally insisted on it," I reply, turning away from her and looking at the books again. "While the subject matter might be a little dark and violent, the days of young people growing up needing little more than *The Andy Griffith Show* and reading Judy Blume are pretty much over."

"Hmm, well, I'll say my father would disapprove, but I understand what you mean," she says, stepping closer. "You know, Mr. Goldstone . . . mind if I call you Tom?"

"If you wish," I reply, sizing her up immediately. She must be up to something, she's coming on too hard, too boldly.

It wouldn't surprise me if she's been sent here on a mission. Her father's a weasel and would see no issue with using his only daughter this way.

She takes my arm, as if she expects me to suddenly escort her and be happy to do so, giving me a false coquettish giggle. "Ooh. I've heard your reputation Tom, that you're pretty *rigid* in your fitness routines, but wow, this tux is hiding a *beast* underneath all this worsted wool."

"Clean eating and good habits," I reply, already tiring of her and her lazily flirtatious innuendos. She tries to lead me back to the main wing, and I follow along simply to avoid any issues, but when she sees one of the press and starts trying to angle us in that direction, I pull my arm free. "Excuse me, Miss Langlee."

She looks surprised, anger hiding in her eyes. I doubt she's used to being denied. She reaches out and grabs my arm again, pulling herself close.

"Come on now, Tom. I'm sure we can find a little bit of fun."

I can't tolerate this any longer, and I pull away, my voice tight. "Sorry. I haven't had my rabies booster this year."

I walk away, cursing myself at that last crack. Turning her down cold? That's one thing.

But essentially calling her a disease-infested slut was probably too much.

"One of these days, you're going to piss off someone important," she says threateningly to my back. When I don't reply, she stomps her foot like a petulant toddler, loud enough to cut through the hubbub of the party as she calls out, "Bastard!"

Everything stops, and I nod, glancing back over my shoulder at her with a charming smile. "That's one of the things they call me."

I keep going, and as I pass by the governor, he gives me a dirty look. Reaching out, he puts a hand on my arm.

"You know, my daughter—" he starts, already conciliatory, which makes me think he knew exactly what Meghan's game was tonight.

I don't let him finish. I just shrug him off, ignoring the snapping cameras. I only pause at the door to reach into my jacket and pull out an envelope that I slide into the donation box.

It's unmarked . . . but that's just what I want.

CHAPTER 3

BLACKWELL

*T*he shadows of the unused wing conceal me, just as I planned. There are no lights up here, just the glow from down below, which is just how I like it.

Why should I waste my time mingling among the players on stage when I can be the director, up here in the shadows until the right moment for my cameo?

The velvet rope across the stairs to the upper floor sends a tasteful but pointed point to the people down below, giving me the privacy I want.

I sip my glass of Seleccion Suprema, enjoying the subtle tones of the fine tequila while watching Thomas Goldstone storm out of the library, the governor outraged and his little tramp of a daughter staring dark murder at him. It's exactly what I wanted.

"Scurry home, Golden Boy," I whisper, sipping my drink again. "Storm out of here, showing the whole world your weakness."

I've studied my adversary from afar for years, ever since The Golden Boy turned his attention from minor league playing the market and posting dramatic percentage gains to actually slinging weight in Roseboro.

I'll admit, I underestimated him at first. I laughed when Goldstone established his first 'headquarters' and even rented him the first building. The old three-story building had sat empty for awhile, caught in that gap between small business and big business and too difficult to divide up. I figured it could come to some use at least that way, but I'd thought Goldstone would crash and burn after a few years.

Little did I expect to have to look out of my office window to see Goldstone's own building, nearly as tall as my own, every morning.

I shake my head, wondering where I'd gone wrong. It should have taken him another decade or more to get to where he is now. It makes no logical sense for the Golden Boy, at just over half my age, to have already closed the gap on me so quickly.

I'd run the numbers and taken the time to double-check the figures personally . . . and knew the day after Goldstone cut the ribbon on that shining monstrosity a mile from my own tower that if I didn't do something to destroy Thomas Goldstone, he'd steal my throne as the richest man in Roseboro.

Goldstone is poised to relegate me to the list of also-rans, the men who were big but not the biggest.

History remembers Secretariat, not the horses who finished second behind him.

I have no intention of ending my life as anything other than the undisputed master of my domain. Some may call me a dictator . . . but at least they'll remember me.

And so I plot, and tonight, I confirmed a suspicion I've had for a long time. Thomas Goldstone's infamous temper is very real and rather raw when it comes to beautiful women.

He didn't show it outwardly, and I'll give him that much. There was no yelling, no screaming like I've heard rumors about. But to just impetuously pull his arm away from Governor Langlee like that? Ill-advised, to say the least.

I chuckle and watch the governor console his stupid, status-seeking daughter while trying to get the focus back on tonight's charity cause.

Men's dress shoes click on the tile flooring of the landing. I refuse to let my wing of the library be sullied with anything as plebeian as fuzzy carpet like Goldstone has in the children's wing. There's a reason they're called rugrats, after all.

Still, the shadows are so thick that even up close, I know the man can't see my face clearly, although the obsidian cufflinks on my tuxedo clearly reveal my identity.

Not too many people can pull off obsidian and platinum cufflinks while not mingling with the crowd.

"Sir, I assume you saw that?"

My operative is dressed like most of the men downstairs, in a suit that is appropriate for the evening but not a tuxedo. No, only the crème de la crème are wearing tuxedos, and I need my man to stay anonymous.

Which, in many respects, is very hard to do in a gossipy upper-crust crowd who eyes any newcomer with scrutiny and obvious analysis of their financial bearing. And unfortunately, my operative is as status-hungry as the governor's daughter, in his own way.

Not quite a peacock . . . but definitely not a chameleon. He's not quite seeking recognition though, which is useful to me. I need a snake, not a chameleon.

"Of course," I reply after a moment of savoring my tequila. Forget the flavoring, the mixings. Just let me savor the oaky vanilla tones of the extra anejo tequila while the agave essence sort of plays in my nose. "It went well."

"I apologize that he didn't leave with the girl. When I pointed her in his direction, I assumed he'd—"

"Never assume anything," I say, looking over at the man. Intelligent, and with striking eyes that most people assume is a product of his upbringing. I know different, and know the fire inside them burns with hatred for Thomas Goldstone. Yes, he's definitely not a chameleon.

But he's not half the hunter he thinks he is, either.

He expects that by playing Judas to Goldstone, he will garner himself favor with me. I can't blame him for the blossoming hope, since I planted the seed myself and have watered it with unspoken promises over these past few months.

The man has a future, as long as he keeps his eyes open. The very same knife he's helping me to slip into Thomas Goldstone can quickly be turned on him as well if he decides to think beyond what he's told.

"It doesn't matter. The Golden Boy has shown his weakness. All that glitters isn't gold."

"Excuse me, sir?"

I sigh and finish off my tequila. Perhaps my operative isn't quite as smart as he pretends to be. But at the same time, it reassures me. The man isn't smart enough to realize he's being played.

For a man who is betraying his employer, he still has an ironic blind spot. He's not very good at planning, just executing the plans of others.

"Piece of advice. There is a time when you set up, and plan, and project, and scheme. But there comes a time to just push that first domino and see what happens. Knowing when to do each . . . that's power."

My man says nothing, watching as the governor clears his throat and the party starts back up, tension starting to melt away . . . but I can see that many people won't forget the scene Goldstone created.

Least of all, the governor.

"Sir . . . what shall we do about him?" my man asks. "Any man confident enough to just walk away from Governor Langlee like that . . ."

I can't help but grin as I think through my plans. Goldstone is on his way to becoming a large enough problem that drastic measures will need to be used. It's not that I'm averse to that methodology, and in fact, I've nurtured a healthy relationship with operatives beyond the law.

But I prefer to stick with the quieter approach I've plotted, so as not to draw more attention to the famous Golden Boy.

I want the man crushed . . . not a martyr.

And there are so many, many ways to cut your enemy's legs out from under him. Quiet or loud, mercilessly or kindly, with confrontation or from the shadows.

"I have an idea . . . but for now, enjoy the party. After all, you have connections to make yourself, yes?"

CHAPTER 4

MIA

$\mathcal{I}$ gather myself as I knock on my supervisor's door. Bill Radcliffe's been my boss for the past two years, and though I might feel nervous coming up here for any other boss, Bill's been a great one.

Best I've worked for, going all the way back to my part-time college gigs. And this week's update meeting should be a slam-dunk considering I'd completed his rush job with time to spare.

But I'm still awkward and uncomfortable up here in the land of the automaton office zombies, feeling like people are glaring at me.

"Hi, Bill," I greet him, adjusting my jeans. It's Friday, which means denim is more than fine, and I like being as casual as I can. Although I might be pushing it with the Ahsoka Tano T-shirt today. "Uhm, you said you had something you wanted to talk with me about?"

"Yeah, come on in and close the door," Bill says, leaning back.

I sit down, a little nervous. This seems odd. Usually, Bill's to the point, but I can see him gathering his thoughts.

"Uhm, is this about my BTS T-shirt last week? Or that mix I played earlier this week? I promise you, I didn't realize the lyrics at the time until I was halfway into it."

"The wha . . . never mind, no, there's no problem at all," Bill says, chuckling. "If I had a problem with your music, Mia, I'd have said something two years ago when I first walked into your office and you were screaming Nine Inch Nails at me."

I blush, nodding. It had been a 'rough time', as Izzy likes to say, and so my music had been a little rougher too. Still, your new boss walking into your office while you scream *I want to fuck you like an animal* is not the impression you want to make.

"Yeah . . . so, what's up?"

Bill takes a big breath and turns his laptop around. "You've been called upstairs. It seems that someone has recognized what I've seen for the past two years, and those Sherlock skills of yours are going to be put to the test."

I read the document he has up, a standard company email, and gulp. "I'll be reporting to Mr. Goldstone? Starting Monday?"

"Not quite," Bill says. "You're still with my group, but this assignment is for a short-term project team, something The Ruthless Bastard likes to do a lot. Ad hoc teams."

The Ruthless Bastard. I've heard more than one person call Thomas Goldstone that, though no one ever says why. Mr. Goldstone must actually like being called that because I can't imagine Bill saying it to me otherwise.

"So, what can I expect?"

"The team will be some of the best talent in Goldstone," Bill says, "and the rewards for a good performance can be substantial. You might even earn a ticket out of the basement, if you want, although I think you might actually enjoy being on your own."

"I could use a window," I joke. "I get pretty pale come summertime. But yes, I do enjoy it."

Bill rubs at his cheek. "Listen, Mia, if it were anyone else on the team, I'd send them up there without much more than a 'watch your ass' comment, but you . . . well, I happen to like you. You do damn good work, and despite your quirks, you make my life a lot easier. With you on the team, I don't feel so bad about taking the demotion I asked for years ago. Those bonus checks you help us get come in handy."

"Why did you ask for a demotion, Bill?" I ask, curious and glad for the opening to pry. I'd heard rumors but had never had the chance to ask him before.

"Six years ago, I was one of those folks who was burning up the corporate ladder. I'd come to Goldstone from Silicon Valley because I wanted in on the ground floor of an upstart again and saw potential almost as soon as Thomas Goldstone launched the company."

"You're an OG?" I ask, surprised. "I didn't know."

Bill chuckles. "Yeah, well . . . in my first three years here, I'd worked myself up. Literally, because when this building opened, I had a nice office on the twentieth floor. But I learned the same thing a lot of people have. This company's great to work for. The pay is good, the bennies are great . . . but the closer you get to Thomas Goldstone, the more you need them to tip the scale in your favor. Goldstone truly demands perfection, and the expectations and stress levels go up exponentially with every floor."

"'High achievement always takes place in the framework of high expectations.' Charles Kettering," I quote, but Bill shakes his head.

"Mia, before I joined the corporate world, I did four years in the Army, including a tour in Afghanistan. I did Ranger school, even if I don't look it now. A year being shot at in the mountains of Kandahar, a year of Ranger school . . . and Thomas Goldstone broke my ass in one project team. Nope, I'm happy here on three."

I nod, thinking. I never knew that about Bill, but I'm not really surprised. He strikes me as that sort of easygoing leader who still gets his people to perform and sort of makes do with what he has available.

"Okay . . . and what if I were to turn down the assignment?"

"It'll be reassigned to someone else but noted upstairs that you turned down the opportunity, which isn't a great look for you," Bill says. "This company has plenty of data analysts. You're just the best . . . in my opinion."

His compliment means a lot to me, and I sit back, thinking. "I'll do it. I mean, a window in my basement cave would be sweet." I wink because we both know that'll never happen. "And, well . . . I want to prove what you said. That I'm the best. Challenge accepted."

Bill nods. "My wife's going to kill me for this. My daughter needs braces and those are expensive as hell, and with your reassignment, my quarterly bonus just poofed into thin air, but you're right . . . everyone's entitled to their shot. More than one, if they want to take it. So let me give you some pointers. One, be prepared to work harder than you ever have in your life. I mean, you need to be on point every minute of every day. That means when you're in a meeting, you need to listen and be able to comment on anything. One of Goldstone's things is he'll ask people their feedback on something that doesn't seem to be in their lane. It's both a test and a way for him to get fresh insight from different perspectives. Second . . . I hate to say it, but Goldstone's a bit old-school, and at least for meetings and stuff, you're going to need to be more . . . traditional."

He gestures at my attire and my dyed hair. I get the point, but he didn't need to say that. I wouldn't show up wearing my usual casual wear.

"Right," I murmur, nodding. I tug at my hair, which today is totally awesome with a blood-red fringe on the lower two inches, wishing it a silent goodbye. Hello, boring old blonde Mia. "Got it."

I stand up, but before I can leave, Bill holds up a hand and grins. "Oh, one other thing . . . got any ideas on the news?"

"Which part?" I ask.

"The White Knight," Bill says. "He struck again." His gleeful curiosity is apparent, as is his joy at being the one to spread the gossip to me.

Ah, the White Knight. He's almost a local myth, and any anonymous act of charity in the Portland/Roseboro area is attributed to him. They say he's even done stuff up in Seattle as well.

"How much was it this time?"

"Half a million," Bill says with a smile. "That's going to help a lot of homeless vets."

Vets this time.

Last time, it was an animal shelter, and before that an orphanage and a drug treatment facility, originally starting off with an at-risk children's center.

Each time, a white envelope with a cashier's check or a white paper-wrapped package of cash was delivered totally anonymously.

Rumor has it the local news is stumped because the checks are connected to some shell corporation out of the Bahamas. It's just . . . urban legendary.

"Honestly?" I reply, shrugging my shoulders. "I think whoever it is wants their privacy, so I figure we should respect that. Whoever it is, they're doing good. Why mess with that?"

Bill nods. "Yeah, guess so. Still, if you told me I could work for the White Knight instead of The Ruthless Bastard, I'd take that offer in a second."

⌇

"MY SWEET LITTLE GIRL, YOU LOOK BEAUTIFUL," MY FATHER GREETS ME, grabbing me and kissing me noisily on both cheeks. Some things he'll never give up. "How is my little Anastasia?"

"Papa, how many times must I beg you to stop with that?" I ask. "I'm no princess, and she ended up dead."

"Bah, that's just what the Party wanted everyone to believe," Papa says, waving his hand. "She still lives on in the hearts of all true Russians. Even now, her daughter is somewhere, waiting for her country to need her."

I shake my head. Papa will always love the Motherland in his heart. Even if we're meeting in a Thai restaurant for dinner. "Whatever you say. Come, let's enjoy dinner. I have good news."

He sits rapt as I tell him about my day, his smile growing as I tell him about the project group. "See? I have always told you, Mia, you have the brains of a genius and the beauty to match. Now you have your opportunity to show the rest of the company the same thing."

"Papa, they're looking for my brains, not how I look."

Papa scoffs, sipping his beer. "Nonsense, sweetheart. You are as beautiful as any of those girls in magazines and on the television. All peasants compared to my Mia!" His voice rises like he's singing my praises not just to me, but the whole room.

I'm blushing, staring at my appetizers as Papa finishes his declaration, wishing he'd be a little less supportive. "Papa, I'm just brains. God made me smart, not . . . that!"

Papa lowers his voice a little, almost to a whisper. "Oh, but you are a beauty. And one day, you'll pull your nose out of your numbers, look into a mirror, and finally realize what I've known all along."

I smile. Papa has always spoiled me with compliments, even when money was tight. I'm sometimes amazed I haven't ended up weirder than I am.

"Anyway, back to the job. I've heard that the stress is pretty high on these projects. There's a real risk of failure, flopping on my butt in front of the boss and the whole team."

Papa shakes his head, his smile dimming. "That's not going to happen. You are smart, and you are capable of being anything you want to be. And now you have the opportunity to show your bosses, of grabbing your future with your own two hands."

He grabs at the air, fisting his hand to emphasize his point. "And in that, I will always be proud of you."

"Don't ask for it," I whisper, and Papa quirks his eyebrow. I shake my head, smiling. "Nothing, Papa. Just something you said reminded me of Eureka Seven, one of my animes. A character says, 'Don't ask for it. Go out and win it on your own.' You just made me think of that."

"Those Japanese cartoons of yours," Papa says, tsking. "I suppose it would be too much to ask that you'd just want to enjoy normal television that I know? Watch *The Bachelor* like an American girl, or the news so we could discuss politics."

I laugh. Papa has never understood my fascination with nerd culture . . . but he lets me be me. And for that, I love him more than I could ever explain.

"Yeah, well . . . right now, what I want to be is well-fed," I reply, seeing the waiter approaching. "What'll it be, Papa? My treat."

Papa sighs and quickly looks at his menu. "What on here won't give me heartburn?"

CHAPTER 5

MIA

The conference room on the twenty-fourth floor seems huge, but maybe it's just the people involved. I mean, there are only six people here, and the table's no bigger than the team meetings I would have on Bill's team.

But the power in this room means a lot, and the view out the windows . . . I know I'm being silly, but I swear that at any moment, a cloud's going to come drifting by and a bird's going to roost on the little antenna sticking out below the window. I think that's a cellphone point, but my tech knowledge is in using the system, not designing it.

"Can I have everyone's attention?" the man at the front, a handsome, broad-shouldered guy with slightly wavy black hair and a chin that would make a cowboy proud, says.

He's got startling blue eyes and teeth so white I wonder who makes his bleaching product. Still, the thousand-dollar suit he's wearing, and the fact that he's put his tablet at the head of the table, tells me he's somebody.

"Let's go ahead and get started, shall we? For those of you who don't know me, my name's Randall Towlee, Vice President of M&A here at Goldstone. Since some of you might be new to this sort of format, let's go around and do introductions. Just your name, your department, and your specialty."

The other five are all from different departments in Goldstone. One's an accountant, another is in real estate, while there's a lawyer and finally, a contracts specialist. They all seem okay. Nobody's breathing fire, at least.

Last of all, it's my turn, and I do my best to not fidget as I fight the urge to scratch my neck and shift my thighs in the unfamiliar 'professional' pencil skirt I've got on.

"Hi, everyone. I'm Mia Karakova. Uhm, I've spent the past few years working with Bill Radcliffe's team down on the third floor, though I house in the basement."

Shit. Why did I say that? They probably know about the weirdo girl in the dungeon. *Shake it off.*

"I'm a data analyst. Most of the time, I do metadata trendspotting, but Bill likes to call me Sherlock." I smile like it's a funny joke, but no one laughs.

Short, but not too short. Nothing too embarrassing. Okay, first hurdle passed.

"Nice to have you with us," Randall says, flashing me a smile. "Everyone, I was the one who asked Mia to join the team. I've had the chance to read her reports and analyses for the past few quarters, and she really is a trend detective. And we've been handed a corker of a problem."

Janice, the accountant who's been looking at Randall like she wants to eat him alive, cock first, gives me an appraising look. There's some frost, and maybe a touch of aggression.

Okay, well . . . she can have him. I don't want drama, and Randall doesn't do anything for me.

"What is the problem, Randall?" Janice asks. "It must be some sort of M&A issue if you're leading the charge, although nobody matches wits quite like you, so it could be anything."

Oh. My. God. She's laying it on thick.

Randall beams at her praise. "Actually, Mr. Goldstone is looking at expanding into the healthcare field and you've each been selected to help us address any issues with this new direction before he proceeds."

"If you don't mind," Danny, the lawyer, asks, "where *is* Mr. Goldstone?"

"Busy, but he told me this morning that he'll stop in," Randall says, his picture-perfect smile not dimming in the least. He launches into the details as he hands out a short document with the bare bones on the deal.

It's stupid and petty, but just another thing I don't like. He's got a tablet, this room has a giant freakin' display screen, and we've all got email. Did he really have to kill the trees to hand out a document he could have shown us digitally? It's the twenty-first century, for fuck's sake.

"So, bottom line," Randall says, reaching the end of his ten-minute speech, "Mr. Goldstone wants to buy a hospital. I'm sending you each an email now."

He clicks around on his tablet, and I hold back my smirk that he could've just done that in the first place. Redundancy, meet Randall.

"I've included the list of hospitals in the area that could be targets. We're not looking at launching a whole project from scratch. That's just not happening here. All the hospitals are in the PNW area, and it's going to be your job to research them. Figure out how we could get control of each of them, what the financial outlays are, projections on growth, things like that. Feed all your results through Mia. She's going to be meta on this, but Mia, I want you sharing your analysis back out. We double-check everything around here, got it?"

I nod. That's something I expected. "Got it."

"Good," Randall says, clearly aiming his attention back at me. "Okay, everyone, let's scatter, and you know the deal. Noses, grindstones, and all that."

The five of us get up, heading for the door, when I hear Randall say, "Mia, if you'll hang behind a moment?"

Janice gives me a look, but I can't tell her out loud that I'm not trying to run clitorference on whatever game she's got with Randall. And she doesn't seem to get the message I'm sending with my eyes.

Randall is shuffling his papers, and I stand by the window, admiring the view for a moment and hoping that Randall isn't about to kick me off the team already.

It isn't until I'm turned around that I remember that this skirt's a little tight through my hips and I'm definitely giving him a show. I turn back around, crossing my arms over my chest and looking down.

"What can I help you with, Mr. Towlee?"

"Two things. First, I know what it's like to be on your first action team here at Goldstone," Randall says, mostly sounding like a nice guy, but I didn't miss the way his eyes shot upward when I turned around. "You're going to be nervous, and I know you're probably not used to other people checking your work."

I shrug. "I do work alone, but I'm sure someone does check whatever I send up. Bill usually, but others too. I'm just probably not the best at verbally explaining it because most people hear 'data analysis' and instantly get bored."

"Okay. You do your data magic, and I'll handle the talking," Randall reassures me, standing up. "I'm pretty good at speaking tech, and I promise that you'll get your name on the report."

I nod, not really saying anything. I expected my name to be known if I am on the team and doing the work, so it's not like he's offering something I wasn't already entitled to.

"Also," Randall says, lowering his voice and stepping a little closer, "if you'd like—"

"Towlee!"

The name booms through the air so loud I swear that whoever said it is actually in the room, but it's not until two seconds later that the door opens and my breath catches.

It's the first time I've seen Thomas Goldstone in the flesh. And the PR photos don't do him justice.

Rich brown hair, sharp cheekbones, and eyes that blaze with green fire, lit from within with an intelligence and intensity that take my breath away. And that's just from the neck up. His shirt looks custom-tailored over an upper body that I'm pretty sure is carved from granite, almost to the point of looking like a superhero in disguise, Bruce Wayne in the boardroom.

Even his suit looks absolutely perfectly tailored to fit his body, or maybe he just has the perfect body for suits. I can't tell, and I know something about suits.

But Thomas himself . . . he's just that powerful. He's magnetic, a man with his own pull and charisma that might be able to overpower the force of gravity if he so desires. Though he's only one man entering the room, it suddenly feels infinitely smaller with his aura pressing in against mine.

"Thomas," Randall says, clearing his throat and stepping back like he just got his hand caught in the cookie jar. "How can I help you?"

"What is this garbage you sent me about the Yakima project? I told you to give me a detailed analysis of their advertising budget usage over the last decade."

For the next three minutes, I stand to the side, trying to stay small while I watch in fear and fascination as Thomas Goldstone performs an absolute verbal castration on Randall Towlee. It's an exercise in utter mastery of the English language.

He never curses.

He never gets personal.

Other than his initial name callout, his voice never even rises.

He just carves the document apart with a tongue like a scalpel, pointing out half a dozen places where the report didn't meet his standards.

It's totally professional . . . and totally emasculating. By the end, Randall, who was John Wayne in the group meeting, looks like a little kid wearing cowboy boots with his diaper as Thomas flips the report dismissively onto the table.

"Get me a *proper* analysis," Thomas finishes up. His eyes for the first time glance over at me. He looks me up and down but doesn't say a word, and then he walks out.

In the silence, I look at Randall, who's trying to gather together the last tattered remnants of his manhood that are left after Thomas just finished slicing, dicing, and feeding them to him by the handful.

"So that's what we call being put on blast," Randall says with a weak, watery laugh.

"And everyone has to handle things like . . . like that?" I ask, wondering how I'd react if Mr. Goldstone really put me on blast. Would I wilt like a flower in the face of an August windstorm, or would I find the strength to stand my ground?

Randall somehow laughs again, already recovering from Mr. Goldstone's onslaught. "That? That wasn't even that bad. You'll learn soon enough. You've got a lot of work to do and a short timeline to do it in. Welcome to the team."

"Thank you," I reply as Randall walks out, leaving me alone in the conference room.

In the suddenly empty space, I can't help but think about what I just saw, think about Thomas Goldstone. My knees shake a bit as I catch the slightest whiff of his cologne. It smells powerful and impressive, just like the man. And I feel fear . . . and arousal? Yes, that uncomfortable clenching in my gut isn't my belly, but decidedly *lower*.

Fear . . . and arousal.

CHAPTER 6

THOMAS

*T*he warning alarm on my computer dings, as it always does at 4:45, reminding me it's time to push away from my desk and to review the 'regular day'.

It's one of my *things*. I've tried to push the habit down on the rest of the company, but most don't take to it. Work hard, work fast, and do it by taking two fifteen-minute spots to intentionally do nothing except think.

By taking the first fifteen minutes of my day, I lay out exactly what I have to do. I review my long-term goals and then break them down into what I'm going to do that day. Then I get to it.

Of course, the day isn't always going to go to plan. In fact, a lot of days, things get torpedoed before I even get to lunch. But that's what this time is for. To reflect, to adjust, and to update my priorities.

There's nothing fancy to it. I don't have a meditation rug or trippy ambient music to put me in the proper mood. They're not needed. I turn away from my desk and close my eyes, letting what happened today wash over me.

It was a good day. The reports I got, the results generated, the plans that I sent out . . . they came back to me in good time and the quality was acceptable.

Still, everything didn't go to plan. I had to lay into Randall Towlee for his report on the Yakima project. It may not have been as bad as I made it seem, but I expect more from him, so he at least partially deserved some feedback.

Thinking of that early morning confrontation, I feel my heart quicken in my chest and my blood start to flow a little faster. It's not the memory of Randall Towlee's report causing it, either.

Randall, for all of his qualifications, is someone who only does what needs to be done. It's gotten him a long way, but that's not what I'm about.

I want perfection.

I want to exceed expectations.

But what my mind keeps going back to is the girl. With a few clicks, I review the email list to figure out her name. Mia Karakova. Amazingly, she's worked for me for years without my seeing her. Apparently, she's been trapped in the basement with Bill Radcliffe's team.

But in a glance, I can't wait to see her again. Her blonde hair hung in cornsilk waves down her back, with a few strands curling over her shoulders, framing a face that shouldn't have been as pleasing as it is.

Her eyes, while beautiful, are too wide-set, almost doll-like behind funky plastic frames, and her nose was a bit too upturned, naturally pixie-like, and her lips just a bit uneven, as though she'd been biting her puffy bottom one. But all together, somehow, it is sweet perfection.

Everything about her is impossible. Her body's no lines, all curves, all of them going in different directions but somehow coming harmoniously together in a multifaceted ballet that's interjected itself into my thoughts.

Her demure, almost shy sexiness inflames me, and I can barely focus for the rest of the fifteen minutes of my meditation. In fact, when five o'clock comes, I realize that I've spent the entirety of my meditation time researching her.

But in her very beauty, she scares me. I don't have a great history with beautiful women, and that history goes all the way back to my childhood.

"You know, Tommy, you're a very lucky little boy," Mrs. Franklin tells me

as my friend Ben and I enjoy some midafternoon cookies. "What with the mommy you have."

I don't really know what she's talking about. Mommy's . . . Mommy. I mean, they all have their good points. Mrs. Franklin, for instance, makes the best chocolate chip cookies in the world.

They're even better than Keebler's.

"Why?" I ask, trying to use words to explain all my thoughts. It's really hard, I think because there are ideas running around in my head that I don't even have the words for yet.

They say I'll learn more when I go to big kids' school next year.

"Honey, Grace Goldstone is a classic beauty," Mrs. Franklin says, her voice sounding both happy and maybe a little angry. "Every time we go shopping, I'm reminded just how much so. Most women would kill to have looks like hers."

I think about Mommy and shrug. The long cloth thing hanging by the fire-place that says Miss Teen California and the pictures of her with that sparkly thing in her hair say it too. But Mommy's job until she had me was to be pretty. That's what she said, at least.

"Honey, before I had you, people paid me thousands of dollars to take my picture," she'd say. I didn't quite understand why people would do that, but if Mommy said so, then it was true.

Ben and I finish our cookies, and then it's time for Ben's bath, so Mrs. Franklin walks me to the corner. I'm a big boy now. It's okay for me to walk the other half block to my house by myself. I know to stick to the sidewalk, and when I get to my house, I turn and wave at Mrs. Franklin just like I'm supposed to.

She waves back, and I walk up to my front door. But I stop with my hand on the screen handle as I hear arguing inside.

"How could you, Grace?" Daddy screams. He's very angry. "In our own bed?"

"It wasn't like I planned it, Dennis!" Mommy yells back. "It's not like you've been here anyway!"

"What does that matter? I put in long hours—"

"Hey!" I call out, opening the door. "I'm home!"

37

The memory hits me hard, and I shake my head, trying to blink it away, but it's already rolling like a movie screen in my mind.

The bus drops me off, and I hurry inside. I open the door, and everything's quiet. That's pretty normal. Mommy's been taking afternoon naps a lot recently, and she sometimes forgets to set her alarm. Checking the bedroom, I see her lying under the blankets, and I let her be.

Adults are weird sometimes.

At school, they make us take naps, and I hate it. Why nap when there's fun to be had?

But adults, who can stay up late and watch the cool movies, take naps by choice.

Whatever.

I go back to the living room, where I watch cartoons for I'm not sure how long. I just know it's time to turn it off when the stupid 'Power Princess' cartoon comes on.

Finally, I get really hungry, and I put my toys away. Mommy's still not up, but I can't really wait anymore, so I walk into the bedroom where she's still lying on the bed. The lights are off and the shades are pulled down. "Mommy?"

She doesn't move, her eyes closed and her hair all loose over her face like she does when she's asleep. I pat her shoulder through the blanket, but all she does is wiggle a little.

"Guess you're on your own, buddy," I tell myself, using the nickname Mommy sometimes uses for me.

That's okay, I'm a big boy now, so I go into the kitchen. Using the step stool, I get the box of chicken nuggets out of the freezer before looking at the microwave.

I'm not supposed to use this, but I've seen it used a lot of times and it's not that hard. A few minutes later, I'm eating from my plate of hot nuggets when the door to the garage opens and Daddy comes in, his suit coat still on and his tie pulled halfway down.

"Hey, buddy."

I smile, hoping he doesn't ask how I got these nuggets.

"Where's Mommy?" he asks, putting his briefcase on the table.

"Uhm . . . she's taking a nap," I admit, looking down. "I got hungry so I made these myself," I say, nodding to the plate. "I'm sorry, Daddy."

Daddy looks worried, and I'm afraid I got him angry, but he says nothing as he goes to the bedroom. I stuff my last nugget in my mouth and get up to take my plate to the sink. I'm halfway there when Daddy's scream scares me, and I drop my plate.

For some reason, the sight of the Batman shattering on the floor of the kitchen is what I'm going to remember most.

I sit up, gasping for air as I'm jerked back to the present.

Sleep . . . she wasn't sleeping. Six years old, and she'd left me.

The most beautiful woman I've ever known had cheated on her husband and killed herself afterward.

CHAPTER 7

MIA

"Well, well, if it isn't the beautiful stranger," Charlotte teases me as I slide into the booth at The Gravy Train.

The diner's busy, but this is a Friday lunch on payday, so it's not too unexpected. "I swear you've been a ghost the past week. No texts, no phone calls . . . if you hadn't shown up, I would have had to come down to your office just to get proof of life."

"Sorry, girls," I reply, sighing gratefully as I stretch out, "but I've been busting my ass with this project."

"Yeah?" Izzy says, trying to sound encouraging. "What's it about?"

"Well, I'm not supposed to spill any details. It's all corporate hush-hush, but I've been pulling long hours all week. There were team meetings four days this week, and after that, I had to really put the pedal down and bust my butt to even get home before ten o'clock."

I chuckle, though it sounds more like exhaustion escaping than mirth. "I haven't seen the sunset in a week."

"Damn, girl," Charlotte remarks as our lunches come. "Is it worth it?"

I shrug, trying to wrap my head around Thomas Goldstone's presence. He's been at every meeting, at least stopping in for a quick check-in.

And each time, I walk out of the room feeling like I just stuck my fingertip into a light socket.

"I don't know. But I do get seen by Mr. Goldstone . . . the boss."

"Yeah, well, he sounds too demanding for me," Izzy says, jumping in. "He'd better be worth all your attention."

Oh, my God, if she only knew. That man is sex on a stick. He could demand anything from me and I'd give it willingly, even if he does come off as an ass.

But I don't tell them that.

"I've heard people say he can be a jerk," I reply, stirring my soup and taking a sip, "and I get it. He maintains a lot of pressure on us to perform, but . . . we've got the heavy lifting done now, I think, so I guess his tactics work."

"So, no more pressure? No more crazy hours?" Charlotte asks, and I nod.

"I sent my report to Randall, our team leader, right after this morning's meeting. So while the project isn't done yet, I think most of what I'll have left is convincing the others why I think my analysis is correct."

Defending my ideas . . . that's definitely my weakness. While so far, corporate politics and turf fighting haven't come into play, the idea of standing in front of Thomas Goldman and trying to say anything coherent makes my head pound and my gut churn.

The man's just too handsome, whether it's in slacks and a dress shirt or jeans and a T-shirt. Oh, yes, I did manage to catch him in casual wear one evening when I was working late and went upstairs. I would've thought he'd look odd, so much power in such a rough wrapper, but the soft wear on the jeans had given me all sorts of dirty thoughts about teasing my hands along his thighs.

And now I don't know which fantasy image I prefer—rough and casual, or slick and formal.

His burning gaze, the powerful clench of his jaw as he chews over what other people are saying, the flex of his muscles straining against his shirt even as the fabric panics to release its hold on his perfect flesh . . . I might be getting home after ten, but I've been up until midnight just trying to get my mind calmed down.

Not that a man like that would notice a girl like me. I've barely spoken up in the meetings, spending most of my time burying my head in my tablet or pretending to be obsessed with the PowerPoints everyone else is putting up like experts.

Yeah, I've answered questions when someone's directed something my way, but for the most part, I've put all of my effort into my meta analysis, and that's not something that can get broken down into daily PowerPoint presentations.

"Earth to Mia, anyone there, cosmonaut?" Charlotte teases, waving a hand. "You spaced out for a minute there."

"Sorry. Guess I'm just mentally drained. What'd you say?"

"I said, is he as hot as he is on paper, or is it just airbrushing?" Charlotte asks. "Gah, he looks like Prince Charming to me."

"Prince Charming?" I ask, snorting. "Sure, he's good-looking." I make sure to play it down. Good-looking doesn't even begin to describe Thomas Goldstone.

"But he's not charming in any way, Char. He's less prince and more god-like." Before they get too excited, I continue, "Really pretty packaging on an arrogant, controlling center. Watch me control the winds, the lightning . . ."

I stab my fingers in the air like I'm directing weather forces and throw my head back in a villainous laugh.

Both girls grin at my antics. "Yeah, yeah, yeah. Babe, I'm not asking if he's *actually* charming," Charlotte laughs. "You know what I meant, and I think I got my answer. 'Really pretty packaging.'" She mimics my words with a waggle of her brows and a smirk.

"Okay, yeah, I guess I did answer. Fine. He's *really* nice on the eyes," I admit. "Still, that's all he is."

"Ooh . . . a hot but arrogant control freak?" Izzy sums up. "I don't know, I could work with that. For one night, at least."

I nod, matching her smile, but inside I'm not so sure. It's strange, because yes, Mr. Goldstone's been hard and domineering, just bordering on going over the asshole line most of the time he has been around, but there's something in the way he delivers each rebuke, each time he tells the team to work hard. To do more.

It seems to come from a place that . . . I don't know.

Maybe I'm just better at understanding numbers than people.

After lunch, I head back to my office, where there's an email from Kerry. *Please report to Mr. Goldstone's office at four thirty this afternoon.* My stomach drops and my heart races. Why would he want to see me? We just gave preliminary reports this morning.

I quickly grab my laptop and go upstairs to Bill's office. "Hey, Bill," I say, thankful for his open-door policy as I knock on the doorframe of his office, "you didn't get cc'd on this. What's up?"

Bill looks over the short email, his lips narrowing as he hums. "I'm not sure, but be careful. I don't want to scare you, but that's always been Goldstone's 'killing time'. He brings people up at four thirty to pink slip them personally. Guess it saves them the humiliation of walking out in the middle of the day, but at the same time, it feels like a long ride down to get your shit together. I know how I felt when he and I had our face to face about my transfer down here."

"But I've been busting my ass on this project," I protest, and Bill nods, giving me a supportive smile.

"Good. Then make sure he knows if he doesn't already. That's one thing about him. He does respect strength, Mia. Don't forget that."

I go back to my office, and for the next two and a half hours, I do everything I can to review what I've done this week. I play out the meetings in my mind and go over the numbers on the spreadsheets once more.

I can't find a flaw in my analysis. I looked at each of the properties and ranked the top four from best investment on down, highlighting the methods needed to gain influence, the hurdles in the way, the outlays, the sunk costs, the potential returns on investment . . . everything.

Four properties, fifty-eight pages of work including charts. I even did an extra five-page summary so that someone could gain a quick grasp on the subject if they needed.

Finally, at four fifteen, I grab my laptop and head upstairs to the twenty-*fifth* floor. Goldstone's floor. I've never been up here before, and I'm surprised at just how . . . efficient everything looks.

The hallway layout is simple at best, with only four doors excluding the shared bathroom . . . at least, I guess it's a shared bathroom. There's only one sign sticking out.

It only takes me two minutes to find Mr. Goldstone's office, or more specifically, his secretary's. We've swapped emails, but this is the first time we've met face to face. She's a well put-together woman, probably in her mid-thirties but could be a young forty, her black hair pinned up stylishly and her makeup flawless.

"Hello, Kerry? I'm Mia Karakova."

Kerry turns around, nodding as she looks me over. "Of course. You're right on time. He's expecting you."

Nervously, I cross the space toward Mr. Goldstone's door, my heart in my throat as I reach up and knock softly. It feels like I'm being asked to enter my own execution chamber.

"Mr. Goldstone?"

"Come in," he growls from the other side of the door, and I quiver and glance over my shoulder to Kerry before remembering what Bill told me. Strength.

He respects strength.

Tugging on the hem of my T-shirt with one hand in my best Picard Maneuver, I wish I'd dressed better today. We'd had a meeting today, but past the first introductory one when I'd dressed up, I've reverted to my usual more semi-casual wear. Thank God I at least have on a denim skirt and flats with my T-shirt, considering it's Friday.

I open the door and step inside. If I thought that the outer office was designed for efficiency, then Thomas Goldstone's inner office is like the epitome of Spartan efficiency.

"Mr. Goldstone, you asked to see me?"

He looks up from his desk, where he's set aside his keyboard to look at a bound folder instead.

"Sit down, Mia."

He indicates the chair in front of his desk, an uncomfortable looking black metal and nylon chair that at least has a little padding under my butt, which barely touches the cushion before his eyes start blazing.

"What have you been doing all week?"

"Sir, I'm not sure what you—"

"When Randall said to give you a chance to join the action team, I was initially hesitant. You've put up some good results but have a bit of a reputation as an oddball. I wondered how you'd work with a diverse team, especially when I expect so much. And now a week in, and *this* is what you turn out?"

He tosses the binder aside like it's nothing more than Charmin in a portfolio.

"I—"

Nope, not going to get a word in edgewise. Instead, for five whole minutes, I feel what it's like to be 'put on blast' by Thomas Goldstone. Every word is like a battering ram to my confidence, every word a cut to my pride.

Just like with Randall, he never loses his temper, but he chews up my report line by line and spits it out.

"Like this," he says, his voice dripping with bitter disdain for my work. "Fifteen million in debt servicing and issuance of new stock for the Columbia River Community Hospital. What led you to—"

"Stop."

I don't know where the strength in my voice comes from, but it cuts through Mr. Goldstone's monologue, and he slams his palms down on his desk, his computer monitors shaking but nothing tipping over.

"What did you say?" he asks, seemingly shocked and for the first time bordering on true anger.

"I said stop," I repeat, whipping open my laptop and pulling up my files. "You've been downing my report from the moment I walked in the door. But what you just said . . . it's wrong."

"Wrong?" It's said with a silky edge of darkness.

I need to keep up my momentum. "Give me a minute to explain, sir."

He looks at me, and I wonder if he's going to grab me in those massive hands of his and hurl me through the window.

Stupidly, my brain tries to calculate just how long it would take for me to fall twenty-five floors before I impact on the street below. But instead, he sits down, his brows knit together as he crosses his arms over his chest.

He nods. "Proceed." It's more challenge than permission, but I jump in.

"Mr. Goldstone, for a whole week I've worked my ass off doing analysis for this project. I took figures and work from the other team members, re-did half of them myself, and then gave you a spot-on analysis. Here's what I've been doing this past week."

I stand up, boldly moving around to his side of the desk to set my laptop down in front of him. Standing at his side, I pull up my files.

"Now, CRCH . . . first off, I didn't even put that in my top four list for the exact reason you stated. They're absolutely drowning in debt. And it's in an area that already has three hospitals, two of which are part of state university systems, which doesn't help CRCH's case. There's no edge to it. It's not a Goldstone brand move. How that even made it into the possible acquisitions you're reading, I'll never know."

He grunts, and I know I'm gaining some wiggle room. I've turned the corner on this meeting, and a manic energy fills me, telling me to seize as much advantage as I can.

I use my energy and take the next twenty minutes going over what I produced. I show him everything, the analysis, the data . . . I even show him the muck on the wall Excel spreadsheet that I created to allow me to group and extrapolate the trends that I used.

His eyes follow my every word, from number to number, line to line, and I realize that not many people understand me when I deep-dive into the figures this way. But he is catching it all. Not just the data, but the extrapolations and analysis. He understands what all this dry information actually *means* the same way I do.

When I finish, a sheen of sweat coats my forehead, and I'm afraid a drop or two may have run down my neck to disappear into my T-shirt. I'm breathless, flushed . . . and my nerves have changed into pride at what I've done.

"I know my numbers are solid, Mr. Goldstone. And I am confident in my decision when I say you should invest in Pacific Cascade Children's. It makes financial sense, and while it's not my area of expertise, the less tangible image rewards of investing in a children's hospital make it the best bet on every front. So if you're going to fire me, do it. Go with whatever other choice you think is better. Just remember what I said when I'm proven right."

I turn around, leaving my laptop on his desk because I'm sure that I just got myself fired with my big mouth. I can't imagine that anyone says much other than *Yes, sir* to Thomas Goldstone.

In fact, I bet when I open this door, building security will be waiting for me, ready to drag me down the stairs and out the door if I don't go quietly.

But I'm not going to give them the satisfaction. I cross the room with my head held high, reaching for the door handle when Mr. Goldstone's voice rumbles across the room again.

"Stop."

My hand freezes an inch from the handle and I turn around.

Mr. Goldstone taps his fingers together, his eyes still sparking with anger . . . but I swear behind that, I can see something else.

"You think you've got it all figured out, don't you? You handed me your little perfect analysis, drop the mic, and strut out the door like this discussion is over. I do believe it's my turn for rebuttal now."

"I . . ." I reply, hating the quaver in my voice as I do. "I didn't plan on the mic drop. I figured I just got myself fired."

Goldstone frowns. "Why would you think that? Have you not done your research on me? That surprises me."

"I . . . I've done some analysis on you," I admit, a blush creeping up my neck as I realize how that can sound. Guilty as charged though. A lot of my analysis has been of him physically, though I did Google the hell out of him after that first meeting.

"I'd like you to share that analysis, and perhaps we can discuss my take on your hospital recommendations. Tonight, eight o'clock?" he says, the question not so much a request but an order couched in just enough politeness as to not make it totally sound that way. "I'll pick you up at your place."

I can't decide if this sounds like a date or a continued business meeting, but my racing heart in my throat knows which I want it to be.

"But how—"

He ignores me. "Dismissed," Mr. Goldstone says, this time a clear order. "Remember, eight o'clock. A dress. Formal. Have Kerry help you if that's a problem."

He looks me up and down, and I fight the urge to twist my toe into the carpet, wondering what he sees when he looks at me.

Nerdy? Cute but careless with my appearance? Those are definitely true, but the light in his eyes says he might see just a little something more too.

"And Mia?"

"Yes, Mr. Goldstone?"

"Call me Thomas . . . never Tom."

CHAPTER 8

THOMAS

*A*djusting the knot on my tie, I check myself out in the mirror. It's only seven fifteen, but I told Mia I'd pick her up at eight and I don't want her to wait.

For a week, I've wanted her. From that first glance, images of Mia Karakova have burned themselves into my mind. I can't get enough of her, but I've had to push myself away from the meetings, from drinking her in and obsessing over her. She's got a thousand and one little ways that she's teased me and she doesn't even know it.

The way she bites the end of her pen, her lips nibbling at the plastic making me want her mouth and teeth on my skin.

The way her eyelashes flutter behind her lenses as she absorbs someone else's prattle. I want to make her eyelids flutter like that as my tongue sends shivers up her spine.

Lust isn't the word to describe the driven thirst coursing through my veins for her. I've never felt this way about any woman before, but by some miracle, I've been able to stay professional.

Until this afternoon.

The first time I had her alone, I caved.

I'd needed to prove a point, to myself and to her, that I'm in charge. So I'd burst in with both barrels blazing, taking control of the conversation. And at first, it'd worked as she shrank beneath my criticism.

But then . . .

The way her eyes sparkled behind her eyeglasses, the intensity in her voice, the way her breath quickened and her body seemed to grow before my eyes. I couldn't resist, and watching her storm out, her ass flexing in her denim skirt, made me thankful I'd instituted denim Fridays at the office.

But nothing was as much fun as the few moments where I'd teased her. She tried to stay strong, and she could be, especially after the way she said she's analyzed me. I'd been glad I was behind my desk because my cock sprang to full attention at that comment, with the way her cheeks blushed and she unconsciously bit her lip.

It doesn't take me long to drive to Mia's apartment, a decent place in a decent part of Roseboro. Still, I know she can afford more than this. She must have either some outstanding debts, or more likely, knowing what I do about her, she's socking it away, because while it is a nice enough place, she could afford more.

I walk up to her second-floor apartment, knocking on her door just as my watch says seven fifty-eight.

"Just a moment!"

One minute later, the door opens . . . and I'm floored.

She's a goddess, wrapped in a black, deep V-necked cocktail dress with floral accents along the top of the thigh-high slit that makes every inch of her flawless alabaster skin look succulent.

I'm almost tempted to push her back inside her place and take her right here, taste her to see if her skin's as creamy sweet as it looks.

She's even changed her glasses, going with some black frames that give her perfection a subtle quirky, geeky twist that only highlights just how unique she is.

"Mister . . . Thomas," Mia says, biting her lip but still smiling. "Uhm, I hope this is okay? I don't often dress formally."

"It's perfect," I reassure her, checking her out all the way down to her open-toed heels that show off toes so precious I want to suck them until she giggles or orgasms, whichever comes first. "You look beautiful."

It's so true that my stomach clenches tightly, threatening to send this date careening off the rails before we even get to the restaurant.

I grew up with Grace Goldstone as the epitome of female beauty in my mind. She was my mother, but as I grew up, I could still admit how gorgeous she was.

And she'd abandoned me.

But Mia isn't Grace Goldstone, I keep telling myself, and it helps me calm down a little. *She's too . . . unorthodox.*

I'm more surprised than ever when we get out to the parking lot and she pulls away to run her hand over the fender of my car.

"Whoa . . . Acura NSX with a hybrid twin turbo. Super-rare here in the States."

"You like cars," I comment, and she turns, blushing a little. "No?"

"Not exactly. I'm just a geek," Mia explains shyly. "One of my favorite animes has a character who drives an NSX."

I nod as though I typically discuss cartoons with my dates, but I tuck the information away, escorting her around to the passenger side and opening the door for her.

She gets in, revealing a long stretch of subtly toned thigh that has my cock jumping in my pants again, and I have to take a moment to adjust myself as I go around back and get in the driver's seat. I look over at her, where she's wide-eyed, checking out the interior.

"Never saw the inside of one."

"I've customized it some," I admit. "It's a better driving experience for me this way."

It's about this time that I expect Mia to try to play off the fact that my bank account dwarfs hers with either an unfunny joke or an obvious money grab. In my experience, that's what women tend to do when faced with an in-your-face show of my wealth. Instead, she smiles, relaxing a little as the leather seats of my car support her body.

It's not a long drive. Roseboro's not large enough for anyone to have to worry about a long drive anywhere, but what the city lacks in size, it more than makes up for in quality. Quality I help cultivate with selective loans, support, and donations.

Case in point . . . Moreau-Laurent's. A husband and wife partnership, they may not have the huge name that comes with having a restaurant in a bigger city, but they do have a James Beard award, and more importantly, they have passion for their cuisine. And they've done so well in Roseboro that they paid off their loan with me in record time.

"I've driven by this place but never been here," Mia admits as we sit down, the white damask tablecloth just draping to our laps. "What do you recommend?"

I grin, seeing how she's not trusting in the waiter but in my opinion. "I tend to always get the smoked salmon, but . . ." I let my voice drop deeper and quieter as if I'm sharing a secret. "I know what I like."

I'm looking directly at her, and judging by the way she squirms in her seat, I think she recognizes I'm not talking about the food.

"Oh?" Mia asks, lifting an eyebrow. "I thought we were here to discuss the hospital figures?"

It's a challenge wrapped in flirtation as she traces a finger along the rim of her water glass and looks at me through her lashes.

She's testing the waters, wanting me to make my intentions crystal clear before she steps off the corporate straight and narrow, which doesn't surprise me about a number cruncher like her, even if she's definitely not a rule follower.

But I left that path a week ago when I first saw her, and I'm the bastard who's going to pull her into the deep end with me, regardless of whether she can swim with the sharks or not. I'll hold her, protect her, buoy her, if need be.

"Mia, though there's absolutely no pressure either way, I think we're both well aware that this dinner has nothing to do with the project." I pin her with my eyes, daring her to disagree.

"Aren't we—and by 'we', I mean you—getting a little ahead of ourselves?" she backpedals, but I can see the fire in her eyes.

The longing is so clear, and I realize that for all her sexiness, perhaps she's shy or inexperienced. The former is surprisingly adorable, a word I don't think I've ever actually used, not even in my mind. The latter can be delightfully corrected.

"Maybe . . . but when I want something, I go for it. Question is, Miss Mia Karakova, do you?"

She pushes her hair behind her ear, meeting my eyes as she lifts her chin defiantly. And it's game on.

Dinner is delicious, but more sumptuous is Mia. She keeps the conversation light, even touching on Roseboro and Goldstone Inc. But I don't mind, because intermixed with the first-date conversation, it seems we're tossing innuendo back and forth like this is a tennis match.

By the time the check comes, the sexual tension is like a tractor beam pulling us together, and it feels natural to let my hand fall to her waist as we walk out.

"So, what did you think?"

"I think I haven't tasted a damn thing since the chicken was taken away," she admits. "The company was too magnetic."

"Too bad. You missed a great dessert."

Mia's lips twitch, and I laugh. "Yes?"

"Oh, I was just waiting for the come-on line about how you've got another dessert waiting for me," Mia says, and I can't hold back my smirk.

"You said it, not me."

I drive back to the Goldstone building one-handed, my right hand resting on Mia's thigh, squeezing and stroking the muscle higher and higher over top of her dress. She's biting her lip again, but I can see her nipples hardening through the top of her dress, and I grin. If she's wearing a bra that thin . . . she's been thinking the same way I have.

"Why are we back here?" she asks, a little confused as I pull into the parking garage in the sub-basement.

"Just trust me. You'll love this," I reply as I lead her over to my elevator. There's one floor that's not accessible on the touch panel, only available when I insert my key card, and the motor starts.

As we start to ascend, I crowd Mia against the side of the elevator, pulling her glasses off and tucking them in my breast pocket. "Thomas—"

I kiss her hard, claiming her mouth, and she freezes in shock for half a moment before giving in to me, her hands coming up to my neck and pulling me in deeper.

Her kisses are soft caresses against my lips combined with the strong, powerful twist of her tongue as she greedily tries to taste me, our mouths opening up to each other.

I breathe her in, her unique scent searing its way inside me before I give the air back to her and she moans in ecstasy.

My hand runs up her thigh, lifting the hem of her dress as I trace the delicious contour of her leg, realizing that she didn't wear any stockings. The soft sexiness I've been watching all night was just her natural skin. My cock throbs in my pants, pressing against her hip.

"Is that . . . for me?" she asks, moaning as I grind against her.

I grin, promising her with my eyes. The elevator dings, and I take her by the hand, pulling her out into my entryway.

"Welcome to my home."

I don't give her time to respond as I pull her to me, crushing her in my arms as I consume her with another powerful kiss. I'm barely able to watch where I'm going as I drag her to my bedroom, ready to conquer her.

Somewhere along the way, her dress gets unzipped and my jacket and tie get pulled off, a button popping and bouncing away noisily before we're in my bedroom. My shirt is half undone, exposing my chest while I look at Mia on my bed, her breasts cupped in a lacy midnight-blue bra with matching see-through panties.

"Gorgeous, naughty girl."

Mia lets out a seductive smile and reaches for my belt. I step back, shrugging my shirt the rest of the way off and undoing my pants, stripping naked for her while she watches. Her fingertips stroke her nipples and drift between her legs, and she gasps as I come into view, fully hard and ready for her.

I lie down on the bed next to her, pulling her to me and kissing her again, licking over to her neck to nuzzle against her ear.

She moans, and I growl in triumph, cupping her ass and squeezing hard as I explore her body. Every inch of her skin pressed against me is an erotic revelation, a symphony of sensation crackling up and down my nerves until my cock is twitching, oozing clear drops of precum even before I have her panties off.

I push her onto her back, my need taking over. Mia barely has a chance to take a breath before I tug her panties to the side and thrust two fingers deep into her pussy, making her cry out.

"Oh . . . fuuuuuuu—"

I love the way she draws it out, her eyes rolling back as I nip and suck on her throat, sucking hard enough to mark her and give her a hickey. My thumb brushes against her clit, and electricity leaps through her body, making her cry out as her hips lift up to meet me.

She's tight, so tight my fingers are squeezed almost numb as I pump them in and out of her, and dimly, in the part of my mind not taken over by my animal passions, I'm glad that I'm doing this to prepare her instead of taking her hard with my cock first.

I don't want to hurt her.

But another side of me wants to be rough. It wants to hear her cry out as I pound her, and that side eventually takes over, though I hope she's ready for me. I pull my fingers out, licking them half clean before shoving them in Mia's mouth, startling her into sucking her own juices off my fingers.

"Like that, don't you? You taste so fucking good."

Mia's eyes close, and she moans around my fingers, but I pull back. "That's enough. I'm just getting started."

She whimpers but spreads her legs wider for me. I look down at her pussy for the first time, my inner beast tamed just slightly by the beauty that I see. Her pale lips are puffy with need, slick with her desire, and her core is deeper pink, beckoning me to come closer.

As I guide my cock inside her, I take it slow so I can watch her pussy suck me inside, each inch stretching and disappearing inside her. Mia moans, her eyes rapturous as she watches too until I'm all the way in, my hips pressed against hers.

"More," she whispers, and in her quiet plea I hear damnation and salvation. I grab her wrists, pinning her to the bed as I pull back, pausing for just a moment before thrusting hard into her again.

Her pussy is the tightest, most amazing embrace I've ever felt. With each thrust she pulls me in tighter, wanting more of my cock, and each time I pull back, her body clings to me, not willing to let go until she's wrung every bit of pleasure she can out of me.

I let go of her wrists to clutch her tightly, greedy to feel her skin against mine, her lips against mine, her tongue wrapped around mine.

She *must* be mine.

My bedroom fills with the deep animal sounds of our fucking, my hips slapping against hers as she tilts her hips up, begging me to give it to her deep and hard. I'm growling, pounding her with everything I have as my inner beast is unleashed.

I grind against her, feeling her body tighten and squeeze around me, her orgasm rushing through her like a thunderbolt.

"Thomas!" she screams, her nails digging into my back, but I don't let up. If anything, I thrust harder, faster, filling her clenching, spasming pussy with my thick shaft until I feel my balls tighten. She's moaning deeply too, her eyes open and staring into mine as she feels me swell. "Please . . . I'm so close again . . ."

It's ten seconds of eternity, holding back my climax until Mia comes again, this time deep and savage as she grunts out a curse.

I cry out, my balls exploding as I fill her with my cum, my body spasming and shaking as I press her body tighter against the bed. My back and neck arch to the point I can feel crackles going up and down my spine even as the last droplets leave me, but I stay inside her for a moment, enjoying the depth of the connection.

I collapse on top of Mia, and she holds me close, sighing happily.

CHAPTER 9

MIA

"Oof," I grunt to myself as I settle into my chair on Monday morning.

Never have twenty hours done so much to my body. Wanting more in the morning turned into a double-dose of aggressive, intense sex with Thomas that left me so weak and unable to move that morning quickly became four o'clock Saturday afternoon before I could drag myself away, part of me still wanting to stay behind.

Twenty hours . . . and I've never been more grateful for having a Saturday night alone. I'm not too sure if my body could have taken another night of Thomas Goldstone.

Even today, my body aches in all the right ways. My nipples are chafing pleasantly in my bra from where Thomas almost gnawed them half off, my pussy still pulses with my heartbeat, and as I settle into my chair and pull up eight hours of chill-hop to let me just glide through the day, only one thought goes through my head.

When's our next date?

I'm just getting through a weekend's worth of bullshit emails when there's a knock on my door and it opens to reveal Randall Towlee, looking bright-eyed and bushy-tailed. He's freshly shaven, with a recent hair trim, and his suit looks like it just came from the dry cleaner's yesterday.

"Hey, Mia, how was your weekend?"

"Not bad," I reply carefully.

Oh, God, does he know? "How was yours?"

"Eh, same old, same old," Randall says. "Listen, I know this might be a little weird, but last week during the meetings, I kept feeling a vibe in the air. You did too, right?"

Huh? Is Randall asking about me and Thomas? "I'm not sure—"

"I'm asking because I was figuring, since the group's pretty much over with now, just a few once-a-week meetings . . . how about we go out and celebrate? Six thirty tonight? I know a good little bar that has your name on it."

It's hard not to thump my head on the desk. Seriously, I feel like I've just walked into the *Twilight Zone.*

Has something been dumped in the water of every man in Roseboro over the past few days? I've gone six months without a guy so much as looking at me, and now I've met two men, both of them handsome, intelligent, and more than well-employed, and they've asked *me* out.

Me.

The girl who spends most of her time buried in numbers to create meta-analyses that most folks couldn't understand even if I could explain it to them.

The girl whose idea of 'making an effort' is to pull her hair back into a ponytail and who treats her hair like one of those tablet dress-up apps. Pink and green? Cool!

The girl who wears glasses, watches anime, and scream-sings trance metal music . . . in Russian.

But when I'm suddenly smacked in the face with the fact that both Randall Towlee and Thomas Goldstone seem interested in me, the choice is pretty easy.

"I'm sorry, Randall. I'm flattered, but I don't mix . . ." I start before realizing that whether I'm trying to say 'no' nicely or not, I'm not going to be a hypocrite about it. Mix business and pleasure? Uhm, I mixed it three times between Friday night and Saturday afternoon, and I came seven times in the course of doing so.

I may not think Randall's sexy at all compared to the human video game god that is Thomas Goldstone, but I'm not going to lie to him.

"It's just not a good idea. Sorry."

His face gets cloudy and his eyes pinch in, like it never occurred to him that I might say no. "Are you sure about that?"

"I'm sure," I reply, surprised at the strength in my voice. "But I think we've done some good work on the hospital project. I'm looking forward to this week's meeting update." It's an obvious redirect back to professional ground, but Randall doesn't exactly take the hint.

"What are you working on now?" he says, leaning against the edge of my desk and eyeing me up and down, though he can only see to my waist since I'm sitting.

I feel like he's trying to get under my skin. "Well, considering it's nine in the morning on a Monday, I'm just going through my emails, getting a start on my week." I hope he'll hear that I'm busy, because while I'd kind of love to tell him to go back upstairs where he belongs, I can't really kick a VP out of my office.

"You are always a morning person. One of the reasons I chose you for my team over some other analyst. You don't start slow. You hit the ground running."

Under normal circumstances, that'd be a compliment. But the way Randall says it makes it come off flirty. A few days ago, I probably would've been excited to have a cute guy flirt with me a little, but it's different now, though I can't explain to Randall why that is.

Awkwardly, I stand and go around the other side of my desk, heading for the door to put some space between us. My voice is bright and falsely high as I say, "Yep, as Mr. Goldstone said, gotta get out there and sell those cookies!"

I'd actually laughed at that one the first time I'd heard Thomas say it. Comparing our work to the Girl Scouts probably isn't politically correct, but it'd struck me as funny.

Randall walks toward me and pauses in the doorway. "You're sure?"

I nod. "I'm sure. Thank you for the invitation, but I'll have to politely decline." It's as gentle of a letdown as I can give because I want to be crystal clear.

"Let's not let this become unprofessional."

"Don't worry," I reply sweetly, so saccharine that a Tic Tac wouldn't melt on my tongue right now. "I won't."

He leaves, and I sit back down, wondering what fueled all that. I mean, first off, asking me out? I just don't get it.

I'm not some uber-hottie. If this were *Scooby-Doo*, I'd be Velma, not Daphne.

So why are two guys who are certifiable studs making moves on me?

~

SO, HOW WAS YOUR DAY?

I glance at the text message, grinning. Of all the silly things to be doing, I'm at home, it's eight o'clock at night, and I'm swapping texts with Thomas.

OK. U know how much I luv my little cave. New music mix today had me jamming.

Oh? Who?

I laugh, shaking my head. *U don't wanna know. Total geekdom.*

I happen to like the fact that you're an unabashed geek.

Really? Y?

Because you're smart. Smart is sexy.

I feel a tingle between my legs, and I smile, letting my free hand drift down my shirt. Yup, I've got high beams going too.

Even if I dye my hair?

What do you mean?

I like to put streaks in my hair. I change it almost every week. I cut two inches of Bright Blood-Orange-Red out for the project meetings to look professional. I might be a little salty about it still. ;)

Hair doesn't make you professional. And I'd take you salty or sweet.

He adds a tongue emoji and I can't decide for a moment if that's cute or cheesy. I decide it's a bit of both and that I like it because it reminds me of his tongue licking me all over.

I know. So . . . U don't mind?

Not at all.

Whoa. I grin, a bit surprised because I'd expected him to be a bit more traditional and prudish about my wild hair, but maybe I should've given him more credit because he has been inordinately accepting of my vast musical taste and anime chatter. I type again, looking for ideas. *So . . . what's your favorite color?*

Depends. What does the old jelly bracelet code say?

Oh, the flashbacks that brings up . . . and if you choose the color, you get what that means?

No, Thomas sends back. *I'll get what I want either way.*

I should be turned off . . . but I'm not. If anything, his swagger and confidence have me even more turned on.

Somehow, that doesn't surprise me.

Speaking of what I want, he says, shifting back to the full spelling he uses from time to time, like he's back to being 'professional', *tomorrow morning, come to my office.*

Uhm, that doesn't sound like the smartest plan?

That's putting it mildly. I can't just waltz into his office like nothing has changed. Hell, Kerry will be able to read it all over my face as soon as I step off the elevator, and the last thing he probably wants is gossip about the basement girl coming and maybe *coming* in his office.

That was an order, Miss Karakova.

Why?

Our next date. It's a political fundraiser down in Portland, and I need you fitted for the event.

Wait, next date? He didn't even ask, he just . . . *Is my cocktail dress not good enough?*

Not for this. You need a full-length gown, and I have a stylist coming in. They'll do the fitting tomorrow, and Friday night's the fundraiser. We'll discuss details tomorrow after your fitting.

I have a chance to say no. I mean, he didn't ask, he's just demanding.

But I could still tell him no, especially about something big and public like this. He's assuming that I want to go with him, and that I . . . *OK. What time?*

9:15.

OK. Then let me get my beauty sleep tonight. See you in the morning?

You're already beautiful, but sleep tight. Goodnight, Mia.

Goodnight . . . Tommy.

He doesn't reply, which I take as a sign of approval. I didn't mean to call him Tommy when he made me come that next morning, but once I did, it just fit. Like it was something just between us.

CHAPTER 10

MIA

$\mathcal{T}$he executive meeting room on the twenty-fifth floor is perhaps the most luxurious room I've seen in the Goldstone Building.

In a place that's designed around efficiency at every turn. This room's dripping in luxury, from the carpeting so thick it looks like it could cushion a tap-dancing elephant to leather chairs that creak only to mellowly remind you of how buttery rich their upholstery is. And the *piece de resistance* is the crisp display paneling the far wall, so large it's almost over the top.

All in all, the room's amazing.

You could throw the Super Bowl party of all Super Bowl parties here.

But right now, corporate meetings are the last thing this room's set up for. Instead, there's a trio of mirrors, a huge rack of gowns, and a bunch of other stuff that I honestly don't quite grasp the use of.

But the biggest thing in the room is truly . . . huge. As in, a bald man who looks like he's nearly seven feet tall, with a barrel-shaped upper body that's clad in . . . lilac velvet?

"Hi, uhm I'm—" I start before the giant of a man turns, a huge smile spreading across his face.

"My next canvas to show the world how fabulous life can be," he says melodramatically, his voice sounding nothing like I would expect, given what he's wearing. It's as deep as James Earl Jones's voice. "Come in, come in. I'm Damien Rayie, the artist who will transform you into the princess you should be."

It's a hell of an introduction, and I feel weird as I step inside, closing the door behind me. "Hi, I'm Mia Karakova."

"Lovely to meet you, Mia. Come now, let's start with that hair. What did you do with it?"

"Uh . . . black and green streaks?"

Damien shakes his head. "Not that, I mean the style, the style! Oh, we have our hands full today!"

He sits me down as an assistant pops out from behind the rack of dresses, and for the next hour, my head's the center of attention while Damien talks constantly.

"So this event, it's a political fundraiser, which means I'll have to restrain myself. It's a shame, because I have rarely seen such a perfect set of raw materials for me to work with. Such is life, but maybe we can have another opportunity." He winks conspiratorially.

"Wait," I ask, sipping at the tea that another assistant gave me. "What do you mean, perfect raw materials?"

"What do I mean?" Damien asks, looking like I've taken leave of my senses. "What do I mean? Do you really not know, or are you mocking Damien and his vision?" He eyes me sharply, and I get the sense that he's seeing into my soul.

"I'm not mock—ow!" I answer as the person on my hair tugs a knot free. "Come on, I condition my hair three times a week. It can't be that bad!"

"Hush now, darling. Stella knows what she is doing. I do think those streaks are very you, and yes, when I say raw material, I mean *raw material*." He lifts my chin with one finger, looking deeply into my eyes. "I don't think you realize how beautiful you are, but don't worry. If you didn't before, you will when we're done."

After the hair, Stella moves around to focus on my makeup.

"Why are we doing all this now? The fundraiser's not until Friday."

Damien hums. "Trial run. And to choose the proper dress, one must be conscious of the total vision. I can't have you trying on gowns with a messy bun and a bare face." He shivers like the mere thought is off-putting, which makes me laugh.

Stella huffs her annoyance, and I straighten, sitting up tall and still for her to work. I close my eyes, letting the brush strokes along my face soothe my nerves.

This is crazy, like some sort of fairy godmother shit, and though I don't want to get my hopes up, there's a piece of me that hopes Damien can do something with me to make it so that I feel right when I walk into the fundraiser on Thomas's arm. Otherwise, I'm afraid I'm going to stick out like a sore thumb and be an embarrassment, not to Thomas but to myself.

Stella intones, "Open." I open my eyes to see her scanning my face critically. "It'll do."

And that's exactly what I wanted to hear, I think, holding back the eye roll but saying, "Great. Mother Russia is not amused."

Damien doesn't even get caught by my weird little jokes to myself. "Now, the lingerie! What are you wearing now?"

I've never felt so deconstructed but at the same time supportively rebuilt. Damien forgets nothing, scheduling a mani-pedi and full-body waxing for Thursday evening, then picking out a set of lingerie for me that feels . . .

"My God, where did you find this?" I ask as I look at myself in the mirror. It's not slutty, but sexy and supportive at the same time. I feel like my breasts have been lifted by magic, and they look damn good, from what I can tell.

Damien's being nice, letting me try everything on in a little ad-hoc changing room behind a curtain, but I almost want to show him how good this looks. "It's amazing!"

"Damien has his suppliers, darling," Damien replies behind the curtain, chuckling. "As I said, a true artist does not depend on labels but on the materials. This comes from a little boutique in Seattle. Now for the dress!"

We go through a dozen dresses, each one more fabulous than the previous. Damien doesn't let me look at the results though, just him and his assistants as they study me. "No," he says at the first. "With hair like hers, that tone just isn't right."

Next.

"Washes out her skin, and I don't want to risk that silk with a bronzer."

Next.

The fifth, he laughs at, shaking his head. "Only if we want someone to call you Elsa . . . no, try the yellow-gold one. It's dramatic, but maybe that's what we need."

Finally, he hits on *the dress*, and Damien's face blooms into a wide smile. "Yes! That's the one!"

"Can I see?" I ask, and Damien nods. He points to his assistant, who uncovers the mirrors, and I turn.

The sight of me takes my breath away. The skirt is full and elegant, clinging to my waist before puffing out just a little in golden yellow waves that are a shade darker than my hair, while the top shines with encrusted crystals, framing my stomach and breasts in contours that highlight my figure.

I blink, and my fingers shake as I adjust my glasses, which somehow compliment the whole ensemble even though these are just my work glasses.

"I . . . I'm beautiful," I murmur, but it's more than that.

For the first time in my life, I see myself as not just brains, not just 'meh' looking, but beyond beautiful. I'm fucking *gorgeous*. With my hair piled on top of my head the way it is, my neck arches gracefully like a swan's, and the ringlets that have been allowed to escape the updo frame my face and make me feel . . . "Damien, thank you!"

"It is nothing, darling," Damien says, grunting as I turn and hug him tightly. "Mia, my dear, is this your first time understanding?"

Tears threaten to spill from my eyes, and I nod, looking up at him. "Papa calls me his princess, jokes I'm Anastasia, but . . . but . . ."

"But he is your Papa, and that makes it easy to dismiss," Damien says, patting my shoulder gently with his massive hand. "Trust me, I understand. Now, we are not finished. A few accessories, not too many. As you said, you are beautiful as you are. Just enough to accentuate, not distract. First . . . a necklace to match your glasses. Or do you wear contacts?"

"Never," I admit. "They irritate me."

"Come, I have a dark crystal set that'll go perfectly with that and the hair colors."

I just get the necklace, obsidian and pearl with a smoky dark gray diamond in the middle, clasped around my neck when there's a knock on the door, and Thomas comes in.

"I came to see—"

His voice stops as he sees me, and I gulp, doing my best little curtsy for him as I smile widely. "What do you think?"

Damien looks eager to hear praise as well, but Thomas's eyes never leave mine as he studies me.

Silently, he crosses the room, taking in my hair, my skin, and my curves and looking at me with a fire burning in his eyes that both scares me and turns me on. Either he's about to explode . . . or he's about to *explode*.

"Everyone out," he says, his eyes fixing on mine. "Now."

Damien opens his mouth, snapping it shut after a moment and waving his assistants out. He tosses me a wink and a big grin before calling out, "Lovely to meet you, Miss Karakova."

Thomas walks them to the door, closing it and throwing the lock while I stand next to the conference table, trying to figure out whether he's angry or turned on.

"Thomas?" I ask, and he crosses the room, grabbing my waist and pulling me to him before crushing my lips in an intense kiss.

Question answered.

CHAPTER 11

THOMAS

I'd waited as long as I could, for hours as Damien laid claim to the executive conference room. I knew that he was going to take his time, and when he was done, Mia would see and feel what I see in her. But he's an artist, and artists are . . . inefficient in their genius. So I tried to be patient, imagining what they were doing in there.

But I'm still shocked at the vision before me as she stands in her heels, her body wrapped in golden silk that makes her glow in the midday sunlight coming through the windows.

"Thomas?" she asks, but my animalistic instincts have kicked in, and I'm barely able to keep myself together long enough to lock the door before I'm on her, pulling her to me and claiming her as mine.

My hands tug at the gown, lifting the hem as I push her against the table, her lips and tongue finding mine. I move down her jaw and neck, my mouth fastening on her skin again, inhaling and tasting her unique scent.

She's not wearing perfume. It's just her natural essence driving me wild and making my cock harden instantly inside my pants.

I've never done this, not here, not like this. But in this moment, I don't care about appropriateness and rules. I want her and I'm going to have her.

This isn't like me. Though most would say I'm a risk-taker, every gamble I make is after solid research and thoughtful consideration, and only then do I throw everything in the kitty. But with Mia, I'm going about it differently, no brakes, no brains, no bluff. Just all in from the get-go, mentally obsessed and physically addicted from just one taste.

I didn't even want to let her leave on Saturday afternoon, and just texting back and forth last night was murder on my patience, something I'm definitely not known for. I had to resist the urge to jump in my car and drive to her place to take from her what I needed. The only thing that held me back was fear that in doing so, I might scare her with my possessive need to be with her, around her, inside her.

Now having her like this, her silky thighs pressed against me as I slip my hand under her dress to grab a handful of her taut bubble ass, is more than my senses can take. I grip the firm flesh, almost pinching as if to make sure she's real and not some figment of my imagination. She responds by pressing her tits against my chest with a throaty moan I can feel as I trace the pulse in her neck with my lips.

"You're so fucking sexy," I growl, reaching for my belt and undoing it, freeing my cock from the painful restraints of my slacks and underwear. Mia's eyes drop down, her jaw dropping open hungrily when she sees my thick hardness. I stroke myself with a tight fist, teasing us both, and she whimpers in need. "I want to see you, all dressed up like a fucking queen, sexy and sullied with my cum. Get on your knees."

I shove her down, but she hurries to obey, swallowing my cock even as I thread my fingers through her hair and thrust forward. Her mouth is amazing, and my cock lights up with pleasure as I pump in and out quickly, groaning with pleasure.

"Look up at me," I rasp as my hips pump all of my thick inches in and out of her eager lips. "That's it . . . you want my cock, don't you?"

"Mmpfh!"

The vibrations of her reply make my knees quake, but I can tell she's agreeing with me. "You're mine, Mia. I'm going to fuck you, take you, and never let anyone touch you. You're totally mine."

I know I'm promising things too quickly, but I can't help it. The words pour out unfiltered and dangerously full of truth. And though she doesn't say anything back, her mouth too full of cock to speak, I can see the hope shining in her eyes as she looks up at me.

Suddenly on the edge, I pull my cock out and jerk her to her feet before turning her around and pushing her chest-first into the table.

'I'm going to claim every inch of her, but right now, with the promises hanging around us like fog, I need to be balls-deep inside her to come the way I want.

Lifting her skirt is like revealing the world's sexiest Christmas gift. She's spread her legs automatically, giving me access to the beautiful, perfect half-globes of her pale ass, just barely parted by her thong. She's writhing, grinding in search of relief, and I steady her with a hand on her cheek, then trace down her leg to the stockings she's wearing.

I can smell her arousal. Whether it's from me or from her finally recognizing just how sexy she is, I don't know and don't care.

Instead, I smack her right ass cheek, planting a bright red handprint on it and making her yelp.

"Ah!"

"You're wearing foundation over my mark. I left it on your neck intentionally," I murmur ominously into her ear as I lay over her, pinning her to the table with my weight, but the with the threat, I tug her thong to the side and rub the head of my cock over her pussy lips, coating it with her honey. "You're not allowed to," I decree, as if my word is law. But for her, for Roseboro, it is.

"But people will see."

"Let them," I roar, slamming my cock balls-deep inside her. She's so hot and tight, and both of us cry out as I ram home inside her perfect body. The heels she's wearing have brought her pussy and ass up to just the right height. I don't have to adjust at all as I pull back and thrust again, grinding deep inside her. "Show them all that you're mine."

I grab her hair, lifting her tits up off the table as my hips thrust hard and deep inside her. I pull the dress's bodice down, cupping her left breast and tugging on her nipple.

In response, a fresh gush of Mia's wetness coats my cock, so I repeat the motion, twisting the nub until she squeals in equal parts pain and pleasure. I watch in Damien's mirrors, overwhelmed as the view of her from every angle amplifies the sweet agony of her velvet walls gripping me.

My cock hammers in and out of her, my mind washed with wave upon wave of intense pleasure. I know this is dangerous, but in this moment, I am more animal than man, more primal than civilized, and I rut into her like a savage. Miraculously, she meets me stroke for stroke, not shying away from my roughness, and in her ability to handle me, small cracks shatter in my façade.

I am not Thomas Goldstone, billionaire entrepreneur. My most important title is . . . hers.

And she is not Mia Karakova. She is simply . . . mine.

My chest heaves, my heart pounds, and with each slap of my hips against Mia's upturned ass, I feel myself bound tighter to her.

I want to etch myself on her skin. I want to claim her as mine forever, my captive to keep and do as I wish. I want her to be my angel, my fucktoy, my . . . my everything.

It's insane, but right now as my cock throbs deep inside her and I hear the symphony of her gasps of pleasure, I'm allowed insane thoughts.

Letting go of her nipple, I grab her around the waist, spreading my legs a little for strength before I start hammering her as hard as I can. I look down, my mouth watering as I watch the obscenely sexy vision of my thick, glistening cock blurring in and out of her tight pussy, her lips clinging to me even as I go harder and faster, thrusting with everything I have.

"Oh, fuck . . . Tommy . . . Tommy . . ."

"Say it again!" I roar, not caring if anyone hears me. Or her.

"Tommy!" she cries out as she comes, her pussy clamping around me, and I roar in triumph as I feel my balls contract, my seed spilling and marking her inside and out as I cry out senselessly. I give myself over to the breakdown of everything as our shared climaxes wash over me and I surround myself in her warmth, her comfort, her beauty.

We stay there, connected as one until our hearts slow, and I pull out by inches, regretfully rearranging my clothes and pulling my underwear and slacks back up. A Neanderthal impulse inside me revels that I'm coated in her cum, and with a glance at her abused pussy, a cocky smirk takes my face that she is just as messy with mine. Mia rearranges her thong, attempting to put herself back together, but she's still so weak from what just happened that I have to reach out and help her with the dress.

"So . . ." she says after a moment, her upper body still heaving as she catches her breath, "I guess that means you like the dress?"

"I fucking love it," I reply, adjusting my tie. "Though we might need to have it dry-cleaned before Friday's fundraiser."

She smiles at the lewd joke, brushing her hands across the skirt and smoothing out the wrinkles where I'd bunched it in my hands.

Mia looks up, her eyes flashing with happiness and questions behind her frames. "I can't tell if you're bullshitting me or not."

I know she's not just talking about whether I like the dress but if *this* is something more. She'd let me walk away, I know she would.

She'd write off the possessive things I said while we fucked as dirty talk, and we could go back to some semblance of professional stasis. It's too fucking bad that that's not at all what I want. I meant every word, both the ones I said and the ones I thought but bit back.

"I never bullshit," I say evenly. "I might skirt the truth from time to time in business . . . but I never bullshit."

The tension builds between us, and though we don't say it aloud, we both know something powerful is changing between us in this very moment. An acknowledgement from us both, an acquiescence on her part, an acquisition on my part.

Finally, she turns away, going behind what looks like a changing screen, and I hear her unzipping her dress and then shuffling as she changes.

"I'm not ashamed of what we just did," Mia says, coming out from behind the partition still wearing the high heels she had on but dressed more like she normally does for work. She looks just as stunning, but I can see that she's armored herself against me with the T-shirt and slacks she must've worn this morning. "I mean, we probably took the corporate conduct rulebook and lit it on fire . . . but I'm not ashamed."

"That's good, because—"

"Wait," she says, holding up one finger to make me pause. "I'm not ashamed, Thomas, but I have to say one thing. I'm not going to be your 'office girl'. This isn't *Mad Men*, and I'm not going to trade on whatever attraction you have for me. God made me smart, and apparently, Russia made me beautiful . . . or at least that's what Papa tells me. But I make my own future, with my brain and no other body parts."

I nod, relieved that this is her only concern. For a moment, I'd been able to see the weight on her shoulders and had thought she was going to write me off.

Like you deserve. Waste of oxygen, thinking you're worthy of a goddess like her. She'll realize soon enough.

"You're much more than an office girl, Mia. I think we can both feel that." I pull her to me, kissing her softly and swallowing the soft sigh that passes through her lips as I pray that she doesn't find me lacking and leave me so soon.

Keeping my arms wrapped around her, I tap her temple. "Actually, Miss Smarty Pants, you were right, and I don't say that often or lightly. I looked over your computer when you mic dropped out, and the file you showed me and the report that hit my desk were two different things. I need to look into what happened in between to update the numbers and see if it'll change our direction, but in the meantime, I'm not going to go easy on you just because of this."

Mia smiles but then snarls comically as she adopts a thick accent. "Good. Because in Mother Russia, hardworking analysts fuck you."

I growl, dropping a hand to squeeze her ass and grind against her a bit. "Yes, you did." Her laughter is infectious, making me smile broadly. "Hey, what's with the heels?"

"Damien says I need practice," she says simply, looking down. "Although I'm really going to have to figure out how to coordinate these with my normal wardrobe. Maybe my friend Izzy will have something I can borrow. She's sort of a discount fashion queen."

From outside the door, the bustle of the office working away gets louder and reality starts to creep back in.

"I should probably get to work. My boss is a real asshole if I slack off." She winks as she teases me. "Anyway . . . see you later?"

"You definitely will," I reply. She opens the door, and I call out, "And Mia?"

She turns, her smile warm but melting into a more professional version. "Yes, Mr. Goldstone?"

"I expect great things from you."

CHAPTER 12

BLACKWELL

*T*he park is small, but the pond in the middle of it is perfectly picturesque and the shadows around the south shore deep as I sit on the bench, watching the basketball game.

Footsteps approach on the gravel path, and I look over, my man appearing precisely on time. He sits down, trying to look casual and failing.

Me? I don't care if someone sees me. I control this game. I am above most of the rules.

"Sir."

His tone holds excitement, news he's eager to share. And because of that, I make him wait, drawing out the moment of anticipation, both for my own delight and the man's frustration.

"Look at them," I start in conversationally, keeping my voice low.

I indicate the game across the pond, where the sweaty group of young men continue to pound the asphalt with their rubber ball, wasting their time with their stupid game.

"And they wonder why they'll never get close to touching power or influence. Some of those boys have been out there for over an hour."

"It's a fun sport," my man says, looking across the pond. "When I was in high school, I played on my school's team. Small forward. I even got All-Conference my senior year."

"Hmph," I reply, unimpressed. I'm finished with the rare attempt at small talk I used to delay the man's delivery. If he won't learn from the crumbs dropped from my table, he'll learn the hard way eventually. "You said you have an update?"

"Yes, sir. It seems that our mutual . . . acquaintance is dipping his pen in a company inkwell."

"Is that so?" I ask, amused. The Golden Boy, Mr. Perfect, finally doing something that could be turned to my advantage? The timing couldn't be better. "And how do you know this?"

"Everyone in the vicinity of the twenty-fifth floor on Tuesday around lunch knows," he says with a degree of disgust. "It was . . . obnoxious to hear his name screamed so loudly. Oh, and she called him 'Tommy'." The man's eye roll is worthy of a teenage brat.

"Hmm, I would've thought the Goldstone Building had better soundproofing."

My man laughs bitterly, nodding. "It does. She's just that loud."

Something about the way he sneers is almost more telling about his thoughts than the actual words. He dislikes this woman. Or maybe likes her, and feels affronted anew by her actions with the Golden Boy.

Curious.

I file the information away in my mental rolodex of data in case it ever becomes useful. Frankly, it's those little tidbits of information that people hand away all the time that make my life possible.

"And Goldstone, he's enamored with this woman?" I ask, and his man nods. "Interesting."

"He's taken her out once, they're attending the fundraiser on Friday, and he fucked her in the meeting room," my informant says. "I'm not sure how serious it is, but it's certainly a vulnerability, even if it's only because she's an employee."

"Then we simply need to apply pressure at the right times, in the right ways," I muse, feeling the first nebulous tendrils of a plan start to swirl in my mind.

"I want you to bring me every bit of information you have on this woman. We'll push him, even if there are risks. But we need to move relatively quickly. This deal is worth more than millions. It's worth a legacy. *My* legacy."

"I understand."

My man gets up and leaves, and I lean back, watching the young men across the pond continue to waste their time playing their stupid game.

I have never been one for such a dirty game. Power is more than your ability to toss a rubber ball through a metal hoop like a trained monkey. Even growing up, I shunned the common games of my classmates for pursuits more befitting someone of my class. Chess, polo . . . even a bit of squash to maintain the heart.

Still, I have to admit, the strength that sports like this form in the young men is admirable. They don't know it, but it's building the muscle and dumbing down the mind so that later on, they can become good little minions in the games of the truly powerful.

Like me.

And that, I muse, gives the basketball players a sort of noble futility, poetic in their usefulness. So let them play their games.

"After all," I whisper, getting up while still remaining totally in the shadows of the warm summer evening, "we all have games we enjoy playing."

CHAPTER 13

THOMAS

The Friday morning sunshine is warm, and Kerry doesn't say anything when I tell her I'm leaving on a personal errand. She knows that I don't shirk my work that often and probably figures I need to get ready for the fundraiser tonight.

Besides, she's probably glad that I'm getting out for a little bit. While I doubt she's already got the tequila flowing and is dancing on her desk, she is probably happy to take her foot off the gas for a few hours.

At least I won't be able to dump any more work in her lap.

But starting yesterday for no apparent reason, I just couldn't get the voice out of my head.

Hammering me.

Weak.

Stupid.

A failure.

So I knew I had to get out or else explode.

Going up to my penthouse, I go into my closet, where I quickly change into my disguise for the day, a baggy old-school Clyde Drexler Trailblazers jersey, shorts, custom-fit blond wig, and a snap-back hat. Armed with a small duffel bag and using my keycard, I lock everyone out of the elevator all the way down to the sub-basement parking garage, where I get in my ten-year-old F150 that I use when I don't want to be noticed.

I wish I could go talk to Mia. It might help. But I can't. For two days, the prospect of having to do this event tonight has ratcheted up the pressure cooker that is my temper and my soul, and I can't let her see me like this. I need to have my head on straight when we waltz into that room tonight because I won't let her down when a public appearance like this is a big deal, and we both know it.

I need to let some of the anger and rage and pain out. And this . . . this helps. In fact, until this past Friday, it was just about the only thing that did help for more than a few hours.

Roseboro is beautiful as I pull away, a picture perfect warm blue sky with a few clouds that scream for kids to be running beneath them, pretending they're one of their sports heroes.

As I drive, I wish for the millionth time that I could learn to enjoy days like this like normal people, maybe go for a walk or have a picnic and appreciate the gift of the sunshine, but I'm anything but normal. I can't be normal . . . was never brought up to be anything of the sort. I was raised to be hard, suspicious, a hard shell wrapped around a dark pain that I could never discuss.

The eastern half of Roseboro is my destination for the day. This part of town is decidedly not the best, a far cry from the downtown bustle and the quaint suburbs. While Roseboro doesn't have any real inner-city ghettos, it does have its bad areas.

And it's from those dirt-lot parks full of single-wide hellholes that the kids I get to see today come from, orphans who were either abandoned by their families or just taken when their parents decided that alcohol or meth were more important than taking care of their progeny.

I get out of my truck at the Roseboro Boys' Home, looking around at the old but well-maintained building. It's been a personal project of mine, no publicity, no naming of any buildings . . . just my place to have a release. Slipping on my sunglasses, I get out and stretch, eager for what's about to happen.

"Hey, Tom!"

I normally hate that name, but when I hear it from the excited mouth of an eager nine-year-old boy whose face is split with a huge smile as

I approach the fence to the orphanage, it's more than worth the instinctual flinch I hide inside.

"Hey, Frankie," I greet my young friend and mentee, one of a dozen that I work with here. Going around to the back of the truck, I grab a big plastic cooler, wheeling it behind me. "How're you looking for school next week?"

"You know how it is," Frankie says. "I mean, I do okay, but what's the point?" He shrugs dismissively, his eyes more haunted than any child's should be.

"You know what the point is," I reply, unzipping my bag and pulling out a football. "How're you going to ever play for the Seahawks if you can't get into college?"

Frankie grins, the old fantasy still having enough tread between us to at least let him hope for a moment. He's barely a shade over four feet tall, and if he weighs fifty pounds, it's because he's soaking wet and someone's put bricks in his pockets. But he's a good kid, and he solidly catches the ball when I toss it to him.

After checking in with the orphanage staff using my fake ID, I follow Frankie out to the best part of the facility, a large grassy play area. It's not big enough for all forty kids to play at once, but for the dozen who wander out to play some pickup football with me, it's more than enough.

"Okay, guys, now who's going to play QB?" I ask, waving my hands when everyone points at me. "Oh, no, I told you guys last time you'd have to work on your spirals. I want to catch once in a while too, you know."

In the end, I actually end up not playing at all, which is what I want. Instead, I act as a ref, coach, and cheerleader as the kids strike up a spirited, sometimes rough, but still clean game of touch football.

Laughter, some smack talk, and joy fill the air as the ball flies back and forth. Frankie even catches a touchdown, which he celebrates with a half-respectable spike before all is said and done.

After the last pass, I open up my cooler, passing out Gatorades to everyone as they gather around.

"Okay, guys, good game today," I tell them, closing the cooler and sitting down on the lid. "So listen, I heard what everyone was jaw jacking about during the game . . . seems you're *excited* about Monday?" I'm trying to rename their emotions in a positive light, even though their chatter was full of nervousness and anxiety.

The groans around me are universal. Frankie's not the only kid who's not looking forward to school on Monday.

"Yo, Tom," one of the guys says, "why should we be excited? Same bullshit, different year. Kids are gonna rag on us about our clothes, rag on us about being losers, all that shit."

"Maybe they will," I admit, and the guys nod. It's probably what gives me a chance to connect with these kids better than a lot of the so-called volunteers who come down here. I give it to them straight, but at the same time, I encourage them.

So I'm going to be bluntly honest because that's what they respect.

"I know most of you are going to say that I'm full of shit, but let me give it to you. A lot of kids, you know what happens to them? They sort themselves into some slot in their heads right about the same age you guys are, and they cruise in those slots. You see it now, the kids who just sort of know in their heads that they're going to go to college, those who're going to be blue collar, and then . . . well, you guys."

"You mean the losers?" one of the boys says, copying his cohort's word choice, and though they all laugh, I'm betting they've heard that and worse.

But I don't laugh. "A lot of people probably already see you that way. Teachers who won't give you that extra chance to fix mistakes that they're giving Timmy Bank Account who comes from a 'good family'. Other kids who have no idea what it's like to wonder where your next meal is going to come from are going to bag on your PB&J lunch. You get a bit older, and you're going to be pushed into a few categories. Those of you who have skills, folks will sometimes encourage you, especially if you're good with a ball."

There are cheers for Jeremy, who is a pretty sick point guard, and he flashes a thumbs-up. "Good . . . go for it, man. The rest of you, it's not too late, and sports aren't the only way out."

A few of the boys look down, and I clear my throat. "Don't let *them* write your future for you," I tell them. "I come down here because I look around and I see possibilities. I see a ball player, a lawyer, a writer, a business owner."

"Man, I ain't ownin' no business," someone says, and I shake my head, growling.

"The only thing stopping you is you. It isn't going to be easy, and it won't be fair. You guys, more than anyone, know that life isn't fair. But that's okay. Because having to fight that much harder means you're going to be that much stronger. So when I look at you guys, I see someone who's going to be a man someday, maybe with a wife, a couple of kids, and a good home. And he's going to look back at this place and see what he's accomplished."

I look at the building behind us, bland and institutional. "Turn around and look. That building right there—that's *where* you are, not *who* you are. Where you're at right now is beyond your control, but who you are? That's your choice, today and everyday. Make the right choices and ultimately, you'll get to be where you want to be too." I let that sink in before adding, "Anyway, I'll stop by sometime next week to see how school goes. I expect to see your heads held high. Deal?"

Of course it's a deal. A lot of these boys are desperate for affection in any form, and more than one of them sticks by me as we gather my stuff up and get ready to leave. For a lot of these boys, it's the only time adults give them the time of day, and it pains me to think that I'm somehow acting in a big brother or father figure role for a lot of them.

They deserve better than me.

The office door finally cuts me off from them, and Reba, the staffer on duty right now, signs me out. "How were they today?"

"Good boys," I reply before starting to cough. "Sorry, Reba, you mind grabbing me a cup of water or something? Little dusty out there."

While Reba's back is turned, I slip my envelope into the incoming mail, wait until she comes back, and sip the water. "Thanks."

"No problem. The boys here really are glad you come by."

"I told them I'd be back sometime next week. I'll give you guys a call, see what we can work out," I reply. I figure she wants me to continue to come by but didn't want to ask directly. She doesn't need to. I enjoy this.

In some ways, I need this as much as the boys do.

"Thanks again, Reba."

"Have a good one, Tom," Reba says as 'Tom Nicholson' walks out of the Roseboro Boys' Home. I get back in my truck, and I'm able to make it out of the parking lot and all the way to the nearest supermarket parking lot before I have to pull over, the memories too strong to deny anymore.

The Cadillac waiting outside of school is expected but unwanted as I come out of Briarwood Elementary, my bag over my shoulder and my new jeans still stiff and uncomfortable.

I didn't get to 'break them in' like they call it. Nobody wanted to play with me . . . again. Since Kenny Tyson came to school talking about Mom and what his dad, who's a cop, told him, everyone seems to not want to play with me.

But that doesn't mean I'm looking forward to the ride in the big black Cadillac.

Still, I don't want Dad honking like he does if I go too slow, so I hurry across the parking lot and get in, buckling my seatbelt.

"Hi, Dad."

"Tom," Dad says coldly. It's the only thing he says for the whole ride to his office, where my 'after school corner' is set up in the firm's coffee room. I know to go right to work and sit down, looking at the math worksheet Mrs. Higgins sent home with me.

But homework doesn't take me long, and by five o'clock, I'm done. I even read my library book for the third time, but the story about the frog and the pig is just boring by now.

Getting up, I go out to the hallway, walking carefully down to Dad's office. The other lawyers in the office seem nice, but I don't want to make them angry. Dad says I'm not to bother them or else.

But Dad's secretary, a pretty girl named Christina, is nice. "Hi, Thomas!" she says, smiling as I walk in. "What can I do for you?"

"Uhm . . . I'm done with my homework," I say, but before I can say more, Dad's office opens and he walks out, stopping when he sees me.

"Go back to your work," Dad says, barely even looking at me. "You're not—"

"Sorry, Mr. Goldstone. I asked Thomas to help me with some stapling," Christina says quickly, smiling at me. "He's already done with his work, and I figured, well—"

"Whatever," Dad says, leaving the office and walking out. I let out a sigh, wishing Dad would be like he was before Mom died.

"Come on, Thomas," Christina says in that voice adults make when they're not happy but don't want us to know, patting the chair next to her. "You can help me do . . . something."

Actually, something turns out to be fun as Christina puts me behind her computer, pulling up a game website. Protecting my castle from the monster blobs is fun, and I'm starting to smile when a little bubble pops up that says Email: RE: Autopsy, Grace Goldstone.

I don't know what an 'au-top-si' is, I think, sounding out the unfamiliar word like Mrs. Higgins taught me, but Mom's name makes me click on the bubble, and a new window opens. It's a picture of some kind of paperwork, and a lot of it I can't understand, but I recognize Mom's name, our old address, and a few other things.

The first thing I see is Cause of Death. A lot of the words make no sense, but I learned what it meant later . . . suicide.

Something else highlighted makes my eyes fill with tears. Time of Death . . . three thirty PM.

I know three thirty . . . that's when Animaniacs comes on.

"No . . ." I whisper, and suddenly, Christina's next to me, curious as to why I'm crying so hard. I want to be a big boy, I'm not supposed to cry, but I can't stop.

"Thomas, what . . . oh, Jesus," Christina says, seeing the screen. She hugs me, stroking my hair. "Honey, you weren't supposed to see that."

"Is it true?" I ask. "Was . . . was Mommy alive when I got home?"

Christina pulls away, looking into my eyes. "Thomas . . . Tom, never, ever blame yourself for that. What your mother did is her fault, not yours."

"But if I'd not watched cartoons, if I'd checked on Mommy earlier—"

"No!" Christina says, hugging me again. "Never, ever blame yourself, Tom."

But I already did. I wipe my eyes, blinking back the pain. Starting up my truck, I drive back to the Goldstone building, parking and going up to my penthouse. I smell, I'm sweaty, and I need to shower before I get ready for the evening.

As the water runs over my shoulders and I'm letting the conditioner soak into my hair, I think about things. Twenty years from that day, and Christina's words still ring hollow.

Because I do blame myself.

If I had focused, if I hadn't been weak . . . if I had been a good son, I could have gotten the ambulance there in time.

I could have had my mother . . . and I could have really had my father instead of the cold, distant man who's never shown me love since that day.

You deserve it. You failed her.

Maybe that's why I go to the orphanage to help out from time to time. I especially go before events like this dog and pony show tonight.

Those kids, from Frankie to Jeremy to even shy little Shawn, who've got issues even deeper than mine, understand. Like understands like, and they see that, regardless of whether my father's still alive or not, I'm just as much an orphan as they are.

CHAPTER 14

MIA

The Sentinel Hotel is one of those places I've driven by a multitude of times, mostly on my way to the famous Powell's Bookstore that's nearby, but I never thought that I'd actually be walking through the lobby of the restored classic hotel.

"There's a red carpet," I murmur as Thomas and I arrive in the limo he's arranged for tonight. "You didn't mention a red carpet."

"Well, there will be VIPs from all over the Tri-City area," Thomas informs me. "We make enough of an impact on the state that the governor wants to keep us in the loop."

He doesn't say it, but I can hear in his tone that he doesn't really like these events. I adjust my glasses and take his hand.

"If you can do it, I can do it." I get out and glance down. "Still, I didn't think the carpet would actually be red."

The cameras are almost blinding, and I'm shocked that so many people would be interested in taking photos of Thomas. Not that he isn't the hottest guy in like, the entire universe, but he's no sports star or actor or anything. He's a businessman, and a relatively private one at that.

"Why so many photogs?"

"The governor's looking at angling for a national presence next election," Thomas whispers as I take his arm and he stops us to pose for a few seconds before leading us on. "It's why he wanted this on a

Friday. It'll be too late for the local coverage, but he figures he can get on the weekend news cycle, get invited onto *Meet The Press* or *News Sunday* or something."

I nod, still sort of awestruck as I recognize some of the celebrities in attendance. Sports players, some movie stars, but Thomas doesn't seem all that out of his element. When one of the sports players gives Thomas 'the nod', I'm surprised.

"You know that guy?"

Thomas smiles a little, giving the guy 'the nod' back. "Yes. He runs a charity for kids in Portland. I helped out some last summer. Decent guy . . . terrible cook though. He served up more bricks at his barbecue than he did all last season on court."

I don't really know what to say, just chalking it up to the growing wonderful mystery that is Thomas Goldstone.

Holding onto his arm tightly, though, I walk with him upstairs to the fourth floor, where I'm stunned by the opulent room we walk into.

Thomas notices my gawking.

"The Governor's Ballroom," he says as he also takes in the scenery. It's beautiful. White-fluted marble columns flank each of the huge windows along the walls while inlaid decorations and a rich mostly blue carpet make the whole space look like a European palace. There's even a quintet of classical musicians, a string quartet with a French horn adding their tones to the whole surreal experience.

"It's beautiful," I whisper, ignoring whether anyone's looking as my head goes on a swivel, trying to take in everywhere at once. There are people, music, and even waiters with drinks and appetizers mixing through the room. I snag a flute of champagne, and Thomas follows. "I knew Damien was like a fairy godmother, but now I truly feel like I just walked into a fairy tale."

"Too many people for a fairy tale," Thomas whispers, giving me a smile that makes me blush as he toasts me. "And though Damien may have worked some magic, the beauty has been in you all along. He simply let you see yourself the way I do."

I blush, dipping my chin and unconsciously shaking my head. I know I look good tonight, had even stared at myself in the mirror in disbelief for more than a few minutes after Damien and his team had left my apartment, but Thomas's bold words lay my insecurities bare.

"You're the most beautiful woman I see at this party. Take a moment and look around again . . . you'll see that I'm right."

I do look around, but as I do, I feel even more like a fish out of water. The women all look stunning, but it's more so that they have an air of confidence and comfort in this environment, something I lack even if I'm decked out like one of them tonight.

But Thomas never even glances at them except when they greet him, and in every conversation, he makes sure to include me.

"Mia, this is Willa," he says, introducing me to a famous local TV anchor. "We met years ago when she interviewed me for a piece about Goldstone. Willa, Mia's the best data analyst I've ever met. She'd put three-quarters of your stock market people out of work if she wanted to. However, she has one significant flaw." He pauses dramatically, giving me a sly smile. "She has terrible taste in men, which is how I've found myself lucky enough to accompany her tonight."

"I see." She raises an eyebrow, giving me a smile that's warm, but at the same time, I can see her mind working because it's a look I wear myself quite often. "I love the hair and glasses. Just the right touch of uniqueness at a cattle call like this. Please tell me they're not non-scrip?"

"Nope, I can't see a thing without them," I reply, relaxing a little that she's not putting my odd choices down. "If I didn't have them on, I couldn't tell you from Beyoncé."

She laughs. "Well, rest assured I won't be busting out in song and dance moves, so if you see Beyoncé, let me know and I'll squeal with you." She smiles, and despite the perfect face, the telegenic smile, and the look that's been practiced so long it's probably second-nature to her, Willa seems to be not that bad. She points in the general vicinity of my head. "The streaks are a great look on you. So how long have you known Thomas? I met him for a profile piece I was doing for the station."

"I, uh . . . I work in the company, but we just met recently," I reply, not sure how much Thomas wants everyone to know about our situation. But when I glance at him, he's smiling easily.

A man comes by and pats Thomas on the arm, whispering in his ear for a moment, and Thomas nods. "Of course . . . Mia, if you'll excuse me, the governor would like to have a word with me. Back in five minutes, ten at most."

"Okay," I reply, and Thomas disappears into the party. As he goes, Willa smirks, and I turn to her, lifting an eyebrow. "What?"

"He's into you," she says, grinning. "*Really* into you."

"Why do you think that?" I ask, trying not to shy away. Thomas wouldn't want me to, and after all the work I've done this week to prepare for this thing, I plan on keeping the empowered feelings that started Tuesday rolling. "He needed a date for the event, that's all."

"Uh-huh. He's been showing up stag for these snore fests for a while now. I don't see why this one would be any different," she replies, nodding as though she's putting the pieces together. She must see the look of panic on my face, though her words delight something deep inside me. "It's okay. I'm not working tonight, so it's all good. But the main reason I can tell is the way he talks to you. He's actually . . . nice. It's like you tamed the monster. You're the Beast Whisperer!"

I blink, trying to think about the way Thomas and I talk to each other. I guess I've seen it with him grilling the team, and he started out that way when he called me to his office that first time, but since then, he's always been . . . Thomas.

Willa notices I'm not quite following and rolls her eyes.

"Oh, please," she says, snorting. "The reason he left you with me is because he's going to have to deal with the governor, and Thomas is . . . mercurial around people like that. When I went with him to one of these things three years ago, purely professional as part of that profile, he had no problem showing me that he's three-quarters asshole, one-quarter genius."

"No, I know what you're saying, and I've seen that side of him," I counter. "I mean, he basically put me on blast in our first real meeting."

"And yet you're still here tonight? Gutsy." Someone calls her name from across the room, and Willa turns, raising a glass. "Excuse me. It was a pleasure, Mia. Good luck."

She leaves, and I'm left confused. Good luck? Good luck with what?

Thomas? I would chalk it up to cattiness, but she sounded totally honest and heartfelt in her words.

"Maybe it's just the TV side of her," I wonder aloud, sipping my own champagne and wiggling my nose at the bubbliness. "Or maybe she meant something else."

Slightly disturbed, I try to set aside my worries and just enjoy the party, not gawking too much at the luxury and splendor around me. I've always prided myself at being levelheaded and not so shallow as to get wrapped up in all the fine clothing, expensive jewelry, and fancy décor, but I can't help it when it's on display like this.

"Papa would be so surprised to see me right now," I murmur as I start playing a mental game of ranking the hierarchy of attendees. It's perhaps a bit tasteless, but it's the way my mind works, finding patterns in the randomness. Actually, it's interesting, seeing the generational trends of couples grouped by age, race, and even flashiness of jewelry.

"Mia!"

I turn, surprised when I see Randall Towlee approaching. Like many of the men, he's wearing a tuxedo. And while Randall looks good, he's still a pretender compared to Thomas.

"Randall, this is a surprise."

"Stepfather's a state assemblyman," Randall says, nodding toward a rather rotund man in the group near the governor and Thomas. "So I get a mandatory invite to all of these sorts of events. I think he wants me to follow in his footsteps."

I nod, unsure what to say next. Since his failed attempt at asking me out, he's sort of avoided me, except for one meeting on the hospital team, and that was strictly professional. And I'd love to think he's let the whole thing go, but there's just something in the way he looks at me that tells me that he's not giving up after being rejected.

"You look lovely tonight."

"Thank you." That feels safe enough, platonic and common for this environment, even if I'd squash him for commenting on my appearance at the office.

"So, what are you doing here?" he asks boldly, lifting an eyebrow. "I mean, I've heard rumors, but . . ." He lets the syllable linger, like he wants me to ask him exactly what he's heard.

"Thomas asked me to be his date," I answer him, trying to sound confident but casual. "I didn't want to make a deal about it at work."

"Oh, I can understand that," Randall replies, and though there's not malice in the words, it feels like a bad dream coming true. Like I can see the moment where he loses respect for me and I have to remind myself that his perception is his problem. I haven't changed and neither has the quality or content of my work.

At that moment, Thomas returns, his face cloudy but clearing when he sees me and I smile back.

"Hello, Thomas."

Never mind, the clouds are back. "Randall, didn't think your father would invite you to something so . . . dry."

"Oh, this is exactly the type of thing he loves for me to attend," Randall says, grabbing a champagne. "He says that it's events like this where I'll learn how politics really work. I keep telling him I'm not interested but . . . well, you know how family can be."

Thomas's eyes tighten, but he gestures with his head. "Of course. If you'll excuse us, Mia, I have someone I'd like to introduce you to."

We walk away, Randall giving us a little salute with his champagne as we go.

"Thomas, I'm sorry. I didn't expect him here, and when he asked—" I rush to explain.

"You said you're my date," Thomas finishes for me. "Good." His soft smile reassures me that I did the right thing. It's funny. When it's just the two of us, everything feels right and easy, but in the stress of this room, these unfamiliar expectations are getting to me.

There actually is someone for me to meet, the president of a small computer manufacturing company in the area. We get into an interesting discussion about computer systems, nerding out over processors, RAM chips, video cards, and more. By the end, I somehow feel like I've just placed an order, and as Thomas leads me away, I look at him out of the side of my eye.

"What was that?"

"That was you meeting someone I felt you'd have something in common with," he says with a smirk. "You're definitely not his typical customer, but I'm sure your enthusiasm made his evening."

"Who is his typical customer?"

"The alphabet soups," Thomas says, chuckling again when I look at him in confusion. "DEA, CIA, FBI, IRS, FDA, all those government agencies that take big names and shove them down into three little letters. He makes high-speed, high-security computers for them. And if he starts recruiting you to steal you away from me, I'll have to make sure the alphabet types step in to help."

It's a bit outrageous and possessive, but it makes me laugh.

The governor gets on stage to make his speech, and while it's short, I immediately see what Thomas means about how he's angling for national attention.

About halfway through the speech, out of the corner of my eye, I see Randall, who's watching me intently while drinking another champagne, totally ignoring the speech.

"What's the deal with Randall? I didn't know his stepdad's a politician."

"It's part of the reason I hired him," Thomas says mysteriously, clapping at a line in the governor's speech that I've totally missed. "He wants to make his own way, and his ambition is . . . useful. I just have to remind him from time to time that I don't care who his family is, whether he was president of his frat in college, or who his father knows. I just need him to give me his best effort."

The governor finishes his speech, and things sort of morph into that cocktail party that everyone's seen in a dozen movies but up until this moment, I've never actually thought I'd get to attend.

"This feels a lot like my high school prom," I tell Thomas at one point. "Although the band's a lot better."

He chuckles and takes my hand. "Then how about a dance?"

He leads me into the center of the room, where a sort of nebulous dance floor has emerged. The lights are dimmer here, and as I take his hand and put my other one on his shoulder, I'm glad I've spent the past week working with these high heels. There's no way I'd be able to do this comfortably otherwise.

"Uhm, Thomas? I can't dance for shit," I whisper. "I can't even macarena."

He laughs lightly at my candidness, a deep rumble in his chest that reverberates in the space between us.

"Just follow my lead and relax."

His touch on my hip is strong but gentle, and as we weave in and out of the half-dozen other couples out here dancing to something jazzy and classical, I let him take control of me.

Moving our bodies together just feels right, and my heart starts to race, my body flushing as I look up at him. His eyes burn with an inner desire, a fire that tells me that if it weren't for the few hundred people in this ballroom right now, he'd have no problem claiming me right here in the middle of the dance floor. I almost want it to happen.

"You're having naughty thoughts," he says, pulling me closer. "Want to share?"

"Not if you want to stay for the rest of the party," I tease. "Let's just enjoy this and see what happens after that?"

As soon as our dance ends, someone approaches us, requesting Thomas's presence again.

He looks to me questioningly, and I tell him to go. I'm a big girl and can mingle at a party.

I decide to go over to the refreshment table, thinking that I'll either get some stimulating conversation with the small group working their way around the table or at least some delicious food. My stomach is rumbling, and I've barely had a cocktail shrimp all night. I grab an *hors d'oeuvres* I don't recognize but that looks pretty, and I almost have it in my mouth when Randall approaches again.

"You looked beautiful out there on the dance floor. I'd be remiss if I didn't ask for my own turn."

"Sorry, Randall," I reply. "But no, thank you. I'm here with Thomas."

"And that's twice now he's left you to do what? Schmooze?" he asks, stepping just inside my personal space zone. "You deserve better than a rich bastard who'll use you and desert you."

I'm surprised at his nerve, both presumptive and erroneous. But mostly just ballsy as fuck, considering Thomas is his boss. And like Willa said, he's quite known for being an asshole.

"Randall, let me be clear. I enjoy our professional work relationship, but that is all I'm interested in," I reply, turning away to scan for a familiar face . . . ideally Thomas, but I'd take Willa or Gene, the computer guru. I'm walking that line, the one between where I tell Randall off in a blaze of glory that'll definitely draw some unwanted attention at a soiree like this and the one where I can control my urge to slap the shit out of him.

And then I feel his hand on my shoulder, and I turn to him in anger, my palm itching.

"She said to leave her alone," Thomas says out of nowhere before I can give him a piece of my mind, his voice rumbling just below a roar.

Randall turns, his own eyes flashing as he goes nose to nose with Thomas. They're nearly the same height, both athletically built, but the rage flashing in Thomas's eyes is like a force of nature, even as Randall stares back, his own ego making him stand up.

I think they're about to come to blows when finally, blessedly, Randall remembers himself and yields.

"Just entertaining Mia. You know how awkward these events can be when you don't know anyone and your date disappears on you."

The barb is supposed to be sharp, but Thomas doesn't flinch. His voice is a quiet version of his reputed 'blast'.

"Randall, she said no politely. At this point, I'm both concerned about your personal ability to accept a decline and your professional responsibility to recognize harassment. Where she has been nice, let me be clear. Mia is *mine*."

The threatening tone in Thomas's voice is clear, and Randall recoils as if he's been slapped. But then his eyes narrow shrewdly, and when he speaks, it feels false and sycophant-esque. "My apologies, sir. I didn't realize it was quite that serious."

Something in the way he says it makes me think that all of this was just to get that admission from Thomas, and I wonder what Randall plans on doing with the information.

I'm suddenly foreseeing a whole host of judging eyes glaring at me on Monday after Randall spreads the news of how I spread my legs for the boss. It's not like that, or at least it doesn't seem that way to me, but I have no doubt that Randall will make it sound as seedy as possible.

Randall steps back, turning to leave, and Thomas watches him before he looks at me. "Let's get out of here."

The ride back to Roseboro is confusing. It's not even an hour, but neither of us says anything as I look out the window, the lights flashing by as my mind tries to make sense of it all.

What had Randall hoped to gain by still hitting on me? I turned him down clearly at the office, and he should have seen in our first talk tonight that I'm not interested.

But then Thomas saying I'm *his*. He didn't say it like I'm his date but like I'm his. Like I belong to him, a possession. It should turn me off, but instead, as I look across the bench seat of the limo at him, I'm tempted to climb into his lap and see if we can do a few more movie fantasy scenes in the time we have left.

I shake my head, trying to figure out what I'm feeling beyond lust, when we get off the Interstate and we're back in Roseboro. Thomas looks over at me, his eyes calmer but still that fire burning in them as he looks at me.

"We'll be back at your apartment soon."

I clear my throat and suddenly make a decision. Though tonight was odd, with more going on below the surface than I was prepared for, I desperately want Thomas right now. There will be time enough for analysis and evaluation, but right now, I'm going with the time-honored tradition of following your gut. "You want to come up?" I ask, reaching over and taking his hand.

He doesn't even think about it and without answering reaches forward, hitting a switch on the control panel. The partition to the driver drops down, and Thomas rumbles. "Change of plans. You'll be dropping both of us off at the first location."

CHAPTER 15

MIA

*T*homas reaches for me as soon as the door to my apartment's closed, but I step back, putting a hand on his chest. "Would you like a drink?" I ask, playing hostess. It's a slight stall, and though I can feel my heartbeat in my pussy, I do feel like we should talk about what happened tonight.

Thomas nods and shrugs off his tuxedo jacket, looking around for somewhere to hang it up.

I take it from him, hanging it up before leading him into my living room.

Blushing a little, I tell him, "Make yourself comfortable. Let me get changed." I slip off my heels and carry them down the hall to my bedroom.

I quickly slip into something more *me*. My dress is gorgeous, but stepping back out into the living room wearing cotton shorts and a *Sailor Moon* T-shirt, I feel more comfortable, more in control of myself and the situation.

This is perhaps the first time I feel like he's in my world versus me being in his. I pause for a moment to relish it as I study him.

He's sitting on my sofa, his back to me as he looks at the arrangement of game controllers and remotes on my coffee table. He picks up my newest acquisition, an aluminum-bodied, unbreakable wireless PS-style controller, turning it over in his hands and pursing his lips.

It's adorable to see his mild confusion by something so routine to me, and yeah, my heart melts a little as he quietly whispers, "pew, pew" at my television. How can I not get all gushy over that?

"I've always been a bit of a tech nut," I say, interrupting his study. Thomas sets my controller down, turning his head and looking me over appreciatively as I come around and sit down next to him. It's a little strange, me in what you could call pajamas while he's in three-quarters of a tuxedo, and it only highlights the differences between us.

But at least he's undone his tie and slipped his shoes off, almost like a sign that I'm getting him to relax incrementally. It feels like a win to see the precise, tight grip he holds himself under loosen.

"Mostly around the house, it's gaming, although the PC here is hooked to my TV too. You ever play?" I'm pretty sure I know the answer before I ask the question, but it seems the obvious next inquiry. What I don't expect is the shadow that crosses his face.

"No, not since I was a child. I last played some game with blobs attacking my castle. After that, I never . . ." He pauses, and I can see that he's somewhere else in his mind. It's on the tip of my tongue to ask him what's going on in that brilliant mind of his, but he shakes it off and says, "I like your setup. It's . . . efficient."

I can hear in his words that he means it. And considering being *efficient* is one of the most important things to him, I take it as a compliment. I do wonder what it is that drives a man who seemingly has it all to be so unrelenting in his drive for more. But that seems rather like a truth that is revealed slowly, not a question to be answered, so I let my curiosity sink and stay with the topic at hand.

"Thanks. It probably seems a bit too nerdy to you. But it's . . . me. Papa would try to get me to get out and do things when I was younger." I mimic his voice, "How about ballet, *dochenka*? Softball? Let's go for a walk!" Returning to my own voice, I finish with, "But he realized quickly that wasn't for me."

"Papa? Doche . . . ?" He stumbles over the endearment.

"*Dochenka*. It's Russian for daughter," I explain.

"Oh, yeah, I remember from your file. Your dad is Russian?" Thomas asks, and I nod, chuckling.

"As Russian as vodka. He was still a young man, barely nineteen when he first came to New York, and the issues with the crackup of the Soviet Union caused him to leave. He struggled for a while."

Thomas hums, nodding. "I could see that. It must've been quite the shock to his system. What did he do?"

"He put himself to work. He had enough savings to pay up his apartment for a few months, and it was above a tailor's shop. He started off as a shop assistant, running errands and stuff, and worked his way up. Eventually, he worked his way up to doing his own work. He used to laugh, too, because my grandmother insisted that he learn how to sew when he was in the Soviet Union. He hated that, said it was so unmanly . . . yet it was what put a roof over his head."

"So your Papa becomes a seamstress . . . but it was a while before you were born," he points out. "What happened?"

"Don't let him hear you call him that," I say, laughing. "He says he repairs and adjusts clothing the Old Country way, and therefore, he's a tailor." I smile, having heard the phrase a number of times over my life. Continuing on with the story, I say, "The fact is that Papa's very talented. He mostly does men's clothing, suits and things, but he likes to dabble from time to time, and he made dresses for me and my friends that were better than anything in the stores. Anyway, Papa met Jennifer Appleman. She was Upper East Side, and he was . . . the opposite.

"He thought it was forever love, and I guess at first, they were happy. Papa was beneath her, he says, a tailor to her family money. I suspect she was playing at slumming it with the immigrant bad boy."

Thomas lifts an eyebrow in silent question, and I clear my throat.

"Anyway, she left him. I think if I hadn't come along, they would have split even earlier, but when Jennifer got pregnant, she faced a lot of pressure to get married. She may have been New York money, but there are those who flaunt it and live it up, and there are families whose asses are wound up tighter than a banker's on tax refund day. Jennifer's family was the latter."

Thomas snickers, lifting an eyebrow at my terminology, but he keeps his composure mostly, sobering as my face tightens.

"So, she just left?"

"Two weeks after my second birthday," I say quietly. "I don't even remember them living together. All I remember is that they lived in separate places. I'd go from house to house, and when I was with Jennifer, it was . . . I felt like an annoyance and a game piece. Everyone made sure I was quiet and out of the way, but then Jennifer would buy me things to try and turn me against Papa. I spent more time with a babysitter than Jennifer or her parents, even though it was their house."

Thomas growls lightly, reaching out and stroking my shoulder. "What was it like with Papa?"

"We had almost nothing some weeks. He worked hard, but New York is expensive and sometimes, he had to make difficult choices on which bills to pay. I remember one time we spent the whole week 'camping' around the stairwell in the living room. We did that so we could catch more of the heat drifting up from the shop downstairs, because Papa didn't want his boss to know how tight things were. Honestly, it was one of my favorite weeks because he made it seem fun and like an adventure. Ironically, it was that week that led to his getting full custody of me."

"How so?"

I lean back, sighing a little. "I was still cold, and Papa took off his jacket, laying it over me. He only had a short-sleeve T-shirt, but he wanted me to be warm. I noticed that Papa had a Band-Aid on the inside of his elbow. I asked him what it was, and he took it off, showing me a fresh hole on the inside of his arm. He'd started going to a couple of plasma centers, lying about how often he was donating to get enough money to support us. The day before he'd picked me up, he donated twice. He showed me the hole in his other elbow, and I told him it was like the holes in Jennifer's arm. She had a whole line of them going up the inside of her left arm. I was too young and naïve to know what that meant."

"Drugs?" Thomas asks, and I nod. "So he told his lawyer?"

"And his lawyer had a cop on Manhattan Vice who owed him a favor. One tail of Jennifer Appleman while I was with Papa, one trip to the right nightclub, and boom . . . the family courts don't look kindly when you're picked up in the biggest drug bust of the year. I don't know all the details on what happened to her. I just know Papa got temporary full custody that ended up permanent. We moved to Roseboro soon afterward so Papa could open his own shop, and I haven't seen her since then. I even reached out to her and her parents. Papa helped me write the letters. The last two were unopened, just marked *Return To Sender*. That's all I needed to know. It's been me and Papa ever since."

Thomas nods, giving me a sympathetic smile. "I was wondering why you didn't call her Mama. I . . . I lost my mother when I was very young too. She died when I was six years old."

He looks lost in his thoughts, and I wonder how many people know this about him. I certainly didn't before now, and I've checked out his corporate profile and online presence like a tenth-degree clinger. There's a lot about Thomas's education, his rocketing up the business world, and the accomplishments he's had as the head of his own corporation, but nothing about his family life. It's as if he sprang forth as a fully-grown man in college, having never existed before age eighteen.

"What happened?"

"She . . ." he starts but then swallows thickly. "I can't talk about that," he admits, and while it's not the same information dump I just shared, his confession feels like he's giving me a vulnerability, trusting me with a weak spot and hoping I won't pick at the scab. He clasps his hands together between his knees, head dropped low, and I want to reach out to him.

He clears his throat, blinking rapidly. "Suffice it to say that while both of our mothers might have left us with our fathers and the resulting baggage of that loss, my subsequent relationship with my dad was not full of fun adventures." I can feel the pain it costs him to say those words, and I doubt he's ever let them pass his lips before.

He sighs and plops back on the couch, shoulders hunched, back rounded, and I think it's the most real I've ever seen him, like he's too exhausted to maintain appearances. I like that he's willing to do that with me, like he's letting me in bit by bit, sometimes with big leaps and sometimes with small steps, but closer to the core of who he is all the same.

"Sorry. I think we've brought up enough bad memories for the night."

I kiss his lips softly, rewarding the gift he's given me tonight. Not the fancy outing with limo and expensive clothes, but his truth. "It's okay. So . . . you want to play a video game?" I ask lightly, wanting to give him a chance to reset and re-center. "Nothing hard, just a little beat 'em up?"

Thomas busts out a small laugh, and we slowly walk away from the abyss of his childhood. We swap little tidbits back and forth as we play, mostly me telling him about myself as I beat him at every turn. But when my clock beeps and I see that we've come up on midnight, I've seen more of Thomas than I think anyone else ever has.

"So, tell me," I ask, setting the controller down and taking his hand, "you made some rather serious claims tonight. Are you sure you're ready to handle a woman who's kinda nerdy, likes to play video games while listening to death metal and techno, makes weird leaps of logic that you might find hard to follow, and has a father who's taught her how to curse fluently in Russian?"

"I suppose," he says with a smirk. "As long as you're willing to deal with a man who has a deep streak of asshole in him for reasons he sometimes isn't really sure about himself."

He seems less sure that I'm going to accept him as he is.

I chuckle, rubbing his shoulders. "Will it come with the good side of you too?"

"Like what?" he asks. "Oh . . . I forgot. You like my car."

I laugh, leaning over and kissing his cheek before climbing in his lap. "I can think of about two dozen things I like about you more than your car. It's a sweet ride, but that's not your good side."

"What is?" Thomas asks, his hands naturally coming around my waist to rest on my hips as he looks up at me, his body reacting even as his eyes search me, like he's trying to figure out what the answer is himself.

"You've got something to you, Thomas Goldstone. It's hard to see sometimes because you keep it under layers of barbed wire and jagged glass to keep anyone from getting too close." I trace a finger along his smooth jawline and then outline his lower lip.

He swallows. "I know. I want to be . . . a better man."

"You're already a good man. I'm just the lucky girl who gets to see it."

He shudders, and I think something in my words might've healed a small crack inside him, but then his eyes light up with devilry. "I've got something else you can see too. If you want."

I smirk back. "Let me see it all."

CHAPTER 16

THOMAS

I carry Mia down the short hallway to her bedroom, letting her give me directions as we go.

I inhale her scent with every step, marveling at how some words can change things so much. It's the same woman, the same silky skin, the same soft hair tickling my nose . . . but it feels so different. Because now she is mine. And we both know it.

Her bedroom's just like Mia, a quirky mix of nerdy and sexy, and I take a moment to notice everything as I set her down on the mattress and stand up, stripping off my tuxedo shirt. I want to memorize everything she is, never forget anything, because she's just so . . . her.

Her bed's just big enough for the two of us, with colorful sheets and a little pink blanket sitting at the foot. She's also got one of those furry Russian hats on top of her dresser, along with a snow globe, of all things.

But all the baubles and trinkets in the world can't distract me for long with this beautiful vision in front of me. As my pants fall to the floor, Mia finishes pushing her shorts off, leaving her in sexy lingerie that matches the dress she wore tonight. That she left it on when she changed tells me she's wearing it just for me.

The pale gold lace is a few shades darker than her creamy skin, drawing my attention even more to her lush curves. Her nipples, pink jewels on top of snowy peaks, peek through the golden veil, and between my legs, my cock rises to full, almost painful hardness.

"Hmm, and I've barely touched you," Mia jokes, brushing a pink-tipped toe up my thigh to trace my cock through my underwear. "Should I wear this more often?"

"If you let me, I'll buy you a whole wardrobe of stuff like this," I promise her, capturing her foot in my hand. I resist the urge to attack her this instant, my desire for our emotional bond overwhelming my primal need to fuck her senseless. "But it's not the wrapping. It's the package itself. It's you who does this to me, Mia. Just you."

I climb onto the bed on my knees and kiss the arch of her foot, making my way up her leg. She moans louder when I lick the back of her knee, and inside my mind, I'm memorizing every reaction, learning how to bring her the most pleasure with a single touch.

As I reach her core, I see how wet she is through the soaked lace and groan, not sure if I can take this slow any longer. She has a way to bring the beast inside me out.

I lean forward and lick her from bottom to top with a wide, flat tongue, savoring the bouquet of her taste and scent while Mia moans.

"Oh, God . . . how are you so good at that?"

It's simple, really.

I love her taste.

I want to consume her, to have her ground into every pore of my skin, to carry her with me everywhere I go, every moment of the day. So I suck and lick, feasting on her from behind the lace until neither of us can hold back.

She lifts her hips, rolling her panties down until I pull my mouth away just long enough for us the get them out of the way before I'm on her once again, pushing her knees up and back, making her watch as my tongue dips deep inside her.

Mia bites her lip, gasping as I tease her inner folds, tracing and snaking my tongue along her pussy. "Hold your legs open for me, Mia."

She does as I instruct, hooking her legs with her hands but spreading them wide, knees near her shoulders.

Freed, my hands come up to cup her breasts, my thumbs rubbing over her lace-covered nipples while I flick her clit slowly with my tongue, making her squirm while pinned underneath me.

"Feel good?" I tease as I pull back, lowering her body back to the mattress as she trembles, keeping her on the edge.

"More," she pleads.

I kiss up her body, taking my time tasting wherever I fancy until I reach her lips. I hold myself above her, our skin just brushing as our mouths and tongues wrap around each other, sliding and lighting our bodies on fire.

It's a game for me, a challenge to hold myself back while bringing Mia to the quivering edge again and again. Through denying us both, prolonging the torturous agony, I'll bring us both to new heights, making the wait worth the reward.

I use my fingers, my lips, even the press of my body against her as I explore her, dipping my fingers into her tightness before swirling them over her clit, stroking until she's breathless, her head thrashing back and forth before I finally give her the final stroke she needs to shatter into a million pieces. It's a gorgeous display of release, my Mia at my hand.

"Enough?" I ask, and she nods, tears of ecstasy rolling down her flushed cheeks.

"Yes! Goddammit, Tommy, please fuck me!" she begs, reaching over and pulling me on top of her. My body's more than ready, and I sheathe myself in her pussy in one savage thrust, her legs locking around my hips as she cries out. She instantly comes on my cock, the convulsions almost continuously washing through her since she's barely recovered from her first orgasm.

Her arms lock around my neck while I watch her rapturous face and feel her velvet walls spasming around me, tempting me to let go with every pulsing squeeze.

I don't let her come all the way down before I pull back and thrust again, my inner animal fighting at my mental leash. I've been restraining myself all this time, torturing myself even as I've given her ultimate pleasure, and now my control's nearly frayed.

No woman has ever gotten this far past my defenses, made me reveal so much about myself. I was weak in front of her, and my ugly self-hatred wants to turn that back on Mia, punishing her for making me think about things best left buried. But rationally, I know it's only punishing myself to delay the inevitable.

So I don't hold back.

Punishing her, punishing me. Pleasuring her, pleasuring me.

With every stroke, I pump harder, deeper, relentlessly grinding against her even as her pussy swells around my cock. I kiss her hard, pulling the very air from her lungs as I fuck her brutally.

Inside me is the nice guy who wants to keep giving her the sweet dream she likely wants. The nice guy wants to keep things gentle, not test the limits of what her body can take and not dole out the depth of what I can dish out.

I want to worship her, to show her that I think she's an angel and that I'm enraptured with her, that I want to give myself fully to her just as she shared her pain with me. She's so strong, and I want to prove to her that I can be that strong as well.

But that side of me is not in control.

Instead, the beast inside me is, and it's going to punish this blonde goddess for daring to see through my façade. My hips slap against hers, her tits bouncing out of her bra from the hard thrusts.

She shouldn't be able to take all this. And she'll likely see me for the monster I am after this is over. But I'm being driven by lust and . . . fear, sweat dripping down our bodies from the effort and stinging my eyes.

But I don't let up, my cock growing with each plunge, my soul enraged as she cries out not in pain but in pleasure, grabbing my forearms and holding on as she comes again, her voice an angelic scream of release that obliterates my blackness. And I cry out, coming deep inside her. Not with fury and pain, for she's somehow cleansed that away for a freeing moment, but with utter happiness.

My back arches, and I purge myself, giving her everything as she accepts me, miraculously. I gather her in my arms as I collapse, holding her tenderly as tears mix with my sweat . . . but somehow, Mia doesn't mind. Instead, she holds me until the darkness swells over me and I let myself fall into sleep.

~

YOU DON'T BELONG HERE.

Go away.

Twenty years I've been hearing this voice, the familiar deep disdain and hatred. Every day, every task, every night, it's there.

Can't it at least give me some peace at a time like this?

How can you even think of ruining this girl with your pathetic weakness? You think you're going to do better this time?

I wasn't responsible for that. She was thirty-one. I was six!

And? You failed her . . . your own mother. You let her die.

I didn't! I didn't feed her those pills!

You failed . . . and you'll fail Mia too.

I sit up, my chest heaving and night terror sweat rolling down my face. The sun's just creeping up over the horizon, and next to me, Mia sleeps, a soft smile on her lips as she murmurs in whatever dream is in her head.

I don't want to wake her up from that.

Shakily, I get up and find her bathroom, where I take a morning piss before washing my hands and face, looking at the haunted eyes staring back at me from the mirror.

What am I doing here?

I'm being greedy, that's what I'm doing.

Mia's beautiful, inside and out. Instead of letting her personal tragedy strike her down, she's come out stronger, smarter, and simply more than a man like me ever deserves.

I shake my head and know that I need to get out of here.

Going back into the bedroom, I find my clothes, pulling my pants on before sitting down next to her, brushing a lock of hair out of her face. Mia hums, her lips twitching.

"Tommy . . ."

"Shh, Beautiful," I murmur, kissing her forehead. "Go back to sleep. I'll . . . I'll call you later."

Fucking coward. Too weak to even walk away like you should. Can you do anything right? You know you're just going to disappoint her. Like you do everyone else.

"Tommy?" Mia whispers, her eyes fluttering open. "What do you mean? Stay."

I shake my head and kiss her lips softly. "I want nothing more than to stay. But I need to go." It's the truth. I wish I could curl up in bed with her and use her body and cries of ecstasy to drown out the twisted voice in my head. But that would be wrong. I don't want to abuse her that way. "There are some things I need to take care of, and I don't want to ruin your morning by obsessing over them instead of you."

It's not a lie, but it's not the full truth, and it tastes bitter on my tongue.

"Then don't," she says. "It's Saturday. Can't you take the day off? You're the boss, you know?" Her smile is sleepy as she sits up on her elbow.

I smile back, shaking my head, so damn tempted to lie back down with her, to watch the sunlight brighten on the walls of her room, and to share coffee or something, maybe even go out to breakfast in last night's tuxedo while she wears . . . well, whatever she wants. I imagine her in a cartoon, no, an *anime* shirt. That's what she called the shows she watches last night.

But the hated voice inside me won't be denied much longer, and I know if I stay, I'm going to destroy what my good side wants so desperately. It's a sharp-edged balance, one I don't truly have experience walking. But I won't risk her, risk this, by pushing too far. The ugly whispers are already getting louder.

"I'm sorry, Beautiful, but this one won't wait. I'll call you this afternoon. Maybe we can get together this evening?" It's a weak promise but one I hope that I can keep.

"Maybe," Mia says, humming as she drifts back off. Her voice strengthens with wakefulness, "Oh, wait . . . I promised my friend Izzy that I'd stop by The Gravy Train. She's working a double and can really use the tips."

"Sounds like a date to me," I reply, smiling hopefully. "Seven?"

Mia smiles and lies back, her breasts so enticing as the sheet falls from them. "You don't have to. It's just a diner."

"I want to," I return, standing up. "I'll call you this afternoon, okay?"

I grab a cab back to my penthouse, where the elevator can't take me upstairs fast enough. Running to my bedroom, I change clothes and go to my gym, where the spin bike awaits me. With four switches, everything is prepared, and as screaming guitars, angry bass, and lyrics fill my ears, I get on the bike.

Two minutes on, thirty seconds off. It's rough, a brutal level of high-intensity intervals, but it's what I need. I'm not interested in the training effect. I'm interested in . . . absolution.

In pain.

In brutalizing my body to the point of exhaustion so that the voice shuts up and gives me a few hours of peace.

So as the lactic acid builds up in my quads and my lungs burn, I scream along with the music, the veins in my forearms bulging as I race away from my inner demons. Electric fire pulses through my nerves, making my muscles cramp before my veins carry the pain back to my heart and lungs, only to be recycled into my brain.

But still the past lashes at me, each memory a whip that drives me another round, and another round, and another. I shouldn't be able to do this. The flywheel on the bike is so warmed through that I can feel it like a baking hellish coal between my legs while my demons cackle in the background.

Finally, the machine can take no more. In a loud *twang*, the over-loaded tension belt snaps and the machine rolls totally free just as my vision clouds over and I collapse against the handlebars, my stomach heaving as sweat pours off my body to puddle on the floor.

Weakly, as the stereo continues to scream at me, I stagger off the bike, pausing with my hand on the mirror before flipping the switches, cutting off the music just as the bass riff starts to wind down and the anger ramps up.

Leaning against the wall, I wait for my vision to clear before going to the bathroom. I shower with scalding hot water, scrubbing the salty sweat off my body and wishing it were as easy to wash away my painful past. Even though it's Saturday, I still shave before putting on a T-shirt and jeans. My stomach's so queasy still that I skip breakfast before opening my laptop.

I didn't quite lie to Mia. I do have work I should catch up on. Emails, correspondence, and reports piled up yesterday as I played with the kids at the orphanage and then got ready for last night's event.

While Kerry handled as much as she could, I still have a pretty significant string of unopened messages, decisions to make, and things to reply to.

The chance to immerse myself in work instead of my inner doubts and hatred allows me to escape even more than my workout did, and I'm so immersed in the numbing regularity of work that I don't even hear the beep from the elevator or the sound of shoes on the tile in the entryway.

It isn't until I hear a familiar, hated double-knock on the kitchen island granite that I stop and turn around in my home office chair to see my father standing in there, for some reason still in a suit even though it's a Saturday.

"Dennis."

It's been years since I've called him 'Dad,' and we're maybe beyond the point of even caring any longer. Then again, I did give him a card access to the executive suite and the penthouse, so maybe . . . I don't know.

"Tom," he says, the same way he has for over twenty years. Bastard, motherfucker, cocksucker, cunt . . . none of those can hold a candle to the way my father can make my name sound, and none of them can cut me as deeply. "You didn't answer your phone yesterday."

"I was busy," I reply, standing up and purposefully walking past him to the kitchen. I give him my back, something I wouldn't have done in my younger years, but things are different now. But still, I've found it's safer to have something physical between us, although the reason's changed over the years. He hasn't laid a hand on me since I turned fifteen and he realized his 'boy' was no longer going to take his shit.

But he doesn't need the physical threat anymore. He has other weapons that he can use.

"I assumed that," my father says, standing on the other side of the island while I grab some eggs from the fridge along with butter and leftover vermicelli. "I see you still like Rita's recipes."

"Yeah. For a housekeeper, she was a good cook."

She was also the only person in the house who cared for me back then.

"Too bad you chased her away, but then again, you do that with most people in your life," he says, turning the same screw he always does. I squeeze the egg in my hand so hard the shell shatters, but luckily, I'm over the skillet, and most of the shell fragments stick together. He chuckles. "I see you're still a clutz in the kitchen."

He's trying to get a rise out of me, but I'm not going to let him. "What brings you here on a Saturday?"

"Where were you last night?" he asks, hands in his pockets. "I came by your office to discuss the quarterly dividend, and your secretary said you'd left early. She wouldn't tell me where."

"I was preparing for the governor's fundraiser," I reply, staring at my skillet while I add the already cooked vermicelli and start scrambling it all together like fried rice.

"So you were slacking off," he retorts, sighing. "How you're able to turn a profit with this clusterfuck of a company you run is beyond me. Guess it proves PT Barnum right. There's a sucker born every minute."

"This company is beyond reproach and has been profitable every year of operation," I remind him for what has to be the thousandth time. Sighing, I set aside the bowl of food and turn to my father, not ready to eat yet. "Everything you need to know about the dividend was in the quarterly report." It's a tactic I learned long ago. Don't ask him questions and don't give him a lead-in, because by giving an inch, he'll take a mile.

"I want to know why you declared a quarterly dividend of only fifty cents a share when the finances clearly show you could have declared fifty-five!" he yells. "Your ineptitude cost me thousands of dollars!"

"As the report showed, and you're well aware, I did it to reinvest it in the company," I reply, trying to keep control of my emotions.

"That five cents a share means a lot of capital for the company to expand and acquire—"

"Who gives a shit? It isn't like you don't have enough leverage to get more! For fuck's sake, you don't just call the bank, you *own* the goddamn bank! Take the capital out yourself, not out of my money."

The argument goes back and forth, although like most of our discussions, it's a one-sided affair. No matter what I do, no matter how I explain it to my father, there's always a flaw in my thoughts, in my planning, in my reasoning. It's always been this way, and I wish I could go back in time to warn my younger self not to take his paltry investment in my upstart. At the time, it'd seemed like a turning point for us and I'd wanted to believe that he finally saw something worthwhile in me. The small percentage of shares in a company I hadn't even begun hadn't seemed like a risk. Now, I can see it was just another way to keep me tied down, to control me even as I finally made something of myself in spite of his influence.

"You know what, Tom? Monday, you will declare another dividend and make this right!" my father explodes after fifteen solid minutes of ranting. It's an order, a command. "If you can't run your company right the first time, you can at least make up for it." He rolls his eyes and murmurs, making sure I can hear him, "Such a stupid boy, useless waste—"

I slam my hands on the counter, my patience lost. "Shut up, Dennis! I've made you a lot of money. I've repaid you a thousand times over for the small investment you made. If you think you can do better, cash out your shares and invest in yourself. Or approach the board and see what your voting rights get you."

My father snorts derisively. "You can be outvoted, you know. I could take your own company right out from underneath you. You own fifty percent, but every move you make needs a majority. I could take you out at the knees."

I lift an eyebrow at the threat. Once upon a time, he did literally take my legs from underneath me with a hard push. I'd been young enough that I'd repeated his description of a 'fall' to the ER doctor when he'd asked how I banged my head on the ground hard enough to get a concussion. But this threat about my business, it's something he's never dared to voice.

"I trusted my own hard work and backed myself. Then and now. You could try getting every other shareholder on your side. But you'd fail."

My father's lips lift in a snarl, and he's pissed. Good. "You little . . . you should have been the one taking those pills, not—"

"Get the fuck out!" I yell, finally pushed too far. As I get closer, I warn him, "Get out of my house, and don't ever come back!"

He shrinks for a split second, like he knows if I take this physical, the way he used to, he's already lost. But though I'm a monster, I'm not him.

When he sees I'm not going to strike him, he looks like he's about to argue, but then he takes the smallest step back and smiles wanly, adjusting his tie. "I will be filing a formal grievance, as per Goldstone corporate rules."

He leaves, and I clench my fists, holding back the explosion until he's gone before picking up my bowl and hurling it in the direction he just went, the whole thing exploding in a giant mess on the wall. The fact that I now have to clean it up as well as not have any breakfast yet infuriates me more.

Never. I can't . . . I can't see him again.

A crazy thought drifts through my head, and it helps me calm enough to get the broom and start cleaning up.

The Gravy Train.

She said the food there is good.

CHAPTER 17

MIA

"You've got a boyfriend," Izzy sing-songs like we're ten.

I laugh, nodding as Izzy sits down across from me for our standing Friday lunch. It's just the two of us today. Charlotte's got some sort thing going at her job that has her working extra time, so she texted her regrets with a picture of a sad brown bag lunch.

It's not the same without her, but Izzy and I have been buddies since we were sharing Oreos on the playground, so we're used to the Two-Girl Power Trip.

"I guess so. Though calling that man a boy-anything is a little strange to hear," I answer, chuckling as I think about Thomas. No, even with the little I know about his childhood, I can't imagine him as a little boy running around in dirty sneakers and a tank top.

Izzy smiles, and I press her. "So, what'd you think?" She's one of my best friends and I trust her opinion. I want her to like Thomas just as much as I do.

She sits back, humming. "I mean, on one hand, the man left me a $150 tip on a twenty-dollar order. For that alone, I'm giving him a chance. But Mia, I just . . ."

Izzy's voice trails off, and we're distracted for a moment as we give our orders. While I wait for my drink to arrive, I sip at some water, eyeing her.

"Come on, Izzy, spill it. We've been friends long enough that nothing you say is going to hurt our friendship."

She sighs and runs a hand through her hair. "It's just that . . . okay, maybe it's me. I mean, I'm the first to admit that I've got a pretty dark view on men."

"Ohh . . . you don't say?" I ask sarcastically. But then my smile drops. "So you didn't like him?" I replay our dinner over in my head. He'd picked me up last Saturday just before seven, had seemed perfectly comfortable in the ragtag diner, and had been his usual charming self. What's not to like? Okay, maybe not quite his usual charm. There'd been a bit more of the "professional" Thomas in his manner- isms, not rude or Ruthless Bastard style, but a little colder than he usually is with me. I'd chalked it up to nerves at meeting my friend, the way I'd been a bit awkwardly star struck at the fundraiser.

She shakes her head, putting a hand on mine, "It's not that I didn't like him. The whole thing just seems . . ." She pauses, searching for the word she wants and then settles on, "Fast. I don't want your hormones to run away with your brain. Like, you've been on a couple of dates, but I could tell that man thinks you are *his*, in the possessive sense of the word. That's just a bit brake-worthy to me."

I don't tell her about him claiming me that way at the fundraiser and how it had made me eschew the brakes and go full-throttle, pedal to the metal. Instead, her words remind me, the story falling out unbid- den, "Do you know what he did on Monday?" I don't wait for her answer, continuing, "He tried to get me to move up to his floor. It was an 'invite' but I don't think he thought I'd have a problem with it. Mother Russia was not amused."

Izzy cringes. "What'd you say? What happened?"

"I reminded him that I don't want any favors at work, so unless he was moving the whole data analyst team up there, I was staying where I am. Plus, I reminded him that while he thinks my quirks are cute and eccentric, most people, myself included, prefer me to work in the quiet basement where I can rock out and geek out in private. And then he saw the error of his ways and apologized . . . on his knees."

Izzy gasps, eyes wide with shock. "In the office?"

I nod, grinning. "In his office, overlooking all of Roseboro."

Izzy plops back against the booth and fans her face. "Dayum, where do I sign up for that benefit package?" Her face sobers, and she purses her lips. "Look, babe, everyone's got a good side, though Thomas Goldstone is more known for his asshole side."

I interrupt her, holding up a finger. "As crazy as it sounds, I think he's actually uncomfortable showing his nice side. Kinda the opposite of most guys where they put on the nice front to cover the asshole lurking underneath. Tommy wears a mask of a jerk to hide his good side."

She presses her lips together, thinking about that. "If he's good to you, good for you, enjoy the ride. Have fun, go do some one-percenter stuff that we never thought we'd get a chance to do, and get yourself royally laid. But be prepared for the crash."

"The crash?" I ask, thinking of the darker side of Thomas. Already, his nickname of The Ruthless Bastard has been yammered in my ear constantly, and while Bill Radcliffe's been cool about things, especially considering the influx of looky-loos who want to see the data analyst crazy enough to date twenty-five floors above her station, he's not the only person who's thrown in the towel when it comes to trying to put up with Thomas's hard-charging nature and angry outbursts. More than a few warning stories people have shared about him call him a user, and while not an abuser . . . I've raised a few eyebrows among both the men and women around the Goldstone building.

"The crash," Izzy confirms. "Come on, don't make me spell it out for you. You're in the fairy tale phase of the relationship, and that's cool. Everything's refreshing, sparkling, you've got more pep in your step than I've felt in . . . shit, I can't even think of the last time I felt as happy as you look right now. But there are too many instances where that fairy tale turns into a bad dream, babe. I'm just saying . . . fairy tales don't always come true. You know that from your own history, or did your dad being Soviet Cinderfella not teach you that lesson?"

I sigh, nodding. Reaching into my pocket, I pull out today's gift and set it on the table between us. "I know, Izzy. But then there's this."

Izzy picks up the card, looking it over. It's black, unmarked except for the chip embedded in the surface. "He gave you a credit card?"

"No . . . something more important," I tell her. "It's a keycard to his penthouse. He gave it to me this morning, saying that he understands why I don't want the office upstairs . . . but that if I ever need to, I have access to his penthouse and his office. To him, anytime and always. He said that after this weekend, I'm one of three people with those cards. The other is his secretary, and he has one. Everyone else has to be buzzed in. He's quite literally letting me inside."

"Wow," Izzy says, pursing her lips before sighing. "Okay. Like I said, any guy who's willing to give me a hundred and fifty bucks on the sly is worth a shot. But be careful, and if things to go to shit, I'll be here for you."

"I know," I say as our lunches arrive and I put the keycard away. "I've got you and Char for sure, and if anything, Papa said he could give a call to some people he knows."

"You dad knows Russian Mafia?" Izzy asks, surprised, and I laugh, shaking my head.

"No, the closest he knows to Russian Mafia is Father Vasiliev at the Orthodox Church. If you've ever heard him give a sermon asking for more donations . . . now *that* man's a gangster."

∼

UP UNTIL NOW, I'VE BEEN A PRETTY BIG PC AND VIDEO GAME NERD, BUT that was before I really started getting in deep with work and Goldstone. I guess 'adulting' has its consequences.

Gone are the games that need daily logins or lots of grinding. So byebye to *Eve Online*. Bye-bye even to *WoW,* or *Final Fantasy Online.*

I refuse to get beaten down to *Fortnite* level yet, so instead I've started up *TERA.* It's action-packed, lots of fun, and not so complex that I can't leave my character for two weeks without major problems.

And tonight's the night to get my game back on. I'm just about to fire up my PC and log on when my phone rings. I see it's Thomas, so I pick up my phone, leaning back on my sofa.

"Hey, Tommy, what's up? Please don't tell me you're still in the office. I know it's hump day, but you don't actually have to be at the top of your mountain of paperwork to slide into Friday."

"Nope. I stick to my policy of leaving the office by no later than six," he says. "Though sometimes, I take work upstairs with me, but that doesn't count." He laughs at his own joke and I grin. "Actually, there's something I wanted to talk to you about, but I wanted to wait until after work because I didn't want you to think I was trying to hit on you in the office."

My smile falls as I sit up, clicking into a more serious headspace. "I appreciate that. What's up?"

"I've been presented with an opportunity for Goldstone. And I need to put together another project team. This is a big one, so I'll be taking the lead on it and selecting the team myself. I'd like you to be on it, but I understand if you think that's muddying the waters too much. You're the best choice, but I won't be offended if you'd rather not." His voice is serious, showing how much he has listened to my rants about people gossiping about us and how it's not right that everyone looks at me as playing up, not him playing down. Not that either of us is playing at this point.

"I can keep it professional. I mean, we wouldn't be together all the time, right? We're twenty-five floors apart. How hard can it be?"

"That's the thing," Thomas says. "The deal isn't one that can be done in the office. Do you have a passport?"

"Uhh, yeah. I got one for a trip to Vancouver last year. Why?"

"The job is in Japan. I'm putting together a team for a week-long trip overseas to tour a resort location and their company headquarters to see if it's a good fit for a capital investment. We leave a week from Friday. Until then, we'll be buried to our eyeballs doing prep work. What do you think?"

I grin so hard my jaw aches. "You realize you just asked me if I want to go on a business trip to the home of anime, video games, and all sorts of nerdy paradise that gets my geeky heart going pitter-patter, right?"

Thomas's laughter is silent, but I can still hear the way he's breathing. He's gotta be almost heaving on his end of the line. "Is that a yes?"

"Of course!" I half scream, trying not to boogie on the couch.

"But honestly, it's just because you'll be working with me, right?" he teases, knowing that he's basically offered me a dream gig. Japan, a work opportunity, and him.

Thinking of him, I say, "Now, you've got two options. Either you let me get off here so I can play the game I was about to start, or you get your ass over here and help me work off this energy another way."

There's a two-second pause on the other end of the line, and then Thomas growls. "Pack a bag for work tomorrow. I'll be by in ten minutes to pick you up."

CHAPTER 18

THOMAS

*W*hen I incorporated Goldstone, I didn't set things up the way a lot of corporations do. Quite frankly, the idea of an elected board with politics and horse trading being the primary reasons certain decisions are made disgusts me. It's as much an issue of covering your ass as it is 'good corporate governance', so I avoided it.

Pretty easy when I'm the largest single shareholder.

But still, as an olive branch to my initial angel shareholders who gave me the boost I needed—including, regretfully, my father—I do have meetings with them, usually including my senior executive vice presidents on a semi-regular basis to give a recap on their respective areas. Mostly, they're informal things that go according to plan. As long as my dad doesn't make one of his rare appearances to decree Goldstone a failure and demand more profits.

But before projects like this, we have a more formal sit-down to address any concerns before proceeding.

I've given the basics of the project and the potential growth we could achieve if this investment plays out, and thankfully, everyone seems to be on board. "Okay, so we'll be flying into Tokyo Narita, and from there we'll—" I say, going over the travel plan as a bit of a wrap-up.

One of my executive VPs, Stanford Truscott, clears his throat. "Yes, Stan?"

"Thomas, I have no concerns about this project, but something connected to it," he says, tapping the table in the way he does when he's got something uncomfortable on his mind. He's a great lawyer, head of my legal department, in fact . . . but the man's got enough tells that I'm shocked he's ever been able to win a court case. Maybe that's why he does his hardest negotiations around a conference table instead of in a courtroom. "It's about Mia Karakova."

Her name on his lips freezes me and I narrow my eyes. "What about Mia Karakova? She did great work on the last project."

Stan glances across the table at some of the other VPs, who give him a supportive nod. It seems I've walked into something of an ambush. But Stan's the one who has apparently been elected to face the executioner. The fact that he agreed to challenge me almost makes me respect him a bit more and lessens my impression of the remaining men and women sitting around the table like lemmings.

"I don't think anyone disagrees with that. And it's not that we don't want you to have a social life, but she works in the company."

"Your point?"

Stop getting your dick sucked by your analysts?

Not that damn voice. I don't need it here.

"By all reports, she's a bit of an odd wunderkind with numbers. In a month, she's gone from being given a chance with a team here in Roseboro to being seen with you at a major public event, and now you've given her a jump up the ladder to an off-site team. To say there are whispers of . . . influenced decision making is an understatement. And as your lawyer, it makes me concerned."

I look around the room, noting the faces looking at me. There's a lot of experience in here, 'advisors' and executive VPs who have been with Goldstone since the beginning. Still, I know their thinking, and I know their number-one concern is quarterly reports and stock prices. Not a one of them cares about me beyond what I can do to fatten their portfolios.

"I'm only going to address this subject once," I reply, pushing back from the table and glaring at the entire assembled group. "My relationship with Mia Karakova has nothing to do with her being part of either research team. It has everything to do with the fact that her professional results speak for themselves. She was given a shot on the hospital team because of her work for Bill Radcliffe. And her analysis was spot on. In fact, you all voted for Goldstone to proceed with her recommended course of action, the one that forecasts record returns on your investments in less than two years' time. She did that."

I can see that some of them are nodding now, on my side, and the fact that they are so easily swayed by dollars and cents only proves my point that money is all they care about. They just wanted to hear me say it.

"Still, Thomas, I've reviewed Miss Karakova's employment history," Stan says, trying to stay on point. "There's a rumor you tried to have her office moved up to your floor?"

"That's not a rumor. That's a fact." I've had enough of this, and my patience is wearing thin. I lean forward, planting my palms on the conference table where I fucked Mia just weeks ago. Fuck, has it only been such a short time. It feels like I can't remember a time before her, like I've blocked it out in favor of the happiness she brings me, even if only for a short time.

"Let me be transparent here. Mia Karakova is a factor in my life, and that's *not* going to change. But she is not affecting my business decisions any more than I take her analysis into account the same way I do each of you. You have all made millions of dollars from trusting my decisions. This one should be no different. But at the end of the day, it's my name on the building out there, and I'll stand by my actions. If you can't, feel free to let Stan know and we'll begin dissolution paperwork of your relationship with Goldstone Inc. Any questions?"

I cross my arms, fixing every person in the room with a stare. No one says a word, most of them unable to meet my eyes. I know I have a reputation for putting people 'on blast', but I certainly hadn't thought this was how today's meeting was going to go.

With a sigh of disappointment, both in my board and in myself, I tell them, "Meeting adjourned."

Everyone files out, leaving me to fume. Who are they to question me on bringing Mia into this project? If it weren't for my decisions, we wouldn't be a billion-dollar company right now in less than ten years.

It's pure luck, no skill on your part, stupid boy.

It's not her fault, but I'm brooding and I barely give Kerry a glance as I head into my office, closing the door behind me and sitting down. I close my eyes and will myself to relax. I'm not going to let them hold me back, and I'm not going to let them force me to doubt myself.

If I'm going to be worth anything, I have to be the best, and I can't be that by being pissed off that someone questioned my decisions. I am better than this. I have to be.

You'll never be worth anything anyway. No matter what you do.

There's a quiet knock on my door, and I open my eyes, shutting the voice down with a growl. "Yes?"

Kerry opens the door, sticking just her head in. She probably saw my face, heard my tone, and wants to make sure I'm not about to rip heads from shoulders.

"Excuse me, sir. Mr. Truscott's here. He was hoping to have a private word?"

I take a deep breath before nodding, sitting back as Stan comes in. Kerry asks if he'd like a coffee, hurrying off to get a cup for him while Stan sits down in my guest chair and stares me down.

I asked him to be my legal VP for a couple of reasons, not the least of which is that he can deal with my fiery temper when it comes to work and isn't afraid to ask the tough questions.

So I remind myself why he's here in the first place. I hired him exactly for this.

"Something else, Stan?"

"Thomas, believe it or not, I came in here to see how you're doing," he replies, unbuttoning his jacket and getting comfortable. I raise a challenging brow, and he says, "And maybe to share a little advice. That is, if you'll listen."

"I have a few minutes," I say, sitting back and refusing to give him a banal response of 'fine' about how I am because we both know that's not true.

Stan didn't need to come to Goldstone. He'd already made a good life and career for himself as a named partner in his own firm. He earned my respect before ever stepping foot in the building as an employee, and he has done even more to impress since coming onboard, even if I do think he's too conservative on his business ideas most of the time.

"Did you know," he says, pausing as Kerry comes back with his coffee and he thanks her with a polite nod, "before I agreed to join the company, I did my research on you?"

"I'd have expected nothing less. What did you find?"

"I found a man who's smarter than the average bear, that's for sure," Stan replies, "but who's no genius. Now don't take that the wrong way, because there are too many geniuses in this world who are cashing welfare checks for me to draw any relationship between brains and success."

"So, what's brought me to the top in your estimation?" I ask, curious what he sees.

"You're successful for the same reason Jerry Rice, Michael Jordan, and every other overachiever is, at least if you look at what people thought of them when they got started. You want to prove people wrong. You compete with yourself, with what others expect of you. That desire to be the best is second to none, and you're willing to work hard to be number one. I also know what fuels it."

His analysis is not incorrect, which makes me wonder what he thinks my driving force might be. "What's that?"

Stan shakes his head, sipping his coffee. "You know, you could create the world's largest company. You could become president. You could craft world peace . . . and it won't matter. Not to *him*."

The fact that he throws that out there so casually infuriates me, but I school my features into a poker face, refusing the tell that would give me away.

"Your father," Stan says, acknowledging the elephant if I won't. "My research and discretion are more thorough than most. That's what you pay me for, after all. And after meeting Dennis at my first board meeting, I felt some inquiry was prudent. Not to be condescending, but you deserved a childhood far different from what you had. You may have had things when it came to money, but money isn't everything, as you're well aware. The way he treats you" —he leans forward, meeting my stare— "and treated you after your mother's death, is criminal. And that's coming from a lawyer."

He's pretty spot-on, but this is a little too deep for Stan and me, so I just want to move this along. "You said you had some advice for me?"

"Yes," Stan says. "Mia Karakova is the first person I've seen in my five years here who seems more important to you than your drive to be the best."

"It seems like that would be a good thing. A more well-balanced leadership?"

Stan smiles sadly. "You'd think that'd be the case, but you're a jet engine on stage-five afterburners, just about two steps short of blowing up if you keep going the way you have been these past few years. And all it takes is for you to be put in just the right situation, the right circumstances, and those two steps will hit you like a ton of bricks. In a situation like that . . . you could hurt yourself, you could hurt her, and you could hurt the business. I'd prefer if you didn't reach that point."

"So, what are you recommending? That I stop seeing her?"

"No," Stan says with a laugh. "I wouldn't dream of asking that of you. What I recommend, what I advise, both professionally and personally, is caution and consciousness. Be aware and be wary, of her, of yourself. And even of others' perceptions, not because they are true but because they can affect your placement as the best on whatever scoreboard you're keeping. Dennis isn't going away, but you can be happy. Not in spite of him, but simply because he no longer has any hold on you. That is what I would like for you."

It's probably the most caring, dare I say *fatherly*, speech anyone's ever given me. That Stan sees beyond the face I present, whether because he's looking for my tells from knowing my history or because he actually cares, is oddly reassuring. His willingness to broach this conversation, both in the meeting and again in private, speaks to his character, and I respect that, and therefore, his advice.

"I would like that as well," I offer.

He stands, offering a handshake that I return. But before he goes, he says, "Investing in a woman isn't like investing in a company. You can't just cut your losses, follow the contract guidelines, and walk away when it's all over."

He's right . . . and wrong.

I know what I'm doing. Mia isn't just an 'investment'. She's someone special. And I have no intention of walking away from her.

And all the old bastards in the company can doubt me. They can doubt my decisions and my skills . . . but I won't let them stop me.

Even Stan doubts that I can have the perfect ending, worries that I can't have my company and Mia.

We'll see.

CHAPTER 19

MIA

*W*atching Tokyo unfurl underneath me is like a dream come true. Sure, at several thousand feet in the air, it pretty much looks like every other city I've flown over in my life, but at the same time . . . it's different.

"You look like you're ready to geek out," Thomas whispers from the business-class seat next to me.

"I am . . . but it's all good."

I was surprised that he's back here with the rest of the team, but when he sat down next to me, giving me the window seat in the front row of business class while he took the aisle, I was so excited that I've barely slept the entire eleven hours.

Instead, I've binged on movies, talked with Thomas, and tried to keep my voice down as he's made me laugh even as the people around us have slept.

That was hard, as somewhere over the Pacific where I could just see the aurora borealis out my window, he insisted on whispering things he wanted to do in Japan into my ear . . . very few of which we could repeat out loud. The ideas that go through his mind fill me with heat, and more than once, I had to stifle a moan as he teased me with naughty thoughts about what we're going to get up to.

And that was without even touching me as he reminded me of my demand for professionalism. I'd been *this close* to saying fuck it and skipping down the aisle to the tiny bathroom to join the Mile-High Club, and he'd known it. He'd delighted in it, in fact.

All work and no play? Thomas likes to pretend that's how he is, but it's the exact opposite. His hard, efficient work means he plays just as hard, and for hours over the Pacific, he told me exactly how he wants to play.

My excitement fades a little as we circle into Narita Airport and go through the exhausting rigmarole that is customs. Even Thomas's money and influence don't swing any weight with these guys, and by the time we step out into the underground train station that links the airport to the rest of Tokyo, I'm already exhausted.

"Please tell me this takes us directly to a hotel."

"Sorry," Thomas says, shouldering his bag while wheeling his other behind him like any other traveler, "but our limo's waiting for us at Tokyo Station. And at least the train's fast."

Fast is one thing, but more importantly, the Narita Express is *quiet*, and Thomas doesn't seem to mind that I use his shoulder as a pillow while I close my eyes. It's comforting, watching him act so normal but so protective. It lets me sort of half-doze, and I have good dreams as I feel his warmth against my cheek the whole trip.

"Come on, we're here," he says, gently nudging me.

Our team isn't that large, only five people, but the other three don't seem to give a second thought to Thomas's possessive closeness with me. In fact, in the last couple of weeks, nobody's said anything to me at all about Thomas and me going 'public' with our relationship, probably for three reasons.

One, almost nobody comes down to my office anyway since the gossip-mongers all got their fill.

Two, I'm still busting my butt for Bill and he's pretty much the coolest supervisor I could ask for in this situation.

Three, I'm pretty sure Thomas's simmering anger and reputation have made anyone who considers saying anything keep their traps shut out of fear of 'the blast.'

I don't care. I'll prove the naysayers wrong the same way that I've won Thomas's respect . . . with my results. I'm strong, I'm powerful, I'm one sexy bitch . . . but most importantly, I'm smart.

Emerging onto the streets of Tokyo is like a dream come true. The crowd, the sounds, the music, the signage . . . I feel like I've just walked into one of my animes.

"It's beautiful."

"Too bad we won't be able to see what it looks like at night," Thomas reminds me, looking around before turning to Kenny, who's serving double-duty as translator and Japanese legal expert. He directs us to our ride, and we make our way over.

The limo's not quite a limo but more of a large, luxurious minivan that takes us where we need to go. I want to watch Tokyo city life blossom around me, watch the hustle and bustle, the children walking to school in groups with their uniforms, hats, and back-packs, the young people looking much more colorfully arrayed, and the housewives on their bicycles. I want to watch the herds of 'salary-men' on their way to work . . . but it all passes too quickly, even if we are dealing with city traffic.

It turns into a hazy slide show, and before I know it, we're at Odaiba Bay, where we get off in front of something I can't believe. "A seaplane?" I ask.

"I figured it'd be more fun than the ferry, and I want to look at incor-porating this service," Thomas replies as we climb aboard the sleek, modern-looking plane.

The flight's about ninety minutes, and while nowhere near as quiet as the business-class airliner we took to get to Tokyo, the view's worth it, and I'm reminded of old reruns of *Fantasy Island* as we come in for a landing.

The island's beautiful, a tropical paradise, one of a small grouping, volcanic hills hunching out of the deep blue Pacific and covered in deep green forests. Along one side there's a small town, beaches, and a dock.

It's about as far from the *normal* image of Japan that I've seen, and while the view up here is amazing, I'm excited to get on the ground and see it.

"My God, it's beautiful," I whisper as we land in a huge spray of water that's amazingly smooth, considering what we're doing.

Thomas nods. "When we get off the plane, take mental notes," Thomas says to everyone, all business as we approach the dock. "I want your impressions, market ideas, everything. We know our preliminary research, but I need confirmation."

～

Colors. Every day, I'm reminded of just how Technicolor this resort is. Five days of waking up in a tropical paradise to the sound of waves, tropical birds, and a gentle wind stirring the curtain outside my window should be enough for anyone to unwind and relax. I sit up in the morning and look out into a riotous collage of blues, greens, whites, and natural browns, of birds dipped in reds and yellows, of fish that dance like golden sparkles and starlets in clear blue bays.

I should be putty in bed, lounging around. I mean, I don't even need to wear pants. Everyone around here wears shorts most of the time.

I should be relaxed . . . but I'm anything but. Part of it, of course, has been that I haven't been able to spend much time with Thomas. While he might be the most efficient worker I've ever met, the locals are on their own idea of what good work means.

Unfortunately, that means a lot of 'work longer, not better,' and he's had huge chunks of his time taken up with meetings, teas, and the like where there's a lot of nodding, a lot of professional smiling, and not much else. I think poor Kenny is getting a sore throat from all the translating back and forth.

By the time Thomas gets back every night, he barely has time to catch up with the rest of the team, to share a small bit of time with me, and to shower before he has to crash and be ready for the next day.

As for me . . . I've got my own challenges.

After a breakfast of rice and *furikake*, a seaweed, salt, herb, and fish flake mixture that's used as a seasoning on top of a lot of stuff all around Japan, I try to go back to work.

Which brings me to my main problem, the working situation.

While the proposal Thomas has been presented with is to buy the resort, with its twenty-eight guest rooms and two meeting spaces, and turn it into a high-end escape for Fortune 500 types who want to mix their business with pleasure, the professional capabilities are severely lacking.

Our team's work room isn't much bigger than my office back in Roseboro, and while there are only three of us in here, we're having to share four outlets for three tablets and six laptops. There's no way we can even fit everyone in here at once unless we want to share bad breath.

To top it off, the Internet is ridiculously slow. As in, I could send a carrier pigeon back to Roseboro faster than this.

"And . . . I'm going to go do my hair," Randy Ewing says, shaking her curls, which are much frizzier than when we arrived, and pushing back from her space. She's responsible for looking at renovation ideas and has been working harder than anyone. "All this heat and humidity is terrible. I'm already planning a salon trip when we get back, but for now, I just need this mop braided and out of my face. I figure by the time I get it done, my email might actually be finished downloading." She taps the laptop she's working on like her harsh words might make it connect faster. "What about you, Mia?"

I mutter a few tasty curse words in Russian and glare at one of my two laptops. Looking up at her, I shrug. "At least you've got something. Did you know the current owner keeps all his business records on paper? Not even an Excel spreadsheet . . . handwritten entries in a bound book like it's 1985. Seriously, how am I supposed to see any trends with that?"

"Best of luck," she says, shaking her head. "By the third time I had to bicycle all the way into town to even check my texts, I'd made up my mind. We'd have to sink too much into this place to make it anything close to what Thomas is thinking. God knows what it'd take to get a proper renovation team up here, and that's before the actual materials cost even kicks in."

Randy leaves, and I chug away at my information as best I can. Finally, just before noon, I see Thomas come in, his eyes red from last night's activities.

"Ugh . . . I don't know what they put in the local version of *sake*, but it smelled like kerosene and kicks like a mule."

"Good morning to you too, sunshine. Or good afternoon," I grumble, slamming my laptop closed. "Please tell me that you're making progress on your side of things?"

"I think I am," Thomas confides. "I feel stupid that I haven't learned Japanese and have to rely on Kenny to translate for me, but I've gotten the flow of how they do things around here. Somewhere in between *Dancing Queen* and *Gimme Shelter* at the karaoke bar, there was a nod, a little grunt passed in between two men who were pretending to be drunk but were nowhere near as wasted as their singing excused, and I've gotten the approval of the village head honchos. If we want to make the deal on the resort, we can. I hope it's worth the headache, and I hope Kenny forgives me for my bad rendition of Elvis. Apparently, the karaoke bar in town doesn't have the most up to date database."

"Databases . . . ugh. God, what I'd give for a fucking database right now. I'd run algorithms, maybe even make a chart. Databases," I say longingly. I lean back, growling at the word while I tug at my hair. I've reached my limit. I never thought I'd be tired of being in Japan . . . but the Japan I want to see is nowhere near here.

"What's the problem?" he asks, rubbing at his temples. "Internet is on the list of needed upgrades. Along with a revamped power system."

"It's not just that. You need data analysis, but I can't get my hands on the data. You want me to spot trends, but without having the ability to see the complete picture, I simply can't. I've got twenty-year-old technology, fifty-year-old data collection systems, and a power grid that can't even keep up with what we're asking of it. I'm working one-armed and in the dark. And I don't want to let you down."

"Mia, figure it out. That's what we're here to do," he says dismissively, sitting down in the empty chair. "You're smart. Think outside the box."

"Excuse me?" I ask, my frustrations boiling over. "Thomas, I've been stuck in here because the tools I need to use—"

"Use your brain, not the technology!" Thomas snaps. I stop, shocked at how he's pushing me. It's not that I think I'm immune from his 'blasts', and in fact, have demanded that he treat me the same as everyone else, but this is the first time he's actually done so, and the charge in the air between us is staticky and buzzy.

He pauses for a moment, taking a breath before continuing in a calmer voice. "Computers are tools, yes. But that's just it, they're tools. They're never going to replace what's inside your head because that brain's better than any computer can ever be. I do need your skills to dissect the clusterfuck this resort is, judging by everyone's complaints. But that can be done at home if the technology isn't here. There's more here to evaluate than just dry figures."

Somehow, it feels like he doesn't even know me. I live for dry figures, columns of numbers that magically add up correctly every time, and the things I can learn from rows of data. But he says there's more?

"What do you mean, 'more'? *This* is why you brought me," I say, gesturing to the laptop in front of me.

Thomas, amazingly, chuckles. "We're not making a decision and cutting a check today. If we do want to move on this deal, it's going to be a fiscal year at least while all the right people put all the right signatures on all the right pieces of paperwork. I honestly think this island's held in place in the ocean by paperwork. But while we're here, I need the team's insight—no, I need *your* insight—into this deal."

I pause, surprised by the meaning in his words. I venture, "Do you realize that we've been on this island paradise for four days and I've barely had time with you as my boyfriend and not my boss? I know we're here on business, but maybe we can take a small break?"

He presses his lips together, and I can already hear him telling me that he can't budge from his schedule. "How about if you spend today compiling every bit of information you can get your hands on and getting your numbers pulled together to take home, and tomorrow, we take twenty-four hours just for us? I'll give the whole team the day and let them pull their own impressions too so we have a solid look at everything this proposal has to offer."

I grin, giving him a little sass. "That was the most unsexy request for a date I think I've ever received."

His smirk is full of arrogance, and he raises an eyebrow. "Not a date, Miss Karakova. We're keeping things professional, remember?"

I bite down on the end of my pen pointedly, remembering how he told me he thought I'd been intentionally driving him crazy in our first meetings. His eyes zero in on my mouth the way I'd hoped they would, and I tease him further. "Anything you say, Mr. Goldstone." My voice is pure sex and suggestion.

"Starting tomorrow when you wake up, you'll be totally unplugged. And totally mine, Mia."

CHAPTER 20

MIA

"Good morning."

Two simple words, but the way Thomas looks at me tells me so much more as his eyes explore me. I'm not naked. I've pulled a tank top on over my bikini top, and I swear I've slathered so much sunscreen on my arms and face that I must look like a ghost, but Thomas's eyes tell me that he doesn't mind in the least.

"Good morning," I reply, putting my backpack over my shoulder. "How'd you sleep?"

"I'll be honest, upgrading beds is on my agenda here," Thomas says with a stretch. "Seriously, futons are not my thing. Come on, let's get some breakfast. You look lovely, by the way."

"My Russian roots are going to do a number on me tomorrow. I'm gonna be sunburned neon pink tonight," I say with a laugh as we leave the resort. "What is for breakfast, by the way?"

"Just down the road, you'll see," Thomas reassures me. "And what other roots do you have, if you don't mind me asking?"

"Not at all. According to what I was told in the little bits I remember, the Appleman side of me is mostly English. So you've got pale and paler. How about you?"

"American mutt, from what I know," Thomas says casually. "Honestly, I sort of treat heritage like zodiac signs. It's an interesting factoid, but it doesn't define us as people. You can toss it out as a

143

conversation gambit, but it doesn't define you. Even if you're from the Motherland."

"Hey, I'm mostly joking—" I start but stop when Thomas takes my hand, entwining our fingers.

"That's culture, not DNA. You can be proud of that and what your father taught you. You've taken the good and hopefully dropped the rest. At least, I'm hoping you aren't planning on wearing a babushka or stuffing me full of borscht?"

"Gotta admit, I hate borscht and my headwear is more headband than babushka."

Thomas grins, giving my hand a little squeeze. "Good. Here's breakfast."

It's a fruit stand, and the selection's stunning. I don't know what the vendor offers me, but as I bite into the softball-sized golden fruit, sweet and sour and utter deliciousness roll over my tongue and I find myself gorging myself on whatever it is as Thomas hands me another piece.

"Mmm . . . this is like the food of the gods."

"Isn't it?" he asks, biting into a green thing that has a deep chromatic red flesh inside. He hums happily, his eyes twinkling before he offers me a bite, and I eat from his hand, licking the juices from his thumb with a flirty look.

He brushes the fruit over my lips, and I suck it for a sultry moment before biting into it with a chomp. "Delicious," I say, grinning at the quick change of his expression from arousal to fear. "Don't worry, I won't bite into you that way, at least not anywhere important."

We laugh and start off walking, exploring the island. There's a lot to find, starting with the small town with its tropical slice of Japanese life, complete with a seeming unending plethora of convenience stores, vending machines, posters adorned with cartoon characters, and other little things that just sort of pop out of nowhere.

"I know I sound like a total tourist right now, but that's just strange," Thomas says as we pass a construction site. Instead of regular signs to warn people, the plastic temporary fence posts themselves are shaped like a man in a construction helmet, his hand up warningly, a bubble coming out of his head to say something in

Japanese. I can only guess it means *Caution*, or *Warning*, or maybe *Stay the Fuck Out*.

"It does get the message across though," I point out as we swerve around the metal poles. "What made you look here to invest, anyway? It's a bit beyond your usual scope, though I know you've invested beyond Roseboro, obviously."

"Because of the unrealized potential," Thomas admits. "Well, someone realized it, hence the resort we're looking at purchasing, but they weren't able to make it a reality. I've heard that the owner is a motivated seller."

"What's his weak point? Financial? Health?"

"Not quite. His daughter and grandchildren live in London, and he's ready to retire and be closer to them," Thomas replies.

I nod, setting aside business as we keep walking. We don't push the pace. We just wander, and after a light lunch at a noodle shop in town, we head back toward the resort, exploring the fifty acres of land there. As we do, the afternoon heat starts to soak in and I strip off my tank top once we reach the shaded privacy of the walking paths that ring the property.

Thomas grins and pulls off his own T-shirt, exposing his chiseled muscular torso and leaving him in just some board shorts. "Need some more sunscreen?"

"Nicely played, though not exactly subtle," I tease, taking the bottle and rubbing a fresh layer onto my thighs, calves, chest, and belly.

"And you think you're being sly stripping down to a bikini top that shows me damn near everything? You started it." The way he looks at me leaves me feeling a lot more than the tropical heat, and as I hand him the bottle, I know my nipples are starting to tighten inside my top.

"Think you can behave?" I challenge.

His hands on my back are thrilling, rubbing lotion into my flesh while at the same time kneading my shoulders, lighting up my body, and leaving me glancing around to see if we're alone.

His hands drift lower, to the curve of my spine, and I almost want him to drop below the waistband of my tiny denim shorts to grab ahold of my ass.

"I can behave . . . when I want to," Thomas purrs in my ear, a thumb rubbing up my side and sending a delicious tickle straight to my heart. "But do you *want* me to behave?"

"For . . . for now," I admit, turning around and putting my hands on his chest. "You know this is hard, right?"

"Getting there," he jokes. But when he sees I'm not being salacious, he asks, "How so?"

I hum as I run my fingers through the light hair on his chest. "Because I want this, but there's a part of me that is still worried. Nobody is saying anything, at least not anymore, but I can see it in their eyes. And I don't want the reputation as the girl who slept her way to the top. I want to earn my spot because I deserved it. Because I do."

"I agree," Thomas says, placing his hands over mine. "Mia, of course work's going to play a role in all this because that's part of who we are—a brilliant analyst and a dashing CEO." He smiles and touches his forehead to mine. "But I do want us to be . . . *us* as well."

It a good answer, and one that I can respect. "I want us to be us too."

It feels like we both just made a major confession, or perhaps a promise. Our version of one, a vow to not change each other and to accept each other as we are in all our geeky, scary, bossy, analytical ways.

I look up at Thomas through my lashes, taking a deep breath. "So, what do we call this? Izzy said you were my boyfriend, but that just seems so . . . not enough." I'm still analyzing, labeling, and he smiles.

"The name doesn't matter. The feelings do," he declares, wrapping his arms around me. In the shaded privacy of the heavy forest, I lean against his warm body, feeling Thomas's aura envelop me, making me hum in happiness.

"How do always know just what to say?" I murmur, rubbing my hand over his forearm and biting my lip as I feel his muscles tremble.

"I tell myself that everything in the universe is in balance. For every dark, there's a light. For every luxury, there is a sacrifice. And for every beast . . . there is a princess. And I just say what I think my princess would like to hear."

His words strike me to my very heart, and I look back at him, somehow loving that he called me his princess even though on some level, it pisses me off that I like it because I'm not that girl. But I'm going to take a lesson from Papa's rulebook and let it go and just enjoy the endearment without judging myself. I'm about to press back into his shorts when we hear voices, and we step apart, keeping our hands locked as we keep going. I don't know what trails we're following. I don't care. I just trust in Thomas.

Suddenly, we're headed downhill, and the jungle opens up, revealing another unexpected scene from paradise that seems to dot this island like gems to be discovered, one after another.

I gasp as I look down on the sheltered lagoon below us. We're on the eastern side of island, and the hills below us slope down to a narrow pristine beach.

By some miracle of erosion, the entrance to the lagoon is covered by a natural stone archway, leading to a pool that's not much larger than a small, deep pond . . . but what it lacks in size, it makes up for in utter beauty.

Thomas leads me down the path, his grin audible in his eager breathing. There's a bounce to his step, a joy and lightness to him that I've never seen before. It's another view into the man Thomas could be . . . and the man he is . . . and the man I realize I'm falling for.

Falling? Fallen? It's an analysis I'll have to do later because for now, I'm living in this moment, enjoying this beautiful day with him.

Getting closer to the crystal-clear water, we both freeze, watching fish swim in front of us. The schools of tropical creatures are so colorful, I almost feel like I'm in a pet store or in one of those BBC nature documentaries.

Slowly, we sit down on the sand, just watching until Thomas looks over at me and grins. "Thank you. For giving me a chance."

I lean in, cupping his face as I sense the meaning of so much behind his words that I can't imagine he said lightly. He doesn't have to question, and maybe that's the funny thing. He's spent so much time being this hard-driving neo-Alpha perfectionist that not many want to get close, if he'd even let them.

"Tommy—" I start before a rumble booms overhead, and both of us look up to see storm clouds coming in quickly over the mountains. I curse the sky as the first drops fall. "The Motherland is *not* amused!"

He chuckles, and we get to our feet and I cast a final look at the lagoon, reminding myself that this forest and this beach bore witness to the leap Thomas and I both made today. It feels special, like a secret only we share, and someday, I want to come back here.

We get back on the path and hurry back, the trip up much harder than the one down. The rain hits hard just as we're cresting the hill. The trees help some, but in less than five minutes, both of us are soaked to the skin.

"Well, this is why I said swimsuit!" Thomas says while we take temporary shelter underneath a tree. "How are you doing?"

"I can't see shit!" I complain, pulling my glasses off. "Here, near-sighted is better than blind as a bat. Can you put this in my back-pack?" I hand him my frames and turn so he can unzip the bag to slip them inside.

"Here, hand it to me," he says, taking the bag. "The straps are already rubbing you pretty raw."

I look down, seeing the faint red marks, and help him adjust the straps to fit over his broad back. It's actually funny and cute, seeing Thomas's muscular frame carrying a miniature pink backpack.

"I'm so taking a picture when we get back," I tease him, wiping my eyes before pulling my hair back over my shoulder. "You look cute in pink."

"And you look hot in white," Thomas says, his voice full of heat as he looks at my bikini top which might as well be translucent by this point. He pulls me in close and kisses me, but before we can do more, lightning splits the sky and thunderbolts pierce the clouds and crack almost directly over our heads. It's so close that both of us jump, and I can feel the hair on the back of my neck trying to stand up despite the deluge.

"Should we make a run for it?" I ask.

"I think we're safer under cover," Thomas says, and we watch as the path turns to mud before our eyes. We go deeper under the heavily fronded palm tree, letting the leaves create a semi-shelter against the torrent.

And suddenly, we're kissing, ravenous for each other. I don't care that we're outside. I don't care about the rain or my soaked feet. I don't care that the drips coming through the imperfect foliage roof are sending chills down my spine, because Thomas's hands are equally hot, cold and heat blending inside me and sending my heart racing.

Thomas reaches up, rubbing a thumb over my nipple through my soaked bikini top, and I moan, reaching down to cup the huge thick heat of his cock, tugging at the drawstring of his shorts.

"Fuck me," I moan in his ear. "Right here, right now."

"I can't wait to be inside you," he whispers, pinching my nipple before sliding his hands around to cup my ass through my shorts, kneading my cheeks and making me moan louder. "You're mine."

"I'm yours," I whisper, tugging the Velcro fly of his shorts open and wrapping my fingers around the warm girth of his cock. He's huge, masculine, and thick, with the flared mushroom of his head pressing into my fist as I stroke back, making him gasp. "All of me. And right now, you're mine."

I emphasize my point with a swipe of my thumb over his head, collecting the pre-cum there and spreading it down his shaft.

"Always," he groans. "Not now, always."

He pulls me to him, my hand and his cock pressed between us, and he grabs my ass with a punishing grip as I buck my hips into him. His fingers drift toward my rear cleft, and I nod, whimpering when I feel a single digit stroke down my ass and over my hole, thrilling and naughty.

"There?"

"Even there," I promise, pumping his cock with my hand. "Do you want it now?"

Thomas's finger probes, but he withdraws, shaking his head. "Not yet. Turn around."

I nod, letting go of his cock and pressing my shoulder against the tree. I feel his hands on the waistband of my shorts, but out of nowhere, a horn blares.

Thomas pulls back, quickly tucking his cock back in his shorts. "What the fuck?"

"We were worried! Went looking for you!" the voice calls, and out of the rain, a man appears. It's the same resort worker who picked us up from the dock. I think he's probably the only guy besides the owner of the resort who speaks any English, and he's grinning widely while I hurriedly try to hide behind Thomas and unzip my backpack to grab my tank top. Everything's a matted mess, and the first thing I get out is Thomas's shirt, but I don't care. I yank it over my head while Thomas shelters me.

"How'd you find us?" Thomas asks, and the man smiles widely.

"Saw the pink bag in the distance!" he says, and I'm struck with the insane coincidence that I was just about to have sex, outdoors, in the middle of a rainstorm, and it was interrupted because somehow, the guy driving around looking for us saw my bright pink nylon bag hanging from Thomas's back right before he was about to get my shorts down.

Of all the fucking luck.

Thomas gives me a wry smile as we follow the man, and both of us are surprised when we realize how close we were to the main road. At least the heater in the truck is blasting, chasing the chill from my body a little bit.

"We still have the rest of the afternoon," Thomas whispers in my ear. "My room's more private than yours."

And I feel a warmth rush through me that has nothing to do with the truck's heater.

Unfortunately for us, as soon as we step out of the vehicle, Randy's there along with Kenny, who're looking thankful that we're back.

"It's getting nasty out there, Thomas. I'm glad you're safe," Randy says, a hand on her chest. "Uhm, I hate to bring even more bad news, but Randall Towlee's been calling non-stop."

"What the hell does he want?" Thomas asks, confusion marring his face.

"Something about the hospital project, he says it's important that you talk to him immediately."

Thomas turns to me, a regretful twist on his lips. "Looks like work calls."

CHAPTER 21

BLACKWELL

"*Your* report?"

I don't like talking on the phone. I feel like it's a needless risk, but at times it is needed. I just have to be careful what I say.

I grew up in an era where tapping someone's phone was a simple matter. Anyone could tap a landline with two alligator clips and a headset. Meanwhile, cellphones have gone from bricks the size of my thigh to things barely larger than an old-fashioned cigarette case, and because of that, I distrust the electronic gadgets in an inherent, primal way that cannot be explained away. And with technology comes more and more ways to exploit it for eavesdropping.

But my contact uses them casually, carelessly. I'm not sure if it's a condemnation of the man or the times we live in. Probably both.

"My friend says that he's distracted for sure," my contact says gleefully. "Reports from Japan show that he spent time with *her* every day, sometimes just minutes, other times much longer." The man's disdain for Goldstone's action is obvious. "He's due to come back in two days."

"Here's what I want you to do," I command, leaning back in my black leather club chair and letting my operative know what I need. It's nothing too complicated, mostly taking guts, timing, and a little bit of work . . . nothing he will be unfamiliar with

Of course, what my operative will do with the results . . . ah, now that is the crux of the matter. The simple, beautiful blow to Goldstone's reign over Roseboro.

If discovered, it's at least a firing offense, if not a felony.

And my operative is not exactly someone trained in the methods of the CIA. So the risk is real, but calculated.

But the operative hates the Golden Boy nearly as much as I do . . . and hate makes a man ignore the risks easily. Still, a more prudent man would wonder if I was using him. A truly cautious operative would consider every angle of the possible repercussions, but this man is blind, malleable.

Just the right kind of operative.

"Sir, no offense, but this could be dangerous. There's no way I'll be able to hide my presence on the security cameras if someone suspects and checks."

Not stupid . . . just malleable. "But you are capable of forging the time and date stamps on your work, correct?"

"Of course, sir. If anyone even checks."

I can feel his hesitation, even through the buzzing line.

"Remember, the prize is often left unclaimed because victory favors those willing to take the risks to grasp it." I pause, letting the words sink in until they're pregnant, roiling in this man's brain, festering until they're a pimple ready to burst. Only then do I squeeze. "So, what kind of man are you?"

The release is immediate, poisonous, and just what I desire. "I'll call you when the job is done."

CHAPTER 22

MIA

"Good job, everyone," Thomas says as the team gets out of the van in Tokyo, and I notice it in the way they're acting. They're not sure what to make of a smiling Thomas. And because of that, they don't trust it and are waiting for the other shoe to drop.

On the island, we all sort of relaxed. Now, they're more professional, but Thomas is probably more jovial than they've ever seen before.

Kenny glances at me while Randy gives me an appraising look. She grins, and so fast I think I might've been seeing things, she flashes me a thumbs-up and grins before schooling her face back to neutral.

"Enjoy your flight," Thomas offers. "Considering you're getting empty seats next to you, you should be very relaxed for our meeting on Tuesday."

Kenny pales a little, and his and Randy's eyes meet. Thomas might be relaxing, but he isn't *that* relaxed. "Of course, Mr. Goldstone."

When they're all loaded up, I look at Thomas, half in shock and half in amazement. He turns, giving me a raised eyebrow.

"What?"

"What?" I reply, smirking. "Tommy, you have to notice that you're acting . . . *strange.*"

To say I'd been shocked when he'd suggested that we stay back for an extra two days of pure vacation time on our own would be an understatement. Actually, I'd laughingly asked if he'd ever been on vacation and he'd thoughtfully said no. That he wanted to do this with me was somehow . . . everything. And more than I could've dreamed.

Thomas shrugs, reaching out for my hand. "Maybe I've learned a thing or two from you. Or maybe you just make me happy. And guess what? From now until we get on the plane back to SeaTac the day after tomorrow, I'm yours. You'll have to show me how to 'vay-cay-shun' because I'm not sure I know how."

I laugh at his childlike sounding out of the word. "You may come to regret that," I joke as we head toward the train station. I already told Thomas that if I'm going to do Tokyo, I'm going to do it the right way. Forget taking taxis around everywhere. I want to experience the real thing—the subways, the trains, everything.

The hard part is that there's so much I want to do, but my inner geek knows there's one place I want to go first.

"So . . . what do you know about Japanese pop culture?" I ask as we buy our tickets at the little electronic machine. "Ever watched anime or listened to the music?"

"I've looked up some of the bands you've mentioned," Thomas says, warming me with his first answer. "I actually found one to add into my workout mix. Don't ask me what it was, but I liked it."

I clasp my hands to my chin, batting my lashes melodramatically behind my lenses, cooing. "You know just what to say to make my heart go pitter-pat. I'll make a nerd out of you yet."

His face lights up, and for the entire forty-five minutes it takes us to make our way to our destination, I do my best to make him smile again and again. I do it because this is the Thomas that I think nobody else in the world gets to see. Just for me. Mine.

It's not his professional smile, roguishly charming or great-white threatening, depending on the need. It's not his ironic smirk or his amused half-smile. This is the full-on, blindingly beautiful teeth and secret dimple that I adore smile.

That's the smile I want, the smile I keep getting from him, and with every flash of it, I find myself falling deeper and deeper for him.

Yep . . . *falling.*

But somewhere in the middle of that rainstorm on the island, as we slogged through impenetrable curtains of rain and I was miserably wet, I knew I wouldn't trade it for anything else in the world. I wanted to be with him, and I knew I'd fallen.

But I just keep falling, more and more, deeper and deeper.

I'm not just going to date him. I'm not just going to explore what it's like being 'his' or letting him fuck me three ways from Sunday and seeing if I can crawl out of bed the next day or if all my bones are still jelly.

There are still a lot of things we don't know about each other, and those unknown things could sink us like the Titanic meeting an iceberg, minus Celine Dion. But I'm climbing on this ship willingly and excitedly, ready to take the trip with him wherever it may go, even if we sink to the bottom of the Atlantic Ocean. As long as it's with him.

"What's on your mind?" Thomas asks as I smile secretly to myself. "You look like the cat who just got the cream."

I chuckle and kiss him on the cheek. "I feel like the girl who just got the fairy tale. Girls like me, it takes a lot to get underneath all the layers to our emotions."

"But what I've found underneath is worth the searching," Thomas replies, pushing a lock of hair behind my ear and cupping my face.

My heart leaps with joy, and as we make our way off the train, I announce, "Welcome to the Mecca of All Things Geeky," I tell him. "Akihabara!"

"Wait . . . Akihabara . . . you mean that group you were teasing me about?" Thomas asks, and I nod. "You're serious."

"AKB 48 . . . Akihabara 48," I explain to him as we walk. There's music, lights, noise, and neon everywhere, even here in the middle of the day. "This area's known as Electric Town, and it's the pulsing, nerdy, slightly pervy heart of all things anime, manga, and video games in Japan. If you've seen a Japanese game, if you've listened to a Japanese song, if you've seen an Internet meme about weird shit in Japan . . . nine out of ten chance it came from here."

We see it all. Thomas shocks me as right out of the gate, he asks to stop at the first store he sees. Thankfully, it's on my checklist too, and we go into the famous Don Quijote discount store. We fight our way through the crowd, laughing at the crazy wildness as a whole gaggle of teens sing and dance to the video playing on the huge screen.

"What are you doing?" I ask, laughing as he holds up his phone and snaps a photo of me in front of some plush figures from *Naruto*. "I'm a mess."

"You're the most beautiful woman I've ever seen," he reminds me, snapping another pic. And then he flips it around and takes a shot of the two of us together.

We both admit that the crowds are a bit much after a few more minutes, and the incessant jingle playing through the speakers is more than our American ears are ready for.

Everywhere we turn, it's another advertisement, another crush of people, another speaker screaming for attention or lights flashing or . . . "I swear, shopping in this place is like going through Vegas!"

Thomas laughs. "Vegas on New Year's Eve!"

We move on, out into the slightly quieter streets, and Thomas is great. He listens as I explain my love of anime and manga in the stacks of a used bookstore, watching me hunt down treasure after treasure.

He insists on buying them, but I refuse, explaining to him that it's not the books that are important to me but the stories themselves.

"So why not keep them as collector's items?"

"Mr. Efficiency is telling me to pick up collector's items?" I ask as I pluck the *Eureka Seven* DVD out of his hands and put it back on the shelf. "Tommy, first, I have this entire series downloaded onto a flash drive back home in full HD. Second, I don't speak Japanese, and these don't come subtitled. While the purists will say that there's nothing like listening to it in the original Japanese and going with subs if you need them, that doesn't mean I need them like this. I just want to see them, hold them for a minute." I pause to see if he understands my weird logic, and when he shrugs, I tell him, "Besides . . . you're buying lunch."

"Lunch? Where?"

I grin, knowing exactly the type of place I want to take him to . . . if I can find it. "Come on, you're gonna flip over this one."

Twenty minutes later, we're seated in a cafe while a girl in a French maid's uniform takes our order, her obscenely short skirt barely covering her ass as she giggles and gives us both looks while flirting shyly with Thomas the whole time. As soon as she walks away, though, he rolls his eyes.

"I've said it a dozen times today . . . this place is nuts."

I look around the cafe, which does its best to mimic an old-fashioned French chalet while still keeping to modern architecture, and nod. "Yeah . . . but it's a bucket list thing. Don't you have a few items on your bucket list?"

"Sure," Thomas acknowledges as he sips his water. "I'd like to learn how to fly a helicopter, I'd like to go hiking in the Rockies sometime, and I'd like . . . never mind." I swear he's blushing a bit as he dismisses whatever dream crossed his mind.

I reach across the small table, taking his hand. "It's okay. You can tell me, you know."

"I'd like to start a school . . . or a scholarship," he says quietly. "For kids . . . give something back to them."

His words shock me at first. It seems so unlike the staunch businessman who chases profits and annual reports. But as they sink in, I realize that this dream is more *him* than anything inside the big gold building back in Roseboro. And I love that he shared it with me, letting me in deeper, closer to the root of his soul. "Then do it," I tell him, smiling. "If you want, we can even do it together. Well, not the scholarship thing. I'm pretty sure any scholarship I can fund wouldn't even be able to pay for textbooks. But I can help in other ways, research and stuff."

"You'd do that?" he asks, surprise widening his eyes.

"Hell, yeah. I'd also hike those Rockies with you and climb in the helicopter with you. I'm afraid to say, you might be a little stuck with me, Tommy."

Thomas swallows and smiles bravely. "Even if I crash and burn?"

I feel like he's not talking about a rough landing in the helicopter he doesn't know how to fly, but something more abstract. But I keep the metaphor going.

"I've never, in my entire life, known someone who has a smaller chance of crashing and burning than you do. I think . . . I think if the blades came off the rotor and it was falling to the ground, you'd keep that helicopter up by the sheer force of your will, if necessary. I trust you that much."

Thomas flushes and nods even as his face pinches a little. I wonder what inner demons are whispering in his ear but don't push. He's letting me in bit by bit, even as he's gushing to support me. And I want to give him time, to trust me and to want to share his story with me. It's his past to reveal whenever he's ready, and I'll accept that as long as he's making his present and future with me.

After lunch is over, we continue exploring, working the back streets just as much as the main drag of 'Electric Town.'

We visit a small shrine, elegant wood and water nestled in between two large shops that somehow seem to be in their own quiet little sub-universe.

We poke around in 'recycle shops' that are filled to overflowing with used computer parts, haggling with shopkeepers over prices on stuff I don't really want or need.

But mainly, we do a lot of people watching.

We see people in Super Mario costumes whizzing down the streets in go karts while anime ninjas patrol the sidewalks, magicians do tricks, and guitarists are somehow trying to make themselves heard over everything in between.

"Oh . . . my . . . GOD!" I scream at one point, totally fangirling out as I see a poster hung on a wall. "They made a new movie?"

"A new movie of what?" Thomas asks as I grab his hand and drag him over. It's even better than I could have imagined. "Mia—"

"*Sailor Moon!*" I yell over the throngs of people gathered around an outdoor screen. "It's the new movie!"

Thomas obviously doesn't get it, but he's smart, and as I join in with the dancing crowd, yelling excitedly, he joins in. I wish I had it on video because the image of a man built like Thomas in the midst of all this and jumping around with me has to be a sight.

Afterward, the noise quiets a little and he pulls me aside.

"Sailor what?" he asks.

"*Sailor Moon,*" I repeat. "It was . . . I guess it still is my favorite anime. When I was a teenager, I was really struggling with some body image issues, some other stuff. For the first time, I sort of missed my mother. Well, not *my* mother, but having *a* mother, know what I mean? Puberty had hit, and Papa, for all his love, wasn't quite sure how to handle his little girl becoming a young woman."

"So, how does that relate to the show?" Thomas asks, leading me toward a cafe. This one's a cosplay cafe, and ironically, our server is dressed as none other than Sailor Moon herself. As we sip our cream sodas, I give him the down and dirty about the show, and he listens intently the whole time.

"So in the end," he says, stroking his chin, "the girls transform from normal girls into these . . . Sailors, go kick ass, take names, and look good while doing it?"

"There's more than that. There's a lot of interpersonal stuff, relation-ships, all of that," I admit. "I mean, it was like, ninety episodes or something that I've chunked down to five minutes here. But it was *so* cool and made me feel like I could handle things too."

Thomas smiles, chuckling. "I get that by how you talk about it. So what's this about cosplay?"

"Getting dressed up like the characters," I say, pulling out my phone and showing him some pictures. "I know it sounds stupid, but we could . . ."

"We?" Thomas asks, lifting an eyebrow. "I hope you mean the guy in the tuxedo."

"Of course, although I'm sure we can find a costume your size in this part of town," I joke. "You'd make a *great* Sailor Pluto."

"Ha-ha." Thomas looks at the picture, then at me, his eyes gleaming and his voice low. "This isn't something you can wear in the office."

"No," I purr, leaning in, "but maybe in our hotel room? You did make a reservation tonight, right?"

"You'll see. Fine . . . but you're going to owe me for this," he says, pointing at a pictures of a rather slutty version of a Sailor Moon costume.

We go to a few shops, but eventually, I find what I want, even if it does cost more than I'd ever spent on a costume. But Thomas sees my eyes light up as I try it on.

"Thomas, this—"

"Looks great on you," he says, his voice husky with desire. "And at least you don't need the wig."

It feels strange, walking around for the next two hours while the shop makes the adjustments to my costume with the promise that it'll be delivered to our hotel. Thomas doesn't even reveal what hotel that is to me, merely humming, a twinkle in his eye that leaves me wondering just how in charge I am of our little jaunt through Tokyo, even if it is more my bucket list than his.

I don't care. I'm having fun and enjoying time with Thomas as we watch the sun go down and the lights of Electric Town really light up.

"This place," Thomas says, watching the hustle and bustle that never stops, "it's special. It's weird, it's unique . . . but I like it."

"It's been fun," I admit, holding his arm, "and thank you. This was near the top of my bucket list and has been the best day I could have imagined."

"It's not over yet," Thomas promises me. We flag a taxi to get to our hotel, and as we pull up in front of the Ritz-Carlton, he holds my hand. "My lady."

My lady. I do *feel* like his lady, and as we check in, I look forward to being his even more.

Our suite is luxurious, looking out over the city lights, and as soon as the bellhop leaves, I turn to Thomas, my eyes brimming with tears. "Tommy, all of this, I—"

He takes me in his arms, holding me close as he brushes my hair back and shakes his head softly. "I'm doing this because I want to," he murmurs, touching his forehead to mine. "I'm not a good man, Mia. So I'm doing this for selfish reasons. Because seeing you happy makes me happy. Because I savor your happiness."

"Then . . . how can I make you happy?" I whisper, hugging him. "Because I want to see your happiness too. I think I have here lately, but I don't want it to end when we leave."

Thomas crushes me in his grip, and I wrap my arms around him. There's no passion, that'll be for later, but instead the comfort and closeness of our burgeoning relationship.

Forget titles. Forget boyfriend, girlfriend, Mia, Tommy . . . forget all of it.

Instead, I give myself to him in this hug, in the closeness of our bodies, and he gives it back to me just as much, two separate souls slowly growing together.

When we step back, I can see it in his eyes too . . . or maybe it's always been there and we're just seeing it for the first time. I think he's about to say those three little words, but he swallows and says, "I'll call room service if you want to get settled in."

I'm not disappointed he didn't say it. I can feel it, and I know we'll get there and are in fact making progress. The thought warms me. "I'm going to rinse off. After you order, why don't you put on that mask you bought when you thought I wasn't looking?"

Thomas grins at being caught and nods. I sashay away, going into the huge bathroom where I strip and give myself a quick wash. I don't want to get my hair wet, so I just spray off the city smell I've soaked up.

I want to transform for him.

My costume's hanging on the back of the bathroom door, and as I take it out, I feel my body responding. I can't believe I'm doing this, but I am.

I skip the bloomers to put on the short blue skirt, the shiny satin whispering against my thighs and ass and making me hum in desire.

Looking into the mirror, I can see my nipples tightening, and if Thomas came in right now, I'd let him have his way . . . but instead, with shaking hands, I get my hair pulled up into the iconic twin curled ponytails with tiara. It's not quite long enough to match the character, but I don't care. I love it, and I do a quick touch-up to my makeup before pulling on the top.

The tailors made it so I don't have to wear anything underneath, and the silk lining tingles against my naked skin, my pussy clenching lightly as I tuck the zipper tab underneath the red bow on my chest.

Last are the boots, knee-high red heels that cling to my calves, followed by the white elbow-length gloves with their red cuffs. Looking in the mirror, the only thing different from my anime fantasy are my glasses, and I slip them off, marveling at myself.

It's hard to hold myself back from going out there, but I force myself to wait until I hear Thomas sign for the room service and for the server to leave. Thomas gives me another few minutes, then clears his throat.

"Mia?"

"Are you ready?" I ask quietly, my heart in my throat. I feel sexy, I feel powerful, but I'm also so vulnerable right now. This character, what she helped me with when I was an awkward teen . . . this isn't play to me.

Thomas hears me, though, and I hear him moving around on the other side of the door, and a switch flips. "I'm ready."

Swallowing my worries, I open the door, my breath immediately taken away as I see what he's done. The room's filled with candles, at least two dozen golden lights around the room turning the suite into a romantic chamber.

Even more impressive is Thomas. His tuxedo isn't quite perfect. It's a modern style instead of the cape and tails from the anime, but considering he's pulled this off somehow on the sly while I was getting fitted and adjusted, it's amazing. And his mask is textbook perfect, the red carnation on his lapel iconic. He's even got a top hat in his hands. He looks me over, bowing when he sees me.

"Fucking beautiful."

I thought I was turned on before, but watching him as he adjusts his mask and holds out a hand fans the flames inside me. I cross the room to him, putting my arms around his neck and kissing him, chuckling as for the first time, *I'm* the one who has to adjust to the other person wearing something on their face.

"This means so much to me," I whisper.

"You mean so much to me," Thomas replies, gasping as I reach down and grasp the clasp on his tuxedo pants. "What about dinner?"

"Later," I promise, slowly lowering myself to my knees and opening his pants.

Like me, he's not wearing any underwear, and his cock emerges from the black zipper already hardening as I wrap my lips around his shaft and start to suck.

I'm no blowjob queen . . . in fact, I'd refer to myself as a relative newbie. But the feeling of Thomas's cock sliding over my tongue and lips as I look up into his eyes is pure molten heat. He tastes like a man, feral and powerful, satiny skin over a steel core that pulses when I pull back.

I swallow him again and again, moaning when his cock gives me a delicious bead of precum that I suck down greedily. I hum around the head of his cock, making him growl, and I realize that *I'm* in charge.

I bob up and down on his cock, and my pussy quivers, arousal dripping down my inner thigh. I want to touch myself, but I'm in total control here, and Thomas is what I'm devoting myself to.

"Oh, fuck," Thomas moans, gripping one of my ponytails but letting me control the speed. "That feels so good. Suck that fucking dick."

I look up at him, swallowing him as I seal my lips around his shaft, my hand and my mouth working together as I speed up. He moans, his hips taking over some and thrusting in and out of my eager mouth, both of us giving to each other as I worship his masculinity while he abandons himself to me.

I'm guided by his sighs, the deep throaty rumbles in his chest as he's pushed higher and higher. I can tell he's trying to hold out and enjoy the experience even as I push him to give me all he has. I feel him swell, his breath catching in his throat before he groans deeply and the first splash of his salty, tangy cum hits my tongue.

I love it.

It's just like Thomas, unique and manly, thick and creamy that pulses out of him to fill my mouth until I'm straining to hold it all in.

I don't let a drop out, though, instead pulling back to show him the naughty, sexy sight of my cum-filled mouth before I swallow, licking my lips and moaning as my pussy clenches beneath my skirt.

"Fuck," Thomas says, pulling me to my feet and carrying me in his arms to the bed. He sets me down, and I get onto my hands and knees, bending over to let him see my gleaming sex while he strips out of his pants and shoes, leaving him in just his open tuxedo shirt, jacket . . . and mask. He climbs on the bed behind me, his voice dripping with fresh desire. "So damn gorgeous, Mia. Look at this pretty pussy dripping wet from sucking my cock. Delicious."

I can't see him. My skirt is hanging down, blocking my full vision, but I can feel his breath on my pussy and his hands on my ass, rubbing softly and making my hips squirm in time to some silent music going on in his head.

"I'm only going to say this once," Thomas says, "and maybe I'm a coward for not being able to say it to your face. But when we started this, I didn't know what came over me. I just wanted to fuck you, I'll admit. But that's changed. My life's never going to be the same. It's all changed since I met you."

I don't have a chance to reply before his tongue invades me, knowingly finding every spot that has me burying my face in the bedspread and my hands balling up, moaning.

"Tommy . . . oh, Tommy, yes . . ."

He doesn't stop, his hands massaging my ass while his mouth voraciously consumes my pussy from behind, sucking and slobbering and licking until I wantonly shove my ass in his face, desperate for release. He reaches his tongue out further and strokes my clit, just once, and I explode, coming hard while his mouth sucks my juices out, kissing my lower lips in a deep, naughty open-mouthed Frenching that has me shaking, crying out.

I collapse into the bedspread, but a jolt galvanizes my spine when I feel his tongue trace up, leaving my pussy to tickle the space in between before he pulls back, his thumbs spreading my cheeks as he blows warm breath over my ass.

"You said this is mine," he says, his voice low and the breath warm on my tight hole. "Is it?"

"Yes," I rasp, breathless after just coming. "It's . . . only yours."

"On the right night, I'll claim it," he promises me, and a wave of such utter devotion floods me as I realize he's heard what I meant to say but didn't.

I've never imagined someone licking my asshole, but when Thomas does, my eyes roll up into my skull. It's amazing, it's wonderful . . . it's the whole fucking thesaurus squeezed into a single sensation and sent from my most private of places to explode in my brain.

I'm giving him my most tender, private place, and he's feasting on me, taking it and telling me with every wide lick, every probing press of a stiffened tip against my ring of muscle, every soft suck, that he's going to do his best to take care of me. It's what makes me open up to him, and I let out a cry of joy, release, devotion, and desire.

It builds me, it stokes my need, and as he darts deeper into me, it's almost like the sensations hit my pussy before exploding in my chest . . . in my heart.

"Tommy . . . I need you," I beg, and he pulls back, his cock ready and stiff again. For a moment, I think he's going to take my ass despite his words, but instead, he plunges deep into my pussy, filling me and making my joy complete.

Complete.

I'm complete when I'm with him like this, woman and man joined together, bodies locked in an embrace of passion and desire. His hands are on my hips, my skirt fisted, as he pumps in and out of me deep and hard, and I push back into him, meeting him as we build to a new peak, higher than we've ever gone before.

Lovemaking . . . not fucking. No, there's a time to fuck, but what we do is different. It's hard and soft, sweat and breath and blood and soul mixing together, delivered by way of cock stretching pussy and pussy gripping cock, electricity crackling through us.

It's pure.

It's honest.

It's beautiful.

My climax starts from somewhere inside me that I didn't even know existed, cascading over itself and sweeping away all other thoughts.

I know Thomas comes too. I can hear him cry out, and this time it's different than ever before. Before, when I've come, everything fades away except the pleasure.

This is different. In an instant, I feel like I truly am superpowered. I see everything, I hear everything, I smell and touch . . . everything. More than that, I can feel Thomas's thoughts, I can feel his heart and his soul, I can feel his pleasure as he gives to me.

It's a moment that I will cherish forever.

CHAPTER 23

THOMAS

"You really want to do this?" I ask Mia as we climb out of the shuttle bus. We've sent everything to the airport except for our passports, phones, and wallets. Our flight's the last one out of Tokyo and we won't need anything else.

"Absolutely sure," Mia says, seemingly totally refreshed after yesterday's long shopping trip and the passionate costumed encounter that led to us eating room service in bed.

My mask was ruined after I ate Mia out and she gushed on my face . . . but I can't imagine a better souvenir than the slightly stained fabric that I tucked into my suitcase this morning.

We approach the ticket gate, and I reach into my pocket and pull out my wallet. Inside is a simple black card, and if you don't look closely, you wouldn't notice the Mickey Mouse ears embossed faintly in the plastic.

"May I help you?" the park attendant asks, her eyes widening as she sees my card. "Yes, sir!"

I let Mia stammer in surprise as we're whisked through the normal gates, a simple signature on my part getting her free access to everything, and suddenly, we're inside the park, although in a part not many people are familiar with. Finally, she can't take it any longer.

"What was that? Are you CIA or something?"

"Close . . . Club 33," I reply, showing her my membership card. "It's sort of Disney's VIP club."

"I didn't know you liked Disney that much."

There are so many questions in her eyes, and I'm on the verge of telling her why I have this card, but now's not the time.

I clear my throat, thinking back with a smile. "I . . . it's a long story. So, where do we start?"

We end up starting with Splash Mountain, skipping the already eighty-minute line to climb right into the front of a log after only five minutes of walking, and as we go over the falls, it sets the tone for the day.

Again, we do a lot of people watching, and as we do, I notice the differences between Anaheim Disneyland and Tokyo Disneyland.

"Is that ten or eleven Snow Whites?" I ask Mia as we walk past It's A Small World while munching on some strawberry flavored popcorn.

"I stopped counting anything after fifteen Elsas," Mia says, giggling as a trio of princesses goes running by. "And I thought we enjoyed dressing up last night."

"I doubt we could do that here," I remind her with a chuckle. "Wrong genre, remember?"

We hit everything. The Mountain Trio, Splash, Space, and Big Thunder. Star Tours. Pooh's Hunny Hunt. In each ride, we get to skip lines, going all the way to the front, even passing up the Fast Pass people to just walk onto a ride. All it takes is flashing the small rubberized wrist bands that we're wearing, and we're able to take the entire park at our own pace.

Even better are some of the 'extras' involved. "This is so cool," Mia says as we walk through the VIP entrance to the Haunted Mansion. "It's like a whole new ride!"

I agree. In the VIP section, the pictures move, the paintings are a little creepier in a fun way, and even the music's different. It doesn't take away from the ride but adds to it, like we're getting the full attraction.

"Each park's a little different in the VIP areas," I whisper to her as we leave the Haunted Mansion. "I remember . . ." I start and then stop myself before exposing too much.

Mia hears it in my voice, and her smile dims. "Remember what?" She says it casually, not prying but just inviting me to share with her.

I shake my head, forcing a smile even as I see another group of happy children and teenagers go by, a knife suddenly jabbing in my heart as a father and son walk by holding hands and laughing. A pang of hurt washes through me, the little boy in my heart wishing for a moment that it had been my life. But wishes don't always come true. Even at the happiest place on Earth.

"Nothing. It's a long story and for another time."

It's not exactly a lie. It is a long story, and I redirect while I can. "Come on . . . I'm hungry. Let's get something to eat."

The Blue Bayou cafe, just across the water from the start of Pirates of the Caribbean, is quiet and refreshingly cool after the muggy Tokyo afternoon. Sitting down, Mia waits until after the waiter's come and taken our orders before reaching across and taking my hand.

"Hey," she prompts, and I know what's coming. She's not letting me off the hook that easily, but she doesn't force the issue, just asks, "You okay?"

"Sorry," I whisper, my eyes drifting to another happy family in the middle of the restaurant. "I shouldn't have come here."

"Why not?" she asks, giving my fingers a squeeze. "I mean, yeah, it was kinda strange to listen to Davy Jones in Japanese, but it didn't really take away from the ride."

I can tell Mia has a feeling there's something more going on and is trying to lighten the mood and give me time to corral my thoughts.

"Not that," I admit, taking a deep breath. Yesterday, I could see the nervousness in her eyes when she shared her childlike things with me, but she did it anyway. Now, I'm almost trembling like a leaf, frightened shitless. "I guess this might be the happiest place on Earth, but I never got to go even though it was something I always wanted as a kid."

"Dad?"

The house is pretty quiet, but I've gotten used to that. Since Mom died, Dad never really turns on the TV much . . . when he comes home at all.

"I'm in here."

I enter the dining room, or at least that's what it used to be. Dad had the furniture all taken out. Now it's his home office. With Mom gone, he can't travel for his work as much as he used to. He's still a member of his 'firm' where he's a lawyer, but his career's supposedly stalled. At least that's what he says when he talks at me.

Not to me.

At me.

"Dad, I got my report card."

He turns around in his chair, his face pinched and his eyes already flinty as he holds out a hand silently for the card. I'd like to lie to him, but he knows the school calendar pretty well . . . and I have to bring it back by Friday with his signature.

I fidget from side to side, my shoes squeaking on the hardwood flooring, wishing I could evaporate as he reads off the grades. "Math . . . A minus. English . . . A. Social Studies . . . A. Physical Education . . . A plus. Science . . . B plus."

I can see it in his eyes, and I try not to panic as he folds the report card and puts it back in its cardboard envelope. "I—"

"Pathetic," he says, staring at me. "I provide for you, and the best you can fucking do is a B-plus in Science and an A-minus in Math."

"I screwed up one test, that's all. I'd just—"

"So stupid, that's what you are," he sneers, getting out of his chair. The quiet label hurts more than what comes next as he gets louder and louder. "I should beat your spoiled rotten ass raw! Maybe you'd learn your lesson then! Such a disappointment!"

His hand raises, but before he can strike, I retreat to my bedroom like usual and go to my special hiding place, feeling at least a little secure. But I heard his words as I scurried out, and they echo in my head, even as I put my hands over my ears trying to drown them out. "Run away, just like you did while she died."

I sigh, coming out of the past to see Mia's stunned face. A part of me wants to clamp my mouth shut, keep it bottled up the way I always have, but it's like I've been uncorked and I keep going.

"And Thomas Goldstone for the touchdown!"

My chest's heaving, but after having run ninety-five yards in the fourth quarter of what's been a high-scoring game, I think I'm allowed to be a little gassed. My teammates are all excited. With this touchdown, we've put the game out of reach for Westwood, and those cocksuckers are our biggest rivals. They knocked us out of the playoffs last year, and this year we're going to be the ones dancing on the fifty-yard line while they go home to listen to the state championship on the radio.

Still, as I jog back toward the sidelines, I scan the bleachers for what's probably the hundredth time tonight, and the thousandth time this year, even though I know it's pointless. Because in all of the eight thousand screaming, cheering faces, I know the one person I want to be here most isn't.

"He never went to a single game?" Mia asks, and I shake my head. "Why?"

"He never thought I was good enough. I'd absorbed it and had gotten used to it by then. Honestly, if he'd come, he probably would've just told me what I'd done wrong and made it worse. But there was that little boy inside who still dreamed I'd look up and see him in the stands, smiling and proud, you know? I still feel it even today. That desire to finally impress him, but the practical side that never wants to see him again. Does that make me awful?"

"Of course not! Why?" Mia asks, horrified. "Why did he do that to you? That's so horrible, Thomas. I'm so sorry." Her words tumble out, but before I can answer, she pulls me in for a hug, her arms wrapping around me and taking the edge off the atrocities I've told her.

Pulling back, she looks me in the eye, cupping my jaw. "And why do you still put yourself through it? He's not worth it."

"Because of my mother," I reply before I can stop myself, telling Mia my deepest, darkest shame. She listens intently as I tell her the memory, our food forgotten. In the end, I have to choke out the last few words. "So that's what happened. I watched cartoons while my mother died from a drug overdose. I let her die, and he blames me for it." I've never actually said those words aloud.

I wait for her judgement, her criticism, her horror at what I did. I wait for her to pull away from me once she sees the truth of what a monster I am. And I try to prepare for it, but there's no way to be ready for your heart to be ripped from your body. And that's what she will do if she scorns me now. She holds my heart, my soul, my future in her hands as I hold my breath.

"And you internalized that and are always trying to make up for it," Mia says like she just figured something out about me, and I nod. She looks at me, and there isn't disgust in her eyes, nor pity. Instead, there's just . . . something I'm not ready to name yet.

"I try to break the cycle, but I always get sucked back in. Eventually, I decided if I couldn't be perfect enough to get his love, I could damn sure be perfect enough to make sure he couldn't ignore me anymore," I admit, thinking back to those days as well.

"The day I left for Stanford, he never even said goodbye. I didn't care, or at least that's what I told myself. I went to college, got my degree while using my extra scholarship money to invest, multiplied it, and when I graduated early, I went to him with the plan for my company."

"Why'd you go to him?" Mia asks. "I mean, did you think he'd be happy for you?"

I shake my head, sighing. "No, I knew I was giving him a noose to hang me with, but I was still too young for a bank to back me and I was desperate. So I worked a deal with him. He gave me a loan, and I gave him shares of the company and signed away my inheritance. I took that money and what I'd saved up myself from my successful investments . . . and in three years, I turned it into twelve million. From there . . . well, now you work in my building."

"Which I happen to enjoy, by the way."

I nod, watching as a boat full of a laughing family goes by, making me sad at what I didn't have. "Somewhere along the way, I realized that he was never going to forgive me."

She tries to interrupt me, but I shake my head. "I know, there's nothing to be forgiven for. I was just a kid. But the narrative's been written in my head over and over. So when I realized he was never going to forgive me, was always going to try to keep me down, I decided to stop making my success about him. I work my ass off, push myself harder than even he would to be my best, and I do a damn good job running my company. Not because of him, but in spite of him. And that eats the shit out of him."

I grin, and I know it's tinged with spite, but I can't help it. There's too much history, too much ugliness for it to be anything but a vindictive victory.

Mia reaches over and squeezes my hand. "You're a good man, Thomas. Regardless of what your father thinks, you were not responsible for your mother. And even with a lifetime of his beating you down, you rose. Because deep down in your core where it matters, you're a good man. And I see that."

Her words heal something inside me I thought was a never-ending gaping wound. I memorize the words, wanting them to battle back against the voice in my head when it inevitably returns with snide insults. With her acceptance, her acknowledgement of the side of me only she sees, I feel stronger, better than I have in . . . *ever*. It's comfortable and uncomfortable at the same time, to be so exposed, so seen.

"I think you're the only person who thinks I'm a good man. Most folks would describe me as a monster, an asshole. Oh, a Ruthless Bastard," I say, quipping with the name I know is muttered around the office to describe me. I let it slide, and besides, the reputation helps with making sure people do their best work.

Mia smiles brightly and winks. "Well, that's because you like to put on that mask. But I happen to think you're best without it."

I let the lighter mood wash through me, reveling in the fact that she's not running and screaming from my baggage like I expected. In fact, as she snuggles into my arms, she seems almost relieved that I finally spilled. Shockingly, I am too. Though I hate that she had to hear all that about me, the weight on my shoulders is lessened from the sharing.

I lean down, whispering hotly in her ear, "You didn't mind the mask last night."

She giggles, and I let the sound brighten my soul. And then she looks up at me. "I'm truly sorry you went through all that. Can I ask you a question?"

Without hesitation, I say, "Yes, anything." And I almost mean it.

She bites her lip. "With a shitty childhood like that, how'd you end up knowing so much about Disneyland? Why'd you get that fancy VIP card? Isn't coming here like poking at the bruise from your childhood?"

She's a smart one, I'll give her that.

"That's a story for another day. But suffice it to say that I've been to Anaheim Disney more than a few times, and once to Orlando. Club 33 is just one of the perks of being me." It's almost the truth. After all, Tom Nicholson doesn't have a card, though he's the one who takes kids on a dream daytrip, but Thomas Goldstone is the one with the black card in his wallet. Funny thing is, they're feeling more like one and the same with every healing moment with Mia.

She nods, letting me keep that story, and we're quiet for a moment. It feels like I just ran the most important touchdown of my life, celebrated on the field with the guys, and now I'm blessedly alone in the locker room, replaying and letting the joy wash through me. Except this isn't a game, and I'm not alone. This thing with Mia is real, and it's everything.

Her voice is muffled by my chest, but I hear her anyway. "Do you worry about being perfect, about proving something to your dad, about your past when you're with me?"

I sigh, not taking the question lightly because I can hear that she didn't ask it carelessly. "With you? No, when I'm with you, I just . . . am. I feel . . . free."

I can feel her cheek move against my chest, the smile against my heart warming me. "Good, because I want you to spend your time with me smiling, relaxing, and having fun. I want the real you, the one you hide, the one you don't let anyone else see. Just me. Mine."

I tip her chin up with my fingers, looking into those gorgeous blue eyes. "And you're mine." Our gazes lock, and though we've said so much, there is more left unspoken in the blue seas of her eyes. I kiss her softly and then whisper, "If I'm yours, what are you going to do with me?"

I expect her to say something flirty back. Most women would take full advantage of an opening like that. Mia, of course, is not most women. And somehow, I'm surprised, but not really, when she pops up and grabs my hand. Her eyes light up with childlike joy. "We're gonna make Disney our bitch! Let's ride, Tommy!"

And though a part of me would like nothing better than for her to ride me, she knows on some cellular level that this is what I need. A day in the park, innocent wonder at every turn, an experience I should've had many years ago but one that she can give me today.

CHAPTER 24

MIA

I glance up from computer, my mouth freezing wide-open as I sing Rammstein's big hit *Du Hast*. It's German, not Russian, but the repetitive nature of the chorus means just about anyone can sing it. Though judging by the barely suppressed laugh on Thomas's face, he's not going to join me in the next round.

I curse in Russian, mixing up all my languages when I tell him, "Shit! You scared me!"

He laughs. "I thought it was just a crazy rumor, you know, like fables they tell the new hires. *Beware the psycho in the basement!*" His voice has a mumbo-jumbo, woo-woo waver to it. "But it's actually true, and it really is you."

I roll my eyes, laughing. "Well, yeah. Have to keep up my street cred so everyone leaves me alone to crunch my numbers."

It's still a bit weird to have the big boss coming all the way down to my basement office, but I like seeing him here, in my space. I suspect he likes the escape just as much as I do. He looks around at the spartan space, taken up mostly by my desk and multiple monitors. But there are several pops of color in the framed posters on the wall.

With a grin, I lift my chin toward my latest acquisition. "Like it?"

Thomas touches the frame gently with one fingertip, a soft smile spreading his face. "Sailor Moon? Any particular reason?" His words are laced with memories.

"Got to see the latest movie in Japan. Did a little cosplay. The poster reminds me of good times," I say, the flashes just as fresh in my mind.

He looks at me. "I came down to ask you to lunch. But now I'm thinking of something a little sooner." He glances at the hall outside my door. "Does your office lock?"

I blush, so turned on by his words I can barely think. "Of course, it does. But I've gotta crunch these numbers. Boss is a real stickler on deadlines. And this is a big job."

It's not a flirt, though the words could be construed that way. I really am mid-analysis on the resort figures, and Thomas was right that doing the work at home had been the right way to go. With the data being in multiple locations, compiling it was my first step, and I'm only just beginning to actually make comparisons and projections. "And I don't know that a mid-morning quickie in the office is really the message we want to send."

He sighs, the sound an admission that he knows I'm right, but the look in his eyes says he wants me anyway. "Fine. Lunch it is. You're a tough negotiator, Miss Karakova."

I smirk. "You have no idea, Mr. Goldstone."

He comes closer, tipping my chin up and leaning forward as he locks me in place with his eyes. Our lips are only a breath's space away and I'm ready for his kiss, lips parted and wet and wanting. And that's when he says, "I can be rather persuasive myself."

I feel the heat of his words, knowing that he wouldn't have to persuade me to do a damn thing. I'm putty in his hands, and I slump as he walks to the door, leaving me cold without his closeness.

He adjusts himself, intentionally letting me know that he's just as affected as I am, a small gesture on his part. But then he stands straight and stiff, his professional persona clicking into place like armor.

"Yes, I'll need those figures as soon as possible. Get to work, Mia."

If anyone was in the hallway to hear, it'd sound like he was dangerously close to putting me on blast, but I see the spark in his eyes, so I play along. Though I do it in my own way.

Knowing he's the only one who can see me, I flash him double middle fingers and stick my tongue out like a child. I can see the clench of his jaw where he's fighting back the laugh.

"I'll hold you to that promise. Lunch today, noon."

He leaves, and I'm a swirl of giddy heat. That a man like Thomas is playful with me, while at the same time actually fucking brilliant and powerful, is a combination that hits me right in my heart. And lower.

I get to work, cranking through as much of the analysis as I can, knowing that it'll be a process that takes weeks to truly get a thorough look at the resort's financials. And before I know it, the morning has flown by.

I hurry upstairs, walking into Thomas's twenty-fifth floor office to see Kerry rather obviously listening to a meeting behind the closed door.

"What's going on?" I whisper.

She jumps a foot in the air, eyes going wide. But then she glares at me for scaring her and I shake to keep the laughter quiet.

We're not exactly best buddies, but things are friendlier after our lunch trip to The Gravy Train yesterday. I'd invited her, wanting to get to know her.

"So, I have ulterior motives for lunch today," I'd told her boldly.

"I expected as much. Look, I'm strictly Thomas's assistant. There's never been anything between us, never so much as a wayward glance. On his part or on mine. And it's going to stay that way." She nods her head with certainty.

With a grin, I reassure her. "Honestly, that hadn't even entered my mind, but thank you for that. What I was thinking is that we're all part of the same team, both for Goldstone and for Thomas. I just want to know the woman who controls Thomas's work life and admittedly, get you on our side so that any gossip-hounds won't use you as a source."

I'm never one to beat around the bush, but this is as blatant as I can be.

I can see the leeriness on her face as she carefully says, "Uh, I like my job. Like how it lets me pay for my kid's braces without taking out a second mortgage. So I'm not inclined to do much of anything that'd put my paycheck on the line. And that includes gossip, about you or to you."

"Oh, no, this isn't a twisted way of pumping you for info! I'm going about

*this all wrong, I guess. I just want us to be friends, or friendly. I just . . .
Thomas is important to me." I slouch, feeling in over my head and like my
good intentions didn't pan out as planned.*

*She pats my hand, letting me off the hook. "I understand. Can I tell you
something? Not gossip, but just an observation?" At my nod, she says,
"I've worked for Thomas for years, since he had a tiny office in a building of
suites. Well before he was Mr. Goldstone of Goldstone Inc. with the second-
largest skyscraper in all of Roseboro. Point is, I've seen a lot. And this is the
happiest I've seen him. That's because of you. He's never had someone, not
his family, not friends, not women. But with you, there's something
different."*

*Something in the way she listed out who he's never had gives me pause.
"What do you know about his family?"*

*Kerry shakes her head. "That's getting closer to gossip, and I won't do that,
but I know his dad is on the short list for security to keep an eye on if he
comes in without an appointment. And I know that you have free access to
his office and the penthouse." She smiles, the importance she places on those
things apparent.*

Back in her office, she whispers so quietly I have to lean close.
"Thomas has Nathan Billington in there on blast."

"Eek," I mouth soundlessly. "How bad?"

She presses her lips. "Grade-three on a scale of five."

I shrug, smirking. "Not so bad, right?" Her perfectly sculpted raised
brow says otherwise.

Through the door, we both hear Thomas's raised voice. "Get the fuck
out, Nathan!"

Ouch. I'd call that a four.

We scramble back to Kerry's desk, her plopping in the chair and me
perching on the edge unnaturally. I'm sure we look just as guilty as
we are, but Nathan stomps by red-faced without a glance our way.

Kerry looks at me with the most saccharine of smiles. "Mr. Goldstone
will see you now."

Though we don't laugh, there's a shared giggle in our eyes. She just
might be the Thelma to my Louise yet. At least at the office.

I knock lightly on the door, sticking my head in carefully. "Hey . . .

bad time?"

Thomas is standing by the window, looking over Roseboro with his hands in his pockets. He doesn't look back as he invites me in, his voice calming down as he talks. "No, lunch is just what I need." But the words are heavy, as if they cost him to say.

I go to him, running my hand up his back, tracing the tension in the muscles there. "What happened? I mean, if you want to talk about it."

He turns, and I can see the storm clouds in his eyes as he growls, "Billington had a sexual harassment claim filed against him. Nothing hardcore. He told a classless and tasteless joke, but it was overheard by someone. He's a VP, for fuck's sake. He knows better."

Nathan's jaw works as he grits his teeth, and then he says in a measured tone, "And when I called him out on it, he had the audacity to say that at least he wasn't seeing someone from the office. He didn't use the words, but he might as well have said I was 'fucking the help' like it's 1954 or some shit."

I gasp, shock and discomfort washing through me that Nathan would've dared to throw our relationship in Thomas's face, especially in such a crass way. One, that doesn't seem like a smart thing to do. Two, our relationship is nothing like that. We're consensually dating and being intentionally careful to not do anything that would smack of favoritism.

"*Mudak*. That asshole. Look, we know it's not like that. If he threw that out there, it's because he was desperate and knew he'd fucked up. Don't let him push you to a place you don't want to go. Blasting people or not, it's not about them. It's about you. I just want better for you because I know how hard that is on you."

His shoulders drop, and he looks at me sideways as if he can't fully meet my eyes. "I hear it sometimes, you know? Hear the words coming out of my mouth and hear my father screaming at me. But I don't know how else to push—them or me."

I smile, shrugging it off. "You just choose differently. Not everyone is motivated the same way, so you have to vary your approach to the person you're reaming out. Sometimes soft, sometimes hard, sometimes direct, sometimes in a roundabout way."

"Is that what you do with me?" he asks seriously. "Decide if it's a

'Thomas might break' kind of day? Or if I can take the brutal truth?"

I shake my head, feeling more relaxed. "No, unfortunately, I'm a bit like you too, stuck in my ways and a bit 'take it or leave it', but maybe we can both work on being softer. Together?"

Before he can answer, there's another knock at the door and Kerry bustles in. "Lunch is served." She's carrying two brown bags from a café down the street.

"I thought we were going out to lunch?" I ask, looking at Thomas.

Kerry answers, setting the bags down. "Yep, that was the plan. But every floor from here to the front door is talking about Nathan's little snit, so I figured the two of you walking out hand-in-hand for a lunch date would send the wrong message. I took the liberty of ordering in for you."

Thomas laughs as Kerry winks at me and mouths, "I got you."

"Whose side are you on here, Kerry?"

She pats her hair, grinning. "My side. And that means keeping the boss happy. And that means keeping his woman happy." She points between the two of us. "I also took the liberty of ordering myself lunch. On your card."

As she shuts the door, she calls back, "Don't forget you have a conference call at one."

Her whirlwind has broken the tension, settled the dust from Thomas's anger and my shock, so we sit down to eat, making the most of the few minutes we have.

"Oh, I'm sending out a meeting request to the hospital group for tomorrow. I'm going to announce my decision. I'm going with your recommendation."

"Which one?" I ask, rolling my eyes. "The first or the second one?"

"The real one," Thomas replies, his smile reappearing but still weak. "I still haven't figured out how the file was changed. I had IT look into it because of the discrepancies, and the print order was done from Randall's computer. But they checked his files and the network, and both show the file was unchanged. The changes happened between your email and his inbox, which isn't possible, but it's the only thing that makes sense. And that worries me."

"It's probably just a blip. Just a random ID-ten-T error," I say, confused but mostly just glad we caught the error.

"I'm not an idiot, nor do I think this was a random error. In fact, I was wondering if you'd help me with a special assignment?"

I lick my lips, wiggling my eyebrows. "What'd you have in mind?"

"Well, that too," he says with a laugh. "But the fact that an error like that could happen once makes me curious whether it's happened before. I want you to go back through the last few years' projects, investments, and such. Focus on the ones where we didn't do as well as early projections had forecast. I want to see if there are any trends."

"Well, I can tell you one trend right off the bat," I tease.

"What's that?"

"One person made the final decision each time. PEBKAC." I say with all seriousness.

"PEBKAC?" Thomas asks, and I nod. "I'll bite. What's PEBKAC?"

"Problem Exists Between Keyboard And Chair," I answer. "In this case, it could just be that you've made some bad decisions, Thomas. No investment is risk-free."

Thomas nods, and I see his shiver as he considers my point. I'm saying it clearly that he's possibly made mistakes. He's not perfect . . . he could be wrong.

"Point taken," he finally acknowledges, "but if that's the case, I need to know that too. Focus on the resort analysis first, but after that's done, if you can start the big job, I'd like you to keep me up to date."

"Of course."

"Speaking of dates . . . you up for dinner at my place after work tomorrow night?" he asks, pointing upstairs. "I know it's a long way, but—"

"But you want to give me time to pack some spare work clothes," I remark, getting to my feet. "I think I can be convinced of that . . . if you let me have a little bit of space in your closet to hang things up. I demand at least two hangers."

"Tough negotiator, but I'm pretty sure I can do that," Thomas says.

CHAPTER 25

THOMAS

*T*he 'super warehouse' is huge, 100,000 square feet of just about everything possible in bulk boxes, bulk bags, and bulk crates. There's enough food here to feed all of Roseboro, I think . . . but it doesn't matter.

Of course it doesn't matter. You're just pissing onto a forest fire, thinking it'll make a difference. Like you could make a difference.

Instead, I focus on what I'm here for. The big cart in front of me is already heavy as I load a second fifty-pound bag of rice onto it. Thankfully, this place doesn't do normal shopping carts but industrial-strength carriers that can easily hold hundreds of pounds.

Up next are vegetables. I get a variety, from corn to green beans to carrots. Sadly, there aren't tons of options. I'd love to buy fresh from the farmers, but that would mean leaving a trail, and I can't have that.

I tug my ball cap lower as I turn the corner, and it's sauces. Lots of pasta sauce, then on to pasta itself, spaghetti being the main one, of course, along with a case of that dried cheese that's total shit but kids love.

Sausages, chicken breasts, oatmeal, milk . . . all of that's going to get packed into thermal cases, and by the time I'm done, I'm straining to push the cart. It takes the cashier nearly fifteen minutes to ring everything up. Thankfully, one of the stock boys helps me load up the back of the truck, and he pats the tailgate appreciatively.

"Man, whatever you're planning, I wanna be there. You've got enough here to feed a crowd. Tell me you're buying beer next?"

"Not for this party," I reply, tipping him a ten and a handshake. "Thanks for the help."

The drive takes longer than usual, mainly because I'm going south all the way over the state line, off the main roads and ten minutes into what looks like woods. When I heard about this place, I couldn't do anything at the time, but as I try to coast silently around the back, I start to tear up.

The Cabin looks almost normal on the outside. A large traditional-style house, a little rundown but cared for in a piecemeal sort of way that tells the tale of money coming in in fits and starts. Its eight bedrooms house sixteen kids, all of them rescued from abusive homes.

There are specialized programs here for the kids, therapy and job training, a chance for them to get their lives together. A chance for them to have a fresh start away from the roughness of their early days.

When I approached this place as Tom Nicholson, I'd heard what some of these kids went through. I hadn't been able to sleep a wink that night, the pain from my own past brought to the surface by the shared shittiness of our childhoods. I'd had to put myself through hell in the gym to purge myself of the emotions, and they still nearly crippled me for two days. But I'd gotten over it and set out to help.

Because they're struggling.

While the building itself might have been donated by an Oregonian who had the property and the foresight to see that getting these kids out of the environment they'd been in would help them more than a large urban 'rehabilitation factory', they don't get as much as they need. Politicians see the budget and the number of kids helped, and the bean counters take over.

Which is why I'm out here at nearly eleven at night, doing my best to unload the truckload of supplies onto the covered back porch without making any noise.

Actually, the fact that I'm having any success tells me that the next trip out here needs to include a security camera and some floodlights. Harder for me to sneak in like Santa, but definitely safer for these kids who deserve to feel safe for the first time in their lives.

I know it's stupid, keeping my charity work secret. If the PR team at the company knew about this, they'd be going gaga over it and trying to get my name in every paper up and down the West Coast. They'd probably preemptively clear a space on the wall of the bottom floor somewhere for all the awards they'd expect I'd get.

But that's exactly why I haven't told anyone. It's not for the recognition. I almost don't want to be recognized, actually. It's why I've taken the steps I have, the shell company, the cashier's checks on that account, the disguises, all of it.

Though I've thought about telling Mia. Maybe she'd understand, but I'm not sure yet. Not because I'm not sure of her but because I'm not sure about me.

My whole life, when my father was smacking me around, not giving a shit about me . . . no one really cared. They took me at face value as a charming, good-looking guy, someone who easily got good grades without the teachers' special attention, and who could play ball and win for the team. There were definitely signs something was going on, but no one cared enough to find out. They took the easy way out and I paid the price.

And I don't want the kids thinking I'm doing this at their expense, riding the coattails of their pain for accolades and awards. It's not about that, and if anyone knew it was me, that's what it'd morph into. I won't use them that way. So here I am, sneaking around in the dark.

Stacking the boxes with the two basketballs and the football on top, I reach into my pocket and pull out the white envelope, tucking it under a five-pound can of tomato sauce.

Getting back in my truck, the door closing sounds loud and shocking in the quiet of the night. I wince and put the truck in neutral so it rolls a bit, looking behind me.

I see a slice of light as a door opens, a wide man and a smaller silhouette at his side dark against the bright backdrop. Through the open window, I hear his words carry on the night air.

"Good Lord, look at all this."

Already caught, I crank the engine and gun it for the main road. But even over the engine, the man's yell reaches me. "Thank you! Thank you so much!" His sob touches me, bringing a sharp burn to my eyes.

It's still not enough. Just a drop in a bucket. You'll never be enough.

CHAPTER 26

I don't come to The Gravy Train for breakfast often. It's really out of the way from my apartment.

But . . . I didn't spend last night at my apartment. In fact, I haven't spent three out of the last five nights at my apartment, and I've gotten used to taking advantage of Thomas's amazing shower.

Seriously, two pulsating shower heads will do things to your body that you only dream about. Especially when you're not showering alone.

The shower's not all I've taken advantage of, but I promised the girls that this morning we'd get together, so I pried myself out of bed while Tommy gets an early start on his agenda for the day.

Izzy comes in, looking fresher than I've seen her in a long time. "Hey, Mia, babe, you're looking . . . freshly fucked."

"What? I just got out of the shower!" I joke, even though it's true. "You look a lot brighter and more bushy-tailed than I've seen you in a while yourself. What's up?"

"Just a moment," Izzy says as Charlotte comes in the door. "I figure I just wanna say it once."

"Ooh, someone else on the man train?" Charlotte teases, grinning. "I mean, I figured you'd be trying out for the nunnery after you finished your degree, but maybe you went all Von Trapp on us?"

Izzy rolls her eyes, shaking her head. "I'm not that bad, but I do have good news."

"What's up?" Char asks as she slides in next to me.

Izzy pauses, then smiles big, the excitement she's been holding back bubbling out. "I got the scholarship!"

We all squeal, a harmony of shrill happiness, and clap loudly for her.

"Way to go, Izzy!" I cheer her.

"It's only five thousand dollars, but hey, it's five thousand dollars," she says. "It's some wiggle room for tuition and cost of living."

"So does that mean you're going to stop pulling insane shifts here?" I ask, and Izzy shakes her head. "Babe, come on!"

"No, I can't," Izzy says. "Listen, it's wiggle room, but not *that* much. My laptop's going to shit, and before you say it, Mia, I won't take yours so you have an excuse to buy a new one."

"Too much hentai anime on that thing anyway," Charlotte teases. "I have a strict three-tentacle per hard drive limit."

"Hey, I haven't gone there . . . yet." I laugh, and they both laugh with me.

"Hey, by the way, how's domestic life? I still can't believe you're spending time with us instead of with Hunky McDollarSigns," Izzy says. I give her a sharp look, checking for any sign of jealousy. We all know Izzy has the most money trouble of the three of us, but she's proud and wants to stand on her own two feet. Even so, having a friend who suddenly hooks up with the likes of Thomas Goldstone must make her a little salty. But in her eyes, I only see happiness for me, not a hint of envy, cattiness, or shallow ugliness. And that's why she's one of my best friends. She's good, down to her core good.

"It's not the size of his bank account that has Mia worked up, I bet," Char teases. "Tell me, honey, seriously . . . how long before you kick us to the curb in favor of ladies who lunch and splurge on a cucumber in their water?"

"Oh, please, it's not like that at all. Hell, Thomas isn't even like that. Besides, what would I ever do without you guys?" I ask, and Charlotte laughs.

"You'd be busy, that's for sure," she says. "On your knees, bent over the desk, in bed, in the shower. I mean, I'm sure we can't compare to Thomas Goldstone."

"Well, that's true. *All* of that is so true," I say with a smug shimmy of my shoulders. "But he can't compare to you guys either," I counter. "I mean, seriously, who's going to listen to me complain when I come in all bloated and crampy with PMS?"

"I don't listen to you now," Charlotte jokes. "Do you, Izzy?"

"Nope, never," Izzy teases. "I mean, if we were friends, maybe I would then, but you're just this psycho who comes into my work so much I'm kinda forced to hang out with you."

"Yup," Charlotte says before busting out singing, "F-R-I-E-N-D-S, that's how you fu—"

"Shh!" Izzy says, slapping a hand over Charlotte's mouth. "First of all, I hate that damn song. Second, I do work here still. I don't need you cursing at the top of your lungs and cracking glass with those shrill notes." She rubs at her ear like Charlotte's howling at ear-splitting levels. She's not far from the truth.

Charlotte sticks out her tongue, wiggling it. "Fine, but you know I sing just fine. When I was a little girl, the pastor in church kept saying I was the best at making a joyful noise during the hymns."

"Emphasis on the noise," I tease. "Charlotte, you're not as bad as me, which isn't saying much, but I say this with the brutal honesty only a friend can give you . . . scratch your plans to try out for *American Idol*. You don't want to end up on the loser reel."

She feigns shock, hand to her chest for a moment before conceding. "I know, I know, but I'm still pretty fabulous, if overlooked." She straightens and sips her drink. "All jokes aside, seriously, how're things with Thomas?"

"Really awesome," I admit shyly. It's not that I'm unsure about what we're doing, but sharing just how much I feel about Thomas with them before sharing it with him seems out of order.

Because I am feeling things, a scary four-letter thing. And I've never felt this before, not like this. Not a fizzy, bright bubbliness on top of deep, earthy richness, not a fire so hot I don't know if I can withstand it but all I want to do is try.

But I do feel all that and more with Thomas. And that both thrills and terrifies me. What if I'm not enough? What if he can't get out of his head? What if this is all just physical and new and I'm making it into more than I should because I've fallen for him?

But I know in my heart that this isn't one-sided or casual. I can see it in his eyes every time he looks at me. He's just as new at this as I am, maybe even more so. But that's okay, we can take our time and get there together.

I realize that while my mind has been whirling, Charlotte and Izzy have been waiting expectantly for a fuller answer. "Japan was every-thing I thought it'd be, and then some," I say cryptically, spreading my hands wide like I can't possibly encompass all that I saw, felt, and did into a few words.

"Because of the company," Charlotte adds wisely, and Izzy nods.

I sip at my coffee, agreeing. "Yeah, because of Tommy. He's . . . not what I thought when I first met him. He's so much more. It's compli-cated. He's got this persona as a hardass, but when he's with me, he's gentle and nice. Japan was . . . enlightening."

Charlotte leans to Izzy, stage-whispering in her ear so I can hear, "Sounds like she's literally tamed the beast. Has him wrapped around her pretty little finger."

I smile cheekily and wave my pinky finger at her.

Then Izzy whispers back, "Or maybe he has her wrapped around his thick cock. Did you see her hair when she came in this morning? Definite morning BJ."

Instinctively, I reach for the back of my hair, smoothing it down as my jaw drops open. When they both burst into raucous laughter, I chastise them. "Guys! That's not funny!" But I finally laugh with them, asking through punctuated breaths, "Is my hair really okay? I have to go to work!"

But that just makes them laugh harder.

CHAPTER 27

THOMAS

"*T*ommy?"

I look up and realize I've missed something Mia's said because my inner voice was whispering in my ear again. The same never-ending mantra of how I'm unworthy, but it's enough to distract me.

Shit. I growl lightly, and Mia's forehead creases as she sees my face.

"Sorry, lost in thought about work," I lie, but it at least eases her worries. "What did you say?"

"I asked how your morning appointment went," Mia says, relaxing. "I was looking forward to talking with you about some of the projects you sent me, but you popped out pretty quickly, Kerry said. I know I went to grab a coffee and boom, gone from the Motherland you were."

"It went well," I answer, thinking about the quick run out to the boys' shelter. Most of them were in school, of course, but Frankie's laid up sick with the chicken pox, so I brought him some Reese's Peanut Butter Cup ice cream before helping him with his math homework. That kid's a fiend for peanut butter.

After that, I came back to my place and did a workout before checking in with Kerry, and now dinner with Mia in my apartment. It's been a full day.

I rub at my temples, willing the voice to stay at bay. Just give me an evening of peace, and it can harass me to sleep later.

"By the way," I ask, hoping to change the subject, "how's the research going on the idea I gave you about someone maybe kneecapping me?"

Mia hums, setting her fork down. "I'll be honest. You've got a lot of oars in a lot of waters. It's been a ton of data to slog through on top of my regular projects that actually make the company money."

"I'm sure you can do it though . . . right?" I ask, forcing myself to keep my voice soft even as the voice in my head yammers at me.

Just do it! It shouldn't be that hard if you actually try, you lazy shit!

I take a deep breath. The voice almost sounded like it was yelling at Mia, but I know it's just a repeat of something my dad said to me once when I had a hard time building a mousetrap car in junior high school science class. Not that he could've done it either, and I did eventually figure it out. *Got an A, fuck you very much,* I tell the voice.

Mia nods her head, giving me a smile. "I said it's a lot of data to slog through, but I've got it. I'm starting by identifying the outliers in terms of prediction versus outcome, and that's not as easy as it might seem."

Okay, that I can understand. There's a lot of factors that can screw with a prediction, and some of them are out of our control. "What do you think?"

"I think it's too early to tell, though signs are looking good that I'll find something," she says, but there's heat in her voice and with a glance her way, I know she's not talking about the research project at all. Or at least not *only* about it.

"Oh, you think you've found something good?" I prompt back, playing along.

She bites her lip. "Oh, definitely. You're not perfect, and I wouldn't want you to be. But I'm really happy, Tommy. I'm sure this project is going to yield some very enlightening results, maybe even increase our ultimate profit margin."

Her not wanting me to be perfect is a balm to my soul, more healing than she probably realizes. And her play with work talk and personal talk is turning me on. Maybe that's weird, but I'm a businessman at heart. And apparently, my cock likes a bit of market chatter too, judging by the growing bulge in my slacks.

"So what exactly are you doing to develop these figures?" I let my eyes roll over her figure, taking an extra-long glance at the hint of cleavage on display in her slashed-neck T-shirt. It's from a band I've never heard of, of course, but most of her clothing is like that. I enjoy the way her blush creeps up her neck, pinkening the skin before my eyes as her breasts heave a little faster.

"Well, I can't just look at profit and loss because some projects are short-term, others long." She lets the word drag out sexily. She's geeky, nerdy, and turning me on more with every word from her sexy brain.

I lean forward, refilling her wine glass. "Nothing wrong with a quickie investment. Get in, get the goods, and get out," I rumble.

Her smirk is pure evil, her eyes wide and innocent, and the mix drives me wild. "But other times, to really get the payoff, you have to take your time, be patient, and really work every avenue for maximum impact. Milk everything you can out of it before you're fully satisfied."

She takes a sip of the red wine, and I watch raptly as she licks a droplet from her plump lower lip. I take a sip of my own, wanting to taste her but wanting to continue our game a bit longer.

"Really, getting everything sorted has been a bit of backbreaker, really hard and intense. But I'm making sure I do a good job on this for you, for professional pride but also because I don't want to give you a reason to bust my ass."

She's still playing, teasing about me sexily spanking her, but the words . . .

Get over here! I work hard to provide and all I ask is that you work hard too and stay out of my way. Maybe if I bust your ass, you'll finally amount to something. You asked for this. You knew I'd bust your ass.

Memories of me literally getting my ass 'busted' suddenly course through my brain, and I clench my jaw, regretting my action immediately as Mia takes it as my admonishing her for her sexy words. "Tommy?"

The mood is broken, the heat in my body replaced by a coating of cold sweat on my back. And judging by the way she's eyeballing me, I must be pale because Mia looks worried.

I hang my head, not able to meet her eyes. "Sorry . . . just a bit of a flashback."

She puts her hand on my back, rubbing me gently. "It's okay. Happens to everyone, about good things and bad."

Her acceptance of my freakout when we were mid-flirtation should make me feel better. Instead, I've never felt smaller, less like a man. I revert to what I know, dry business talk to distance myself from the shit show in my head. "It's just that I've figured out there might be some level of corporate espionage and sabotage. Maybe something going on for a long time. And I'm furious and disappointed in myself for not realizing it sooner."

Mia shakes her head. "This is slick, if there's even anything there yet. Which I haven't decided there is."

"I know," I say with a heavy sigh. And then I admit, "It's . . . I'm learning how to trust, with you. Basically for the first time. And with this over my head, it's even harder now. I'm sorry if that seems cruel to you or if I'm being an asshole. But I guess that's what I'm known for."

In my head, I see me yelling at Nathan Billington. But then superimposed over my face, my father's face appears. Red, veins bulging, hate in his eyes. Am I really that bad? How did it get this bad?

Like father, like son. He broke your mother so badly she killed herself rather than face life with him, with her own son. How long do you think Mia can withstand you? Like father, like son.

Mia shakes her head, taking my hand. The soothing touch pushes my inner demon back for a little bit, and I feel my pulse slow a little as she strokes the back of my hand with her thumb.

"Tommy, I know this is going to be difficult. And honestly, part of me wishes you'd get some help on your issues, even more than what I can do. Your dad did a number on you, but you don't have to let him have space in your mind. Kick him out, for fuck's sake!"

She mutters something in Russian, even feigns spitting on my dining room rug, so I decide she's cursing my dad. As stupid as it is, it helps. It makes it feel like she's on my side.

"But I'm not going to push you on going to therapy. You'll go when and if you're ready. In the meantime, I'll just earn your trust as best I can, because . . . well, I want that. And more."

"I know." I swallow, almost afraid of everything she's asking for. "And this may sound insane, because it shouldn't be this way, but that 'more' is coming faster than the trust." It's the closest we've gotten to saying the words, and she offers me a small smile, letting me know she feels the importance too.

"That's okay. We'll make our own path," Mia reassures me. All I can give back is a nod as I blink the burn in my eyes away.

She leans back, giving me space before clapping her hands as if she can clear the air between us. "As we were saying, with this data mining, it'd help if you had a guess as to who I could start my search with. It's not always a great idea, but with the sheer volume of data I'm combing through, I could use a good yard marker . . . unless you plan on my taking the next two months just doing analysis on all this."

"I don't know." I grit through my teeth. "I've tried tracking back through some emails myself, though I'm no cyber-security expert, and I've searched my brain and the company directory for anyone I thought might either want to hurt me or might benefit from a Goldstone loss. And nothing. Your mic drop performance was the first time I'd really considered that something might be wrong. You helped me."

"How'd I help?" Mia asks. "I mean, I just told you that you were wrong. And it was not a mic drop," she argues again, the same as she had done that day. It seems so long ago, but at the same time, I feel like so much has happened. It helps, seeing that sass and fire. It reminds me that Mia's on my side, and she's smart, and beautiful . . . and mine.

So I don't mind giving her some of my own back, even if it's professional. "You had evidence to back up your claim. Most people just backup their data to the company server. But you hard saved your own copy of the data on your laptop. So I had a place to start the comparison, follow the trail, and compile a smaller group to work from."

"The hospital project group," Mia murmurs, and I nod. "But the only person I sent that file to was Randall."

For some reason, even hearing Mia say his name pisses me off. "I know, but Randall says he didn't make any changes, and like I said, his computer's clean. Also, I looked back through my own files about some of the projects I knew didn't go according to plan, and for some of them, he was nowhere close to the team. It's a start, but I don't think it's strong."

"But you don't like him," Mia points out, and I shake my head.

"I trust him to do his job, but no, I don't like him. It's in his face, in the way he acts sometimes. Like when I had to get in his face at the party. Every once in a while, it's like the mask slips, showing me someone underneath who's my enemy. And if anyone knows about masks, it's me."

Mia chuckles. "Yeah, that party . . . it's funny, Tommy. I know a lot of folks would say that caveman behavior was wrong. Even that I should've left you both standing there, measuring your dicks. But I felt safe with you. I could see that your anger wasn't directed at me."

"And you have no idea how much that means to me. I was surprised at my reaction that night too," I admit, thinking back. "I was angry at how Randall wasn't listening to your polite no, but deep down, I just wanted to beat the shit out of him for daring to look at what was so obviously mine."

"And I'll admit that scares me, but the point is, you didn't. You held yourself back," Mia says. "So you can do better, be better. But Tommy . . . it's also what makes me worry. You're hell-bent on building a world for yourself, and I can see a place for me in it. But it's a world that's being built on a shaky, flawed foundation because you've got all this inner anger, this rage. What happens the first time a really big earthquake comes along and shakes it up?"

I nod and get up, going around the table and pulling her to her feet. "I've had the same thoughts every day. But that's something else you help me with."

"What's that?" Mia asks, her breath catching when I pull her close.

"When I'm with you . . . I feel like for the first time in my life, I feel . . . peace. I feel like when that earthquake does come, maybe I can survive it."

Mia smiles and takes off her glasses, setting them on the table before wrapping her arms about my neck. "Maybe we can survive it together. Ride it out together."

Her words are back to having a double-meaning, this one about acceptance, about wanting me to grow but taking me as I am, fucked-up mind and all. But on top of that deeper meaning, the heat returns between us, flashing fire through my every nerve, burning away my thoughts about work, my family, my shortcomings, and leaving in its wake only . . . need.

I pick her up, carrying her over to set her on the couch, loving the image before me. She's still the quirky woman I first met, still has the streaks in her hair—purple and blue today—but she's been wearing skirts more often. I suspect it's both to drive me wild with the flashes of her sexy legs and to make after-work access that much faster. Today, her skirt is black denim, jagged at the hem in a flirty, sexy way . . . and already halfway up her thighs. I kneel, pushing her knees apart even as she spreads for me, showing me what she's wearing today.

"You wore a thong under that skirt?" I marvel, tracing the outline of the lacy triangle over her smooth pussy. "Maybe you're lucky I stayed out of the office today."

"Mmm, but you would have so loved the mid-afternoon snack I had in mind," she teases. "I was hungry and thought to myself that I could easily fit under your desk."

Though we've been trying so hard to corral our actual fucking to outside work hours, the image of Mia on her knees under my desk, sucking me off while I try to maintain a semblance of normalcy, feels naughty and invigorating. "Tomorrow, maybe. I'll send Kerry out on an errand of something or another," I joke before rising and kissing Mia. I want to feast on her, but after such a hard day, my cock needs attention more than my tongue, and I pull back. "Wait."

"What?" Mia asks, her flushed face looking so fuckable I can barely hold back. But I want more than just torn clothing, tossed aside shirts, and frantic pawing at each other.

I want to be in control . . . of myself. Of her.

"Stand up . . . and strip for me," I reply, getting up so she can stand. As soon as she does, I take her place on the couch, watching her.

She shimmies her way out of her skirt and then begins teasing at the hem of her T-shirt, pulling it up and shoving it down to give me quick flashing peeks. And then with a smile that says she knows exactly how wild she's driving me, she pulls the shirt over her head.

She's a vision in sheer lace, bright pink against her pale skin. Her tits are pushed up high, cupped in a way that makes me want to free them, want to see their heaviness bounce. The lace at her center is but a bare scrap, giving way to thin strings that go over her hips.

I palm myself distractedly, looking for relief from the wellspring she's drawing up inside me. But she notices and with a bite of her lip demands, "Let me see."

I growl, giving her what she wants only because it's what I want too. I pull my shirt open, buttons flying but I don't give a fuck. And as I reach for my belt, I rumble, "Get on your knees for a closer look."

Her eyes flash to mine, and for a moment I think I went too far, not in the words because I know Mia can handle that, but in the tone. Bossy, demanding, arrogantly forceful. Like I'm entitled to have her suck me off. But then I see her blue orbs darken, and she drops in one movement, sagging like someone simply knocked her down. Or like someone took control of her body.

And I realize that someone has. Me. And she's letting me.

I rip my fly open, shoving my pants and underwear down over my ass. My cock stands heavy between us, and she waits for permission, for an order. She waits for me. "Suck me off, Mia. Like you would under my desk. Wrap those lips around me and swallow every fucking inch."

She moves forward, taking me into the hot wetness of her mouth, not inch by painstaking inch but all at once to the hilt. I surge into her throat, grabbing at her head and finding purchase with fistfuls of her hair. She makes a *gluck* sound in her throat and it's my undoing.

I push into her mouth over and over, pleased beyond measure as she swallows me at every interval. Her hums of pleasure vibrate through my shaft, and all too soon, I'm on the edge.

I hold her back by her hair, and she pouts that I've taken her treat away, though I can see the mess I've already made of her, drool and pre-cum mixing and dripping off her chin to her chest.

I guide her up, and she climbs into my lap, our hands exploring each other. I lean in, kissing her chest before sucking on her stiff nipple through the lace, flicking my tongue over the peak as Mia rubs against my cock, the wispy thong preventing nothing but my filling her.

"Oh, God, Tommy . . . I want you every day," Mia moans, pushing my head away to kiss me tenderly. "I promise you, I'll do whatever I can to make you a happy man."

"I promise you . . . I'll never hurt you," I reply. "I'll protect you, even if it's from me." It's a promise I hope I can keep.

She shakes her head, her hair brushing along the backs of my hands where I hold her hips. Though her eyes are closed in pleasure as she grinds against me, her words are crystal-clear. "I don't need protection from you. *You* need protection from you. That demon inside your mind only wants to hurt you. But I won't let it. I won't let it have you. You're mine. My *good* man."

The demon scoffs in my head. *You're barely even a man, much less a good one.*

But when Mia slips her thong to the side and reaches down, rubbing the head of my cock between her wet lips, her words are the ones echoing in my mind, shutting the voice up.

I pause, not forcing her down on my iron-hard member but letting her control it, feeling the electric thrill as she rubs just the crown, her honey oozing over my tip and down my shaft until I'm gleaming, and Mia whimpers.

"Your good man," I reply, needing the power of the words in the air between us. I hiss as she lowers herself onto me. Her pussy grips me in a tight, slippery vise that draws me into her until I push down on her ass, seating my cock deep inside her. "And I've wanted you all day. Now I have you, and you have me."

Mia leans in, kissing me before she starts riding me, lifting her body and bringing her nipples to my mouth. I suck deeply, her other side rubbing against my cheek as she bounces, planting her hands on the back of the couch as she takes me.

I . . . I like this. Like our time in Tokyo, I let her have what she wants, entranced as she rolls her hips, her thighs tightening while my cock plunges deep inside her. Watching her through half-lidded eyes, I can feel my soul yearn for her happiness and pleasure, exaltation sweeping me as she throws her head back, crying out when the head of my cock rubs over her G-spot.

"So good. *Soo* good."

"Beautiful," I rasp, and she looks down, smiling. Reaching down, she grabs my hair and pulls my head back into a soul-searing kiss that ignites the feral side of me like gasoline on a fire.

Grabbing her ass, I squeeze tightly, my fingers digging in and holding her still as I thrust deep into her, her pussy clenching around me as I hammer upward, my hips flexing hard with each savage stab deep inside her. I clamp my lips around her right nipple, sucking hard until she cries out in pain and pleasure.

"That's it," I growl, letting go of her nipple and flexing my arms, adding all my strength into the deep stroking, fucking her with my whole body. Her hips must be aching. She's clapping up and down on my thighs so hard that the sound echoes even above our panting breaths and the roar of my heart beating in my chest. "Take it."

Why pretend? You're not good enough for her.

The whispered voice that I thought had abated drives me into a fury, and I pull Mia off me, pushing her over the arm of the sofa before plunging back inside her, holding her by her hair.

She cries out, but it's not in fear or pain, and she pushes back into me. I pound her, smacking her ass with my free hand while my cock pumps deep into her.

Sweat rolls down my cheeks, and I can hear her groaning as if I'm being too rough, but I can't stop. I just need to give her everything that I feel inside me. I need her to feel what I feel, all the fear and the desire and the hope and the anger.

I give it all to her.

And she takes it, somehow pushing back against me. I feel her pussy choking my cock before she starts to shake, and her climax crashes through her as she clamps down on me.

My name is a guttural howl of devotion on her lips, and I roar, my cum splashing deep inside her as her cry unlocks my release. I feel my balls emptying, the white-hot pleasure and pain mixing and scourging me of my agony, telling me that somehow, I've found my one and only.

The words are right there on the tip of my tongue but I hold them back. Not because of Mia. She deserves my truth, and I'm learning that more and more. But because I need to be stronger, better before I give her that last bit of me. The words are a promise, and I want to be the man she thinks I can be before I make that vow. But heart and soul, she's marking me as much as I'm marking her.

It scares me, but at the same time, I want more of it.

More of her. More of me. More of *us*.

My hand relaxes, and I pull her back, cradling her body in my lap as she shudders, putting her arms around my neck and nuzzling against my neck.

"Thank you," she whispers. "For giving me everything. For not holding back."

"Thank you . . . for letting me be myself."

CHAPTER 28

MIA

I shift in my seat, my ass and neck both aching from last night's hammering. There are times, especially during and right afterward, when Thomas's intensity feels amazing.

And I love the way he protectively snuggles me in his arms when we're done. He's the world's best blanket buddy.

And yeah, I sort of take pride in walking just a tad bit bowlegged when I meet up with Izzy or Char for lunch. Their looks of amused jealousy are more than worth it.

But when I'm sitting at my desk trying to get my work done, an ache in my neck while I constantly shift around trying to get comfortable isn't the best feeling.

Not that I'd trade the feeling that Thomas gives me for anything in the world. The feeling of waking up this morning in his arms, of the safety and security that comes with it, is beyond compare. I even felt just as safe and secure as he was fucking me so hard that my spine crackled last night as I did this morning when he gave me a soft kiss before we came downstairs to start work.

Speaking of, it's time to get to work. I've got a day full of clickity-clacking away on my computers in front of me, analysis and compilation.

But first, I need data. Thankfully, my new position and my new assignment from Thomas give me administrator viewing privileges to everything in the Goldstone database, only one step below Thomas's own access or that of the IT department's VP.

I even have ghost mode, which means nobody but someone who's actively checking the database at the time will know any files are even being looked at. Sneaky . . . but effective.

It doesn't cover everything. I can't see the passwords for bank and other financial transactions, for example, but it does enough.

"Okay," I tell myself as I turn on my favorite Spotify techno channel to get things rolling, "let's put all these multiple cores to work."

Thankfully, my computer can handle the load of running multiple separate database searches at the same time. I went full geek mode on it, and I'm pretty sure it could run The Matrix if needed. Actually, the slowest part will be the data stream to the Goldstone servers, but that's fine.

First, I shunt my resort numbers to my far screen, then I pull up my main search on the other two screens. On the right, I run the first of two algorithms I wrote. The first one scans for server access that falls outside job title parameters I've set, like an HR assistant opening an IT file, which could be sketchy. The second assigns everyone a home floor based on their department location and then scans the data access points of their card usage for anomalies.

That'll help me find out if Susan down on three heads upstairs to the executive level bathrooms at ten every morning, or it will catch if someone is sneaking out to the parking garage outside set factors of lunch and quitting time.

Both checks result in huge heaps of data, but I'm hoping that it'll be useful to catch someone where they shouldn't be, either physically or electronically, and correlate it back to the questionable project figures. It's a long shot, but it's either in-house or an outside threat, and statistically speaking, in-house sabotage is much more likely so I want to scan from every possible angle.

On the middle screen, I work through my project figures of the ones Thomas pointed out as concerns.

The music and the hours go in sync, with the beats and grooving flow of the music allowing me to pull up files on bad deals the company's made.

Not all of them lost money, which is what makes it hard. Whoever's done this has been really, really subtle. There were deals that broke even, or deals that made a profit, but just a small one. The only consistent thing is that they underperformed.

For example there's the real estate deal, a large tract in an expanding suburb of Seattle. Everything around it seemed great, the area was up and coming, and Goldstone had a contractor ready to turn the whole area into a housing development . . . until after the contracts were signed and the contractor went belly-up at the last minute.

While the housing development was done, the cost in the delays, the taxes, and more meant that what should have netted the company tens of millions of dollars barely broke even.

Or an aircraft parts company that was ready to sell to Goldstone until at the last minute pulling out and selling to a Chinese government-backed consortium. It made no sense because the company made military parts, and by selling to a foreign entity, they lost out on twenty years or more of contracts that would have netted the company billions.

The strangest part was, Goldstone had actually outbid the Chinese, but the supplier was privately held and sold to the Chinese anyway.

Those are just two of the anomalies. I keep finding them. I know that at least half of these are going to end up being dismissed during my search as just plain old bad luck. Even with Thomas's superhuman drive to be the best, it's business.

Even in an era where the stock market can gain or lose a thousand points in a week, there's always that thirty to forty percent of investments that go opposite of what the rest of the market does.

But I have to investigate each one, draw out the data and plug it into my matrix. From there . . . trends will emerge, and I'll try to find that one common thread in the whole fabric.

I feel a little bit like a detective searching for clues to a crime . . . and maybe I am. *Like a forensic analyst,* I think, picturing me surrounded by computers with a flap-eared hat and pipe like Sherlock Holmes. I have always been someone good at finding patterns and clues, but this feels different. More challenging. More important.

"Face it, Mia, you just need a dog and some Scooby Snacks and you'll have the entire schtick down," I murmur as I close a file on a chemical research deal that hasn't increased in value but hasn't decreased either. I move it into my list of *Investigate Later* and keep going. "Well, that and a kickass orange sweater. Ooh, knee socks! Actually, those might be kinda hot," I murmur, appreciative again that no one can hear my weird chatter.

By lunch, I take a break, rubbing my eyes and checking in with Thomas, who's plugging away at his computer. He's muttering to himself, but his face looks calm, and when I knock, his first reaction is a smile. I'll take the win.

"Hey, I thought the fat cats at the top of the corporate ladder were supposed to sit around in their offices listening to, I don't know, Huey Lewis and the News or something." I sing dramatically, "It's hip to be square!"

Thomas claps, a laugh teasing at the edges of his smile. "You geek out on the old stuff too?" Thomas asks, sitting back. "What's up?"

"I was going to grab a little bite down the street. You want to join?"

Thomas shakes his head sadly, his mouth narrowing. "I'd love to, but I can't. It seems *someone* is trying to throw a wrench into the hospital deal. I'm getting a request from them. Well, more like a very strong suggestion that I see a doctor."

"What? What's wrong?" I ask, surprised. "I know it's not a performance issue."

"No, not like that," he replies, sitting back and rubbing at his temples but not laughing at my joke, which worries me. "You should have heard what they said, total corporate word salad . . . *In the interest of maintaining our commitment to public health and to good corporate image, we'd encourage you to take advantage of the same perks that all of our corporate officers share and complete a full physical and mental checkup so you can feel comfortable with our offerings* . . . blah, blah, blah. They want me to know what I'm buying firsthand, I guess. Basically, if they're going to sell to me, I have to do this."

"I mean a little ahh while some doc looks at your tonsils isn't bad, but a mental checkup? That seems odd, right?" I say hesitantly. I'm not averse to Thomas getting a little professional help and have even said as much to encourage him to do so, but doing it as a requirement of sale seems beyond the pale.

"I wondered the same thing," Thomas says, glancing out the

window. "Either it's legit and they just want to show off a bit, or someone encouraged them to require this as a condition."

"Ouch. So when's the first appointment?" I ask.

Thomas looks up, lifting an eyebrow. "Who said I'm going?"

I can't help but chuckle. Maybe I am starting to read him because though his face is dead-serious, I can see the twinkle deep in his eyes. "Thomas, I know you, remember? You'd crawl naked through fifteen miles of army ant-infested manure in order to get what you want, and you want that hospital."

"Army ant-infested manure?" Thomas asks. "Where did you hear that . . . another one of your Russia-isms?"

"Nope, that's a total Mia-ism. So?"

"This afternoon . . . in about two hours," Thomas says, and I can hear the dread in his voice. "Which is why I'm chugging away at this."

"How, uh, open and honest are you planning on being with them?" I ask.

"As little as I can get away with being. I don't need a shrink poking their fingers in my emotional wounds and asking how that makes me feel. This is a business transaction. Truth be told, if the return on investment wasn't so high, I'd tell them to shove it. But like you said, I can say ahh, let them listen to my heart, and tell a therapist that life is grand and be out the door with their promise to sign on the dotted line."

"Sounds like a plan. Though maybe skip the bloodwork too? Just suspicious, and I don't want them cloning you from your DNA," I joke, though my Velma senses are still tingling. "So, dinner later then?"

"Do you think we can do breakfast in the morning? I think after all this, I might need to work off a little frustration and I won't be very good company."

His answer disappoints me, but I understand. I've seen how much wear and tear he's put on his home gym. "Sure. You know, if you want, I can introduce you to some of my games. It's not as sweaty as your ways, but there's something to be said for the rush of slashing a troll in half with a giant sword and how it calms the nerves."

Thomas smiles a little, relieving me. He's not that bad off, and maybe he'll do okay today. "I can do that. Say, if things aren't too bad . . . ?"

"You might find that I wouldn't mind a visitor tonight," I promise him. "I'll keep a half-pint of ice cream ready for you, deal? It's another guaranteed stress reliever."

"Deal."

I head to the elevator, my mind still ticking over what's going on. Someone is trying to break Thomas, I'm sure of it. I've seen enough of the data to know that Thomas isn't paranoid in that regard.

And this, now? He's got a lot on his plate, but everyone's well aware the hospital deal means a lot to him. Financially and personally. With that on the line, the last thing he needs is the additional stress of having a shrink, therapist, whatever, poking the bear that is his emotional baggage.

Someone knows this, and they're applying the pressure to him. As the elevator doors close, I promise myself that I'm going to do whatever it takes to help him. Still, as I eat my chicken wrap, I force myself to think about everything but Thomas and his twin mysteries that are on my work plate.

It's part of my secret, just letting my mind work unfettered by conscious steering. Sometimes, it works faster that way.

Not that I plan on a revelation coming to me out of the blue while I'm eating lunch, but stranger things have happened.

When I get back from lunch, my scans are still chomping away, but at least one of the algorithms is done. The last thirty days of access card scans that hit outside my set parameters are compiled into a report. It's not much, just a bare-bones start, but I figured fresher figures would be my best bet to see if this approach will even yield useful information.

I can't help it, my eyes scan for Thomas first. Not to be snoopy or spy on him, but just because I'm curious. Okay, and maybe a little possessive. I like knowing what he does all day. It makes me feel close to him, even if he's twenty-six floors above me.

Nothing too unusual. Data points for him heading back and forth to his apartment mid-day, visits to other floors, but that makes sense for the CEO, and several exits to the parking garage. And I realize with a smile that the last line is his exiting to the garage just a few moments ago.

He is heading to the doctor appointment at the hospital. I'm proud in a weird way. Even if it's only because he wants the hospital deal so badly, the mere fact that he's going to sit down with a therapist bodes well.

I cross my fingers and say a little Russian prayer Papa taught me, hoping that Thomas is protected. From whomever is messing with him, and from himself.

And then I turn back to my computers with a groan and turn up the volume on my music. "I've got a lot more data to go through."

CHAPTER 29

THOMAS

*T*he office is a series of pastel blotches that I've read about in interior design magazines. It's supposedly meant to reduce stress, support positive mental states, and be totally non-threatening.

To me it looks like someone tried to harness their Jackson Pollack, but with nothing but pastels and earth tones. It's Army camouflage meets Lululemon and throw in a good dose of Lena Dunham annoying, and you have the décor of the office.

"Hello, my name's Thomas Goldstone," I tell the receptionist. "I'm here to see Dr. Perry?"

There's no answer for a moment. Instead, the receptionist, who looks very professional in a 1985 sort of way with her puffy hair and tie at the neck of her blouse, just keeps typing away . . . but considering that she's only using the arrow keys on her keyboard, I suspect she's not exactly doing data entry.

"She'll be with you in a minute," she says without looking up from her computer. I swallow my frustration, making mental notes about everything I've seen here as I sit down in a plum-colored chair.

From the front door, everything had been pretty well-maintained. Clean and bright, maybe a little outdated. And the workers on the first floor had been smiling and helpful. Then, I'd met with an internist, Dr. Maeson, who'd basically spent the appointment time trying to sell me on Botox and Juvéderm injections and very little time actually giving me a real checkup. It's a good thing I have a primary care doctor of my own. And now here I am, at the pinnacle of my downfall.

So . . . finally, you've been reduced to this. And I thought you had some pride.

I do have pride, but you were the one who kept telling me pride goes before a fall. I'm not going to fall.

You keep saying that. But you're going to fall anyway. You think you'll be able to get through this interrogation without the doc realizing you're fifty shades of fucked up? Good luck with that!

I squeeze the arm rests on the chair until my knuckles are white as the demon's laugh echoes hollowly in my head, drowning out everything around me.

Dimly, I become aware of someone calling my name, and I look up to see the receptionist. Judging by her sigh, she must've called my name repeatedly before I heard her.

Getting to my feet, I follow her down the short hallway to what pretty much looks like your standard shrink's office, although instead of the couch, it seems Dr. Perry prefers the super-comfy club chair arrangement.

I take a seat, and the receptionist leaves, closing the door behind her and leaving me alone . . . except for the voice in my head.

What are you going to tell her? Maybe you should start with how you let you mother die while you ate chicken nuggets?

The door opens, and Dr. Perry walks in, and I'm cringing already. She's younger than I expected, maybe mid-twenties, but dressed in a buttoned-up, almost prudish way that makes her seem even younger. I have a biting thought that maybe the receptionist is her mother. There's just something about Dr. Perry that screams she has no life experience and would be offended by the most minor peek at my true history.

I'm not normally one to judge people on appearance. I know just how much a fancy business suit can hide, after all. But how am I supposed to 'connect' and share with someone who looks like her biggest concern is whether she should have a bran muffin or treat herself to Mini-Wheats for breakfast?

How am I supposed to share and gain insight from someone I already think has never dealt with the same things I've dealt with?

Not that I have any real intention of getting help from Dr. Perry or anyone else. This appointment is strictly so that I can proceed with the hospital purchase plan.

Aw, you know you can't get rid of me anyway. And this hospital deal is going to be a failure, just like you.

"Thomas, it's a pleasure to meet you," Dr. Perry says, something else that puts me on edge. While I encourage the use of first names within the Goldstone offices, outside I'm always professional. You don't use my first name without getting permission first. "How are you today?"

"I'm here," I reply, cautiously guarded. "You?"

"It's been a good day," Dr. Perry says, and I notice she doesn't offer her first name. Instead, she looks me over before sitting down and picking up a clipboard next to her. "So, let's talk ground rules."

"Ground rules?" I ask, lifting an eyebrow. *Remember the deal. Remember the deal . . .*

"Yes. First, I am going to need you to be open with me. That's the only way to delve into any areas that need clarity. Perhaps we should begin at the beginning. Tell me about your childhood."

The things I do to be the best.

~

THE ELEVATOR CAN'T OPEN QUICKLY ENOUGH AS I GET BACK HOME, MY anger barely held back.

I'd spent the better part of an hour redirecting Dr. Perry away from every hot-button issue I have and trying to steer her toward information pertinent to the hospital sale. But she'd been relentless, almost to point of it becoming an interrogation as she calmly asked questions about my parents, my school years, my business, and my personal life, all the while making checkmarks on her clipboard like the whole thing was an automated process for her. Check yes here, ask follow up question there. And when I'd gotten frustrated at her repeated inquiries, she'd had the nerve to tell me that I need to *accept* my anger, let it *teach* me, and *grow* a healthier future. It might as well have been an inspirational quote from her Pinterest board for all the insight she offered.

She'd basically turned me off therapy, and between Dr. Maeson and Dr. Perry, my biggest concern with the hospital purchase is the caliber of its employees. Well, and that someone had managed to wrangle that whole rigmarole in the first place.

I strip quickly out of my suit and look in my closet, finally choosing the clothes that match my inner anger and rage. The white under-shirt's tattered, bloodstained, and patched in half a dozen places, looking more like Frankenstein's T-shirt than something belonging in the closet of a man who has more money than he knows what to do with.

For two years, I wore it under my shoulder pads for every football game, every team lift, so that by now, it barely hangs together. But it's raw, it's torn and battered . . . and so am I, full of rage, venom practically dripping from my lips as I pull on my heavy compression shorts and go into my gym.

Grabbing my belt from its hook on the wall, I start up the music, Carl Orff's *O Fortuna* setting the right mood as I set up the squat rack.

Time to get ugly, to make the pain flow.

By the time *Venom* pounds through the speakers, sweat stains my shirt, my thighs are flooded with blood, and my chest is heaving as I stare at the 375 pounds on the bar.

Do you think this will make you feel like you've accomplished something? It won't. You're just going to fail.

"That's the fucking plan," I growl, slapping myself across the face. This isn't exactly safe. You're not supposed to push yourself to maximum effort under heavy weight without anyone here to spot.

But I built this gym with that in mind, and I've got the equipment to protect me. The nylon safety straps looped around the upper supports of my power rack are capable of catching the weight when I can't do any more.

I slap myself again, rage and anger and hatred for myself, for my life, for everything that I've been through coursing through me. Jamming myself under the bar, I revel in the punishment of the steel pressing into my back, the inch-thick bar digging into that space right below my deltoids and across my back before I drop into 'the hole'.

One.

You're never going to make it. Your best is twelve . . . you're weak.

College. Standing on stage. Nobody in the crowd for me. I was the twenty-one-year-old *wunderkind* who graduated with his MBA at the same age most people were figuring out which beer they liked best. Dennis Goldstone? Didn't attend, didn't send a gift, didn't send a congratulations.

"Bastard! Two!" I yell as the music screams with me.

High school. The state championships. Giving the valedictorian speech. Never once did he attend.

Three . . . and I can feel it in my back. I've spent so much time over the past month doing things besides putting in time under this bar, my back is tired already. Fighting it, I push my stomach out against my belt, bracing myself and dropping again.

Four . . . five . . . my thighs are flushed with blood, the muscles in there quivering with each breath, sweat pouring down my face and dripping onto the flooring beneath me, but I still go down.

I bet you won't even be able to do ten.

Six . . . God, the pain's blinding . . . seven . . .

You really think you're the best because you can push some pussy weights around? The best perform to their capability every time, always pushing further, deeper, better. And that's just not you.

Junior high. Scoring a perfect on my PSAT, then a 2250 on the then SAT scale in ninth grade. No acknowledgement from my father except to point out that over 400 students got perfect scores.

Nine . . . I take a deep breath, my vision narrowing to a pulsing red-black tunnel that barely allows me to see my depth as I go down again. I feel wetness on my upper lip and realize I've burst a blood vessel in my nose, but I don't stop, going down into the hole again.

Stay down! You're fucking weak, stay down!

My mind flashes, remembering the 'discussions' with my father, the time I told him if he'd come, I'd hit a home run in Little League . . .

I groan, pushing as the world spins around me until I'm standing up, pain pulsating through every fiber of my being. My back's on fire, my legs are numb, I can't feel my fingertips, and my heart's pounding so hard that I can't even hear the music anymore.

But I go down again.

My knees are almost in my chest, and everything's strained in ways that men are not supposed to strain themselves, and for this eleventh rep, the hole feels like the deepest pit on Earth, the weight of the entire building on my shoulders. I'm in hell, and the only way out is my rage and my own will.

My thighs quake, my calves threaten to cramp, and everything becomes a single explosion of pain as I push to get the weight back up.

I'm a quarter of the way there when the cramp paralyzes my left thigh and I pitch forward, unable to stop myself. The safety straps catch the weight just as planned, saving me as I fall face first to the ground, unable to even stop myself with my arms.

I lay there, blood pooling under my face, trying to will my thigh into relaxing. The pain's enormous, and even after my leg releases, I can barely move. I have to crawl like a baby out of my workout room, all the way to the bathroom. I'll clean up the mess later.

My tub is built into the floor, my only obstacle a six-inch lip that I lean on as the water fills and I peel my T-shirt off and use my toes to get my shoes off. I try twice to get my shorts off, but my back and legs won't let me move, so I leave them on, rolling over the lip of the tub and into the hot water.

Luckily, my arms are moving, and I push myself into a sitting position before calling out, "Alexa . . . play Enya." The screaming death metal from my workout room stops, replaced by soft music in the bathroom. It's cliché, perhaps, but everyone jokes about Enya music being relaxing for a reason . . . it is. And with a touch of a button, the jets in the tub turn on low.

I lean my head back, and shame fills me as the voice in my head gleefully taunts.

Told you that you'd fail. You've gotten even weaker, if that's possible. She's done that to you.

"No," I whisper, shaking my head. She's made me stronger, and I can't imagine not having Mia in my life anymore. I have to have her, and I have to keep her with me.

CHAPTER 30

BLACKWELL

"*You* steered him to whom?" I ask.

"Only the worst therapist in the entire system for him. She's young, has a one-track mind, and not in the fun way, and is about as interesting as Cream of Wheat."

I chuckle, sipping at my snifter of brandy. The firelight flickers behind my chair, casting my body into dark relief as my man sits across from me in the study, his vengeful smile slightly off kilter and bloody in the burning light.

While I would not normally risk another face-to-face meeting so soon with such an underling, this one is amusing. He has a twisted sense of vengeance that most people wouldn't associate with him, underestimating him on appearances alone.

"Wouldn't Goldstone just walk all over her?"

My man grins maniacally, shaking his head. "Perry's too stupid to realize if he was. She goes from question one to two to three, no variance. Ever. So he could try to skirt around her questions, but she just wraps back around and around until she can check if off. Maddening woman. Met her at a Christmas party once. She's a good reason to indulge in too much eggnog."

"You have a stroke of deviousness to you."

It's high praise. I rarely meet people who are worthy of it.

"Thank you, sir. I learned from some of the best."

I hum, wondering if the man is giving me a backhanded compliment. I doubt it. He hasn't been under my tutelage for long. And he's experienced enough to know that mocking me is a potentially deadly choice.

"And does the hospital suspect you of planting such a poison pill in their potential deal?" I ask.

The man's smile is wide. "No, they thought my idea to really show Goldstone all the hospital had to offer was genius. I was able to make it as a casual suggestion through a buddy of mine. Made it easy for their board to take it as a good recommendation. But they have no idea about . . . this."

"So are you assured that you've been able to poison the deal?"

"It isn't perfect," my man admits. "You know he's driven, and more than once, through sheer force of will or stubbornness, he's made chicken salad out of chicken shit."

My mouth pinches, and I set my brandy aside. I understand my man's background has taught him such language is acceptable in the company of men, but I have other expectations.

"You should learn that a foul mouth is best saved for only the most exclusive of situations. Overuse of it in inappropriate times only makes you seem uneducated and crass. Although, Golden Boy does deserve stronger language than what you might normally use."

"That's true, sir. I can assure you that the Ruthless Bastard is going to fall. The only question I have is, will I let him know who's slipped the knife in his ribs when he goes down, or will I just enjoy the fruits of my labor?"

I shrug, unconcerned. Still, I know when I'm being asked for advice. "You know what cost Marcus Junius Brutus his life?"

"Killing Caesar?"

I pick up my snifter again, downing the rest of it in a single gulp. "No, his error was in letting it be known that he'd done so."

The truth, of course, is much more complicated. Entire books, entire careers, have been made on studying the political machinations of the transition period between the Roman Republic and the Roman

Empire. It's actually a delightful bit of study that I've indulged in, and far more than what any television show or movie has been able to replicate. It makes *House of Cards* look like *Sesame Street*.

A more nuanced answer would be not that Brutus let it be known, but that he then didn't crush his adversaries when he had the power to do so.

Not that my underling would grasp the nuances of power. He sees power as a blunt tool.

"Of course, sir. May I ask, what will you do while this is . . . ripening?"

I chuckle, a chilling sound that makes even my man shiver. Ripening . . . it's a fine choice of words.

"What I always do. Consolidate power."

CHAPTER 31

MIA

*T*wo more days, and my research has split.

I've been forced into a rather uncomfortable pair of possibilities. And either one is dangerous for Thomas.

One, there's an outside puppet master involved in all of this, someone pulling strings inside Goldstone. If that's the case, I just don't have enough data. This puppet master could have multiple agents inside the company, and I would be chasing phantoms for years without knowing where to focus attention.

Goldstone has so many business rivals, so many enemies, that I'd have to do an active investigation, and I'm no private eye.

I'm just a data hound.

I don't care if I want to call myself Velma while I'm working at this and I don't care how sexy I think I look in glasses. I'm not an actual private eye.

The more dangerous possibility, though, is that there's a high-ranking traitor involved. I consider every angle of how the decisions are being made, from data pulls to meetings to PowerPoint presentations.

As hard as it is, I even consider Kerry as a suspect. I mean, in most mysteries, the butler does it. And while Kerry definitely isn't the butler, she's the one who filters all of Thomas's info to him. Thankfully, after a whole day of work, I can't find any data that supports that and I happily cross her off my mental suspect list.

Past that, I look at those with corporate powers. And considering the number of investments and the scattershot way I've seen them done, it would have to be a major shareholder or one of the Executive VPs. Only they have the ability to see all the projects that the company is undertaking, and only someone with such power would be able to apply pressure in the right way.

But why would a major shareholder or VP want to see the company hurt? Their fortunes rest on the company's continuing to do well. Why would a VP, who would want a good track record with the company even if they wanted to jump ship, undertake a complicated exercise in corporate sabotage?

And why would the shareholders, whose wealth is literally pegged to company performance? Thomas certainly wouldn't, and he's the largest shareholder in the company.

Looking over the list of major shareholders who would have access to enough information to slit the throat of all the projects I've found, there's only one name who'd have potential reason for wanting to hurt Goldstone . . . and it's a Goldstone after all.

Not Thomas. Dennis.

But would Dennis Goldstone really want to hurt his son that much?

Would he be so hateful and hellbent on ensuring Thomas's failure that he would sabotage him just to prove a point? Thomas told me about their argument, but even if Dennis is a greedy bastard, this seems unfathomable.

And then I remember the other unimaginable things Thomas has told me.

I might not be a private eye, but I can at least do some investigating.

I grab my phone, dialing Kerry and saying another prayer that I think she's legitimately a good thing for Thomas. "Hey, Kerry! I had potential lunch plans with Thomas today? Any word on his morning meeting?"

She scoffs, and I can imagine her shaking her head at her desk. "Definitely a no-go. His meeting is running long. He sent me a message a few minutes ago to give you apologies and order lunch in for the whole group downstairs. Bunch of bloodhounds are probably just yammering away in the hopes of getting a free lunch anyway. But he says sorry, and I've gotta run. Unless there's something else?"

I smile, relieved. "You're the best, you know that? But that's all I was checking on. Thanks!"

"Just make sure your man knows that and we're golden!" she replies, and then she hangs up without another word.

It seems like a sign, a perfect maelstrom of opportunity, information, and curiosity. And I'm going to Sherlock the hell out of it while I can.

I use my downloaded records to get Dennis Goldstone's address from the corporate database. Despite his supposed disdain for Thomas, he actually lives in Roseboro, having moved to town approximately one year after the Goldstone Building opened up. He even has a business address, a law office in a suburb just outside Roseboro.

I grab my keys. It's time for a road trip. Feeling good, I flip on the tunes as I drive, singing along in my terrible voice as I head out of town and into the pleasant suburb.

I'm a little surprised when I get there. I expected more, considering Dennis Goldstone's history of being a partner in a law firm. But Dennis's office is small, not much more than a pleasant-looking medium-sized house, and if it weren't for the plain wooden sign out front, I wouldn't be able to tell it apart from any of the dozen other small offices and houses that dot this tree-lined street.

I get out, noticing that there's only one car in the driveway, and go up to the front door, knocking three times and waiting. I wonder, does he work by himself?

Or maybe I'm just here when his staff has the day off?

Just as I'm about to ring the doorbell, the door opens and I get my first view of Dennis Goldstone.

I didn't realize until this moment that I'd expected a monster, not a mere man after the things Thomas told me. But before me is just a man. I can see the resemblance, faintly, if you took away about thirty pounds of muscle from Thomas and replaced it with maybe ten pounds of middle-aged pot gut.

Still, the eyes are the same, and while he's got the same jawline, it's obvious that Thomas got most of his good looks from his mother.

"Can I help you?" he asks.

"Mr. Goldstone? My name's Mia Karakova. If you don't mind, I'd like to talk with you about Thomas."

At the mention of his son's name, Dennis snorts, though nothing is funny in the least. But he steps back, waving me inside. "So you're *her*, huh? Come to see the Boogie Man, I suppose?" His tone is sarcastic, biting, and I can only imagine that it's what the voice in Thomas's memories are like.

I step inside Dennis's office, and I'm immediately struck by two things. One, that while Thomas's sense of style tends toward the efficient regardless of the aesthetics . . . Dennis is just cheap. The man made 1.8 million dollars in dividends on his Goldstone stock last year based off the declared dividends, but his office looks like it was furnished with page 62 of the IKEA catalog.

Still, his desk's nearly military neat, and the carpet looks freshly vacuumed this morning. Okay, he's gotta have staff working for him. They're just not here right now because nothing about this man says he does his own household chores.

The next thing I notice as I look around is the total lack of pictures on his wall. He's got his undergrad and law degrees framed and hanging behind his desk, and he's even got a couple of other certificates, thanks, and awards from various civic groups in Roseboro and other places.

But there are no pictures. Nothing of Thomas, nothing of his deceased wife . . . no family pictures at all. It seems strange, considering it is his office.

"So, what do you want to know?" Dennis asks, sitting down in his chair. I take the other, immediately wishing I had my office chair instead. The foam's shot, and I can feel the seat post actually pressing against my butt.

"What do you mean, sir?" I ask, doing my best to stay polite. Thomas may not like his father for good reason, but that doesn't mean I have to be hostile to him too. Especially when I'm trying to decide if he's the one trying to hurt Thomas. *More flies with honey,* I repeat to myself.

"I saw your picture in the paper with Tom, and there's no reason for someone from the company to come see me. The only people I talk to are my son and that bitch he has screening his phone calls. Unless . . . did he send you?"

Kudos, Kerry. I owe you a cupcake or something.

"No, Thomas didn't send me. He uh . . . he doesn't know I'm here, actually." And the impact of what I'm doing hits me full force. I truly am one of 'those meddlesome kids', thinking I have any right to Velma my way into not only Thomas's company business but his private affairs with his dad.

I squirm in my seat, the post prodding me and making me want to make a run for the door.

Dennis narrows his eyes in suspicion, his face pinching. "But you are dating my son? Are you looking for a payoff?"

I flinch, my jaw dropping in shock. "Yes . . . I mean no." I sigh, calming myself and speaking more confidently, "Yes, I am seeing Thomas. No, I don't want a payoff. That's absurd!"

"Uh-huh," Dennis says, leaning back. "So then you probably want to figure out why my son hates me so much. Like I said, you've come to see the Boogie Man."

"No, Mr. Goldstone, I wouldn't—"

"No, it's fine. He does see me that way, no sense in denying it. I already know it's true. So I repeat, what do you want to know?" His eyes are sharp, challenging me. No, *daring* me. This is a test, I know it in my gut.

This man has belittled Thomas, testing him and setting him up for failure since he was a little boy. And I no longer feel the need for polite niceties and falsely civilized conversation. Dennis Goldstone goes for his son's jugular at every opportunity, and it's high time someone went for his.

"I want to know why you blame Thomas for your wife's death? I want to know why you punished him, a six-year-old little boy, for something that wasn't his fault? And I want to know just how deep your well of hatred goes and what you'd do to hurt him now that a backhand won't do?"

It's harsh. I know it's harsh, but I also know from my time with

Thomas that strength is important. And in this case, it's like son, like father. Dennis stares at me for a moment before grunting, leaning forward and planting his forearms on his desk.

I hold my breath, refusing to bow to the fury swirling in Dennis's eyes, so similar to the anger I see in Thomas's sometimes. I'm already expecting the blow, verbal or physical I don't know, but I'm ready either way.

But I'm not prepared for the way Dennis deflates before my very eyes.

"You're a ballsy bitch, aren't you?" He makes it sound like a compliment.

"I've been accused of it before."

"Fine, you want the whole sordid story? Then here you go." It sounds like he's about to tell a roomful of kids there's no Santa Claus, Easter Bunny, or Tooth Fairy, and dread fills my gut. I almost stop him, knowing this isn't my place, but I need to know too badly. I think it might be the only way I can truly help Thomas. So I don't stop him, instead letting Dennis dive into the past.

"I was a junior associate in one of those big firms when I met Grace. She was so beautiful. And we were happy, for a bit. Until she shattered my soul like it was nothing. Heartless bitch."

His words are deep, dripping with hurt, and I blink, wondering what they mean. "Shattered your soul? You mean the suicide?"

He bares his teeth at the word, like I just bade him to bite into aluminum foil. "No, she killed me long before that. See, what you need to know about Ms. Grace Lewis was that she was a beauty queen, always thought she'd marry up, live a life of luxury. Eat bonbons or some shit, I guess. But that's not what she got. She got me. And I was living in a dog eat dog world back then, working from sunup to midnight just to stand a chance at making partner one day. She got bored, told me she wanted to have a baby to play with. So we had Tom, and I thought she'd finally be happy and leave me alone to work. I was getting close by then, you see? Moving off the grunt work, living the American dream, it seemed like it was all going well."

He pauses, lost in the past, and I prompt him, "But?"

He slams his palm on the desk, his eyes flashing with decades of pain and fury. "But she was fucking everyone from the mailman to the Avon lady behind my back. Some dream!"

I'm shocked and the look on my face says everything. Thomas didn't say anything about his mom cheating, not that it excuses anything, but it's another puzzle piece clicking home.

"Yeah," Dennis growls. "Imagine, coming home early after busting your ass and you walk in to find your wife fucking someone in your own bed. The first time it happened, Tom was over at his friend's house. Grace even tried to defend herself, saying she'd always sent the boy over to play. Made me wonder just how many people were in on her little games. The whole time, I was being played for a fucking chump."

I shake my head. "But why blame Thomas?"

"Because he never said a word to me about going over to this kid's house! I would have known something was going on! While the cat's away, I guess the mice were having a fucking party." Bitter pain drips from the words like venom.

Horror fills me as I realize the depth of Dennis's anger. Somehow, he still blamed his son for all of this. Or at least blamed him for part of it. He hadn't known, had no concept of what she was doing, and maybe doesn't even remember that, but still. And in this moment, I'm just as angry at Grace Goldstone as I am at Dennis.

"I should have left her then, but I didn't." His voice catches, and he swallows before continuing. "I gave her another chance. I didn't even hold it against her. I didn't need to cash in my chip and play tit for tat. I was trying to fix it if I could, even suggested counseling . . . and then she did it again. Walked in on her with my boss, said she was trying to help me at work, then pulled out that if he could get home by dinner time, then why couldn't I? She'd set it up on purpose, I think. I told her then that I was going to talk to a lawyer. Two days later, she killed herself while Tom sat munching on chicken nuggets and watching fucking *ThunderCats* or something."

And there it is.

"Dennis, he was six years old."

"So?" Dennis explodes, his eyes glaring in rage and anger. "He was a smart boy. He could have done something!"

I swallow back my own anger, not wanting to get into a screaming match with this man.

He blames Thomas? Where was *he*?

I'm not saying that Grace was right to cheat on her husband, but he was the one who abandoned her to chase his way up the legal ladder while assuming she was fine being a housewife.

I don't excuse Grace Goldstone for doing what she did.

But I don't blame her for what happened to Thomas, either.

Twenty-plus years of torturing his son mentally, abusing him emotionally and even physically . . . and it comes down to one afternoon.

"Did he tell you I got fired then? I was grieving my wife, trying to figure out what to do with a kid, and I was fired because they were afraid I was going to kill the last man who'd stuck his dick in my dead wife. And he was the one signing my paychecks."

Another nail in the coffin of the life Dennis Goldstone thought he had. And I can't imagine the pain that caused him, but this story doesn't end there. Not for Dennis, and not for Thomas.

"Dennis, I'm not going to tell you not to be pissed at Grace. She was selfish, and she betrayed her trust as both a wife and a mother. But your son has suffered for over twenty years, not because of what she did . . . but because of what *you've* done."

"And what did I do?" he asks quietly.

"You're not stupid. I think you know. I can see it in your eyes," I reply, having come to a realization. Dennis is just as much a pained monster lashing out at the world as Thomas sometimes is, but where Thomas has me, Dennis has no one. His rage and misdirected anger at his wife are hurting Thomas, but I don't think he's the villain in the sabotage scheme. He's definitely Thomas's Boogie Man, but he's not the spy. I'd bet on it, and I only gamble when I know the odds.

I stand up, done with this. "I came here because someone's trying to destroy your son's company. I thought maybe it was you, but from what you've told me, I'm sure it isn't. But Thomas has many enemies and not enough friends. He could use another ally. Even more, he could use a father. But make no mistake, if you hurt him in any way, physical or mental or emotional, I will make you wish for the release of death to ease your pain." I mumble a little Russian threat after I finish. I doubt he could understand, but I'm sure he gets the message either way.

Dennis sits pondering for a few moments before nodding, though not speaking any words.

After two decades, words must be hard to come by.

I give him my office number and email, writing them down on a piece of paper. Dennis takes a look and stands up, offering his hand. I'm so surprised that I shake it, just to see what he has to say.

"You're a strong woman. Smart, too, from what I've heard. Good luck."

We shake, and I leave, heading back toward the office.

I'd thought I might get a little insight on the man behind the monster, see if he was the one pulling the strings to hurt Goldstone, and I definitely got a lot more than I expected. I'm just not sure if that's a good thing or a very bad thing.

CHAPTER 32

MIA

*T*homas arrives at my place right on time in casual sweatpants and a T-shirt. With his hair sort of disheveled like he's just gotten out of the shower and finger combed it, and a touch of five o'clock shadow . . . it's honestly the sexiest look he's ever had.

"Hey," I greet him, pulling him inside before kissing him softly. Tonight will end up with us in bed unless someone sets off a hand grenade . . . but that's still hours away, and I want him to see this side of me more. "How was your post-work workout?"

"Light," Thomas reassures me. After watching him limp for a day or two, it's nice to hear he does know how to throttle it back a notch. I didn't ask him what had triggered him to punish himself so much, but I've made a few assumptions and trusted him the rest of the way. "So, what's on the agenda?"

"TERA," I tell him, leading him over to the couch. "I've already got an account ready to go for you. You just need to pick your character name and we'll walk through the rest."

I turn on my TV and show him the basics of the world, what the deal is behind the game, and all the other stuff he needs to know. It'll be hours before he really gets it, but as he listens and flips through the various options, I can see him nodding in understanding.

"Uhh, what type of character do you use?" Thomas asks, and I grin as I open another window and show him my current favorite character. "You're one sexy elf," he says with a cheesy bite of his lip.

"Thank you. Just remember I can shoot the hairs off your ears at half a mile," I tease him. "You're going to need a lot of leveling up to get anywhere near my skills."

"Well then, since this is just for fun, how about . . . Castanic?"

I grin, the two of us deciding on a Castanic Brawler, his massive fists encased in the 'power gloves' of the game. It's a character and role that'll let him have fun while releasing some tension for sure.

I especially like how Thomas picks facial features that, while not exactly mirroring his own, certainly suggest the handsome man I've got seated next to me.

Thomas picks up the controller while I guide him through playing. Unfortunately, TERA isn't a game where we can both be onscreen at the same time, but that's okay. I enjoy coaching him through the basics.

We decide to swap the controller back and forth, Thomas watching as I hit a few button combinations and show him how to trigger the skills he's starting out with. Still, as he plays, I can see he's tense.

"What's on your mind? The game isn't the kind that you need to grit your teeth. I mean, you're beating up a mushroom right now. Not even Mario gets this tense."

"Sorry," Thomas says, rubbing his hands together. "Just trying to play well, but there's a helper in my head telling me that I'm going to crash and burn. Can you even do that in this game?"

I nod slowly. "Yeah, but you're safe here in this area. It's a learning and training ground. Just relax. This is supposed to be fun."

Thomas nods and takes the controller back when the pizza comes. I grab the large extra pepperoni pizza and bring it back, surprised when I see Thomas jamming buttons, his face flushed and his lips drawn back in a sneer.

"Tommy, what—" I ask just as another player turns him into a pile of goo. He'd attacked a high-level player outright?

Thomas growls and slams the controller into the cushion of my couch. Thankfully, I've nerd-raged a few times myself, and my wireless controller is strong enough to take it. I've learned that one from experience.

"Dammit!" Thomas growls while I come around, setting the pizza down on the table.

"You fought a guy twenty-six levels above you. There's no possible chance to win that."

"I should be able to." He pouts.

I climb into his lap, and he shuts up, his eyes still sparking with anger. "There's a method to the madness, steps and progress to take along the levels. You can't skip stuff. Just like in life, you've got to explore everything."

My sexy tone is melting his anger, turning it into molten lust before my very eyes. "Explore. Every. Thing?" he says darkly.

"Mmmhmm. Every emotion, every nook and cranny, every bit of it so that you're ready for the next level."

I see a flush wash over Tommy's face, and then he whispers hotly in my ear, "And are you ready for the next level, Mia?"

I could take his words as flirtation, because they most definitely are. But there's something underneath the sexy tone, a longing, a plea from this beast of a man, and I look into his eyes, wondering what would bring him to the point of begging. And I know.

He can't be the first to say it. He's simply not able to make that leap first and needs me to lead him there. But I can do that. That's what partners do, take turns leading each other sometimes, walk side by side sometimes, and even carry each other when one needs help.

So I press his palm to my chest over my heart. "Thomas Goldstone, you have let me into your heart and into your life, trusting me when every bit of life experience has told you not to. You may be a ruthless bastard to others, but to me, you're a brave man, beautiful on the inside, scars and all. I love you."

I can see the relief wash through him, the light filling him. I think I even see a glassy shine to his eyes, but I can't be sure because he pulls me down, kissing me hard and taking my breath away. I don't need it, but still my heart leaps when he breaks our kiss, whispering in my ear, "I love you too." And I feel the last wall crumbling between us, exposing even more of us to one another.

I grin like the cat that got the cream, so happy I could burst, and then I laugh out loud, the jiggles of my body rubbing me along Thomas's cock.

"What's so funny?" he demands, but I can see that he's not worried, just curious.

I try to sober but barely get the words out. "It's like Grand Theft . . . coronary. You stole my heart."

He blinks, and I think he doesn't get the reference to the popular video game, a crime against gaming everywhere, but then he busts out laughing too. "God, that's corny. It's a good thing you're cute."

I fake offense, swatting him with a throw pillow, and he smiles back. It feels good, like we said this really big thing, but we're still us.

And as *us*, the heat returns in an instant when Thomas kneads my ass, grinding himself against my pussy.

"I'm all yours, Tommy," I promise him as I swirl my hips, feeling him grow harder in his sweatpants. "Take it . . . *all* of it."

"You know what that means, right?" he asks, and I nod, grinning.

Thomas reaches under my legs, and standing up feels like a thrill ride in itself it's so smooth and powerful. He carries me down the short hallway to my bedroom, where he lays me down on my bed before stepping back, pulling his shirt off.

My heart hammers in my chest, watching his perfectly sculpted body flex with power and strength that's understated but fills the room. His muscles flow and bunch with organic grace as he unbuttons his jeans and slides them down his hips, pausing just before his cock pops out.

"This isn't all on me," he says, using his chin to gesture at my still-clothed body.

I grin, biting my lip naughtily as I sit up and pull my top off, my nipples tightening and my chest flushing as his eyes drink me in. "You're so beautiful, Mia. And so . . . mine. I love you."

The words come easily this time, but I return them anyway, wanting to reward him for the gift.

"I love you too."

I lift my hips and shimmy my pants down in time with him until he stands before me, a hulking, powerful god of love and sex, his cock standing thick and hard from his body.

"Spread your legs," he commands.

I do, stretching myself as wide as I can and letting him watch me, my legs as straight as possible before running my fingertips up the insides of my thighs, stroking my pussy softly for him to watch.

"So fucking hot," Thomas growls, reaching down and wrapping his fist around his cock as I keep rubbing until the warmth reaches its sexy tendrils down the insides of my thighs. I spread myself open for him, his fist slowly pumping his cock as we tease each other, our eyes glued on each other.

His cock is perfect. Even his massive fist can't make it look small as he squeezes it before he strokes back, pumping in and out of his hand. A clear drop of precum oozes out to hang on the tip of his cock like a jewel of morning dew before sliding down and off, a thread of delicious light gleaming in the bedside lamplight.

"I'm thirsty," Thomas says, dropping to his knees, his eyes fixed on my stroking fingers. "I'm going to suck your pussy dry until you come all over my face, but I want you to do something for me. Get your favorite toy for me?"

I nod and reach over with my free hand to open my bedside table. I take out my vibrator and the small bottle of lube just in case, setting them on the bed next to my hip. Thomas picks up the vibrator and inspects it, finding the switch and turning it on.

I blush, and he smirks knowingly as he picks up the bottle of lube. "This . . . this, we'll use later."

He lowers himself slowly, teasing and tantalizing me, his mouth just hovering over my pussy until I can't wait any longer, and I lift myself up, offering myself to him. The first touch of his tongue on my pussy is a dam breaking, and the sound he makes as he sucks on my tender lips is ravenous, starving, animalistic in its intensity.

He consumes me lovingly, his tongue stiffening to drive deep inside me before he scoops out my juices, sucking and drinking me like I'm a fountain for him.

"Mmm, that's it, Beautiful," he says as I toss my head side to side, somehow overwhelmed even though I knew what was coming—namely, me. "Give it all to me . . . and I'll give you more. Make this sweet pussy gush for me."

His tongue strokes my clit, and in the dim, sex-addled recesses of my mind, I hear the sound of my lube being opened. Thomas scoops under my ass to lift me before tucking a pillow under my lower back, and I look down blearily at him as he smiles between my legs, a conqueror ready to truly show me what he can do.

I gasp as his slick finger finds my ass, the breathless sound turning into a deep moan as he sucks on my clit, pleasure and trepidation teasing me as he massages the ring of muscle in time to his strokes.

I know we talked about it in Japan, and his tongue was wonderful, but can I really take him there? I open my mouth to say something when his finger pushes into me at the same time he licks my clit hard, and I cry out, instantly coming around his finger while his mouth sucks on my pussy, literally drinking and draining me of everything.

I don't know how long I writhe, but his free hand holds me still, trapped as his finger starts to probe deeper, slipping all the way into my ass before pulling back as he slowly finger fucks my backside.

"Mmm . . . I can read your eyes, Beautiful," Thomas growls, scooting up my body so that he's reaching between my legs to keep his finger moving against my clit, massaging it at the same time as he slowly slips in and out of my ass. "You think you can't take my big cock in that tight, heart-shaped ass of yours?"

I nod, whimpering as he lowers his mouth to my left nipple and sucks, my fingers twisting in his hair as he bites down lightly, keeping me trembling on the edge of pain and pleasure. My ass is starting to relax, and a deep feeling of accomplishment and wanton lust flood me as I feel him slip another finger inside me, stretching me more.

"Oh, fuck, you'll split me in half," I whimper as he speeds up. It feels so good now, my body taken in a new way while my clit slips and slides against his hand. "But I trust you."

"Then you'll love this," Thomas says, withdrawing his fingers from my ass. I squirm. The suddenly empty feeling has me trembling in need and he knows it.

He grabs my vibrator and holds it up, covering it with slick lube before teasing my asshole with it while at the same time kissing me deeply. I feel his smile and know it's a warning, one last chance to stop this, but I want it. I want it all. He swallows my cry as he pushes, the vibrator sliding into my ass and sending me over the edge.

I cry out, bucking against him as my clit throbs, the vibrator lodged deep inside me as I come around it and Thomas holds me close, his tongue invading me.

"Mmmhmm, one more . . . for now," Thomas says when I come down, limp and almost unable to move. "Trust me, Mia. I love you."

His repeated declaration of his love is what I need, and I nod, lifting my knees up as he gets between my legs. I think he's going to take the vibrator out to replace it with his cock, but instead, he reaches down, twisting it a little as he searches for the switch, but when he does . . .

"Oh, fuck . . . I can't, you'll drive me insane."

I've never tried this before . . . but each second, my body is pummeled with sensation as the vibrator turns my ass into a center of pleasure that I've never thought it could be. It's like he's pushing my limits, taking me, and cherishing me all at the same time, and as the tingles start to spread again, a new type of heat fills my body.

He grins, his cock long and proud as he grabs the lube again, rubbing it over himself . . . and I realize what he's going to do.

"You make me insane every time you look at me. Every time you kiss me, you drive me wild. I'm just giving you a taste of what I feel."

His cock gleams as he wraps his hands around my thighs and pulls me into him. I feel his thickness press against my pussy, but there's no way he'll fit. My body's already being taken over again from the vibrator and—

"Now!" Thomas grunts, driving his cock balls-deep into me in one savage, powerful stroke. I cry out, tears springing to my eyes even as my body comes again, my pussy clamping around his slick cock as he holds me paralyzed with pleasure and pain from the dual intrusions.

So full. I've never been this full.

My heart freezes, the air steel in my chest as Thomas doesn't stop, pulling back before stroking in slowly this time, drawing it out. My mind's exploding, my neck aching as I toss my head back and forth, but I don't know what I'm denying.

Is it that I can't take any more? That I want more? That I'm overwhelmed by what I'm feeling? That I can't believe what he's doing to me?

Yes. Yes and yes and all that and more. He presses into me, my pussy tightly clenching around his huge cock. Thomas presses me into the bed, letting go of my thighs to plant his arms on each side of my head, using all of his massive strength to drive his cock hard and deep into my exhausted, quivering body.

I've heard of this type of never-ending climax. I mean, what nerd hasn't? Wave upon wave of pleasure crashes through me, my body shaking and my muscles losing all sense of control. I'm helpless, pinned underneath him and barely able to feel anything except the constant barrage of white-hot explosions with each stroke of his cock. It's a fairy tale, it's a fantasy, but it's real and it's happening to me.

"That's it, honey . . . take my cock, cream deep all over me, and I'll fuck you over and over. I'll pound you, I'll hammer you . . . but I won't break you," Thomas rasps between thrusts. "I love you."

"I love you too!" I scream with the last conscious thought in my mind, and he howls, his cock swelling as he thrusts as deep as he can one last time. Liquid heat flows through me, pure release, but no sound escapes my lips. I can't even breathe anymore. Instead, I let the darkness take me because I know that in the darkness, there will be my Thomas . . . and I'll be safe in his arms.

CHAPTER 33

THOMAS

*L*ove.

Terror.

It's amazing how similar the two emotions feel as they dance around in my chest and my head, dueling with each other.

On one hand, I am in love. Mia's simple declaration sealed it, and the trust she put in me later melted any doubts I could have ever had from my heart.

I'll fight for her.

I'll conquer for her.

I'll win for her.

If she asks, I'll even die for her.

But can I be a better man for her?

I want to be, and I know I need to be, but am I capable?

And that desperate thought is what has me returning to this well-spring of hell.

I'm back here at Dr. Perry's office, sitting in her chair while she looks at me with eyes that judge me even before I've opened my mouth. Maybe it's fair game since I did the same to her when I saw her, but she's supposed to be the professional.

"So, Tom—"

"Excuse me, Dr. Perry, but if you don't mind, can you call me Thomas? Tom is . . ." I start before searching for the right buzzword to use with her. It takes me a moment, but it comes to me from irony. "Triggering. Being called Tom triggers me."

Dr. Perry lifts an eyebrow and scribbles a note on her clipboard. "Why is that?"

"My father calls me Tom," I explain, clearing my throat and taking a sip of the herbal iced tea that's at my side. At least that's pretty good, I'll give her that. "And since my mother killed herself, it's been used more as a curse than as a name."

"I didn't know your mother committed suicide," Dr. Perry replies. "Tell me about that."

I'm not sure I can. Not sure it'll do any good other than give her a reason to add a checkmark to her list. But this is for Mia. And maybe for myself a bit too. Even if Dr. Perry can't help me, just saying this out loud is an accomplishment. And maybe she will have some insight. Or maybe she'll tell me to switch my breakfast cereal to something less stimulating like bran.

It's hard, and the words start slowly, in little fits and stops until momentum takes over. I hate reliving the memories, the voice in my head damning me the whole time, but I tell her about the day my mother died, trying to purge myself of the bad memories as she hums and says, "Tell me more," at regular intervals.

"After he screamed, I went into the bedroom and my father was trying CPR. I didn't know what it was at the time, and he kept yelling, 'Breathe, you bitch!' I didn't know what to do, and suddenly, he looked up, throwing his phone at me and yelling at me, 'Call 9-1-1!' And I did, but they couldn't save her. Since then . . . things have been bad."

Because you fucked up.

It takes me a long time to go over what my father did to me growing up, the mental and sometimes physical abuse. For the first time, Dr. Perry looks at me sympathetically before clearing her throat.

"Thomas, you have a lot of anger, but part of me feels like you're not being totally clear as to *whom* you're angry with."

"My father."

She looks at me blankly. No checkmark to her clipboard.

Wrong answer, shithead.

"You mean, am I pissed at my mother?" I ask, my hand clenching and my voice raising. "You're goddamn right, I am! I was just a boy and she left me. And ever since, my world has turned upside down!" Shame blasts through me. "I shouldn't be mad at her. She couldn't have known how Dad would react, the things he'd do. She was just a depressed, lonely woman, or at least that's what I heard the ladies call her at the wake while they ate finger sandwiches like it was any regular luncheon."

I'm out of the chair, pacing back and forth on the carpet, and Dr. Perry watches with a detached demeanor that infuriates me. As if I'm not enough already.

"You know it's not your fault," Dr. Perry says. "Rationally, you know that. Suicide is not about the survivors. Your mother likely couldn't contemplate what her choice would do to you because all she could think was what it would do to her. Suicide isn't about ending one's life. It's about ending one's pain."

It's a little mental health brochure-ish but startlingly insightful.

But her life ended just the same. All while you watched cartoons and ate a snack.

I'm getting nowhere, just circling the same drain I always dance around, and I'm done. At least for today, maybe with Dr. Perry, maybe forever. But I need to go.

"That's enough. I'm out of here," I growl, grabbing my jacket. I storm out, ignoring everything and everyone as I jump into my car and fire up the engine. The angry growl of the powerful motor echoes my inner turmoil, but it somehow focuses me enough that I don't crash as I drive back to the office and take the elevator upstairs.

It's just before the end of the work day, and I'm surprised Kerry's already gone, but I don't care right now. I should do my usual fifteen-minute meditation, but that seems like a dangerous proposition with where my head's at right now. Instead, what I want to do is check my email, and then head upstairs and—

"Dennis?"

He's standing in my office, dressed as he always is in his suit, but with him is Mia, who looks up and smiles. They've been talking, obviously, and I blink, stunned. How could she . . . how could she let *that* man into my office?

"Thomas, I'm glad you're back. I'm sorry. I thought your schedule was clear, and—"

"He was probably wasting time," Dennis says in that voice he has. "I've been sitting on my ass for a half hour waiting on you, Tom."

"Don't call me . . ." I rasp, my anger flaring at the name I hate. "You know what, never mind. Just what in the hell are you doing here?" I go around to my chair, needing to put the desk between us. I'm not sure if it's for his protection or mine.

Dennis reads my tone of voice and sniffs, offended. "Well, if you're going to act like that . . . I came because Miss Karakova convinced me that I've been missing out on something by not having a friendly relationship with you. So I came bearing gifts to bury the hatchet." He tosses a box on the desk in front of me.

I glance at it and then back at him, unbelieving. "So that's supposed to be it? A present and that's supposed to wash away the years of abuse?"

He scoffs, rolling his eyes. "Oh, come on, 'abuse'? Don't be melodramatic. I kept a roof over your head, put you through school, even got this ivory tower you like to sit in started for you."

I stand, indignant fury coursing in my blood. "Melodramatic? Are you fucking serious? That roof over my head just gave you a place to slap me around. And the school you 'paid' for? You didn't pay one red cent. I earned that admission and that scholarship in spite of your telling me how stupid I was every fucking day. And the only reason you keep holding the startup money over my head is because you know I'm *better* than you. I did all this," I say, gesturing at my office, "and all you've amounted to is a wife who killed herself to get away from you and a son who wishes you were dead."

I've never been able to wipe that smug look off Dennis's face before, but those words sure did it. Maybe a little too evil, perhaps, but it does surprise him.

He stares at me, absolutely shocked before speaking up. "You should have died with her."

"Get out!" I bellow, crossing my office and grabbing him by the jacket before shoving him toward the door. Dennis stumbles out, and I have just enough time to close the door to my office before I turn to Mia, who looks aghast.

"Why? I told you those things in confidence. Why did you stick your nose in the one place I didn't want you to pry?" I beseech her. But then the fury reignites, aiming directly where I know it'll hurt her most. "I trusted you!"

"Tommy, I'm sorry," Mia whimpers, cowering away as I cross my office and pick up the package. It's a box wrapped in shiny plastic wrapping paper, the kind that looks like sparkling foil if you tilt it this way and that way in the light. "I went to see him about the sabotage stuff, and—"

"And what? You ended up having tea and fucking crumpets with the man who tried every day of my life to destroy me? And you thought, 'Hey, you know what'd be great? If I just blind-side Thomas with his asshole of a dad, and then ta-da, it'll be happily ever after.' How'd that work?" My words are caustic, sharp and jagged as I stab her with her every sarcastic syllable. But I hurt, so badly. And I can't stop the lashing out.

"You pried into my family relations!" I scream accusingly. "You brought that man into my office, knowing what he's done to me. You know better than anyone—*anyone*—why I can't be around him. But still, you thought you knew better."

"I . . . I know," she says, sobbing. Dimly, I realize I'm going too far, but the animal's loose, the rage overwhelming, and I can't stop it with so much emotion boiling over. "He told me about your mother, and then he called me and seemed to want to reconcile. I really thought—"

"No, you didn't think!" I yell, slamming the gift down on the desk.

I slam the gift down again and I hear something inside snap. Maybe it's in me, maybe it's the gift, I don't know. The sound triggers something primal and enraged deep within my soul, and I pick up the misshapen box, using the last of my self-control to turn away from Mia before hurling it against my office window. The thick security glass cracks from top to bottom, making a Y shape that echoes the question inside me.

Why? Why did she do this?

Why did he have to come here?

Why did she have to die?

Why do I hate everything about myself?

Mia gasps, and I hear a loud thump before the door opens, leaving me in my memories.

Dad is yelling as I hold my hand over my bleeding forehead, praying I don't spill any blood on the carpet. "I just bought that bike!"

"Dad, I'm sorry, I didn't—" I try to explain. I don't care what they say about wearing helmets. Smacking your head into a tree branch when a snake pops out of nowhere, sending you tumbling down a dirt hillside, sucks the big hairy one.

But it's going to suck even more if I bleed on the carpet.

"You were careless and clumsy! Don't think you're getting another bike. You ruined that one so you can walk to school, for all I care!" Dad yells. He picks up the remote control to the TV and throws it, where it goes crashing into the fish tank, cracking the glass. Water spills out, and I can see Goldie and Mr. Colors, the two fish my best friend Andy across the street gave me for my birthday, start panicking as their home drains onto the living room rug. "Goddammit!"

"No!" I scream, ignoring my head to run to the kitchen. I know where the big spaghetti pot is. Maybe if I fill it with water in time, I can save them.

I turn, running for the living room, but the water strikes again, or maybe it's that I'm still dizzy from my bike crash. I slip on the wet carpet, my head spinning as I crack my head on the edge of the fish tank, but somehow, I still get water into the pot. Scooping it in deep, I get Goldie and Mr. Colors out, sobbing as I watch them swim in their new home. It's gray, metallic . . . they're trapped. But they're safe.

"When you're done being a baby, clean that shit up," Dad says, his voice still raw and ragged from screaming at me.

He leaves, and I sob, watching Goldie circle around Mr. Colors, his mouth opening and closing. The water ripples, and I realize it's my tears.

I gasp, jerked back to the present as I look at the crack on my window . . . just like the one on the fish tank.

My God. I've become just like him.

No. I've *become* him.

CHAPTER 34

MIA

*W*atching the gift, I don't even know what it is, pinwheel through the air and crack into the window, a Y-shaped lightning bolt splitting the thick safety glass, is one of the scariest things I've seen in my entire life.

Maybe that sounds silly, but seeing Thomas lose control absolutely terrifies me. In a blind panic, I turn and run for the door, but somehow, my hand slips and I literally run headfirst into the door before I get it open, the world spinning as I flee.

I must have hit my head harder than I thought, because the next thing I know, I'm outside of Papa's shop, tears running down my cheeks.

I open the door, and before I can even say a word, Papa sees me, his sewing machine stopping immediately.

Coming around the counter, he wraps me in his arms, murmuring the soft phrases he used to when I was a little girl, little Russian words that gave me comfort then and comfort now.

I'm transported back, back to the days when the world was big and scary, but my Papa was bigger and scarier and could protect me from anything. It's just that his lap has shrunk, and instead, he holds me as we stand up and I sob my eyes out.

"Mia . . . Mia, darling, what happened?" Papa asks after a few minutes of consoling me.

"He was so angry . . . I didn't mean to," I hiccup before fresh sobs rack my body. I feel miserable, like I've wrecked everything when all I was trying to do was help.

"Who's angry, Anastasia?" Papa says, helping me over to a chair and guiding me to sit down. He goes into the back, returning with a bottle of water that he hands to me. "Sip slowly and tell me what happened."

It's disjointed, my head's still not quite working right between my scare and the hit to my head, but I get it all out.

"I . . . Thomas asked me to look into who's been doing some corporate espionage, hamstringing the company," I start, holding the bottle against my head where I feel the biggest throb. "While doing that, I went to meet his father, Dennis. Things were weird, but when Dennis reached out to me, I figured it would be good to try and clear some of the air. Oh, Papa, there's so much between them, really bad stuff, and I . . . I was so scared."

"Shh, it's okay," Papa says softly, stroking my hair again. "Mia, whatever happened, you're safe now. I won't let anything happen."

I nod and struggle to get the rest of the story out. I explain my first meeting with Dennis Goldstone more, and how Thomas and I exchanged our love vows, and how I just wanted to ease the pressure on Thomas.

"Papa, he's under so much self-inflicted torture. I couldn't let him keep punishing himself, driving himself crazy with whatever Dennis has done to him."

"I understand, but Mia, how'd you get hurt?" Papa says, brushing my hair back. "You have a lump the size of a golf ball on your forehead. Did that man do that? I'll kill that son of a bitch if you say yes." The words are quiet but a promise of violence.

Oh, God, I didn't even realize.

"Papa, no!" I cry out, grabbing his wrists. I explain the disastrous meeting, that I bumped my head and it wasn't Thomas, but that the sight of him losing his temper terrified me.

Papa stops, and I can see he's trying not to scoff at me. "Mia . . . tell me the truth. I've heard that before—even on the TV, they say it. *I walked into a door. I fell down the stairs. I slipped on some ice.* You—"

"Papa, I'm serious. I ran into the door when I was running out. I came straight here."

He eyes me carefully, looking for the slightest sign that I might be lying to him. But finding none, he sighs, hugging me close once again.

"Okay, so let me see if I have this straight. You know your Thomas has bad blood with his father, and yet you set up a meeting without his knowledge, no preparation, no decision on his part on whether he wanted to mend fences, as the Americans say?"

Papa's words are eerily similar to Thomas's. Less angry and accusatory, of course, but the gist is the same and I break out in fresh tears.

"Shh, don't cry, Mia. Though it pains me to say it, I believe you have made a mistake. Perhaps this Dennis even used you to hurt your Thomas. Another pawn in their hurtful game."

Papa spits air at the ground beside us, and I wonder if he's cursing Dennis, Thomas, or me. I'm too afraid to ask, because he's right. I made a terrible mistake.

"Oh, God, I need to go back and apologize." I move to pull away, but Papa holds me tight.

"No. You may have made a mistake in judgement, but it was with good intentions and hope for a better outcome. Your Thomas reacted violently, like an out of control toddler. I can't let you go back there. Not now. He may come to see the error of his ways and come groveling back to my princess, but you both need time to settle. Let him calm, Mia. Let both of you calm." His voice is soothing, hypnotizing me into agreement.

I nod silently.

"Good, now you will stay with me tonight. I do not like the look of that bump on your head and want to keep an eye on you." He pokes at my forehead with gentle fingers and I wince. "I will wake you every two hours to make sure you can see properly and know who you are."

"Papa, I have work tomorrow. I have to go home," I argue even though staying buried under a pile of blankets on Papa's couch while he makes me soup sounds like just what I need right now.

"Then go home and get your things. But you should call in sick tomorrow. You have a perfect excuse." Though he looks at my head, most of my pain is coming from a point further south . . . my heart. "You should not work for a man who can't control himself."

I look into Papa's face, and I see a rocky stubbornness that is hard to crack. "Papa, I'm not just going to quit, but I'll call in sick and maybe take a vacation while I decide what to do, deal? And I don't mind staying with you for a few days. Let me go back to my place and I'll pack some things."

He goes to object, but the door to his shop opens and a customer comes in. Papa takes a deep breath and turns back to me, nodding.

"Fine. I promised Mr. Smith his suit by tomorrow and I have to get to work. But you go, and you come back here. Understood? How is your head?"

"It's fine," I assure him. "It hurts, but I'm fine."

"Oh, Mia . . . you have surely gotten yourself into something this time, but if it is right, it will be. Trust and truth are vital parts of love. But so is forgiveness. Let us hope that you both have enough in your heart to give."

We both close our eyes, exhaling and sending the prayer heavenward.

I get back in my car and see my phone flashing. There are two missed calls . . . both from Thomas.

I decide to take Papa's advice and give us both a little space. Instead, I start driving, trying not to think about what Papa said but failing miserably, as it seems I'm not really registering what's in front of me.

A horn blares, and I come to a stop just inches from the side of a UPS truck, the driver glaring at me. "Fuck, lady! Eyes ahead!"

I give him a little wave of apology, wishing it were that easy with Thomas. But I make it to my apartment without further incident, where I start packing my bag with the basics for staying with Papa for a few days.

I don't even know why I'm doing this, other than not wanting to deny Papa. It's not like I fear Thomas coming over or anything, but maybe Papa can help me get my head right. Figure out where I go from here.

A whisper in my head tells me that I just want to hide out, run away from the pain, the embarrassment, and the fear. And I wonder if this is what Thomas's inner demon is like, calling him on his bullshit and not letting him get away with anything. I suspect my inner voice is rather nice and polite compared to Thomas's though.

My phone rings again, and I'm about ready to ignore it when I see that it's not Thomas but Izzy instead. She's supposed to be on at The Gravy Train, and I pick up the call, worried something might be wrong with her.

"Izzy? What's up?"

"What's up?" Izzy asks, frantic with worry. "Mia, are you okay? Are you at the hospital?"

"What?" I ask, confused. "What do you mean, at the hospital? Why would I be there?"

"Babe, why aren't you at the hospital?" Izzy asks. "After what happened, I'd be getting checked out while calling the fucking police on his ass!"

"Izzy, you're making no sense. What are you talking about?"

Her voice is tight as she says, "Flip on Channel Eight. You're top fucking news."

I turn to my TV, finding my remote and turning it on, and a picture of Thomas flashes on the screen.

CHAPTER 35

THOMAS

"*While the outcry from the Internet has been immediate and outraged, so far, there has been no official response from either Goldstone the company or Thomas Goldstone himself.*"

I shake my head as the video plays again behind the voiceover. It's the fifth time I've watched it this morning, and each time, I wince.

It's a video, taken from the hallway outside my office. At first, the visual isn't too damning, but you can hear the yelling, cursing, and hurled insults, all obviously my voice. You can clearly hear every word of my family's dirty laundry as I scream about my mother's suicide and wish my father dead. And then the door opens, showing me physically shoving him out the door. I look mad, crazy-eyed and red-faced. In the background of the image, you can see Mia's pale face, horror written plainly in her expression. Then more closed-door yelling, and the crash as I throw the gift box against the window. But without knowing about the box, the shatter of glass sounds ominous, especially when a moment later, you hear a solid thunk against door. And then Mia runs through the video frame, holding her head with curled-in shoulders and runny mascara tears streaking down her cheeks.

"That's enough."

Irene Castellanos, my head of public relations, hits the pause button on the remote, and the video stops. "Someone's already pieced together a story about Mia, calling her your 'basement babe' and

255

speculating on your relationship. I'll be honest, Thomas. The way they put this whole thing together, it looks like you were out of control and hit her."

"But I didn't!" I argue for the millionth time, rubbing at my eyes. I didn't sleep at all last night and I feel like sand's been poured behind my eyeballs.

Deep breaths . . . just deep breaths.

That's what I'd told myself when Mia ran out. Calm, breathe . . .over and over like a mantra. Dr. Perry would've been proud. Well, except for the raging tantrum I'd thrown. But I'd calmed, or more like collapsed like a deflated balloon, when I'd seen just how far I'd gone.

The news had broken by six, like the network had just been waiting for a chance to throw me under the bus. They aired it first with a lot of speculation and started asking leading questions later. And there have been a lot of them, because the phone calls demanding interviews have been coming in non-stop.

And now they all know what a fuckup you are. Can't hide now!

The voice in my head is gleeful as fuck, dancing around like it's won the lottery of fucking me over. At this point, I guess that's true. Everything's a mess . . . me and Mia, my company, my head.

Irene clears her throat, yanking me from my downward mental spiral.

"Sorry, Irene. You're right, but that isn't what happened. I was yelling at my father . . . for the most part. We have history."

"Yeah, I know. I heard. Everyone knows that now, if they didn't already. Too bad your father so far isn't willing to make a corroborating statement on that," Irene replies, tapping at the notepad in her lap. "I've reached out to him twice since I learned about this, and he's sticking with 'no comment' like I'm a member of the fucking press too."

That Irene cusses tells me just how bad this is. She's a consummate pro, experienced, and has pretty much seen it all. And she's losing her shit. That doesn't bode well for me.

A sudden thought goes through me, and I realize how exhausted I am that I didn't think of it earlier. "Have we found out who sent the video to the news? There's got to be a trail there."

Irene opens her mouth, then shakes her head. "I'm sorry, Thomas. I didn't think of that. I've been handling the PR side, trying to squash it, not track down where they got it since it's obviously real."

"Hold on that," I say, heaving myself to my feet and stepping out of my office. Kerry's frantic at her desk, talking with someone on the phone while typing furiously, and she's refused to even look at me all morning. I don't blame her. I haven't been able to look at myself all morning either.

But right now, I have something I need to find. "Kerry, I need you to call Smithson Security. Have their best investigator here today. If they can't come, see if they can recommend someone who can. And Kerry, be discreet, please."

If looks could kill, I'd be a dead man where I'm standing. "Yes, Mr. Goldstone."

I don't have time for this, but I stand directly in front of her, giving her a hard look. "Kerry, I'm only going to say this once, so listen closely." I can see her bracing herself, ready to be put on blast, or worse. "I didn't hurt Mia. Yes, I lost my temper, but I didn't lay a hand on her."

Her face softens a degree or two, but she's still not happy with me. "Shit, Thomas. What the hell is going on around here?"

Irene clears her throat, interrupting. "Actually, Kerry. You weren't here when all this was going down, correct?"

Kerry turns a frosty glare to Irene, and I intervene, holding up a hand. "Nobody's accusing you of anything. But you were gone when I came into the office. Did you know Dennis and Mia were here?"

She nods, looking pained. "I did. I asked Mia if she knew what she was doing, and she said she hoped so."

I swallow thickly. "Okay, so when you left, did you see anything suspicious? Maybe someone up here who shouldn't have been?"

Though I can see her racking her brain, she's already shaking her head. "I'm sorry, I didn't see anyone. I just headed out for my daughter's recital. I rode the elevator down with a bunch of folks, I don't know who, and then walked out the front door. I waved at Michael, the security guard, and then caught a cab. I didn't know about this until late last night because I had my phone on silent while Cami danced. I'm afraid I'm no help."

I pat her hand, and she grabs mine, holding on tightly. "I'm sorry, Thomas."

I grimace. I scared Kerry, angered her, hurt her trust in me, and I never should have. She's been the one person I could always trust before Mia . . . and I'll make it up to her.

"It's okay. Can you just call Smithson? I really need someone here, pronto."

"On it," she says, grabbing her phone and clicking around on her computer to get the number.

Irene gestures for me to come back into my office and shuts the door as I sit back down. "Okay, so what's the fallout here?"

"So far?" Irene asks, picking up her notepad she'd left on my desk before. "Well, Goldstone, both you and the company, have been condemned by every women's rights group from NOW to LOLA."

"What's LOLA?" I mutter.

"Ladies of Liberty Alliance . . . yeah, I had to look them up myself," Irene admits. "If you could see the sidewalk from up here, you'd find a group of marchers downstairs right now on the sidewalk protesting. I don't know what group they're from except that they're pretty much calling for you to finish breaking that window, preferably with your head, before you go falling to the street below."

The window. Turning around, I look at the Y-shaped crack, haunted by my rage. The gift had ended up being a photo cube, of all things, with pictures of my parents and me when things were happy embedded on each side. I didn't even know those pictures existed and certainly wouldn't have thought Dennis had saved them all these years. And last night when I'd finally opened the box, alone in my office in the ruined tatters of my life, the pictures had seemed more of a taunt than anything healing.

See what you did? If only you'd helped her, this is the life you could've led. But look at you now . . . broken and alone.

That's what the demon had said on repeat last night, and I shake my head, not wanting an encore performance of the vitriol.

"What else?"

"Well, your net worth is highly tied to Goldstone stock . . . and it's down ten points so far today. So you've lost a significant amount of money. Probably a millionaire instead of a billionaire today." It's a hollow attempt at a joke, both of us knowing I couldn't care less about money right now.

I shrug, not giving a shit. For once, business success isn't foremost in my mind. "Forget Wall Street. How's it affecting the company?"

Irene sighs. "So far, not too badly. There's an uptick in callouts. Some in protest, some because they don't want to cross the crowd below. Most of them just opted to work from home for the day, so it's not like anyone is hair-flipping out. I told HR not to say or do anything about it until you gave a directive. I'd suggest letting it slide . . . especially in Mia Karakova's case."

Mentioning Mia hurts, and I look out the window toward her apartment across the city. The simple fact is, I chased her away. She hasn't returned my calls and has ignored my texts, and I'd called down to her manager, Bill, this morning to see if she'd come in. He'd carefully said she called in 'sick' and I'd heard the questions in his voice. I'm not sure if I'm going to ever get her back.

"Agreed," I whisper. "Nobody gets punished for my fuckup, understood?"

My door opens, and Randall Towlee pokes his head in. Like I don't have enough problems to deal with. "Thomas, got a moment?"

I wave him in, sighing. More good news. "Sure, invite everyone in while you're at it. We can get to the execution faster that way. Sorry . . . what's on your mind?"

"Not to pile on, but I just forwarded you an email from the hospital project liaison. Basic idea is that they're cutting ties with Goldstone until this is resolved. There's some verbiage about negative public image, but they're basically running scared."

I sigh. *Of course.* "It's fine. I'll reach out to them."

"One other thing." Looking like he'd rather be anywhere than passing along the news he's got, he says, "The Board has called a meeting to discuss your behavior and the news coverage. Rumor is, they're concerned you've broken your own corporate bylaws."

I nod, exhaustion hitting me like a wave. "Tell them . . . tomorrow."

"They may not want to wait that long, Thomas," he says. "The damage to our corporate image—"

"Can wait at least twenty-four hours," I reply. "Tell them tomorrow, noon, conference room. Thank you."

He leaves, and I look at Irene. "I'm putting you in charge of that. Develop a plan to get ahead of the news cycle. I put us in a nosedive, but I'm going to need you to pull us out."

"That'll need you, Thomas," she says. "I can develop a plan, and I can be the corporate press presence, but to really change things around, the public's going to demand that you do it. Personally, and probably in public, to let them get their pound of flesh from you."

I nod, but I'm too tired. I'm shaken. For the first time in a long time, I actually do feel weak.

"I know," I whisper, heaving myself to my feet. "But not right this moment. You're in charge of that. I know you can pull magic out. If you need me, call Kerry."

I leave the office, point up, and Kerry nods. She'll screen things for me, but right now, I can't handle it. Instead I leave, each step feeling like I've aged fifty years in a single day.

As I enter my living room, something out of place catches my eye, pink and white, and I walk over to tug a T-shirt out from under the edge of my sofa.

I remember this. Mia wore it the last weekend she stayed over. I'd peeled it off her before we made love on the couch, and afterward, we'd soaked in the tub before making love in the bedroom. I guess in all the passion, we just sort of forgot where our clothes ended up.

My eyes burn, and I lift the shirt to my nose, inhaling that soft scent that's unmistakably Mia. She's not someone for perfumes, nothing eye-watering, just her natural scent that's honest, pure . . . and I've hurt her.

I feel wetness run down my cheeks and it isn't tears of rage or shame, it isn't sweat or chopping onions. I can't stop seeing the terrified look on Mia's face from the video.

I hurt the woman I love.

How am I supposed to recover from that? How am I supposed to move forward?

Out of everything I've lost today, she's the most important thing and what I cherish most.

For the first time in years, I don't know what to do, so I lay on the sofa, holding Mia's shirt to my chest while I cry myself to sleep.

CHAPTER 36

MIA

"*Freedom is something you have to fight for, rather than something you're given. Being free means being prepared to carry that burden,*" the rather handsome hairy-chested man on the computer monitor says, flashing a thumbs-up to the young boy watching him. It's been years since I've watched *Eureka Seven*, but next to *Sailor Moon*, it's one of my favorite animes.

Lying in my sweats, my hair a mess and a bowl of Cocoa Puffs in my lap, I have to pause the video, setting it aside to wipe at my eyes. It's been three days, and I still can't stop crying at moments like this. It's part of the reason I still haven't gotten through the fifty-two episodes of the show . . . there are just so many feels.

I keep watching, rapt even though I know what's going to happen, and when the episode ends, I see that it's already getting close to eleven, and I get off the sofa to head for the shower.

Papa's place is a little bit bigger than mine, but most of it's been converted into his sort of home workshop-slash-storage area, so it seems smaller. But still, it feels good to be back, surrounded by the dressing frames, the bolts of cloth, and three broken sewing machines that Papa picked up at an estate sale when I was in college. He vowed then to fix them, and it's become a running joke that he's never so much as turned a screw to start their repair. But somehow, their broken-down presence is just as much a part of 'home' as the whir of Papa's working machines.

I have just enough time to wash up and run a brush through my hair —to ensure I don't have a single obscenely matted blonde dreadlock hanging down my back—and pull on some jeans and a T-shirt before I head out. I stop down in the shop to give Papa a kiss on the cheek.

"Grabbing lunch with the girls."

"Are you sure it is safe out there for you?" he asks, peering out the windows. It'd taken fewer than twelve hours for the press to track me down, first at my apartment, then here at Papa's. Finally, I'd turned my phone off once the voicemail had gotten full. Izzy and Charlotte have been checking in with me via Papa's landline.

But today, the street is blessedly empty and I'm getting out for a little bit. I desperately need to so that I can get out of my head, even if only for a few minutes.

"Seems clear for now, at least, so I'm making a run for it. I'll call you before I come back to make sure no one has set up camp while I'm gone. See you later. Maybe I can help out down here some? I'm getting cabin fever upstairs."

"I would love for you to keep an old man company . . . and I do think I have some buttons that need work," Papa teases. "You know me. I'll make you work for your keep! Oh, and tell Isabella I have something for her to try! A skirt I made!"

I leave with a smile. Papa is always generous with Izzy. It's the first one to appear on my face in days, and I drive to The Gravy Train where Izzy's already waiting for me, twirling the straw in her Coke and looking nervous. "You're late. I was getting scared."

"Papa," I reassure her.

"*Eureka*," she says with a smile.

I laugh softly, nodding. "Yeah, you know me too well."

She reaches up, hugging me before I sit down. Having been forced to sit through many an episode with me, she knows my routine. "Has it been that rough?"

I shrug, looking out the window. "I don't know. I know I'm not ready to go back there. If I face him, I'm going to have to make a decision, or maybe he's already made one, and I'm not ready for that yet. So I've just avoided the whole mess, hiding out at Papa's."

"You know, if you're that upset, you could always have your father talk to someone in the Russian Mafia," Izzy jokes, trying to lighten my dark mood incrementally. "I bet there are a couple of guys who could teach Thomas some manners."

"Papa doesn't know anyone in the Mafia," I protest, but Izzy snorts.

"Tinker, tailor, soldier, spy," Izzy chants. "When I saw the book in the library, I just thought of good ol' Papa Karakov. I've never even read it."

It's my turn to snort. My father's the last man who'd be a spy. "Izz, you've gotta get out more."

She smiles and takes a sip of soda. "Seriously, though, you could walk away. Cut ties with Thomas and with your skills. You could get a job anywhere, even with the notoriety you've got now. Maybe especially because of it. I bet you could even sue his ass for a nice ten-foot-high pile of cash if you wanted to."

"No!" I protest, though I know she's not being serious. But she's pushing me to think, to consider what I want now that I've come out of hiding. "No, I'm never going to do that. I just . . ."

Words fail me, and Izzy sets her Coke aside, which means she's really worried about me. The girl never sets aside calories. She needs them too much with as few as she gets.

"Talk to me, babe. What are you feeling?"

I close my menu, biting my lip as I try to form my thoughts into words. It's been swirling in my head for the past three days, and honestly, it's been easier to just sit back and let myself get lost in video games and anime. But the thoughts never stop.

"I love him," I say simply, and Izzy's shiny eyes mirror my own. "But I'm not sure if he's in the right state of mind to be in a relationship or if he'll ever get there. We were doing so well, and I . . . I really fucked up, Izz. I shouldn't have interfered."

I'm saved from her rebuke by the waitress coming up. I order a cheeseburger and fries and Izzy orders a grilled cheese with bacon. By the time the waitress leaves, I jump back in, not letting Izzy patronize me with words that none of this is my fault. Because it is, and this isn't like Thomas internalizing something he had no control over. This is a mess of my own making. Not the media stuff, but the part between Thomas and me.

"Izzy, there's just something about Thomas," I tell her. "Yes, he's got issues. Yes, he's got a temper and a lot of emotional baggage. But I don't think he'd ever hurt me. I know the world doesn't believe me, but I did run into that door. And my mind keeps flashing back to the little things he's done. I don't even think he knows that I've noticed."

"Like what? The big tip he left me? Honey, I don't care about that. I want to see you happy," Izzy says. "I'd give the money back if it'd help you feel better. If I hadn't spent it already."

"It's not that," I say, thinking. "It's other things. It's hard to even explain, but despite his reputation, there's a gentle side to him. The way he's made love with me is just part of it, and no, I'm not just talking with my hoo-hah. But taking me on a dream trip through Japan, remembering my favorite brand of juice and stocking it in his fridge, and sharing with me, even when I know how hard it was and how much it cost him to appear weak that way to me. Not that I think he's weak for what he went through as a child, but *he* thinks he was. He's got this need inside him to be strong, be the best, and he broke down in front of me, Izzy. He broke down *for* me, trusting that I would help him pick up the pieces. And I tried. I just solved the puzzle all wrong."

Izzy covers her mouth with her hands, and she sighs deeply. "Honey, I am so sorry. Tell me how I can help. Do you want to call him? It sounds like you both have apologies to make."

"I know, but—"

Izzy's phone buzzes, and I see that it's Charlotte. Izzy picks it up, putting it on speaker. "Hey, Char, what's up?"

"Hey, turn on Channel 7," Char says. "You're gonna want to see this."

"Hey, Elaine!" Izzy yells, her diminutive body exploding in the voice of someone's who's worked in a diner for a long time. The waitress on duty pokes her head up, and Izzy points. "Turn on Channel 7, pronto! And turn it up!"

"You got it, Izz," Elaine says. She flips the TV in the corner over to Channel 7 and cranks the volume up as loud as it'll go. "There you go!"

It's the noon news, and the little info bar at the bottom says the camera's set up outside the Goldstone Building. There's a crowd outside, a mix of media and a lot of pissed-off-looking women protesting.

On a quickly setup podium, Irene Castellanos, who I've met once in my time at Goldstone, gets on the microphones.

"Thank you for coming today," she says simply, looking as professional as possible in her tailored suit and skirt combo, somber but not funereal. Dimly, in the part of my mind that isn't stunned by what I'm hearing, I note that she's striking the right tone for a press conference. *"Mr. Thomas Goldstone would like to say a few words."*

The reaction by the crowd as Thomas steps up is loud and ugly. I'm almost surprised nobody throws a tomato at him, but the first thing I notice is that he looks like hell. He's shaved, sure, but the bags under his eyes are noticeable, and he looks haggard, exhausted as he smooths out the paper in his hand on the podium surface.

"Ladies and gentlemen, thank you for being here today. My name is Thomas Goldstone, and I've come to address the recent incident and the video that has surfaced of me."

"Abuser!" someone screams at him, and Thomas winces like he's been slapped. I wince with him, knowing that of all things, that label would be one that cuts deeper than most.

Thomas waits for the crowd to quiet, holding up a hand until he can be heard again. *"There are many things that people have called me over this. And many of them I deserve. There is no excuse for my behavior in the video, though the whole story is not reflected accurately in what you've seen. The truth is, I did lose my temper, and I behaved in a way that is inexcusable, raising my voice and throwing a box at the wall of my office. But, let me be clear. I did not lay a hand on the woman in the video, and she was never in any danger from me at any time."*

"I'm aware of the nickname I'm known by, and the video showed me a man . . ." he says, pausing before continuing, *"showed me a man I do not want to be. So first and foremost, I'd like to apologize to the employees of Goldstone. I've pushed, I've demanded . . . I've been ruthlessly harsh."* His words speak to the ones running through everyone's mind . . . Ruthless Bastard. *"For that, there is no excuse, and no amount of apology can compensate for the hurt feelings, the hurt souls, I've caused."*

"More importantly, though, I owe an apology to the woman in the video. Some of you have found her name, so I feel comfortable saying this. Mia, I'm truly sorry. I'm sorry for scaring you. I have more to say, but you deserve to hear it from me directly." His eyes look deeply into the camera, deeply into my eyes through the TV screen. It's like feeling him right here, in my very soul.

"To the shareholders and the people of Roseboro and around the world who have come to know the Goldstone name, I swear to you that I will work tirelessly to restore your faith in this company. There are good people here, thousands of them. Don't let my mistake ruin all of their hard work. Therefore—"

"The rest of it's mostly just stuff Irene made me put in there," a deep voice says from the entrance.

Izzy and I both look up in shock as Thomas stands at the edge of the booth, still wearing the same suit as in the video but looking even more haggard. I blink, unable to form words while Izzy just gawks.

Finally, I force out, "How—"

"It's on an hour tape delay," he says quietly, barely audible over the TV. Izzy waves to the waitress, and she turns off the press conference, and suddenly, it feels like everyone in the diner's looking at us.

They probably are.

"Listen —" Izzy says, but Thomas interrupts her before she can dismiss him.

"Wait," he says, his eyes shimmering with tears and exhaustion. "Mia, I know you're still angry at me, and maybe you're even scared of me. I've prayed for three days that you aren't, but I have to admit you could feel that way. I'm just asking for a few minutes."

I look up at him, and I can see everyone watching with bated breath to see what I'll say. Finally, Izzy interrupts the drawn-out silence.

"Mia? You need to do this, but you *don't* have to do this now if you're not ready." She eyes Thomas carefully.

"Give us a minute, Izz?" I ask, and she nods, sliding out of her seat before moving to the counter seat closest to our booth and sitting down.

"I'm gonna sit right here, and if I hear even a raised voice . . . buddy,

I don't care how many muscles you've got. I'm gonna have your balls," Izzy says to Thomas with a falsely sweet tone. "And hurry. I'm hungry."

He slides into the seat gratefully and the waitress comes up. Thomas waves her off with a shake of his head and clears his throat. "Mia, I came here because I need to ask you for your forgiveness. I was wrong, I hurt you, and I've probably sent you running for the hills. I'm so sorry."

"You didn't *hurt* me," I remind him. "You did startle me a bit, but I ran into the door myself. We both know that video is bullshit."

"True, but my outburst caused it, so I still feel responsible," Thomas says. "Fuck, seeing myself in that video . . ."

"I get it, Thomas. I love you, but . . ."

"I know," he rasps, his voice thick with emotion. "And I know some people may tell you I'm not worth the trouble. For three days, I've realized that I've become the man I tried not to be."

"Like your father?" I ask, and Thomas nods again. "That is why I forgive you. Because you know that and want to be better. Yes, you lost control, but I was the one who pushed you off the edge, knowing your grip was precarious at best. I didn't realize . . . I mean, I knew what you'd said about how bad it was. But Dennis seemed like he wanted to reconcile, and I just thought I was going to give you this fairy tale ending." I bite my lip, swallowing the sob down. "I'm sorry, Thomas. I shouldn't have forced it. It wasn't my place."

He takes my hands in his across the table. "Don't you see? You did give me a fairy tale, but not with my dad. With you. That's what matters."

The impact of both of our apologies fills the air between us, washing through us, burning up the pain of the last few days and resetting us. Not back to where we were, but somewhere else on our journey, closer to a healthy place because we've both touched the fire and know the burn, know just how close we can get to it without getting singed.

Tears flow messily down my face, and a sniffle from my side tells me Izzy is sobbing too. "The heart wants what the heart wants, and I'm not about to give up on us so easily. I love you, Thomas Goldstone."

Thomas looks at me intently, and the hope in his eyes pierces my soul. Here's the Tommy I've been missing, the one he's hidden from everyone but me. "I love you too, but are you sure, Mia?"

"You've told me what he's put you through, and for so long . . . that's not something you can just brush off, but I know it's not who you are or who you want to be. We will get through it. And call me stupid, but I do hope that someday, you two can . . . I don't know, mend things? On your terms and no one else's. Your mother's death did more than end her life. It ended your childhood, and it ended something in him too." I swallow the sadness down at how the loss of one woman has reverberated through decades, changing everything for Dennis and Thomas, and I wonder if she had any idea about the dominos she'd set in motion.

"But I need you to know, I didn't go to him for that purpose. I went to him to ask him a few questions relating to the sabotage situation."

"I remember," Thomas says. "I remember what you said."

"Right. It wasn't to set all that up. But as bad as Dennis was to you, I don't think he's the one sabotaging you. He's angry at you, but that's just it. He's too scattered, too emotional, too focused on hurting you to do something this calculated. He just can't. So I don't know who it is, and I've been thinking about it for three days to distract myself from us."

"You're probably right about that," Thomas says. "But the company's second. You're the most important thing."

I take a big breath. "Then let's try this again . . . but there's one thing."

Thomas's relieved smile dims. "What?"

"Well, you have your family issues. And I, uh, have mine."

From beside us, Izzy snorts. "Ooh, good luck with that one, boy. You've got one very pissed off Russian tailor who'll cut you into pieces and you'll never be seen or heard from again."

Thomas's eyes ping-pong between us. "Your dad?"

"If it were me, I'd just find a new girlfriend," Izzy interjects, raising an eyebrow when I cut my eyes to her to see her turned all the way around, watching us, amused. "What? I'm just being honest. Your Papa's more stubborn than I am."

"Should I tell him you said that? With that new project of his almost ready with your name on it?"

Izzy's eyes widen, and she shakes her head. "Hell, no! Papa's the nicest, sweetest teddy bear in the whole world!"

"How hard can it be?" Thomas asks, and I nod, giving his hands another squeeze.

"Words of wisdom, something I was reminded of recently and might be useful," I tell him. "Don't beg for it . . . earn it. Do that, and you'll be rewarded."

CHAPTER 37

THOMAS

J remember the time I was just seventeen and stood outside the Dean's office at Stanford. There I was, a kid whose driver's license still practically smelled of freshly-minted plastic since my father wasn't willing to sign the parental authorization form until he realized if I could go to college, I'd be out of his hair.

I'd worn my best shirt and tie, feeling like a fool and wondering how I was going to tell a man three times my age that I deserved to get a full-ride scholarship when my father was economically well off. I was so nervous, I had to go into the men's room and splash cold water on my face before going in. But I'd done it, and I'd gotten the scholarship.

Then there was the time I had to go for my first major investor pitch. This was after I'd sunk everything I had made in four years of online investing into getting Goldstone Inc. off the ground and had even hit up Dennis for ten thousand in exchange for his shares, and I was ready for the majors. This was my first 'big' meeting, and again I was a nervous wreck. But I'd done that too and had gotten the money.

But standing on the sidewalk outside Vladimir Karakov's—in Russian, he's Karak*ov* and she's Karak*ova*—shop and apartment, I'm more nervous than I've ever been in my adult life. My palms are sweating, my throat feels tight, and despite not having drunk anything in hours, I swear I need to pee. Because as much as that scholarship and investment changed my life, this meeting and Vladimir's blessing will make or break my future.

The sun's going down. Mia made me promise to let her go in first to smooth the introductions and to let me handle a little bit of corporate business.

Maybe that's why I'm here. I've spent the past three days thinking almost exclusively about Mia. Anything I said about corporate responsibility or public trust in the press conference? That was put in by Irene. My apology to the workers inside the Goldstone Building? Okay, I did want to do that, but the rest of my thoughts have been about Mia.

But she wants me to take care of myself, of the company.

On our way out of the diner, she'd even made me promise to go work hard, to try and clean up some more of the mess before coming over.

So I did, and now . . . here I am.

I turn, my stomach clenching, but maybe it's that I haven't eaten anything since that 'power smoothie' Kerry got me before the press conference.

I hear the door to the shop open behind me, and I turn around to see a stern-faced man, his cardigan vest and white shirt looking somehow old-fashioned for someone who Mia told me is a tailor.

"Mr. Karakov?"

With a grunt, he jerks his head inside, and I follow him in. I see Mia behind the door inside the shop, and she gives me a supportive thumbs-up.

"Papa, I'll keep things going down here. You said Mr. Smith was going to stop by to pick up his shirts?"

The man turns to his daughter, his icy demeanor immediately thawing as he gives Mia a kiss on the cheek.

"Thank you, darling."

He turns back to me, Siberian winter once again gripping his eyes. "Upstairs."

I follow him, and as we start up, I swear I hear Mia chuckling under her breath as we mount the narrow staircase in the back of the shop. The space is made even narrower with boxes of what look like sewing supplies stacked along the right side of the stairs, and I find my left shoulder rubbing against the wall the whole way up.

He heads into his apartment, and I follow, stopping in the entryway. He turns, eyeing me left to right, top to bottom. With a sound of annoyance and some muttered Russian, he approaches me, his hand reaching out toward my face. To my shame, I flinch, and his eyes soften as he brushes some lint off my jacket. It must've brushed onto me as I touched the stairwell wall. Feeling more comfortable that he's not about to kill me where I stand, I let him do his thing.

He touches the seam at my shoulder. "Custom-made. Worsted wool, handmade buttonhole." He flips open the lapel, examining the inner lining with a hum. As if speaking to himself, he murmurs, "I can learn much about a man by his suit, what he values, what he fancies, where he will cut corners, and where he will indulge."

Feeling like a dog at the dog show, I stand straight and tall. "And what does my suit tell you about me?" I venture.

He grunts, stalking away from me on heavy feet. He heads into the kitchen, and I follow uncertainly, not sure if he's actually inviting me further inside. He takes two tumblers out of a glass-fronted cabinet and pours a healthy measure of a clear liquid in each one. The bottle is completely unlabeled. *Could be water, could be vodka, could be poison, for all I know,* I think as Izzy's words run through my head. He hands me one.

"Drink."

It isn't a question, and as I lift the glass to my mouth, the smell hits me. Whatever it is, I'm pretty sure I could power a rocket to space on it. But there's no question about just sipping at it, and instead, I toss it back, praying that I've got enough 'power smoothie' left in my stomach and bloodstream so as to not make me piss-drunk in about two minutes. It burns hotly down my throat, but I force the gasp down.

Karakov smirks as he drinks his own vodka easily, then sets the bottle aside. "You hurt my Mia."

I nod, clearing my throat before I can speak. "I did, sir."

"My only daughter, who is more precious than the world to me," Karakova continues. "A young woman for whom I'd burn the world down."

"I did. And I'm sorry, sir," I reply honestly. "But I want to be clear that I never raised a hand to her, would never."

Karakov hums and stares at me from across the kitchen counter. "My daughter . . . she says the video was not the total truth?"

"No, sir. Though I did lose my temper, even in my rage, she was not in danger. But in her fear, she bumped into the door herself. I feel awful that happened, even if it was not my direct doing. It was still my fault for scaring her."

"I see. And she says you love her?"

I nod, blinking as the alcohol starts to hit. Jesus, what was that stuff, a hundred and fifty proof? "I do, sir. I know that I'm an asshole. But I'm working on being better for her. I'm not worthy of Mia's love yet. She is a pure and beautiful heart. And maybe that . . . maybe that's why I love her so much."

"Why?"

"Because if there's any hope for me," I reply, the words coming easier, probably due to the vodka, "any chance that I can be a good man and not the beast that I've become, it's her. When I'm with her, I see an end to the pain. I see a future. I see happiness."

"And if you're wrong? If you can't change?"

"I know I can. I won't fail. Because a single smile from her is all the strength I need to overcome anything."

Mr. Karakov nods, his eyes still icy cold. "When Mia's mother left us, I promised myself that I would give her the love of two parents. From what she has told me, when your mother left you, the exact opposite may have happened. You haven't been shown how to love properly."

"You might be right, sir. But with Mia, it feels natural. I don't think I need to be taught. And if I do, rest assured that the woman you've raised will set me straight."

He grins, pouring another two fingers of vodka into our glasses and raising his toward me. "It won't be easy. You'll make mistakes. Every man does, because a woman is a mystery that time, wisdom, and all the efforts of men to decipher have utterly failed at throughout history. But I believe you will still try, because that is what love is.

And you will love my daughter with all your heart, or you will walk away now."

It's a threat wrapped up in an expectation. Something I'm familiar with, but something tells me Vladimir's follow-through would be different from my father's.

I agree, nodding gravely. "Yes, sir."

Karakov smiles. "Then you have my blessing. You're a lucky man, Thomas Goldstone. Mother Russia may be harsh, but Papas . . . we are harsher when it comes to our daughters. Now drink!"

I pick up my glass, sniffing before setting it down. "Forgive me, no disrespect, but I'm pretty sure this is rocket fuel, and I haven't eaten much the past three days. This is probably not the best idea and I'm trying to make smarter choices."

"Oh, but that's when the vodka is best," Karakova says with a soft laugh. "But I understand. Stay for dinner then?"

I nod, grateful as Karakov, I guess I need to start thinking about him as Vladimir, leads me over to the couch. "It'll be nice to have a dinner guest," he confides softly as I sit down and he comes over with a packet of Ritz crackers. It's simple, but right now, they taste delicious on my suddenly ravenous tongue.

Vladimir smiles. "For three days now, the only thing I've been able to get Mia to talk about are her animations and her two girlfriends. That and her data . . . always data with her. Though I understand none of it. But you sit, eat the crackers, and stay for dinner."

~

THE MOON'S ALREADY PASSED ITS ZENITH WHEN I LEAVE VIA THE BACK door of Vladimir's home, adjusting my tie as I do. Thankfully, he didn't insist on any more of that rocket fuel vodka of his, and the world is no longer spinning.

More importantly, though, Mia's with me, and inhaling her scent as I hug her next to my car is all the reassurance that eventually, things will be right between us.

"Thank you," Mia says, wrapping her arms around my waist. "For everything you're doing."

"And thank you for everything you're doing."

It's poignant, both of us having made mistakes, big, ugly ones, but able to still find our way out of the darkness by holding hands and taking it step by step. Together.

"I'd like very much to sweep you off your feet right now, carry you back to my place, and make love to you," I tell her, holding her tight, "but I feel like we need to work our way back to that. Like I need to earn you back."

Mia smiles and gives me a kiss on the cheek. "You already have my love. As for my body . . . you're right. We both need to work back to that, earn each other. And we'll both be rewarded. I'll see you at work tomorrow."

"It's a date," I say with a wink, feeling better than I have in days.

CHAPTER 38

MIA

It feels comfortable back in my office at work after the few days off. And I thankfully get to bury myself in numbers and figures and data. It's my dream come true, except all my reports have been crunching away without me, and now I have mountains of results to analyze.

Today is my first day back, and when I walk into Bill's office this morning, I expect him to chastise me for falling prey to Thomas's charms. But he simply looks up and smiles, welcoming me back with barely a mention of the mess even though I know it left him in the lurch.

"Hey! The gauntlet outside let you through? I got screamed at. I haven't been called so many nasty things since high school homecoming."

"Homecoming?"

"Short version? Rivalry game, star quarterback, smack talk," Bill says. "But seriously, you okay?"

"Once they realized who I am, it shocked the hell out of them. Some of them yelled at me for being weak, while others seem to have grabbed their ball and gone home," I reply, shrugging. "Whatever. Just leave me alone, you know?"

Bill chuckles and stands up, offering his hand. "Welcome back then. To be honest, it's been too damn boring around here without you. I even missed your loud music, though I'll deny it if HR gets another complaint about the volume. Only thing I'll say about this whole issue is that if anyone gives you any flak at all, you tell me. I'll be the one handing out ass kickings and name takings." He lowers his voice, looking toward the door, "And that includes the boss man, Mia. I won't stand for any of my people to be mistreated. He's a lot to handle and fairly fucked in the head, judging by what I saw. You deserve better."

I shake my head. "No, it's not like that."

He lifts a brow, shrugging. "If you say so." I can tell he's not convinced. "Anyway, back to what we do best, data analysis. Go crunch those numbers. Your machine's been beeping like crazy."

He's right, and it takes me several days to get close to being caught up, and that's mostly on the resort figures because I missed a project team meeting in my absence. Finally, I'm starting to have time to split my attentions, getting pulled back to the saboteur puzzle again and again.

But the work has been a great focal point for my days and I feel like things are getting pretty much back to normal after almost two weeks back. I mean, I've yet to go with Thomas upstairs to his penthouse again, but I don't see it as our taking a step back. We've both acknowledged that our feelings for each other haven't changed.

Simply put, I still love him.

And he still loves me.

We hashed that part out the first weekend after I decided to come back on one of our dates. He and I sat at one of those Brazilian steakhouses for hours, mostly because they never give you shit about not leaving, especially when Thomas plunked an extra hundred-dollar bill under his red button the second time the guy with the skewer of beef came around and saw we were talking more than eating.

But with our conversation, I'm surprised I ate even a bite.

"After my mother died . . . well, I told you how my father was," Thomas says, looking about a thousand percent better than he did yesterday. *It's shocking what a decent night's sleep will do for a man. "But I didn't tell you about the voice."*

"The voice?" I ask, still at that point chewing a little bit of picanha. *Maybe I'd been skipping some meals recently too.*

"It first started in junior high school, but it really ramped when I left home to go to college," Thomas says, nibbling at his own sirloin. "It's Dennis's voice . . . and he's just as vicious in my head as he is in real life. Maybe even more so. A bit ironic that when I finally got out on my own, that's when his grip got tightest and he didn't even realize it. He'd just brainwashed me over the years to the point where I didn't even need the real deal anymore."

"That's a heavy weight to carry around in your head," I admit. "I mean, we all talk to ourselves in some way or another but . . . I'm guessing this wasn't rare?"

Thomas shakes his head. "It's like a constant presence on my shoulder, just instead of protecting me or encouraging me like an angel, it's the devil telling me that I'm going to fail, that I'm going to fuck it up. So many times, when people are thinking I'm pissed at them, it's not so much them but me getting angry at hearing my father's voice in my head, and they're just the unfortunate recipient of the cruelty."

I nod and take a sip of tea. "Is that why you actually tried with that, what was her name?"

"Dr. Perry," Thomas says, nodding. "Who, by the way, has already called me, trying to get me to go see her again."

"And are you going to see her?" I'm not going to push him. I've learned my lesson painfully, but I still think a bit of guided processing wouldn't hurt with the book of wrongs Thomas is hauling around.

"No, but I am going to see another therapist. One I can trust, and one who understands me. But I'll find someone who can help. Someone other than you."

"Fair enough. I'll take those times to go hang out with the girls or something," I tease. "Maybe I'll join a Zumba class or hot yoga, work off some of my own stress as well."

"You can always use my place," Thomas offers. "It'd be nice to see someone using that gym as a joy and not a burden."

He tells me about the night he nearly passed out under the squat bar, and that's it for dinner for me. "Tommy . . . the voice pushes you that hard?"

He nods, rubbing at his cheeks. "There was only one thing, before you, that made me feel better. It was . . ."

His voice trails off, and he sighs. I set my drink down and reach across the table, taking his admittedly slightly sticky barbecue sauce-stained fingers. "You can tell me. I'm not going to judge anything you say. I'm here for you, and I love you."

Thomas nods and swallows, and I wait for him to drop some awful huge bomb on me. Drugs, hookers, illegal underground fighting. Okay, that's a reach, but . . .

He shifts in his seat, only making me more nervous. We've conquered so much already. He'd shared such deep things. What could make him this twitchy?

"Okay. Well, I am . . . him."

"Him?" I ask, utterly confused, though he clearly thinks the words have meaning.

What does he mean? The man for me? Duh, I've kinda figured that out. But what's the coping mechanism he's hiding?

He nods and looks up. "I was trying to find some way to quiet the voice. It kept saying all these awful things, and one night, sitting in the dark with just my thoughts, it started in like usual. But that night, I'd been to one of those corporate gala things, just a stupid reason for rich people to get dressed up and feel like they were doing something good while eating fancy food and drinking champagne. And I'd given a check like every other bastard in the room. So when the voice started in, I talked back, like the check had been this major thing. But it helped. Even though I knew the charity probably overpaid its director, and only a portion of the funds went to those who needed them, it helped me. So I did it again."

I nod, not quite getting it. "Okay, charitable giving is a good thing. Unless you're giving away everything you have? Are you telling me you've donated so much you're poor now? Because I'd love you even if you were penniless."

"No, that's not what I'm saying. I'm saying that I'm him. *The White Knight. Maybe I'm partially doing it for selfish reasons, but I keep telling myself that at least it's doing some good, right?"*

And everything started to make sense. Of course he is . . . he was robbed of his childhood, of attention and affection, and so he gives of himself to those who have nothing.

I hug him so hard, right there in the middle of the restaurant. "I knew you were a good man. I mean, I already knew, but this clinches it. My Ruthless Bastard. My White Knight. Why is this some huge secret though? I mean, this is a good thing."

He smiles, looking bashful. "I know, but that's why no one knows. I want the kids to think I'm doing it because I care about them, not some award. I have the people I help, the ones I support, but there are no PR photoshoots exploiting those in need. Just quiet, direct help."

I smile at the memory, warm bubbles rising in my belly, and if I was one of my anime characters, I'd probably have big pink heart eyes right now. My computer dings, breaking my happy buzz.

After a spin in my chair, legs kicking wildly, I focus on the finished report. It'd occurred to me yesterday that I needed to run a specified filter on the card access and see who'd been on the twenty-fifth floor the afternoon everything had gone to shit. Someone there had filmed that video and the suspect pool has to be rather small. Honestly, I was pretty pissed at myself for not thinking of this sooner, but I'd let myself off the hook since I'd been wallowing in the pits of despair, then buried in backlogged data, neither putting me at my best analytical skill level.

I scan through the report, line by line, moving a few folks to my *Look Into* list and dismissing others. After more than an hour, my suspicions are narrowing down.

Uncomfortably. These are people I work with, chat with over lunch, and see on a daily basis.

I turn to my secondary monitor, looking at the list of projects I'd been concerned about before my impromptu vacation, looking for cross-references and connections. And time and time again, my list gets shorter.

Nathan Billington had been on the twenty-fifth floor, a peculiarity for him since he offices on sixteen. But the project data doesn't pan out.

Kym Jenkins is an admin who frequently works on twenty-five, so her presence is logical, but she also served as an assistant on three of the five most suspect projects.

Randall Towlee wasn't on twenty-five at all, but he's been on all but one of the concerned project teams. Technically, I should mark him off the suspect list, and the rational side of my brain almost does it, but my gut roils. He doesn't fit the parameters, but something about him just makes my Scooby senses tingle, so I go ahead and put him on the short list with an asterisk to note that he's an outlier and an unlikely suspect.

I go through several others, and though I hate the answer, I'm pretty sure I know who is sabotaging Thomas. I double-check and then triple-check, even diving into the server files. I need to be sure because I'm about to accuse someone of some rather serious charges. Like felonious. And I don't want to make a mistake. I need to proceed with caution.

But everything I see, it all points in one direction. I save it to my personal hard drive, eschewing the network server, and put another copy on a flash drive, not wanting to take any chances. I feel a little like Sherlock, truth be told, but where he was this fictional brilliant badass, I'm just me. And the trip to the elevator and upstairs feels riskier than ever.

My heart is racing, my faced flushed when I get out on the twenty-fifth floor. I even look up and down the hall, feeling like there are eyes on me. Truthfully, there probably have been since I haven't been back that long, and the gossip mill is still churning inhouse, even if the media has found bigger fish to fry.

But twenty-five is its normal deserted self, and I finally get to Thomas's office and Kerry looks up. "Mia, are you okay? You look as pale as a ghost."

I shake my head, keeping my voice low. "No, I need to see Thomas." I quickstep across the room, heading for his doors, but Kerry calls out.

"He's with someone right now."

Shit. Too late, I've already opened the door and interrupted. Thomas stands when he sees me, worry instantly etching his face. "Mia? What's wrong?"

CHAPTER 39

*M*y door opens, interrupting my meeting, but when I see Mia's face, I know it's for a good reason. Or a bad reason, judging by the complete lack of color in her cheeks. "Mia? What's wrong?"

I ask the question, uncertain if I want to know the answer because I'm not sure I can handle anything else today. Normally, that'd make me feel like an absolute weakling to admit, even to myself. Hell, *mostly* to myself and my demon. But it's noticeably quiet, and I'm a bit emotionally spent. Understandable, I suppose, after my morning session with my new therapist had drained so much out of me.

Dr. Culvington has helped me make some rather quick strides in just a few appointments. He's a former military guy and suffers from PTSD, and the help he received led him to become a therapist himself. His approach today was pretty aggressive too, which suits me.

"Okay, Thomas. Give me the basics of what you know is fucked up and we'll go from there."

"Uh, I don't usually . . ." His eagle eye had glared at me, making me feel like I was in boot camp and my choices were pushups or spilling my guts. While the pushups sounded easier, that was exactly the point, so I took a big breath and went the harder route. *"Mom cheated and killed herself while I watched cartoons in the other room, Dad lost his shit, abused me my whole life, I worked my ass off in spite of him, not to spite him. Got my degree and*

started a successful company, but his voice is in my ear, still beating me down at every opportunity. I need it to shut the fuck up. I want to be better. There's a woman. I love her."

I'd never summarized everything that succinctly before, and when Dr. Culvington had smiled, I felt like I'd already accomplished something. And ever since, we've been making strides. He knows about voices, said he had a few of his own too after a rough tour, so he's taught me some helpful tricks for shutting them up. Mostly, to ignore them as much as possible to lessen their influence, challenge with positive messages, and while it makes me feel silly, to actively praise myself in my head. The awkward 'atta-boys' are weird as hell, but Culvington says I need to create a new methodology for my inner monologue, give it new messages to repeat.

The memory helps me gird my mental loins, so to speak, so that when my inner voice pops up upon seeing Mia's face, I'm ready for it.

I don't like him.

For a moment, I'm almost intimidated again, but I can hear it now, the notes of petulance and fear in that voice . . . the voice of a father who blames me for his failures.

Fuck off. I like Dr. Culvington, I tell the voice.

You can't handle whatever Mia is about to say. She's leaving your worthless ass and you're going to explode again, hurt her again.

I force the breath into my lungs, filling them slowly and carefully as I refute that and let it go, secure that Mia and I have withstood trials and will handle whatever is wrong now.

She rushes to me, shocking me as she hugs me tightly. Not that I'm surprised she's doing it, but that she's doing so in front of an unknown guest in my office. We've been decidedly careful about who sees any of our PDA. But I know who he is, so I hug her back, rubbing the knotted muscles along her spine. My heart thumps as she whispers in my ear.

"I know who's doing it. Get him out of here. We need to talk. Now."

I look down in alarm, my heart thumping for a whole new reason. "You know?"

She nods, and I see the certainty in her eyes but also pain. "Mia Karakova, let me introduce you to John Smithson of Smithson Security. He was just about to share with me what he's found about the video, but perhaps you can share with us first?"

She shakes his hand but then looks at me sharply, silently questioning me if I want to air our company laundry this way. But I brought John in on this personally, and he's had his team examining the video's cyber-footprint as carefully as the FBI itself would.

She sees the answer in my eyes and goes over to my laptop, clicking some buttons as I sit down, giving her some space to work. "I need to remove any server access for this."

"It's all protected so that no one can get into my work. Shouldn't that suffice?"

She shakes her head, talking into the monitor as she focuses. "Better safe than sorry. Easier in the old days when I could just yank the fiber line. So here's what I found."

She's pulled up two files, splitting the screen into rows of data that make zero sense to me, but John leans forward, eyes scanning left to right, back and forth. He's got a background in cyber security and can probably see what Mia's saying faster than I can.

Mia paces as she speaks, like she needs the physical movement for her brain to function best. "I've been running data checks on unexpectedly low-performing projects like you told me to look into. I've identified several of interest," she says, pointing at the left side of the screen. "There are others, but these seemed the most obvious outliers, where the profit margins or the way the project played out made the least sense. Like the Chinese buying the aircraft parts company. So, I had these, but the overlap between players, project team members, departments involved, et cetera, was just too big. And then I had a thought."

"What?" I feel like this is her big build-up moment, but I'm eager to hear the results. "What'd you do to whittle it down?"

"Uhm, this isn't exactly legit, and you didn't ask me to go this far, be this intrusive, but I hope you'll think the result is worth it." I narrow my eyes at her, but John smirks as if he approves of whatever she's done even before she explains. "Okay, so I thought weeks ago that it might be helpful to track people's movements inside the company, both electronic and physical. I was hoping I might find some trend in someone being in the server files where they shouldn't be, on a floor they shouldn't be, or just weird comings and goings."

She looks at me, a slight blush to her cheeks. "I swear, I'm not some stage-five clinger, Tommy. I wasn't just tracking you. I was tracking . . . everyone."

I feign a mad look, then wink. "Stalker," I say. "Besides, maybe I'm one of those split-personality types."

John misses the wink and only heard my rough voice, so he comes to Mia's defense and corrects me. "Security."

He looks up, recognizing he's missed something, and realizes we're sharing a private joke. "Can we get back to what you've found?"

Reminded of why she's here, Mia resumes her pacing. "Yeah, of course. So, I've had that algorithm running for weeks, compiling loads of data. It's like freakin' terabytes worth. But then I realized, I didn't need to know about weird floor access six months ago. I only needed to know who—"

John interrupts, "Who was on the twenty-fifth floor to record the video that one day." Mia nods, and I can see that she's pleased John understands where she's going. "So, did you figure it out? Who was here?"

Mia gulps. "I did. But not only that. I got the list of who was on the floor that day, tracked if they'd exited and not returned, like Kerry. That gave me a shorter list of who was on the floor. But then I took that data and cross-referenced it with the project lists to see if anyone was on both lists. There were several, and I've been whittling them down, trying to figure it out."

She bites her lip, tears springing to her eyes. "It's Bill Radcliffe, my boss."

I search through everything I know about the man. Former military, has worked for me for years, took a move a few years ago, said he needed less stress and more nights at home with his family, but that's all I've got. He's just not a big blip on my radar.

Honestly, the move downstairs is the only thing I remember because it was unusual. Most people who can't cut it just move to another company. I normally even give them a letter of recommendation when they do.

"What? Why? Are you sure?" I ramble, not really questioning Mia's work, because I know it's above reproach, but just trying to make sense of it.

She nods, sighing. "I'm sure. I realized I was going about the project search wrong. It wasn't the team members themselves who were the biggest suspect pool. It was who had access to the data. Bill filters every bit of data through himself as a supervisory measure for those he manages. He didn't have to be on the project team. He could tweak the data itself to whatever he wanted. I found some server accesses that don't make sense, but I suspect he's running something sneakier to change the data. But that's beyond my cyber skills. I'm an analyst, not a security specialist."

I sag back in my chair, and Mia rushes over to sit in my lap. We hold each other for a moment. "I thought this was going to make me feel better, an answer to the puzzle, but this feels like shit," she says quietly, and I realize just how much Bill's actions have hurt her.

"I thought I was going to be mad as hell, rush out to kill someone or at least ream them, and I do want to do that, but mostly, I just feel confused," I admit.

John clears his throat, drawing our attention. "Not to hit pause on your pity party or anything, but I've got some info too." He looks to Mia, his eyes admiring. "First off, I'd like to say good work. The algorithms you thought to run, the data you slogged through, quite brilliant. And if you ever want to leave Goldstone, leave the corporate drudge and mill grinding behind, I'd have a place for you at Smithson."

I growl dangerously at him, holding tighter to Mia. "Over my dead body."

Mia pats my chest, chuckling. "Down, boy. Thank you, Mr. Smithson. But I'm good right where I am."

He shrugs like I'm not about to rip his head from his body. Okay, I'm probably not because then I'd have to set Mia down, and I rather like her in my lap, patting me. But I still give him a harsh glare. We've been professional acquaintances for years, but I can always find another security firm if need be.

"I suspected as much, but I had to extend the offer. Just business, you know?" He looks at me, not apologetic but as if to say *you'd do the same thing.* "So, I took a different approach to your issue, focusing on the video itself because most people aren't tech savvy enough to erase all the markers. Actually, most people don't even realize there are data markers on every picture and video you take with your phone. First, I had to get the video. No small feat because the media was not interested in sharing their source, no surprise there, and copied versions off the Internet did me no good. Let's just say it took some work, but I got the original file and the email of where it was sent from."

I don't know what John had to do to get that access, and I suspect he wouldn't tell me even if I asked, but I trust he did it willingly and smartly. That's why he charges the exorbitant rates he does, because he's good at his job and goes all in for his clients.

"Once I had the info, I had my guys check it out. For your protection and mine, I won't share how we do that, but I tracked the phone back to one owned by Goldstone itself. It's in my report. I assume you can match that up with your records. The email was a blank account, basically the online equivalent of a burner phone, but from the metadata, I got the IP address as well. I think between what I have and what Ms. Karakova has found, it's pretty damning evidence. Prosecution might be a reach because explaining this to most juries is a crapshoot, but it's definitely enough for termination of employment and likely a civil suit."

John sets a plastic-coated folder on my desk, sliding it toward me. "Here's everything I have. Let me know if you need anything further, on this or anything else."

With a handshake, he's gone, and it's just Mia and me.

"What are we going to do?" Mia asks. "I'm in over my head here. I did the data work, but I don't usually have this much invested in the results and what you do with them. But this time, I do. I just don't understand why he'd do this."

I squeeze her tightly, using her body to ground me and keep me from charging downstairs like a raging bull.

"You know, part of me wanted it to be Randall Towlee," I growl lightly. "Since that thing in Portland-"

"I know," Mia whispers. "He's a jerk . . . but there's a difference between being a jerk and being a traitor."

Surprisingly, the urge to charge down at Bill, while definitely present, is something I can stave off. As long as Mia's with me, I have that inch of control I need. But distance is probably a good idea until I work out just what I'm going to do with all this information.

"Let's get out of here for a bit. Go to lunch or something."

"Upstairs?" Mia asks, her voice soft and silky.

I press my lips to her forehead sweetly and grind my cock against her ass roughly as I groan. "Fuck, Mia. I want nothing more than to take you upstairs and use you to make all this go away. Just lose myself in your pussy and pretend none of this exists. But I can't. I won't use you that way. Not for our first time taking it back to that level. When we go there, I want it to be just the two of us. No drama, no voices, just you and me."

She cups my jaw in her hand, looking up into my eyes. "You're a good man, Thomas Goldstone."

And another jagged piece of my soul sears over, the glass heating and reforming solid and whole. She is going to burn me to ash, but I want it because she's putting me back together bit by bit with her love.

She pops off my lap, pulling me to stand beside her. "Come on, I know just what you need. We're going to The Gravy Train and you're getting the biggest, greasiest burger they have, a whole plate of fries, and a milkshake. It's thinking food, and we're gonna think this whole shit show through and figure it out piece by piece, analyze the fuck out of it. Because Bill might have thought he was fucking with Goldstone, but he's fucking with my man. And Russian women, we don't put up with that shit."

She fake spits on the floor and mutters something, and in that moment, she is utterly beautiful. In all her weird streaky-haired, Russian-spouting, anime-loving, videogame-playing, metal-music-blaring, healing angel, avenging demon ways. I love this woman, and I will do whatever it takes to be worthy of the love she gives back to me so freely.

CHAPTER 40

IZZY

I set a refill down on table six, taking a deep breath and schooling my face. How in the hell did I get myself involved in this? Oh, yeah, Mia. Of course. That girl could get me to do just about anything and definitely has over the years.

We've joked that we're each other's 'bury the body' friend. You know, the one you call when you accidentally-on purpose kill your cheating SOB of a boyfriend, and when you call them, they show up with a shovel and the gasoline? Yeah, *that* kind of friend, so this shouldn't be too bad.

In theory. At least that what Mia and Thomas had said.

"You two okay? Looks like somebody pissed in your Post Toasties. And just to be clear, I would never do that to a customer's food," I say with a smile, hoping to get a returning one from Mia at least. I don't know what it'd take to make stone-faced Thomas smile, but Mia's easy game.

"Not really, Izz. Just some work stuff that's hard and sad and infuriating and all the emotions rolled into one, basically." She sighs and reaches for Thomas's hand, comforting him as he returns her sigh.

Okay, tough crowd.

I pour their coffee. "Anything I can do to help? I mean, I'm no corporate genius, but the chocolate cake has solved some pretty serious problems before, especially with a scoop of vanilla ice cream on the side. Free of charge,

293

of course. Benefits of friendship." I frame my face with my free hand, high-lighting the awesomeness Mia gets by being my friend.

"Actually, yes. Cake for lunch is just what we need. It won't solve a damn thing, but I could go for some feeling stuffing right about now," Mia says.

I plop a shareable slice on a dinner plate—no little side plates for my girl— and then add two scoops plus a drizzle of chocolate syrup. Feeling stuffing, coming right up. I've got you.

I set it down between them, interrupting.

" . . . understand why Bill would do something like this?" Mia says.

I can't help it, I hear everything that goes on in this place. It's like tying an apron on makes people forget you're human and they basically ignore you until they need something. Mia's not like that, but I can't help what I overheard.

"Bill? As in your boss, Bill? He comes in here often. Eats quick and leaves, not much for conversation. BLT with double bacon, onion rings, and Diet Coke, like that makes a damn bit of difference with that meal. Nice guy, though, tips me a fiver every time. What'd he do?"

Two sets of eyes turn to me, and Thomas says, "You know Bill Radcliffe from Goldstone?"

"I don't know him, know him. But I know lots of people from Goldstone. We're the best diner around, you know that," I reply with pride and not a bit of sarcasm. It's the absolute truth.

Thomas looks at Mia with an expression I can't read, not that I could begin to read him in the first place. But apparently, Mia can because they start some whole silent conversation with just their eyes and I excuse myself from their weirdness to go serve my other tables.

I return a few minutes later, and Mia asks me if I'll do her a 'small favor'.

This right here, this madness is no small favor. *But I'd do anything for Mia,* I remind myself. I give Elaine a wink, letting her know that I'm about to start my weirdness. I'd had to tell her I was doing something for Mia so that she wouldn't think I'd lost my marbles when this whole farce starts. The door opens, and Bill comes in, heading straight for his usual seat at table ten, right by the window.

I pinch my thigh hard so that tears spring to my eyes and think about those commercials with sad-eyed puppies in the rain, begging for your thirty cents a day. It works, and I get a good cry on before I approach Bill's table.

"Hey, Bill. How're you tonight? The usual?" I say, my voice flatter than Henry's pancakes. Actually, our cook and part-owner, Henry, makes great pancakes. So maybe that's not the best description. Flatter than my Grandma Sue's pancakes. That woman could make frisbees out of food.

"Yeah, that'd be great," he replies, and then he looks up at me. "Shit, you okay, Izzy?"

I swipe a tear from beneath my eye and glower at the window to the kitchen. "Yeah, I'm fine. Henry's just being an ass and it's making for a rough night. I'll get your order in. Maybe the King will deign himself to cook without bitching me out this time." The lie flows off my tongue as slick as turpentine. Henry's a great guy and a great boss, but that truth doesn't serve Mia's purpose.

I place Bill's order and return with his Diet Coke while the food's cooking. Like the heavens part and sing down praises on this ridiculous plan, Henry looks into the dining room and calls out.

"Izzy, fries up, girl. Show some hustle." He's not even in on the plan. His words are meant to be fun and just a part of our camaraderie, but they play right into Mia's evil hands and my twisted luck.

Grabbing the fries, I deliver them to table nine and scoot past Bill's table. A little more attention tonight, nothing too crazy as to raise his suspicions.

He tells me, "Chin up, Izzy. You're doing well."

I sniffle and offer a watery smile.

I grab Bill's food and deliver it to his table with an eyeroll that'd make a teenage girl proud. "Oh, my gosh, he's such a bear tonight. Of course, I might've had a little something to do with that," I say, holding up my finger and thumb an inch apart.

As I hoped, Bill raises his brows. "How's that?"

I glance over my shoulder at Henry and hunch down a little, whispering, "So just between us, Henry is like the biggest, absolute worst caffeine addict in the world. Buys this fancy ground coffee, blah, blah, blah special roast. So when he's giving me an extra-hard time, I offer to make him a pot. Out of the kindness of my heart, you know?"

I add a bit of devilment to my voice and then smirk. "And then he drinks that all night long. What he doesn't know? I don't make his fancy high-octane coffee. Nope, I use grocery store stuff, the cheapest swill I can find. And it's *decaf.*" I say the word like it's poison.

And then I slap my hand over my mouth like I just told state's secrets to the mob, horror taking my expression. "Oh, my God, don't tell him about that. Please, Bill. He'd fire me in a heartbeat. I don't know why I told you that." I look over my shoulder at Henry, who's oblivious to his usefulness in this plan.

Bill chuckles. "No big deal, Izzy. I won't tell. Though you'd better make sure my coffee is the good stuff."

My eyes widen. "Really? You won't say anything? You're a lifesaver. Thank you. I'd get tossed out of here in the middle of dinner service if he found out."

I don't want to lay it on too thickly, but it's my big play, the breath-holding moment in all this charade.

Bill is still laughing. "Really. We all do it to asshole bosses who deserve it. A little decaf here, a little fudged number there. It's no biggie."

I sigh in relief at the flippant share, but I want to really make sure the screw is tight. "That's right, you're a numbers guy. You'd really do that? I'm not a horrible person for getting a little revenge?" I hang my head ashamedly.

He shakes his head. "We all do it in some way. One little slip as I'm typing, and oops, that four becomes a five."

I look up in hope, like his casual comment makes me feel so much better. Then I shake my whole body like I'm letting go of the worry and smile sweetly.

"Thanks, Bill. I needed that. You know what you get today?" I point at the counter with my thumb. "One of our pieces of chocolate cake, on the house. Consider it 'hush cake', and hell, I guess I'd better go make a pot of coffee too. You want some? Caffeinated, I promise. And the good stuff."

"Sure, coffee and cake to go, please."

Minutes after Bill's left, a guy named John comes over and casually pops the bug off the bottom of the table. If I hadn't watched him put it there earlier, I would've been none the wiser. He gives me a subtle nod and is gone.

Operation Spy Izzy: success.

I think I'll get a slice of cake for myself too.

CHAPTER 41

THOMAS

*N*ot every floor of the Goldstone Building is strictly meant for business. In fact, most of the ground floor is open to the public, including tonight's room, the large 'atrium' that can, and has been, rented out for large gatherings.

But tonight, it's strictly for Goldstone purposes, and it's a perfect setup, fun for almost everyone.

Except Bill Radcliffe.

"Thomas?"

I turn around, once again floored at the sight before me. Since we said we love each other again, Mia and I have not spent a night together, ironically. We've shared time during our days and have spent hours over long talks, but that's it. Step by step, bit by bit, better for her, better with her.

The physical piece of it will factor back in soon, and we can hopefully stop our torturous nights of phone calls where we invariably end up hanging up with fantasies roaring in my mind and my cock hard throughout the next two hours.

It's not enough, not nearly, but it's giving us time, and I've got a long and rather creative to-do list of ideas once she gives me the go-ahead. I'm hoping that's tonight, but if not, I'll wait as long as she wants to. Because she's already earned her way back into my good graces, my healing heart, and my soothed soul.

I'm not sure she ever really left, even when I was so hurt and angry, but either way, she owns me completely now. I just want to own her heart again too.

I walk over to her, taking her hand and twirling her around so I can get a better look. Her black gown is satin, hugging her curves sexily, and it's apparently a Vladimir Karakov original. Not bad for a man who says he's just a tailor who specializes in menswear.

But the piece de resistance is the under-layer of the skirt that flashes Barbie pink with her every step and matches the two inches of pink she's added to the bottom of her hair.

"You are stunning. I'm going to be the luckiest man in the room tonight."

She presses her free hand down her dress, smoothing invisible wrinkles, grinning. "Pshh, you're going to be the luckiest man in Roseboro tonight. Not because I can fill out a dress, though Damien and Papa really outdid themselves, but because this mess is finally going to all be over."

I don't want to talk about that right now. I'm a little nervous that everything won't play out as intended, especially with John still handling some last-minute details. I'd wanted to be there for that, but Stan said he'd handle it and John had agreed.

You'd fuck it up. You always do.

"It's going to be fine," I tell myself and Mia. "But let's not jinx it. Shall we?" I offer my arm, and we take the elevator down.

The party's in full swing already, our fashionably late entrance having just the right firework that I'd intended. People clap lightly, and I wave as Mia holds onto my arm for dear life, even though she's surrounded by friends and coworkers.

Or maybe that's why. It's easier to fake it when you just have strangers around you. It makes it different from the charity event in Portland, and besides, there's an air of something potent in the room tonight.

We work our way through the space, small talk here and even a few photos there. Apparently, some of the workers actually do like me . . . or more likely, they realize Mia's stunning.

Kerry signals me, and I make my way to the stage, taking the microphone the DJ hands me.

"Excuse me, if I could have everyone's attention, please?"

Conversation dies down as eyes turn my way. I meet Mia's eyes, gaining the strength I need to say the things I'm about to say.

She blows me a kiss and offers a thumbs-up with a big grin.

"First, I want to say thank you for coming tonight. I know it's been a rough couple of weeks for us, both Goldstone the company and Goldstone the man," I say, pointing over the crowd and then to myself. "But I appreciate your taking the time to come tonight."

There's a polite applause, more out of expectation than enthusiasm, which is understandable. Nobody likes an executive who gets up on the mic and makes it all about himself. Especially if it's a pity party.

"I've been the cause of a lot of concern and some media coverage, and you've paid the price for that along with me. And for that, I'm sorry. I said it in the press conference, but I'm saying it again. Profits don't mean much when they don't consider the people who produce them. And the simple fact is, I've spent too much time over the past six years thinking I had to put all of you on my back to drag this company up the hill. But the reality is, you are the hill, and I'm standing on the shoulders of giants. The giants who work on every floor, every day, busting your ass and not getting credit beyond a quarterly bonus from time to time."

I can see heads nodding and some surprise that I'm being so harsh about how I've run the company, but it's the truth. And I can see that now.

"But that's going to change. It's already changing, and I hope that you can feel that, in the building, in your departments, and in your dealings with me. We have some changes still to make, but it's going to be a new era at Goldstone, starting fresh tonight. I'm still going to ask each of you to give your best, but I'm also going to give you *my* best. And if I don't, I'm sure there's a smart Russian woman who will put me in my place."

I wink at Mia and the crowd laughs. "I watched a cartoon this week," I start.

Mia calls out loudly, "It's not a cartoon! It's anime!"

I grin and conspiratorially tell the audience, "I like to tease her, but I know the difference. God help me, I know the difference between a cartoon and an anime." Everyone laughs again as I look heavenward. "So I watched anime this week, and something resonated with me. It said, 'Don't ask for it, go out and earn it. Do that, and you'll be rewarded.' And that's what I want to do, and what I want you to do. Let's earn our way into making Goldstone the best it can be. We can reach that reward together. Thank you."

The applause starts quietly, and I'm surprised as it grows organically. Leaving the podium, I make my way through the crowd to Mia and take her in my arms.

"How'd I do?"

She smiles, kissing my cheek. "You did excellent."

More rounds of the room follow, and while everyone seems rather accepting of our relationship, especially considering the long weeks that have given time for the shock to wear off, there are still quite a few looky-loos. There are even some faces that let me know not everyone is pleased.

Before, I would've taken that challenge head-on, calling them out for daring to so much as have an opinion about who I keep company with. In fact, recalling one such board meeting, I cringe but then consider just how far I've come and decide the progress is worth celebrating.

Ironically, it's Stan who approaches me as I think back to that meeting and then the one afterward in my office. He'd been correct in his advice, and I think I've followed it in a round-about, messy way.

"Thomas, if you'll come with me. They want to run everything by you one last time."

I nod and start to follow, bringing Mia with me. I need her with me every step of the way on this because I know how hard this is for her. Bill has been a great boss while she's worked for him, and she's told me how hurt she is that he'd do something like this. She's a by-the-book, solve-the-puzzle type, and no matter which way you twist and turn this, Bill's actions just don't make sense. And that's eating at her, slowly but surely.

This needs to be over, for her as much as for me.

But she pulls back. I turn, questioning, "Mia?"

She swallows thickly, keeping her voice low. "I know this is happening, and I want it to happen. This needs to be made right. But while you do your last check, I think I'll go ask Bill to dance. One last time."

I cup her jaw, looking in her eyes. "Are you sure? If you say the word, I'll let it go. I have to fire him, but it doesn't have to be this way." I gesture to the full room around us.

She shakes her head and squares her shoulders. "No, this can't be hidden in the shadows like he's been doing. He needs to be called on the carpet, but not put on blast. And you need to show that you have the utmost control, of the company and yourself. This is where the fresh start begins, with you showing that you're better now."

I press my lips together and nod. "I'll be right back."

I walk out with Stan but glance back over my shoulder to see Mia smiling sadly as Bill sways her back and forth.

In the hallway, John is waiting for me with the city prosecutor and the police.

"Thomas, they feel like there's enough to proceed with a criminal case if you want to press charges."

I sigh, the moment suddenly real. I'm scared I'm going to lose it when I go back in there and see Bill's face as the accusations fly. Especially if he's confrontational.

You're going to make an utter fool of yourself, just like always. You deserve his fucking with the company. You're going to run it into the ground anyway. Might as well let him get a head start.

I shake my head, refusing to let my voice have the final say. *I run a successful company, with the help of a great team. One team member needs to be removed for wrongful actions of his own doing. This is how I keep the company healthy. I will keep my cool.*

The demon quiets, and I give John and Stan a look before nodding.

"Let's do this."

My entrance into the atrium ignites even more fireworks this time when uniformed officers are following me in. I head for Mia as every eye in the room watches. Her eyes meet mine, no doubt in them, and she steps to my side.

"Bill, these officers are here to arrest you." My voice is steady, calm, belying none of my anger, none of my sadness.

One of the officers moves forward, taking Bill by the arm. "What? What the hell's going on, Thomas?" he yells. "What are the charges?"

The silence from the crowd is shattered as whispers start. I can hear the soft murmurs of 'What's happening?' and 'The Ruthless Bastard strikes again.' But I don't let their words touch me, not now.

"We know you've been changing data, which in turn cost the company millions of dollars among the multiple projects you sabotaged," I reply, making sure my voice carries through the entire atrium. "And we know you were the one who filmed the video and sold the lies that I'd physically hurt Mia."

"I didn't. I wouldn't," he argues, trying to pull away from the officer who clamps down even harder.

"Don't resist or I'll have to cuff you, Mr. Radcliffe," he says quietly. "Don't make me take down a fellow vet."

Mia cries out, her emotions bursting through. "I know you did it! I'm the one who found the proof, Bill. I didn't want to believe it at first. All the files you accessed, you were so careful but not careful enough. And the reporter gave you up. Was the ten thousand worth everything? How could you do that to me?"

Bill's face is red, his breathing ragged. "I didn't do anything to you. This bastard did! He's the one who scared the shit out of you and hit you!"

"Don't do that. He didn't hit me and you know it," Mia argues loudly.

Bill rolls his eyes, huffing. "Fine, I sold the video, but you have nothing on the data manipulation." His smug arrogance as he admits to selling the video sends a shockwave through the room. They know how much hell we all went through because of that—the protestors and media presence, the influx of phone calls, and lost stock margins. A lot of the people in this room own shares of Goldstone, and his actions have hurt everyone.

And with Mia and me both explaining repeatedly that, as crazy as it may sound, she really did run into a door, everyone believes the truth. That one of our own could do something so heinous and use Mia that way doesn't sit right with any of them any better than it did with me.

John holds up his phone and Kerry rushes the microphone over. She's good. I didn't even know he was going to need that, but she's on top of things, as always, anticipating everyone's needs better than should be humanly possible. John holds the mic to the speaker on his phone and Bill's voice fills the room.

"Really. We all do it to asshole bosses who deserve it. A little decaf here, a little fudged number there. It's no biggie . . . we all do it in some way. One little slip as I'm typing, and oops, that four becomes a five."

"How did you . . . that bitch!" Bill rages.

"Why?" Mia cries.

"Why not? I served this country for years! Saw shit that spoiled little brats like him would never understand! All I needed was a little fucking breathing room, a fucking break! Take your foot off my neck a bit, you know? Never once did he even give a shit whether I was okay." He sneers at me. "Not that you care, but I was fine. And ready to move back upstairs. And when I asked to transition back, you know what you said? Absolutely nothing. I emailed you, I left you messages, and you couldn't even be bothered to respond. You trapped me and then left me there to die. Fuck you, Golden Boy!"

The officer hitches Bill up by his arm and starts forcibly leading him out of the room. At first, he's frantically looking for help from others. "Guys, this is wrong. He's the Ruthless Bastard, not me."

But when no one moves to help him, he gets more agitated, exploding at the door just before the police take him out. He turns, yelling, wild-eyed and crazy, "This isn't over!"

The threat hangs in the air, mixing with shock.

This is my moment to lead my people, to do better for them. I take the mic from John. "I'm really sorry you had to witness that tonight. And I will say that I probably have hurt many of you in the past six years. I can only say again that things will change. And I hope with a committed team of people who truly want Goldstone to succeed, we can move forward with the fresh start I spoke of earlier. Regardless of what I've done, Bill has been undermining our team for far too long, and I demand better. Not for me, but for you, the heart and backbone of Goldstone. Please enjoy the party tonight, celebrate the good things we've accomplished, and plan for the greater things we're growing toward. Good night, everyone."

I take Mia's hand and together, we walk into the hall. John and Stan give a quick wrap-up with the city prosecutor, and then they leave as well, promising an update as soon as they have one. In a moment, it's just the two of us.

"How're you holding up, Mr. Goldstone?" Mia asks softly, her hand on my chest.

"Better than expected, Miss Karakova. Though I suspect you have something to do with that." I hug her tightly, laying my cheek on the top of her head.

"Let's go upstairs," Mia whispers, and for a second, I think I imagined it, but when she pulls back and looks at me, I can see it in her eyes. Not just lust, but pride and love.

"Earned it?" I ask, cockiness creeping into my voice.

She laughs, tugging on my tie. "Fuck yeah, you earned it."

I kiss her lips lightly, but the passion is already igniting beneath the surface. "Good, because you earned me back a long time ago. You're a hard sell," I tease.

She adopts her thick accent, humming. "Mother Russia is not easily amused, but I could be courted to your point of view."

I sweep her into my arms and run for the elevator, not able to wait another moment to be inside her.

CHAPTER 42

MIA

*B*y the time the elevator opens twenty-six floors up, my dress is already unzipped and puddling around my waist. I'm sandwiched between Thomas and the wall, our bodies on fire at every connection point. His tongue chases mine, twirling and teasing.

He backs me into his bedroom, and when my knees contact the edge of the bed, I fall back into the soft mattress. He pulls my dress the rest of the way off and then makes quick work of my black bra and panty set too, leaving me bare in my heels while he's fully dressed. It feels decadent and sinful, like he's going to use me, pleasure my body while taking none for himself.

But I want him to get pleasure too. This is us reconnecting, moving to a new level after some really tough challenges.

"Take off your clothes. Let me see you too."

Thomas unbuttons his shirt with deft fingers and flings it off carelessly, but when he slides his belt free from his slacks, he pauses and looks up at me.

I'm already expecting a flirty suggestion about him using the belt to tie me up, but what I'm not expecting are his next words. "Mia, I hurt you and I am so sorry. I feel like there's no way for me to prove to you that I won't lose control like that again. But I think ceding control to you might be a start." He offers me the belt. "It's not . . .

LAUREN LANDISH

who I am, but I can do it to prove to you that I have the strength to give you everything, to be the man you deserve."

I sit up on the bed, thinking and asking, "Is this something you want to do or something you think *I* want you to do?"

He shrugs, and I can see the sad boy inside him, the one who would do anything to make his dad happy. But I don't want that type of control over him. I don't want him to give in to me to the detriment of himself. I want to build him up, accept the flaws, and celebrate every change we both make, individually and together. I want a partnership.

"No," I say, and Thomas winces visibly.

He steps away from me, his eyes falling. "I understand. I'm sorry, so sorry."

"No, I won't tie you up because you think you need to prove something. I won't let you punish yourself, physically or mentally, for something we've already moved past. I don't want to change the way we make love unless it's exploring something we both want. I happen to like the rough way you fuck me, take me, and own me, every inch, every cell, every corner of my heart. So, if you want *that*, then take your damn clothes off."

He freezes for an instant, and I think he's actually thinking about it, like I might let him walk out of this room and leave me. He thinks he's possessive, but he's got nothing on a Russian woman, and I'll drag him back in here by his cock if he tries to go.

But then his face breaks out into the most beautiful smile, wide and happy and scrunching up his cheeks so much that little lines crinkle around his eyes. "Fuck, I love you," he says.

"Still not naked," I warn. But as he shoves his pants and underwear down his legs, I say earnestly, "I love you too."

In a flash, he's on me, or more to the point, he's on the bed. But he lies on his back, yanking me up to straddle his face. "Give me that pussy. Fuck my mouth."

Just the spread of my legs around his head feels naughty, but when I dip closer and his tongue licks along my slit, I'm lost, wanton with need that's been building for days. He lets me set the pace as I buck against him, but as my moans get louder and my movements erratic, he holds me still and feasts on me. His tongue delves into my pussy, stiff and fucking me like a precursor to what he's going to do with his cock. And when he slips up to circle my clit with wide strokes, electricity and love galvanize my body into a shuddering release.

I grab his head, holding him against me as I chase every spark of orgasm, and he drinks me down, gulping and slurping to get every drop.

As I relax, I sit back, making sure I didn't smother him to death, but he's still smiling happily. "That was fucking amazing."

All of a sudden, I'm flying through the air and Thomas has switched our positions, putting me on my back as he looms over me. "I think you also asked for me to fuck you rough."

I wiggle my eyebrow, challenging him. "Give me all you got."

He teases the crown of his cock against my slippery folds. "I already have. You have all of me. I love you."

I start to say the words back, but Thomas shoves into me with one powerful thrust, snatching my breath away. He's deep and nearly splitting me in two, and . . . "I love youuu!"

The howl begins before I can finish telling him, but I think he gets it, judging by the cocky smile on his face.

He pounds into me fiercely, our lovemaking raw and primal as our hips slap against one another in a sexy symphony. But through the animalistic fucking, our eyes never break contact.

This is us, our lovemaking. Sometimes rough, sometimes playful, but always a true expression of the deep love we feel for each other and the acceptance for who we are at our cores. There is something extra-special about this time, like it's the final puzzle piece of the rebirth of our relationship. We've been through work wildness, family feuds, and some hard self-awareness growth, but it's all brought us to this moment. Thomas thinks he doesn't deserve me, not yet, but he couldn't be more wrong. I love every part of him, the Ruthless Bastard he's moving away from, the secret White Knight he hides, my boss, my love. My Tommy.

And as he grunts, pistoning into my puffy pussy with his sweat marking my skin from his efforts, I realize he's one more thing. My beast.

CHAPTER 43

BLACKWELL

"*And now in happier news, Thomas Goldstone, head of Goldstone Inc, seems to have found the magic touch again, this time not in business but in his personal life. He has just announced his engagement to Mia Karakova. The couple made headlines just weeks ago—*"

My thumb jabs at the remote control, turning off the TV, casting my office almost totally into shadow. Other than the bloody sunset coming in behind my desk, there's almost no light in the room. It helps me think.

How did my plan go awry? I'd set things up so carefully, years of work slowly ratcheting up the pressure on the Golden Boy, cultivating the connection with Bill Radcliffe, the vengeful Goldstone employee . . . and now my plans lay in ruins.

The hospital announced yesterday that they were accepting Thomas Goldstone's offer, and Goldstone Health is now a reality. Thomas Goldstone's star is even brighter than it was before, and I can already feel the sun setting on my empire like it's setting now outside his building.

My desk phone rings, and I pick it up, knowing select few have this number. "Yes?"

"Sir, please, you have to help me," Bill Radcliffe's pathetic voice hisses in my ear. Yes, he served his country, but obviously, men change. "I don't know what else to do. I've stayed loyal. I didn't mention your name. Yet. But they're saying they can pin the Chinese deal on me . . . that's real prison time. They're talking years if I can't give them something."

I growl, knowing exploitation when I hear it. "Do not threaten me. An attorney, a good one, mind you, has already been provided for you. That is contingent upon two things. One, you will keep your mouth shut. You will never say my name to anyone. Not the police, not a lawyer, yours or otherwise, not even in your sleep. And two, you will never contact me again. You do these two things, and the attorney will do what he can for you. You choose any other option, and you will not be enjoying Federal custody for long."

I hang up before he can respond and sit back, tapping my desk. The grandfather clock against the wall starts to chime, and just as the sixth bong gets somehow swallowed by the cavernous air in my office, the outer door opens and my secretary walks in.

She approaches the desk slowly. "Sir, your evening appointment is here."

"Show him in," I command, watching her carefully.

"Of course, sir," she replies, scurrying out. She's dressed as provocatively as always, her curves on full display as she shows my appointment in, but I have to give the man credit, his eyes never acknowledge her as she leaves. It's a good sign, considering the job I'm hiring him for.

For the target is very eye-catching, and this man must be able to resist such . . . primal urges.

"Mr. Blackwell," the tall man says, his charming face and boy next door smile doing nothing to hide the ice in his eyes from my perception. I've built an empire on both light and shadows, and this man definitely knows the shadows. "It's an honor. I've heard not too many people get invited to meet you here."

"Not many are deserving," I reply, standing up and going over to my wet bar, considering what to serve. "But for the man known as the Fallen Angel, well, exceptions can be made. Drink?"

"Absinthe, if you have it," the man replies. A fine choice . . . unique, but certainly tasteful. "What is the nature of the job, Mr. Blackwell?"

"I recently had certain plans of mine backfire," I explain carefully. Before I reveal any extra information, I want to know if this man is on my payroll or not. "Unfortunately, the main parties involved are, if not beyond my reach, at least high enough in notoriety that I do not want to risk stirring too many pots right now. But there is one person I want eliminated. Their death will send the right message to the right people."

My guest nods, unperturbed by the macabre conversation. I have done my research thoroughly, how this seemingly charming man, as handsome as any television star, with a background that should make him a hero, has instead turned to such pursuits.

While he's not the best in the underworld and definitely does not have the highest body count, his background and demeanor are unique. It's given me leverage, for I just happen to know a few things that could help this man . . . if he does what I ask.

"I see. Hearts and minds?" he asks, lifting an eyebrow. "Show them not to mess with you?"

"Something like that," I admit. "This person's death would rattle my enemy, tell certain people to shut their mouths, and also, quite frankly, please me to no end. They were only an instrument, but even an instrument shares some blame for the damage they cause."

"Anything I should know? And before we proceed further, I assume they meet the aforementioned criteria I gave you?"

"That they do. And they aren't well-protected or even aware that they could be a target. It should be easy to make it look like a tragic accident. An easy payday for you."

The Fallen Angel nods and shifts as he takes the drink I hold out, swirling the glass for a moment before sipping. It's a good absinthe, and he savors the flavor before speaking again.

"Understood. But you realize if I take the contract, I do it on my timetable?"

"I know that is how you operate, but I would prefer a faster resolution to this issue. Wait too long, and the message loses impact," I tell him matter-of-factly.

"And the target?"

I cap the absinthe and pour myself a tequila before walking back over to my desk. Opening the lap drawer, I withdraw the photograph inside and slide it across the desk. It's a good picture, framed properly to give the Fallen Angel a good image to work from.

"Her name is Isabella Turner."

EPILOGUE

THOMAS

"*H*ey, Frankie, this is my friend Mia. I thought she could hang out with us today. That cool?"

He shrugs. He's still too young to really care about girls. "Ms. Reba say it's okay? If so, it's good by me. She can be the cheerleader for the game," he says, laughing. But Mia's having none of that.

"Excuse me, mister man. But just because I'm a girl doesn't mean I'm automatically a cheerleader. I happen to be a brilliant data analyst, a video game virtuoso, and I know more about anime than anyone you know. So just because I'm female, you shouldn't assume I can't play football." She huffs, and I swear I almost see a neck swivel as she sets him straight. And she does curse, but at least it's in Russian so Frankie doesn't understand. She promised me no cursing in front of the kids.

"Oh, uh . . . sorry?" he says, apprehension in his eyes. "So, uh, want to be the QB?"

Mia smiles sweetly, tossing her hair back over her shoulder. "Just messing with you. I have no idea what a QB is. I don't play a lick of football, but you shouldn't assume that I can't."

She winks and laughs while Frankie looks at me and mouths, "Your girl is crazy."

"You have no idea," I mouth back.

And then we're all laughing.

Eventually, Mia does play ball with us, and all the guys are running around, doing their best to make up for her lack of skills. And while she can't catch, she can at least tag, and she runs decently enough to play defense on kids.

But what she lacks in experience, she makes up for with hard work and motivation. She's a natural cheerleader, encouraging the boys and helping them while we play, but I'd never call her that aloud.

Well, not now, at least, but maybe if she was wearing a costume.

Hmm. Might need to pick one of those up.

After the game, we pass out Gatorades and high-fives, along with promises to come back soon for a rematch. I tell Reba a quick good-bye, slipping a white envelope into the mail stack on her desk when she hugs Mia. And then we're back in my dusty old beater truck.

"Thank you for letting me come along today. I know this is kind of your thing," she says softly. "Don't know about the wig though. I like your real hair."

I shake my head, scratching where my scalp still tingles some. "Now it can be our thing, if you want. Look, I know you wished I'd make peace with my dad someday, but that's not going to happen, and I think that's for the best. He's off the board, out of my company, and out of my life. And I finally feel like I can breathe deeply for the first time in . . . ever. I might never be the son he wants, but I can be a role model for those boys at the home. And maybe one day, I'll be the dad I wished I'd had to a son of my own."

It's a big confession for me. Wanting kids seems scary as fuck since I don't know how to parent, and I'm reasonably certain a few hours here and there playing ball doesn't cut it as parental training.

I look over at Mia. She's wearing her favorite black distressed jeans, a rock band T-shirt from a group I've never heard of, and Converse. After a run of purple, her hair is a soft pink from roots to tips, and she has not a lick of makeup on. She's never looked more beautiful. Or happy.

"You'd be a great dad, Tommy."

I'm a bastard, a billionaire, and a beast. A man no one ever cared enough to get to know because of the monstrous mask I wore, but she saw beneath it so easily. Her Papa may think she's a Princess, but I know the truth. She's my savior, my angel.

We're going to be one big happy family, just Mia and me and however many kids she wants to have.

I wait for the demon to argue, but it's silent. Only my positive hopes for the future echo in my head like a promise.

Thank you for reading! If you enjoyed this book, be the first to meet Gabriel, Blackwell's "Fallen Angel." Can he do the job Blackwell has hired him for? Read the first few chapters of Not So Prince Charming here! This will be Izzy/Isabella's book!

Also, flip over for a preview of the first book in my Get Dirty Series, Dirty Talk. If you like Dirty Talking Alpha Males, you're going to love it!

PREVIEW: DIRTY TALK

DERRICK

*M*y black leather office chair creaks, an annoying little trend it's developed over the past six months that's the primary reason I don't use it in the studio. Admittedly, that's probably for the better because if I had a chair this comfortable in the studio, I'd be too relaxed to really be on point for my shows.

Still, it's helpful to have something nice like this office since it's a hell of a big step up from the days when my office was also the station's break room.

"All right, hit me. What's on the agenda for today's show?"

My co-star, Susannah, checks her papers, making little checkmarks as she goes through each item.

She's an incessant checkmarker, and I have no idea how the fuck she can read her sheets by the end of the day.

"The overall theme for today is cheaters, and I've got several emails pulled for that so we can stay on track. We'll field calls, of course, and some will be on topic and some off, like always. I'll try and screen them as best I can, and we should be all set."

I nod, trying to mentally prep myself for another three-hour stint behind the mic, offering music, advice, hope, and sometimes a swift kick in the pants to our listeners. Two years ago, I never would've believed that I'd be known as the 'Love Whisperer' on a radio talk segment called the same thing. Part Howard Stern, part Dr. Phil, part DJ Love Below, I've found a niche that's just . . . unique.

I started out many years ago as a jock, playing football on my high school team with dreams of college ball. A seemingly short derailment after an injury led me to do sports reporting for my high school's news and I fell in love.

After that, my scholarships to play football never came, but it didn't bother me as much as I thought it would. I decided to chase after a sports broadcast degree instead, marrying my passion for football and my love of reporting.

I spent four years after graduation doing daily sports talks from three to six as the afternoon drive-home DJ. It wasn't a big station, just one of the half-dozen stations that existed as an alternative for people who didn't want to listen to corporate pop, hip-hop, or country. It was there I received that fateful call.

Looking back, it's kind of crazy, but a guy had called in bitching and moaning about his wife not understanding his need to follow all these wild superstitions to help his team win.

"I'm telling you D, I went to church and asked God himself. I said, if you can bless the Bandits with a win, I'll show myself true and wear those ugly ass socks my pastor gave me for Christmas the year before and never wash them again. You know what happened?"

Of course, everyone could figure out what happened. Still, I respectfully told him that I didn't think his unwashed socks were doing a damn thing for his beloved team on the basketball court, but if he didn't put those fuckers in the washing machine, they were sure going to land him in divorce court.

He sighed and eventually gave in when I told him to wash the socks, thank his wife for putting up with his shit, and full-out romance her to bed and do his damndest to make up for his selfish ways.

And that was that. A new show and a new me were born. After a few marketing tweaks, I've been the so-called 'Love Whisperer' for almost a year now, helping people who ask for advice to get the happily ever after they want.

Ironically, I'm single. Funny how that works out, but all the good advice I try to give stems from my parents who were happily married for over forty years before my mom passed. I won't settle for less than the real thing, and I try to advise my listeners to do the same.

And then there's the sex aspect of my job.

Talking about relationships obviously involves discussing sex with people, as that's one of the major areas that cause problems for folks. At first, talking about all the crazy shit people want to do even made me blush a little, but eventually, it's just gotten to be second nature.

Want to talk about how to get your wife to massage your prostate? Can do. Want to talk about how your girlfriend wants you to wear Underoos and call her Mommy? Can do. Want to talk about your husband never washing the dishes, and how you can get him to help? I can do that too.

All-in-one, real relationships at your service. Live from six to nine, five days a week, or available for download on various podcast sites and clip shows on the weekends. Hell of a lot for a guy who figured *making it* would involve becoming the voice of some college football team.

So I want to do a good job. And that means working well with Susannah, who is the control-freak yin to my laissez-faire yang.

"Thanks. I know this week's topics from our show planning meeting, but I spaced on tonight's focus."

Susannah nods, unflappable. "No problem. Do you want to scan the emails or just do your thing?"

I smile at her. She already knows the answer. "Same as always, spontaneous. You know that even though I was a Boy Scout, being prepared for this doesn't do us any favors. I sound robotic when I read ahead. First read, real reactions work better and give the listeners knee-jerk common sense."

She shrugs, scribbling on her papers. "I know, just checking."

It's probably one of the reasons we work so well together, our totally different approaches to the show. Joining me from day one, she's the one who keeps our show running behind the scenes and keeps me on track on-air, serving as both producer and co-host. Luckily, her almost anal-retentive penchant for prep totally doesn't come across on the air, where she's the playful, comedic counter to my gruff, tell-it-like-it-is style.

"Then let's rock," I tell her. "Got your drinks ready?"

Susannah nods as we head toward the studio. Settling into my broadcast chair, a much less comfortable but totally silent one, I survey my normal spread of one water, one coffee, and one green tea, one for every hour we're gonna be on the air. With the top of the hour news breaks and spaced out music jams, I've gotten used to using the exactly four minute and thirty second breaks to run next door and drain my bladder if I need to.

Everything ready, we smile and settle in for another show. "Gooooood evening! It's your favorite 'Love Whisperer,' Derrick King here with my lovely assistant, Miss Susannah Jameson. We're ready for an evening of love, sex, betrayal, and lust, if you're willing to share. Our focus tonight is on cheaters and cheating. Are you being cheated on? Maybe *you* are the cheater? Call in and we'll talk."

The red glow from the holding calls is instant, but I traditionally go to an email first so that I can roll right in.

"While Susannah is grabbing our first caller, I'll start with an email. Here's one from P. 'Dear Love Whisperer,' it says, 'my husband travels extensively for work, leaving me home and so lonely. I don't know if he's cheating while he's gone, but I always wonder. I've started to develop feelings for my personal trainer, and I think I'm falling in love with him. What should I do?' "

I *tsk-tsk* into the microphone, making my displeasure clear. "Well, P, first things first. Your marriage is your priority because you made a vow. For better or worse, remember? It's simple. Talk to your husband. Maybe he's cheating, maybe he isn't. Maybe he's working his ass off so his bored wife can even *have* a trainer and you're looking for excuses to justify your own bad behavior. But talking to him is your first step. You need to explain your feelings and that you need him more than perhaps you need the money. Second, you need to get a life beyond your husband and trainer. I get the sense you need some attention and your trainer is giving it to you, so you think you're in love with him. Newsflash—he's being paid to give you attention. By your husband, it sounds like. That's not a healthy foundation for a relationship even if he is your soulmate, which I doubt."

I sigh and lower my voice a little. I don't want to cut this woman's guts out. I want to help her. "P, let's be honest. A good trainer is going to be personable. They're in a sales profession. They're not going to make it in the industry without either being the best in the world at what they do or having a good personality. And a lot of them have good bodies. Their bodies are their business cards. So it's natural to feel some attraction to your trainer. But that doesn't mean he's going to stick by you. Here's a challenge—tell your trainer you can't pay him for the next three months and see how available he is to just give you his time."

Susannah snickers and hits her mic button. "That's why I do group yoga classes. Only thing that happens there is sweaty tantric orgies. Ohmm . . . my . . ." Her initial yoga-esque ohm dissolves into a plea-sure-induced moan that she fakes exceedingly well.

I roll my eyes, knowing that she does nothing of the sort. "To the point, though, fire your trainer because of your weakness and tell him why. He's a pro. He needs to know that his services were not the reason you're leaving. Next, get a hobby that fulfills you beyond a man and talk to your husband."

I click a button and a sound effect of a cheering audience plays through my headset. It goes on like this for a while, call after call, email after email of helping people.

Well, I hope I'm helping them. They seem to think I am, and I'm certainly giving it my best shot. In between, I mix in music and a hodgepodge of stuff that fits the daily themes. Tonight I've got some Taylor Swift, a little Carrie Underwood, some old-school TLC. I even, as a joke, worked in Bobby Brown at Susannah's insistence.

Coming back from that last one, I see Susannah gesture from her mini-booth and give the airspace over to her, letting her introduce the next caller.

"Okay, Susannah's giving me the big foam finger, so what've we got?"

"You wish I had a big finger for you," Susannah teases like she always does on air—it's part of our act. "The next caller would like to discuss some rather incriminating photos she's come across. Appar-ently, Mr. Right was Mr. Everybody?"

I click the button, taking the call live on-air. "This is the 'Love Whis-perer', who am I speaking with?"

The caller stutters, obviously nervous, and in my mind I know I have to treat this one gently. Some of the callers just want to laugh, maybe have their fifteen seconds of fame or get their pound of proverbial flesh by exposing their partner's misdeeds. But there are also callers like this, who I suspect really needs help.

"This is Katrina . . . Kat."

Whoa, a first name. And from the sound of it, a real one. She's not making a thing up. I need to lighten the mood a little, or else she's gonna clam up and freak out on me.

"Hello, Kitty Kat. What seems to be the problem today?"

I hear her sigh, and it touches me for some reason. "Well . . . I can't believe I actually got through, first of all. I worked up the nerve to dial the numbers but didn't expect an answer. I'm just . . . I don't even know what I am. I'm just a little lost and in need of some advice, I guess." She huffs out a humorless laugh.

I can hear the pain in her voice, mixed with nerves. "Advice? That I can do. That's what I'm here for, in fact. What's going on, Kat?"

"It's my boyfriend, or my soon-to-be ex-boyfriend, I guess. I found out today that he slept with someone else." She sounds like she's found a bit of steel as she speaks this time, and it makes her previous vulnerability all the more touching.

"Ouch," I say, truly wincing at the fresh wound. A day of cheat call? I'm sure the advertisers are rubbing their hands in glee, but I'm feeling for this girl. "I'm so sorry. I know that hurts and it's wrong no matter what. I heard something about compromising pics. Please tell me he didn't send you pics of him screwing someone else?"

She laughs but it's not in humor. "No, I guess that would've been worse, but he had sex with someone kind of Internet famous and she posted faceless pics of them together. But I recognized his . . . uhm . . . his . . ."

Let's just get the schlong out in the open, why don't we? "You recognized his penis? Is that the word you're looking for?"

"Yeah, I guess so," Kat says, her voice cutting through the gap created by the phone line. "He has a mole, so I know it's him."

There's something about her voice, all sweet and breathy that stirs me inside like I rarely have happen. It's not just her tone, either. She's in pain, but she's mad as fuck too, and I want to help her, protect her.

She seems innocent, and something deep inside me wants to make her a little bit dirty.

"Okay, first, repeat after me. Penis, dick, cock." I wait, unsure if she'll do it but holding my breath in the hopes that she will.

"Uh, what?"

I feel a small smile come to my lips, and it's my turn to be a little playful. "Penis, dick, cock. Trust me, this is important for you. You can do it, Kitty Kat."

I hear her intake of breath, but she does what I demanded, more clearly than the shyness I expected. "Penis, dick, cock."

"Good girl," I growl into the mic, and through the window connecting our booths, I can see Susannah giving me a raised eyebrow. "Now say . . . I recognized his cock fucking her."

I say a silent prayer of thanks that my radio show is on satellite. I can say whatever I want and the FCC doesn't care.

I can tell Kat is with me now, and her voice is stronger, still sexy as fuck but without the lost kitten loneliness to it.

"I recognized his cock fucking her tits."

My own cock twitches a little, and I lean in, smirking. "Ah, so the plot thickens. So Kat, how does it feel to say that?"

She sighs, pulling me back a little. "The words don't bother me. I'm just not used to being on the radio. But saying that about my boyfriend pisses me off. I can't believe he'd do that."

"So, what do you think you should do about it?" I ask, leaning back in my chair and pulling my mic toward me. "Is this a 'talk it through and our relationship will be stronger on the other side of this' type situation, or is this a 'hit the road, motherfucker, and take Miss Slippy-Grippy Tits with you?' Do you want my opinion or do you already know?"

"You're right," Kat says, chuckling and sounding stronger again. "I already know I'm done. He's been a wham-bam-doesn't even say thank you, ma'am guy all along, and I've been hanging on because I didn't think I deserved better. But I don't deserve this. I'm better off alone."

Whoa, now, only half right there, Kat with the sexy voice. "You don't deserve this. You should have someone who treats you so well you never question their love, their commitment to you. Everyone deserves that. Hey, Kitty Kat? One more thing. Can you say 'cock' for me one more time? Just for . . . entertainment."

I'm pushing the line here, both for her and for the show, but I ask her to do it anyway because I want, no need, to hear her say it.

She laughs, her voice lighter even as I know the serious conversation had to hurt. "Of course, Love Whisperer. Anything for you. You ready? Cock." She draws the word out, the k a bit harsher, and I can hear the sass, almost an invitation, as she speaks.

"Ooh, thanks so much, Kitty Kat. Hold on the line just a second." My cock is now fully hard in my pants, and I'm not sure if my upcoming bathroom break is going to be to piss or to take care of that.

I click some buttons, sending the show to a song, Shaggy's *It Wasn't Me* coming over the airwaves to keep the cheating theme rolling. "Susannah?"

"Yeah?"

"Handle the next call or so after the commercial break," I tell her. "Pick something . . . funny after that one."

"Gotcha," Susannah says, and I'm glad she's able to handle things like that. It's part of our system too that when I get a call that needs more than on-air can handle, she fills the gap. Usually with less serious questions or listener stories that always make for great laughs.

Checking my board, I click the line back, glad that Susannah can't hear me now. "Kat? You still there?"

"Yes?" she says, and I feel another little thrill go down my cock just at her word. God, this woman's got a sexy voice, soft and sweet with a little undercurrent of sassiness . . . or maybe I really, really need to get laid.

"Hey, it's Derrick. I just wanted to say thanks for being such a good sport with all of that."

"No problem," she says as I make a picture in my head of her. I can't fill in the details, but I definitely want to. "Thanks for helping me realize I need to walk away. I already knew it, but some inspiration never hurts."

"I really would like to hear the rest of the story if you don't mind calling me back. I want to hear how he grovels when he finds out what he's lost. Would you call me?"

I don't know what I'm doing. This is so not like me. I never talk to the callers after they're on air unless I think they're going to hurt themselves or others, and I certainly never invite them to call back. But something about her voice calls to me like a siren. I just hope she's not pulling me into the rocky shore to crash.

"You mean the show?" Kat asks, uncertain and confused. "Like . . . I dunno, like a guest or something?"

"Well, probably not, to be honest," I reply, crossing my fingers even as my cock says I need to take this risk. "We'll be done with the cheating theme tonight and it probably won't come back up for a couple of weeks. I meant . . . call me. I want to make sure you're okay afterward and standing strong."

"Okay."

Before she can take it back, I rattle off my personal cell number to her, half of my brain telling me this is brilliant and the other half saying it's the stupidest thing I've ever done. I might not have the FCC looking over my shoulder, but the satellite network is and my advertisers for damn sure are. Still . . .

"Got it?"

"I've got it," Kat says. "I'll get back to you after I break up with Kevin. It's been a weird night and I guess it's going to get even weirder. Guess I gotta go tell Kevin his dick busted him on the internet and he can get fucked elsewhere . . . permanently. I can do this."

"Damn right, you can," I tell her. "You can do this, Kitty Kat. Remember, you deserve better. I'll be waiting for your report."

Kat laughs and we hang up. I don't know what just happened but my body feels light, bubbly inside as I take a big breath to get ready for the next segment of tonight's show.

Want more? Get the full book here.

ABOUT THE AUTHOR

Get Dirty:
Dirty Talk | | Dirty Laundry | | Dirty Deeds | | Dirty Secrets

*Irresistible Bachelor*s:
Anaconda | | Mr. Fiance | | Heartstopper
Stud Muffin | | Mr. Fixit | | Matchmaker
Motorhead | | Baby Daddy | | Untamed

The Virgin Diaries:
Satin and Pearls | | Leather and Lace | | Silk and Shadows

Bennett Boys Ranch:
Buck Wild

Connect with Lauren Landish
www.laurenlandish.com
admin@laurenlandish.com
www.facebook.com/lauren.landish

Made in the USA
Coppell, TX
17 May 2020

25927698R00184